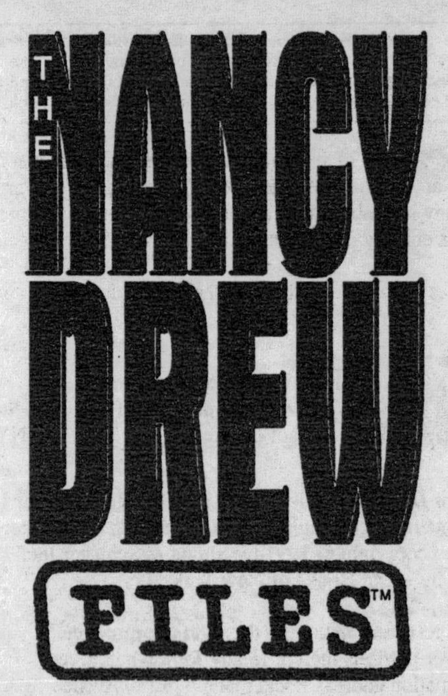

COLLECTOR'S EDITION

Danger for Hire
Make No Mistake
Poison Pen

CAROLYN KEENE

AN ARCHWAY PAPERBACK
Published by POCKET BOOKS
New York London Toronto Sydney Tokyo Singapore

These titles were previously published individually.

An Archway Paperback published by
POCKET BOOKS, a division of Simon & Schuster Inc.
1230 Avenue of the Americas, New York, NY 10020

Produced by Mega-Books of New York, Inc.

ISBN: 0-671-01930-9

First Archway Paperback printing July 1998

10 9 8 7 6 5 4 3 2 1

Cover design by Jim Lebbad

Printed in the U.S.A.

IL 6+

Danger for Hire

Chapter One

"So in conclusion, I repeat that detective work is exciting," reported Nancy Drew, "but it can also be very dangerous. Okay, does anyone have any questions?"

A dozen hands shot into the air. It was Saturday and Career Day for juniors and seniors at River Heights High School, and Nancy was one of three guest speakers discussing careers in law enforcement.

Nancy pointed to a pretty girl sitting in the front row. "Miss Drew," the girl began.

"Please! Call me Nancy," she said, brushing her reddish blond hair away from her face. At eighteen she didn't feel old enough to be a "Miss Drew." "Please tell me your name, too," she added.

The girl smiled. "It's Cindy Larson. Nancy, how do you get your cases? Do you advertise?"

"No," Nancy answered. "Usually people come to me with a problem, and more often than not there's a mystery involved."

"Well, you do have a reputation for solving tough puzzles. Like the Nikki Masters investigation. You know, there's still something about that case that I don't understand. . . ."

She launched into a long and technical question about the evidence. Nancy listened carefully and then began a quick summary of the clues.

Cindy's interest in that particular case wasn't surprising. Nikki Masters was a popular junior at River Heights High, who had been suspected of killing her boyfriend. Nancy thought of that case as *The Suspect Next Door.*

No, Cindy's interest wasn't unusual. What surprised Nancy was that the girl had such detailed recall of the case. It had happened ages ago! She must have studied the news-

paper accounts very carefully. Nancy asked if there were other questions.

Nancy answered them all patiently, until she noticed that the session was almost over.

"Doesn't anyone have a question for Chief McGinnis or Tom Hayward?" Nancy asked, glancing at her two fellow speakers.

Chief McGinnis studied her with a grin. "I doubt it, Nancy. Your sleuthing sounds much more glamorous than police work. Why, I'm wondering if I should go private myself."

"The River Heights Police Department couldn't get along without you, Chief," Nancy said, her cheeks hot. "Besides, police work must be very rewarding."

"Does that mean you'll take the patrolman's exam when you're old enough?" the chief asked.

"Not so fast, Chief," Tom Hayward cut in with a devilish smile. "If anyone's going to recruit Nancy Drew, I want it to be Hayward Security Systems. My company is growing fast, and I need a bright mind like Nancy's. What do you say, Nancy? You'll earn a lot more money working for me than for the River Heights Police!"

Nancy studied Tom. He was remarkably

young to be the president of one of the most successful businesses in River Heights. Nancy knew that he was only in his midtwenties and easily the youngest millionaire in River Heights.

He's probably the most handsome, too, Nancy decided. Tall and athletic, with neatly trimmed sandy blond hair and attractive steel blue eyes, Tom was the all-American dream-boat. Furthermore, his smile was warm and his manner was easy. No wonder he was so successful! Nancy liked him the moment she met him. It was hard not to.

"I don't know," she said and smiled in response to his job offer. "Security is a whole different ball game than solving mysteries."

Tom smiled back and turned to face the students. "I hope that when you finally make a career choice, you will consider the security business. It pays well and there's plenty of opportunity for advancement."

Nancy listened in admiration as he shifted smoothly into a final pitch for his firm.

"In fact," he went on, "I am hiring right now for Hayward Security Guard Services. So far not one of our customers' homes or businesses has been robbed. So think about Hayward, okay? Especially you graduating seniors."

Just then a bell rang, signaling the end of the session. As the students rose and began filing out, Nancy turned to Tom and the chief. "Well, how'd we do?"

"I'd say you did well, Nancy," the chief answered. "I'll bet every one of those kids wants to be a PI."

It was probably true. A few students were hanging back, and they were all gathered around Nancy. Blushing, Nancy fielded their queries one at a time. The last of the group was Cindy Larson.

Cindy was of average height, slim, with an athletic build. Her face was pretty in an innocent, hometown-sweetheart way. Her gray eyes were bright and intelligent, and her glossy brown hair was shoulder-length and stylishly cut. She was dressed to impress, like most of the students, but Nancy got the feeling that she'd be more at home in jeans.

"That was a good question you had about the Nikki Masters case," Nancy complimented her. "Did you follow it in the papers?"

"Oh, I save *all* the articles about your cases," Cindy said. "I keep them in a binder, a sort of casebook. See?"

She handed Nancy a notebook. Opening it, Nancy was amazed to see that it contained a

complete set of newspaper clippings about her. Some of the articles went back several years! Stunned, Nancy realized that this girl was a fan of hers—big time.

Nancy felt both flattered and oddly uneasy. Fans were for movie stars, not teenage detectives. She closed the album and handed it back to the girl.

"I'm honored," she said gratefully.

"No, *I'm* honored," Cindy answered. "I think you are totally amazing. I mean, a hundred other people could have the same clues that you have on a case, but you're the one who puts them all together and catches the crook."

"Oh, I usually have lots of help," Nancy demurred.

"Not always. You must be incredibly smart."

"No, just persistent," Nancy said with an uneasy smile. She was definitely feeling uncomfortable now. It was obvious that the girl idolized her—or at least had an exaggerated mental picture of her. That was too bad. She was bound to be disappointed by the real-life Nancy Drew. Nancy felt that she was a pretty ordinary person most of the time.

"Okay, so you're persistent *and* smart!" her

fan agreed. "That still means you're incredible. My goal is to be a detective, too. Your life sounds so exciting."

"Lots of times it is," Nancy admitted. "But some of the time it's downright scary."

"You always come out of your cases okay, though."

"So far! I've been lucky," Nancy said sincerely.

"It's more than luck. You know how to keep your cool," Cindy insisted.

"I'm also well trained in a lot of stuff, like judo and fencing and—" Nancy stopped herself. She was beginning to sound as if she were bragging!

"I want to learn all that stuff, too," Cindy announced.

Nancy nodded. "Then do it. You'll enjoy it. I know I did. But if you're going to be a detective, you have to learn that there are times when the work is dull—with a capital *D.*"

"Oh, I'm sure it could never be dull!" Cindy said with a grin.

It was hopeless. Cindy was determined to glamorize Nancy, so Nancy decided to quit trying to set the girl straight.

Just then they were startled by the loud crackle of the chief's radio. "Headquarters to PO One. Are you there, Chief?"

At that same moment, Tom Hayward's beeper began to chirp. Shutting it off, Tom swiveled to face the others. "Excuse me."

He left the room to find a phone. The chief, meanwhile, lifted his black police radio from its leather holster at his waist. He punched the transmit button. "Chief here."

"Chief." The radio crackled again. "We need you down at Orange and Duke. We got a major five-five-oh at that location."

"Anyone injured?" the chief demanded.

"Negative. An S.G. was gift wrapped, that's all."

"I'm all done here. Be right down," the chief said. "Over and out."

Nancy grinned at the chief. "A big warehouse burglary, huh? Must have been a professional job—that is, since a security guard was bound and gagged."

The chief shook his head in admiration. "No one slips anything over on you, Nancy."

"Sometimes, but not *usually.* Anyway, thank goodness no one was hurt," Nancy commented.

"No one but me!" said a male voice from the doorway.

Nancy, Cindy, and the chief wheeled around to face Tom Hayward, who had come back into the room.

"That was a call from my office," he said in a hollow voice. "The warehouse that was robbed is guarded by Hayward. So much for our perfect record! I'm ruined!"

Chapter Two

"That's terrible," Nancy said, her blue eyes expressing concern. "About the burglary, I mean. It's not really the end of Hayward Security, though, is it?"

"I'm afraid it might be," Tom lamented. "You see, the whole foundation of our business is our complete reliability. The state-of-the-art alarm systems we put in, plus our security guard service, let our customers feel safe. If they don't feel safe anymore, then *poof!*—we have nothing left."

"One break-in isn't going to shatter the confidence of your customers," Nancy suggested.

"It won't help it."

"But no one's perfect." Nancy searched for a way to help him feel better. "In fact, a break-in was probably inevitable sometime," she said. "And this obviously was the work of professionals."

"That's even worse," Tom moaned. He began to pack his briefcase. "It's the pros that our systems are supposed to thwart. This is a disaster."

Nancy gave herself a mental kick—she had only succeeded in making him feel worse.

"Let's not call this a disaster yet," the chief said. "Maybe these 'pros' weren't so professional after all. If we catch them—"

"Sure!" Nancy interrupted. "If they're put in jail, your company's reputation will hardly suffer at all."

"I guess," Tom said, not convinced at all.

"Well, let's get going," the chief said. "We won't know anything until we check out the scene. Care to come, Nancy?"

"You bet." Nancy turned to her student admirer. "It was nice talking to you. I hope

you make your dream come true and become a detective. I could use some company!"

A second later she was halfway to the door.

Nancy shifted her Mustang and let it glide downhill. It wasn't hard to figure out where to go. A herd of blue-and-white police cars jammed the street in front of a warehouse, their twin roof lights twirling. The long, low warehouse had *CD Revolution* painted in giant red letters across its front.

On her way inside, Nancy noticed the high-tech alarm and lock system that controlled the loading bay door. There was even a control panel on the wall outside. Unusual. With access to the system so easy, Tom was obviously confident that the system was secure. So what had gone wrong?

Tom and the chief were in the glass-enclosed inner office, questioning the security guard who had been tied up by the robbers. A plainclothes detective was taking notes. Nancy, not wanting to intrude, waited outside the door.

"No, I never saw their faces," the young guard was saying. "They were wearing masks."

"Ski masks?" the detective asked.

"No, rubber Halloween masks. You know, the kind that pull over your whole head. Frankenstein, the Mummy . . . like that."

"Gloves?" the chief asked.

"Yeah, cloth. Work gloves."

"Weapons?" Tom inquired.

"Uh—long-barrel automatics."

Professionals, Nancy thought. Eager to ask her own questions, she was glad when the chief noticed her.

"Ah, Nancy! Come in," he said. "You're good at spotting things. Take a look around and see what you find."

Nodding to Tom and the detective, Nancy slid inside and quickly asked, "How much was taken?"

"We're not sure yet," Tom said. "It looks like about two hundred boxes of CDs were lifted. They backed a truck to the loading dock and moved the boxes with handcarts. The whole operation took only seven minutes."

"I timed them on the wall clock," the guard chimed in.

"Fast work," Nancy commented.

"They didn't bother to blindfold me. They didn't have to," said the guard, sounding morose.

"Because of the masks." Nancy nodded. "How did they get inside in the first place?" she asked curiously.

"They came in through the loading bay door. All of a sudden I saw it rolling up, but by the time I got there, two of 'em had rolled underneath and had their guns pointed at me. They tied me up, and—bingo. Seven minutes later they were out of here. That was it."

Nancy narrowed her eyes. "Wait a minute. . . . How did they disable the alarm connected to the loading bay door? To turn it off you'd need a code, and I'll bet you get only one chance to input the correct code on the keypad."

"That's right," Tom supplied.

They all looked at the guard. He shifted uncomfortably. He was tall and athletic and quite young. Nineteen at the most, Nancy guessed. The name tag sewn on his gray uniform said "Adam Reeves."

The police detective shot them all a warning look. He was obviously suspicious of the guard, but wanted to take it slow with him. "Okay, let's get back to the robbers," he said. "Did they say anything to you?"

After a minute a pair of uniformed officers

entered. With them was a worried-looking woman holding a thick computer printout and a pencil.

"We've done a preliminary check of the inventory," she said. She must be the warehouse manager, Nancy realized, called in on her day off. "There are about two hundred and twenty-five cartons of CDs missing. They seem to have picked whatever was closest to the door," she added.

"That's strange," Nancy commented. "You'd think they'd take only best-sellers." Especially considering how well they planned the rest of the operation, she added to herself.

A commotion outside the office interrupted them. A patrolman was attempting to block the path of a dark-haired young woman. She was about eighteen, Nancy's age, and was angrily waving an ID card in their faces.

"I'm with the press," she snapped. "I demand that you let me through!"

Oh, no! Nancy thought. Brenda Carlton!

Nancy could see that the teenage reporter looked as professional as ever in a tailored skirt and pumps. If only Brenda would pay less attention to her appearance and more to responsible reporting, Nancy thought wearily. Their paths had crossed often, and once too

often Brenda had come close to ruining Nancy's investigations. She had even put their lives in danger.

Dropping one shoulder like a linebacker, Brenda rudely shoved past the officer. She was firing off a rapid string of questions as she burst into the office.

Adam Reeves glanced at Tom, who shook his head. He didn't want his guard answering any questions.

"Um . . . I don't think I should comment," Adam said.

"Chief, what about you? What steps are you taking?"

Nancy pressed her lips together to keep from smiling. Brenda was such a cartoon! Of course, she thought of herself as an ace reporter. The truth was that she had a byline only because her father was the owner and publisher of *Today's Times.*

The chief rolled his eyes. He was well acquainted with Brenda's blunt style. "Our investigation is continuing," he told her. "Other than that, I have no comment."

Brenda turned to Tom. "What about you, Mr. Hayward? This break-in is a big setback for your firm. . . ."

Nancy caught the chief's eye and inclined

her head in the direction of the door. The chief took the hint, and both of them slipped quietly into the warehouse proper.

"Chief," Nancy said in a low voice, "if you ask me, these crooks had inside help. Someone gave them the code to that alarm."

"Looks like it," the chief agreed. "We'll work on that angle."

A moment later Tom joined them, having left Brenda to Adam and the detective. "Chief, I've got a big problem," he said with a cautious backward glance.

"I know," the chief said. "Nancy and I were just discussing that. It will take some in-depth probing to uncover the person in your operation who helped these robbers, which is a bit beyond us right now. We've had a big budget cut."

"Yeah, I know," Tom said. He didn't sound bitter, however. "Looks like I'll have to do that work myself."

The chief rubbed the side of his nose with his index finger. "May I make a suggestion?"

"Please," Tom said.

"Since it'll be difficult for you to be objective about your own people, why not get some outside help? I know someone who's already familiar with the case. . . ."

"You mean *Nancy?"* Tom sounded startled.

"Naturally." The chief smiled at her. "She's got a nose for the truth, and a brain that thrives on mysteries. She'll be perfect—if she wants to take the case."

"Oh, I do," Nancy said quickly. She didn't have to think twice.

Tom studied her for a moment, probably wondering if an eighteen-year-old could really help him. A lot of people wondered that at first.

Finally he nodded. After all, he was not that much older than she. "Thanks, Nancy. Why not meet me at my office? I'll pull out some employee records, and we can make plans."

Nancy smiled. She always felt great when she got a new case. "Okay. I think I'll take a last look around here first, though."

"Sure. I've got a few details to wrap up, too," Tom said.

Nancy walked into the heart of the warehouse. There were aisles and aisles of industrial metal shelves. Each shelf, in turn, was packed with cardboard boxes. Glued to each box was a computer-generated label that announced its contents in large letters. It was easy to see which CDs were where. Why had the robbers chosen their loot at random?

Puzzled, Nancy moved still deeper into the building. The only noise she could hear was the soft buzzing of the strip lighting overhead. It was very quiet.

Scrape.

Off to her left, Nancy heard a shoe scuff against the concrete floor. A police officer? No, they were all in the front of the warehouse, waiting for orders.

The next sound was faint—but unmistakable. Someone was walking slowly and quietly. Nancy was not alone.

Chapter

Three

NANCY PEERED THROUGH the gap between two shelves, her heart beating faster. Two aisles away she caught a flash of movement. A jade-colored shirt? After slipping off her shoes, she crept ahead.

At the corner she paused and was just in time to see a lithe figure dart around the corner at the far end of the aisle.

Crouching low, Nancy took a chance and ran forward as quickly as she could. When she was halfway to the front of the warehouse, she turned left and zipped up an aisle. Good,

thought Nancy. The figure was coming toward her.

Nancy waited until the figure was only a few feet away. Then she turned the corner and stood directly in the figure's path.

"Cindy Larson, what are *you* doing here?"

"Aaagh!" With a howl of fright, Cindy scrambled backward. She struggled for balance as she stumbled into a stack of boxes. "Nancy, you scared me to death!"

Nancy suppressed a smile. "Sorry. I wasn't sure it was you at first. Now, you'd better tell me what you're doing. Do the police know you're in here?"

"Well, sort of," Cindy said in embarrassment. "See, I really wanted to come get a look at an actual crime scene, so I came here and told the police officers that I had a message for you. They told me you were back here, and I . . . well, I felt dumb because I *didn't* have a message for you, but I wanted to watch you work anyway, so I followed you back here hoping that you wouldn't see me. I guess I didn't do a very good job of hiding, huh?"

"Of hiding, no," Nancy said. "Of getting past the police—not bad. But you shouldn't

have made up a story. Especially when you could have just asked me to show you around."

"I didn't think you would."

"Oh." Nancy felt bad for coming down so hard on Cindy. An idea came to her just then. It was perfect! "Cindy, I'm going to be helping Tom Hayward get to the bottom of this robbery. Would you like to work with me on this case?"

Cindy swallowed. "Do you mean it?"

Nancy beamed. "Sure! This is the sort of case that has a lot of legwork to it . . . you know, cross-checking schedules, getting information on the phone, that kind of thing. It'd be a lot for me to handle on my own, but with a helper—"

"Oh, this is the most exciting thing that's *ever* happened to me! Wait until I tell my friends! Of course, I'll only be able to help you after school, but don't worry, Nancy! I'll be the best assistant detective you've ever had!"

That's a tall promise, Nancy thought to herself. She was usually assisted in her cases by her two best friends, Bess Marvin and George Fayne. Her boyfriend, Ned Nickerson, had been in on quite a few as well. All had proved themselves to be invaluable.

"Great," Nancy said. "Well, I'm all done here. Let's go." After retrieving her shoes, she walked outside onto the loading dock with Cindy.

"Here's my home number," Nancy said, jotting it down on a scrap of paper from her purse. "Now tell me yours, and we'll arrange—"

Screeeeeeeeeeeeeeeeeeeeeeeeeech!

The air was split by an ear-shattering burst of feedback. Nancy's hands flew to her ears.

As suddenly as the noise had begun, it stopped. Then from the loudspeakers above the loading platform across the street came a booming, gleeful voice. "So! How does it feel, Tom Hayward, you little creep! Not a lot of fun to have a client robbed, is it?"

Nancy's gaze swung across the street as Tom and the chief appeared beside her. Brenda was not far behind them.

"About time you had a setback, son. It'll make you humble. Make you think twice about taking away other people's business! I'll tell you another thing, too, Hayward—I'm glad. You're getting exactly what you deserve!"

The chief yelled, "Bates! Go find out who that is!"

"Wait," Tom said, laying a hand on the chief's outstretched arm. "I know who it is.

It's Stanley Loomis. My main rival. Stanley's had the security business in River Heights all to himself for years—until I came along."

"He's not happy about your success, obviously," the chief observed.

That was the understatement of the year, in Nancy's opinion. The amplified tirade continued for a few minutes longer, and then abruptly ceased. A moment later a metal door on the opposite loading platform opened, and a portly man wearing brown slacks and a plaid sports jacket emerged.

He said nothing. He just climbed into a large tan luxury car and roared away.

"That's Loomis," Tom said. "He overcharged his clients for years. Now I'm offering people better service at a lower price, and he resents it."

Nancy wondered if it was possible that Stanley Loomis had arranged the robbery. Yes, she decided almost instantly. Proving it, though, was going to take some work.

That evening at dinner Nancy told her father, Carson Drew, about Tom's remark. They were sitting at the dinner table with Hannah Gruen, their longtime housekeeper, eating pot roast.

"You're right—that wouldn't have done any

good," Carson said. "Hayward's just discouraged. This is his first big setback."

"He's awfully young, isn't he?" Hannah remarked. "He's not used to business difficulties, I'll bet. But he'll learn. With more experience, problems like this won't bother him so much."

Nancy's father lifted the salt shaker from the table. "I guess he needs more 'seasoning,' eh, Hannah?"

Nancy groaned. "Dad, that was your worst pun in a week."

"Just trying to add some spice to the discussion," Carson quipped.

"Ohhh!" Nancy moaned, rolling her eyes.

"Mr. Drew, you shouldn't joke about it," Hannah scolded. "Tom Hayward is in trouble. He needs help, and I think it's wonderful that Nancy is giving it to him."

Nancy smiled. "Thanks, Hannah. It remains to be seen whether I'll be much help, though."

"I'm sure you will," her father said, setting the salt shaker down again. "In fact, you have one suspect already, don't you? That young guard . . . what was his name?"

"Adam Reeves."

"He seems a likely bet."

"Sure," Nancy agreed. "I'll be checking up on him as soon as I can."

Carson wiped his mouth on his white linen napkin. "There's something I don't understand. If Adam Reeves was tied to a chair, who called the police?"

"He did—in a way," Nancy explained. "The chair the robbers tied him to had wheels. He waited until they were gone, then he rolled himself to a side exit and butted open the door. It had a bar lever, so he didn't have to use his hands."

"How did he untie himself?" Hannah asked.

"He didn't. The emergency exit had a separate alarm connected to it. The alarm went off, and a patrol car stopped to investigate. The two officers untied him and called headquarters."

"Hmm. That's how Brenda found out about it, too," Carson surmised. "Monitoring the police channel."

"Obviously," Nancy agreed.

Hannah rose and began clearing the dishes. "Who'd like cherry pie?"

"None for me," Nancy said, folding her napkin and rising. "It sounds fantastic, but I don't want to be slowed down by a full stomach tonight."

"Going dancing with Ned?" her father asked.

"No, he's staying on campus this weekend,"

Nancy answered a little wistfully. Her boyfriend was a student at Emerson College and didn't get home very often. "I'm going to begin some surveillance of the warehouse district. I have a hunch that we haven't seen the last of these robbers."

"Are you sure that's a good idea? Especially at night?" Carson asked.

"I'll be careful. If they show up again, I'll phone the police," Nancy promised.

In the daytime the warehouse district was crowded with trucks and warehouse workers. At night, though, the area was quiet and seemed sinister, the occasional streetlight dropping an isolated white cone of light into the darkness.

Nancy drove once through the entire grid of streets, carefully noting the location of pay phones and fire boxes. Then she parked near the river, not far from the fat silver grain silos and began to patrol on foot.

She was wearing black jeans, black sneakers, and a worn leather jacket that Ned had given her. It was chilly out. Nancy zipped her jacket to her chin and flipped up the collar.

Late-night deliveries were under way at a few of the warehouses, but most were dark,

their loading bays closed with metal security doors. Nancy was pretty sure she'd be able to tell if a robbery was under way—a truck would be loading at one or another of the bays, but the work would be done with flashlights. She saw nothing suspicious.

After an hour she had worked her way around half the streets. The next block was a long one. Nancy walked down it quickly. All of the warehouses were dark. If she were looking for a place to rob, this was definitely a block she'd be interested in.

Then, passing an alley, she thought she heard a faint sound.

Nancy paused. Alert for the slightest noise, she peered down the alley. There was nothing but some garbage dumpsters, a few stacks of crates, and a door set into one wall. Nancy waited.

Creak.

There! No mistaking it that time. Something—or someone—had made a sound. She started down the alley, then stopped.

Silence. Nancy tiptoed farther. She kept near to the wall because it was darker there. She paused again, letting her eyes adjust to the alley's blackness.

Still no sound. Nancy crept one step farther and stopped behind a ten-foot-high stack of wooden crates.

Creeeeeeeak!

She was close now. But where was the noise coming from?

Suddenly Nancy froze—and raised her eyes. The stack of crates was falling toward her. In less than a second she'd be crushed!

Chapter Four

WITH A SCREAM, Nancy dived to her right. She tucked and rolled as the crates hit the pavement where she had been standing a second earlier.

The top ones splintered and sent a blizzard of white Styrofoam peanuts into the alley. As Nancy began to rise, a dark figure raced past her, shoving her violently to the ground.

"Hey! Stop!" Nancy shouted, but it was futile. She looked up just in time to see a dark shape zoom out of the alley and wheel left.

She was furious. There had been no need to

try to hurt her. Whoever it was had only needed to stand still in the shadows. In a minute or two she would have gone away.

Nancy took off at a sprint and turned left at the top of the alley. The figure was fifty yards ahead of her. As the figure crossed through a pool of light below a street lamp, Nancy saw that he—it was definitely a he—was wearing black. A rubber mask of some sort was pulled over his head.

She ran flat out. Unfortunately, her attacker was even faster than she was. Nancy couldn't keep up. Her heart was hammering and her shoulder was throbbing. She tried to put on speed, but it wasn't enough.

As she turned the second corner she groaned. The street was empty except for a car a couple of blocks away that was careening around a corner. Nancy watched in anger as her attacker's red brake lights flared for a second, then winked out.

He was gone. Nancy stood panting, her breath sending little clouds of vapor into the frigid air. She felt frustrated and unsettled. Maybe her attacker had been checking out a robbery target, but a nagging suspicion told her that his purpose was different. He had

been waiting for her, and she had walked right into his trap.

The next morning was bright and sunny—a perfect fall day. As Nancy descended the stairs, though, she still felt uneasy about the night before. Had she been set up? She still wasn't sure.

Hannah had a pancake breakfast waiting. Her father was already at the table.

"How'd the surveillance go?" Carson asked, smiling over the top of his newspaper.

Nancy shrugged. "I'm not sure. I think I ran into one of the robbers."

Carson put down his newspaper. "Are you okay?"

"I'm fine," Nancy promised.

"I thought you weren't going to tangle with them. You said you were going to call—"

"The police. Yes, I know," Nancy said, feeling a bit guilty. "I didn't have time. It was over in a minute." She took her seat.

Carson frowned. "Nancy, I don't like you putting yourself in danger."

"It wasn't a dangerous situation, Dad," she said. "At least, not very," she added under her breath. The guy had merely shoved her to the

ground, but he might have done worse. *Long-barrel automatics.* This gang used guns.

"Please be careful, won't you?" Carson said.

"I will," Nancy assured him with a smile. "And don't tell Hannah! She worries about me even more than you do."

"Don't tell Hannah *what?"* the housekeeper demanded, sweeping into the dining room with a pitcher of orange juice.

Nancy casually forked two pancakes onto her plate. "Nothing. It's just something . . . uh, something in the newspaper."

"You never lie well first thing in the morning," Hannah observed, taking her seat. "Your father said something about worrying. What have you been doing that would worry me?"

Nancy grinned weakly. "Uh . . . can I tell you about it this afternoon?"

Hannah sighed wearily and, to Nancy's relief, let it go at that.

After a minute Carson extended the front section of the newspaper to Nancy. He said, "Here's a story that will interest you."

Nancy glanced at the paper. "Ugh. That's Brenda's paper."

"Yes, but take a look anyway."

Nancy took the paper from him and scanned

it. The headline read, "Robbery Embarrasses Security Wizard." The byline was Brenda's.

"It figures," Nancy muttered.

She began to read. Brenda's writing style was breathless and sensational. It always irritated Nancy, and now she liked it even less. According to Brenda, the robbery was the most daring ever pulled in River Heights. The police, she stated, were baffled. No clues had been found.

"This is totally exaggerated!" Nancy complained.

"It gets worse," her father told her.

The concluding paragraph read:

> Yesterday's events may be the beginning of even deeper trouble for Hayward Security Systems. A survey of the crime scene by this reporter indicates that a company insider may have aided the robbers. A well-known private investigator was also at the site, suggesting that the company is planning an inquiry by impartial outsiders.

"Oh, great," Nancy said, tossing down the paper in disgust. "Not only does she trash

Tom's company, she also tips off his employees about my investigation."

"Were you planning to work undercover?" Carson asked.

"No, but it's always nice to have the element of surprise when you interview someone," Nancy explained. "People are usually more candid when they're caught off guard."

Nancy finished her breakfast in gloomy silence. She spent most of the day in her room reviewing the employee records that Tom had given her the day before. It was boring stuff, mostly, but Nancy found two items of interest.

The first was in Adam Reeves's employment application. As Nancy had guessed, he was nineteen. He had graduated from Mapleton High School two years earlier and had worked at a gas station from February until November of the previous year. Tom's company had hired him the previous December, and except for a two-week training period, he had been in the security guard division ever since.

What, Nancy wondered, had Adam done between his graduation and the following January, when he began working at the gas station? Six months of his life was unaccounted for!

The other interesting item that Nancy found was that both the security guard division and the crews who installed the alarm systems reported to the same man—the vice-president of operations, Neil Masterson. If anyone could tell her who could obtain the alarm code, it would be he.

Nancy was resting in her room before dinner when Bess Marvin and George Fayne swept in.

"Hannah says you've got a new case," George said, breezing over to Nancy's bed and flopping down. She was trim and highly athletic. Her curly dark hair was cut functionally short, and her dark eyes sparkled.

"Why didn't you tell us?" Bess complained, crossing to Nancy's full-length mirror for a quick check of her makeup. Although they were cousins, Bess was George's opposite. Her eyes were blue, her figure was curvy, and she wore her blond hair long.

"Give me a break!" Nancy said, laughing. "I only got this case yesterday."

"Well, where do we come in?" Bess demanded.

Nancy filled them in on the details. "As for you guys—well, I may not be needing your help this time around."

"You mean we're fired?" George asked with a grin.

Bess gave her hair an exaggerated toss. "Well, talk about *gratitude!*"

"Cut it out, you guys." Nancy giggled. "After all, you're always griping that I drag you into these things against your wills. Especially you, Bess. And this time I've got the help of a volunteer."

Nancy told them about her fan, Cindy Larson, and how she promised her she could help. "This case looks so straightforward, it'll probably be boring. I'll interview the suspects, check their backgrounds, and make my report. That's it."

Bess shook her head. "Oh, sure. I've heard *that* one before."

Just then Nancy's phone rang. She lifted the handset. "Hello?"

"Nancy, it's Tom. Can you meet me? Another warehouse has been robbed!"

Chapter Five

LEAVING BESS AND GEORGE with a hasty apology, Nancy raced to her car. The sky was twilight pink as she parked at the location Tom had given her. The warehouse in question was larger than the one that had been robbed the previous day. A sign over the loading bay door announced that it belonged to Jumping Jeans, a clothing chain.

Tom was inside with Chief McGinnis. "What happened?" Nancy asked, rushing to the inner office.

"Exactly the same thing that happened yes-

terday," Tom reported grimly. "The thieves got inside by disarming the alarm. It's the same gang, no question."

"Chief?" Nancy asked.

"Looks likely. Their method of operation is nearly identical. What surprises me is that they struck again so soon after their last job."

It was a bold strike, Nancy had to agree. They hadn't even waited for the "heat" to die down from the previous day.

"Where's the guard?" Nancy asked. "Did he see anything?"

Tom rubbed his temples. "Unfortunately, this warehouse isn't guarded on Sundays. The client felt that our alarm system would be enough."

"Tell me—how much did they take?" Nancy asked.

"That's the funny part," the chief said. "The warehouse manager has checked the inventory. They took only enough jeans to fill up about a quarter of your average truck."

"That's odd. They had all the time in the world," Nancy mused.

"Maybe, maybe not. They were operating in broad daylight," Tom observed.

"True, but on Sunday this area has got to be

deserted," Nancy reasoned. "If there was no guard around, who called in the complaint?"

"The robbers left the loading bay door slightly ajar when they took off. A patrol car eventually noticed and checked it out," the chief said.

"You had a car patrolling the area?" Nancy asked, surprised. If that was true, then the robbers' crime had been doubly brazen.

"Yes, and I wish I had assigned more than one," the chief said ruefully. "Unfortunately, like Tom, I didn't expect that they'd strike again so soon."

"Who did?" Nancy said sympathetically. "It looks like they'll consider making a hit anytime the area is fairly empty."

"Thank goodness it will be busy again tomorrow morning," Tom said. "I feel awful about this. And to think that I spent the day trying to relax! I was sailing on the river with some friends. I should have been at work instead."

"Don't blame yourself," Nancy advised him. "By the way, Tom, there's something I wanted to ask you. Do you remember I told you that I was going to do some surveillance last night?"

"Yes."

"Did you happen to mention my plan to anyone else?" she asked casually.

Tom frowned. "No, I don't think that I—wait a minute. I believe I mentioned it to my VP in charge of operations, Neil Masterson."

Nancy's eyebrows rose. "No one else?"

"No. Neil was the only person I talked to. How'd it go last night, anyway?" Tom asked.

"I ran into one of the gang."

"What?" the chief and Tom cried in unison.

"Where?" Tom went on.

The chief demanded, "When? And what did he look like?"

"He was tall, trim, and in excellent shape," Nancy told them. "He outran me by a mile. Other than that, I can't tell you much. He was dressed in black and had a rubber mask over his head."

"Nancy, maybe you'd better forget about doing any more surveillance," the chief said.

"But if there's a company insider involved, then he or she will keep the gang one step ahead of us all the time. My best chance of getting a line on the gang is to catch them in the act."

"I don't know, Nancy. It sounds risky," Tom said.

"Sure, but without risk there's no reward," Nancy countered.

The chief puffed out his cheeks and expelled a long breath. "Nancy, I think Tom is right. This gang seems to be fearless. From now on I want you to let me know every time you patrol the area. I'll make sure there's a cruiser around."

"Okay." Nancy nodded. She'd be glad to know that the police were standing by. She added, "With a little luck we'll put a stop to these robberies soon."

"How soon?" asked a girl's voice behind them.

Nancy turned in surprise to see Brenda furiously jotting something down on her pad. She was wearing designer jeans and an expensive brown leather jacket.

How much had Brenda heard of their conversation? Nancy wondered.

"The RHPD is continuing its investigation," the chief stated blandly. "Other than that, I have no comment."

"Mr. Hayward? Two of your customers have been robbed in one weekend. How can your other customers be certain that they won't be robbed, too?"

"Because Hayward systems are the best,

that's why," Tom said, losing some of his composure. "It's the people who rely on the other security services in town who should be concerned."

Brenda zeroed in. "Are you telling me that it's just coincidence that both robberies happened to clients of Hayward Security?"

Tom went on to defend his record. Nancy thought he was foolish to let himself be baited by Brenda. Her only interest was in getting a good story. If necessary she would twist his remarks to make him say anything she wanted.

Leaving them, Nancy privately told the chief of her destination and headed off to search the alley where she had been attacked the night before.

At nine the next morning, Nancy swung her Mustang into an empty parking space at Hayward Security Systems. Her examination of the alley the night before had revealed nothing, and she was now determined to try a fresh angle. The company's headquarters were in a low steel and tinted glass building in an office park on the outskirts of River Heights. She locked her car and walked to the front doors, which whooshed open automatically.

Inside, she was escorted to the office of Neil Masterson. He was in his early thirties, tall and dark haired. He seemed remarkably relaxed, given what had happened over the weekend. His handshake was firm and friendly.

Before Nancy took a seat opposite his desk, she noticed a framed photo on his desk.

"That's my wife and daughter," Neil said proudly, turning the photo so Nancy could see the pretty woman and laughing baby girl. "Tasha—that's my daughter—is eighteen months old."

"She's cute."

"Smart, too. Do I sound biased?" he asked with a grin.

"No, of course not." Nancy smiled, too, in spite of herself.

Leaning back in his desk chair, Neil got down to business. "Tom said that you're doing an independent investigation. That's great. An outside opinion is definitely called for under the circumstances. How can I help?"

"I need some information about the alarm system at the two warehouses. For instance, who makes up the access codes?"

"It's not 'who' but 'what,'" Neil answered. Swiveling, he patted the computer that occu-

pied one corner of his desk. "This is programmed with a random code generator. Once a month it changes the access codes for each of our customers' alarm systems by telephone."

"Then how do the guards and the warehouse managers find out the code?" Nancy inquired.

"Do you see that printer over there?"

Nancy spotted a computer printer to her left. A string of envelopes was rolled into it. The envelopes were the type with carbon paper lining and tissue-thin sheets of paper sealed inside, so that a message could be printed without having to open the envelope.

"When the computer assigns a new code," Neil continued, "it prints a sealed copy. Once a month the guards and the warehouse manager report to this office in person, and I hand them the envelope. They memorize the code. Then I run the envelope through our shredder."

"I see," Nancy said. "What happens if a guard calls in sick? Or the warehouse gets a new manager? Do you print out extra copies of the code for their replacements?"

"Well—no. I have to print a new envelope, of course, but when I do, the computer generates a new code."

Nancy nodded. "Clever. Whoever designed

this system seems to have thought of everything. It sounds amazingly secure."

"We thought so, too—until this weekend."

Nancy frowned. "So if only authorized users have access to the codes, then only an insider could be behind these thefts," she said after a moment.

"Unfortunately, that's the only possible explanation," Neil confirmed.

"Well, the next step, I guess, is to see if there is anyone who worked at both warehouses," Nancy said.

Neil tapped a yellow legal pad on his desk. "I started working on that angle this morning," he said.

"And?"

"Well," Neil said, "there's only one name that crops up at both locations. It's one of our guards, I'm afraid."

"Adam Reeves, right?" Nancy guessed excitedly.

"Yes."

She grinned. "Then he's our man!"

"Not necessarily," Neil said cautiously. "You see, he was assigned to the Jumping Jeans warehouse for only one month. The alarm code has changed several times since then."

"But perhaps he or another member of the gang bribed someone to leak it. What's your opinion of Adam Reeves?"

Neil shrugged. "We screen our employees very carefully. Other than that, I really can't say. I hardly know the guy. I assume he's okay, though. He's been working here longer than I have."

"I see," she said thoughtfully.

After chatting for a few more minutes, Nancy thanked him and left. To get to the bottom of this, she realized, she would have to dig much deeper.

Nancy's home was in one of the nicest neighborhoods in River Heights. It was an area of broad streets lined with graceful trees, sweeping lawns, and large houses.

As Nancy pulled into her driveway, she saw that her father's car was parked there. What was he doing at home on a Monday? she wondered. After shutting off the engine, she leaped out of her car and walked around the house to the kitchen door.

Hannah was in the kitchen. "Your father's working in his study," she reported. "Some corporate work, I gather."

"Poor Dad," Nancy said sympathetically.

Nancy's father was a well-known lawyer whose first love was criminal cases. Still, he did some corporate work, as the hefty fees paid by his corporate clients were hard to turn down. He did take the work, but grumbled whenever he did.

Nancy tapped on the door of his study and went in. Her father was talking on the phone. He waved her into one of the leather chairs opposite his desk.

"Incredible," he was saying into the phone. "Down two points in one hour? That'll mean some problems for—"

The person at the other end of the line began to speak. Carson nodded, then frowned, then shook his head sadly.

"Well, keep me posted," he said finally. "Goodbye."

"What's going on?" Nancy asked as her father hung up.

"That was my stockbroker in Chicago," he said. "He called with some information I requested, but then we began to chat. He told me that Brenda Carlton's latest article about Tom Hayward has been picked up by a wire service, and it ran in this morning's Chicago papers."

Carson went on. "The article makes it sound

like Tom's company is in bad trouble. Investors are dumping their shares in Hayward Security right and left."

"Bad news, huh?" Nancy asked, concerned.

Carson nodded. "You bet. The price of a share has dropped almost twenty-five percent this morning alone. Since Tom is the majority shareholder, that means he has lost a small fortune."

Nancy gulped. "How much?"

"I'd say"—Carson took a breath—"a quarter of a million dollars at least!"

Chapter Six

"YOU'RE KIDDING!" Nancy exclaimed. "He lost a quarter of a million dollars in a few *hours?"*

"Yes."

Nancy was incredulous. "Dad, how can that be? Tom's *company* isn't losing money—not yet, anyway. And it didn't shrink in size overnight, either."

Her father nodded. "True, but that company is owned by its shareholders. Those shareholders value their stock only as long as Tom's company is able to show a profit."

"So what you're saying is that when the outlook for future profits goes down, the stock loses its value."

"Right. And because Tom's fortune is tied up in his own stock, he's losing like crazy."

Nancy whistled. "Boy, that means in another day or two Tom could be broke!"

After lunch Nancy started to dig. Her first calls were to the two warehouse managers. Both gave her descriptions and lot numbers of the goods that had been stolen. Stolen merchandise was usually sold, and that meant that it could be traced. It was a starting point, anyway.

Next, she rechecked the backgrounds of the guards currently assigned to the warehouses in question. She already knew about Adam Reeves, but he was only one of three guards regularly assigned to the CD Revolution warehouse. Jumping Jeans also had three regular guards. Except for the six months "missing" out of Adam's life, they each had spotless records and excellent references.

She was copying names and numbers from the phone book when Cindy Larson arrived after school.

"*This* is your room?" Cindy asked as Hannah showed her in. "Gosh, it's so—"

"Ordinary?" Nancy supplied.

"Yeah. I sort of expected—I don't know, a crime lab or something."

"I'd love to have one, but then where would I keep my stereo?" Nancy joked.

"Okay, how do I start?" Cindy asked.

"First, we'll try to find the stolen goods and trace them backward," Nancy said.

"You mean we're going *shopping?*" Cindy asked in amazement. "All right! And you said that detective work was dull."

Nancy grinned. "Don't get out your wallet yet. We'll be doing our 'shopping' by phone. I've made a list of local odd-lot retailers," Nancy said. "That means they carry merchandise that didn't sell at full-price stores. A few of them may also sell 'hot' goods. You're going to call them up looking for specific jeans and CDs."

"So if they've got what I'm looking for, we go check to see if the stuff came from the stolen lots, right?" Cindy concluded.

"You got it." Nancy was pleased.

Cindy smiled. "You mentioned two things. What's the other one?"

"We're going to research and write a profile of Adam Reeves," Nancy announced.

"Uh-oh," Cindy said. "This sounds like homework."

Nancy smiled and opened a drawer to pull out a sheet of stationery for a business called Highway Auto Supply. It had no address.

Cindy's eyes went wide. "What are we going to do with *that?*"

"Get Adam's credit history," Nancy explained. "Find out about his debts, credit cards, bank accounts—stuff like that. We want to know how much money he spends and where he spends it."

"Nancy, that's so personal! Who's going to tell us all that?" Cindy wondered.

Nancy leaned back in her chair. She was proud of this idea. "A credit bureau. We claim that Adam wants to open a charge account at our 'store,' and we want to know if he is a good credit risk. The bureau will tell us—in great detail—for a fee."

"Wow, I had no idea."

Nancy's tone grew determined. "Cindy, that's just the beginning. By the time we're done, we'll know things about Adam that *he's* forgotten."

* * *

They worked until dinnertime and then Cindy left.

Nancy drove back to the warehouse district because that was where she would have the best chance of getting a lead on the gang.

Before going she informed the chief, as she had promised. Two cruisers would be in the area all night.

Nancy had a large-scale map of the area from the city assessor's office with her. It showed each building, and Nancy had used a green marker to highlight those that were guarded by Hayward Security Systems. About a third of the buildings on the map were highlighted.

A light drizzle was falling when Nancy turned into the warehouse district. She flicked on her wipers and slowly drove through the streets. Within ten minutes she passed both patrol cars. As she did she turned her headlights off and on to identify herself.

The patrol cars answered with their lights. She felt good knowing that help was near.

Two hours later she decided she'd see more on foot. She parked near a cluster of fifty-gallon oil drums. Pulling up the collar of her leather jacket, she set out. Her sneakers squished on the wet pavement.

Finally, around 1:30 A.M., Nancy gave up and walked back to her car.

Slipping her key into the door, she unlocked it and climbed in. Her neck felt stiff. She rolled her head to stretch the muscles.

Nancy started the engine and snapped on the headlights. Something was different.

She tensed.

What was it?

A box was strapped to the fifty-gallon drum directly in front of her. Taped to the box with thick silver duct tape were two cylinders made of waxy red paper. Plastic wires looped from the cylinders to the box.

A bomb! Without a moment's thought Nancy slammed her car into reverse and jammed the accelerator pedal to the floor. Someone wanted her off this case in a major way!

Her tires shrieked. The Mustang fishtailed backward. Before she had gone ten feet, however, the world in front of her windshield erupted into a sea of white-hot flame.

Chapter Seven

FOR A FEW BLINDING SECONDS the air outside the car boiled like the surface of the sun. Nancy felt her heart hammering in her chest. She was terrified.

But the Mustang was still racing backward. Fifty yards later she hit the brakes, yanked the ignition key out of its slot, and leaped out.

There were two patches of flame on the hood of her car. Nancy whipped off her jacket and beat the flames until they went out.

She heard the loud crackling of the burning

drum and watched as the one next to it ignited. Then a third caught. Nancy crouched. Off in the distance sirens began to wail. A patrol car screeched around a corner several blocks away and came flying toward her, its roof lights strobing. She started to tremble as the enormity of what had almost happened to her began to sink in.

The patrol doors of the patrol car flew open as it skidded to a stop on the wet pavement. "Are you okay?" an officer yelled as she ran toward the detective.

"Yes—no! Well, I'm not sure. I guess I am," Nancy said in a shaky voice.

"You look okay," the woman said, shining a flashlight in her face. The flashlight's beam swung to the Mustang. "Your car will need a new paint job, though."

Nancy smiled weakly. "It deserves it. That car saved my life."

"What happened?"

"A bomb was strapped to one of those oil drums," Nancy explained. "Whoever planted it must have been waiting nearby with a remote-control detonator, because a few seconds after I started my car, it went off."

"Then the guy might still be in the area!"

The officer quickly lifted her radio from her belt.

"Forget it," Nancy said, suddenly feeling angry at herself. "He's gone by now."

A few seconds later a fire engine arrived. The fire fighters quickly contained the blaze by spraying the area with chemicals. Nancy repeated her story for the fire chief, several detectives, and finally, Chief McGinnis. "That gang of thieves is definitely on to me," she concluded.

"Perhaps they saw you patrolling the area," the chief suggested.

Nancy shook her head. "I don't think so. If they did, why didn't I see *them?* No, I'm pretty sure they were told where to find me."

The chief's eyebrows drew together. "Who told them, do you think?"

Nancy gazed upward. The rain was letting up. Between the clouds she could see patches of clear, starry sky.

"I'm not sure," Nancy admitted, "but I'm going to find out."

The offices of Loomis & Petersen seemed to have survived unchanged for decades. The front door led into a retail store with large wall

displays of locks, alarms, and intercom systems. A salesman took Nancy's name and disappeared up a flight of stairs at the back of the store.

A minute later he returned. "Stan says go right on up."

"Thanks."

Nancy climbed to the second floor, which was as out of date as the store below. The floor was bare wood, the paint on the walls was faded, and the hall was illuminated by long strips of fluorescent lighting.

Stanley Loomis occupied a corner office. Its large windows let in plenty of the morning light and offered a beautiful view of the river. He rose, presented a beefy hand to Nancy, and settled back into an old-fashioned wooden desk chair that squeaked every time he moved.

"I've read about you," Loomis said. He reached for a package of cigars on his desk, but then changed his mind. "You seem like a smart kid. Why are you working for Hayward?"

"What makes you think I'm working for Hayward?" Nancy asked.

"C'mon! Why else would you be here? Anyway, I saw you with Chief McGinnis and that Hayward punk on Saturday."

"I see." Loomis was shrewd, Nancy decided.

"You're wasting your time here. You know that, don't you?" Loomis barked.

"What makes you say that?" Nancy asked.

"Those robberies had to be an inside job," Loomis said. "That means you should be investigating Hayward's clients, or maybe Hayward's own employees. But not me."

"I have to cover all the angles," Nancy said evenly.

Loomis laughed nastily. "And what do you think you're going to get from me? A confession? The only thing I can tell you is that those computerized systems that Hayward has been selling are about as secure as a bureau drawer. If you're covering angles, start there."

Nancy was surprised. "You're saying Tom sells crummy alarm systems?"

"Not crummy, exactly," Loomis admitted. "But they're no better than mine."

Nancy was tired of playing games. She went on the offensive. "Mr. Loomis, on Saturday you baited Tom over a warehouse loudspeaker system. How did you happen to be at that particular location that day?"

"Coincidence," Loomis said, studying his nails.

Nancy didn't believe in coincidence. "Oh, really?"

"Prove that it wasn't," he challenged.

Nancy was silent. She couldn't prove it, and he knew it.

"Oh, don't look so gloomy," Loomis said, smiling. "Look, I'll tell you why I was there—I was checking out a customer's facility for a possible upgrade of his system. I'm planning some moves that will take the wind out of Tom Hayward's sails."

Nancy speculated upon hearing this. Did his "plans" include robbing Tom's customers in order to ruin Tom's business?

"You seem to resent Tom's success," Nancy stated plainly.

"Of course I do," Loomis said. He leaned forward all of a sudden and pointed a finger at her. "Hayward tried to buy me—us—out. Us! After thirty years in business!"

Nancy kept her face impassive. Now she was getting somewhere! "But you wouldn't sell?"

"*I* won't. But my part—" Suddenly Loomis cut off. "Well, that's none of your business. Drop it."

Nancy knew that she was getting warm. Loomis was clumsily trying to hide something. Before she could dig deeper, however, there was a knock at Loomis's door. The door swung open, and a thin, gray-haired man wearing a

baggy suit stormed in. He had a piece of stationery clutched tightly in his fist.

"Stanley, I won't let you send this letter to young Hayward! It's insulting. If he reads this, he'll forget all about—" Suddenly the man noticed Nancy. "Oh, I'm sorry. I didn't realize you had company."

"This is my partner, Roy Petersen," Loomis explained. "Roy, this is Nancy Drew."

Petersen's face lit up. "You're the young detective, aren't you? I'm very glad to meet you, young lady." He offered Nancy his hand. "You know, it's nice—"

"Clam up, Roy," Loomis said rudely, cutting his partner off.

"Stanley!"

"Nancy is helping Hayward investigate those robberies," Loomis said.

"Oh—yes, a terrible business," Petersen said. "I hope you can get to the bottom of it, Nancy."

Nancy listened to the exchange in fascination. The partners were as different as night and day. She also suspected that they were in the middle of a major disagreement—a disagreement that had everything to do with Tom Hayward. But what was it?

"Anyway, Stanley," Petersen went on,

"about this letter. We shouldn't be so quick to brush off young Hayward. His offer—"

Again, Loomis cut off his partner in midsentence. "Roy, I told you that subject is closed!" He quickly turned to Nancy. "Miss Drew, would you please excuse us? We have some business here—that is, unless you have more questions?"

"None for now."

After leaving Loomis & Petersen, Nancy turned her Mustang out of town and into the farmland that lay beyond the city limits. She needed time to drive and think.

Questions were swimming around in her mind. Had the thieves known in advance that she would be patrolling the warehouse district? Who had told them? Why did they steal only moderate amounts of loot? And what about the codes? How had they gotten hold of them?

More than anything else, however, she was nagged by the feeling that she had missed something during her talk with Stanley Loomis. Something he had said was more important than it seemed—but what? She couldn't figure it out.

Nancy checked her rearview mirror. A hundred yards behind her a beige-colored car was

keeping pace with her. Nancy slowed down, so the car could overtake and pass her, but it didn't. She shrugged and returned to her thoughts.

A few minutes later she checked her rear-view mirror again. The car was still there. It looked familiar. Hadn't a car just like it stopped behind her at a red light back in River Heights?

She sped up. The car behind her sped up, too. Without signaling, Nancy quickly braked and swung onto another road. The car behind her turned, too.

Nancy clenched her jaw and pressed down on the gas pedal. There was no doubt about it. She was being followed.

Chapter Eight

NANCY CONTINUED to drive normally. She didn't want to lose this tail. She wanted to identify the person.

The road rose and dipped over a series of low hills. Nancy was pleased to spot a barn roof over the next hill. A farm was just what she needed.

As Nancy topped the rise, she jammed the gas pedal to the floor, and in a few seconds she reached the farm. Swiftly she braked and swung into the muddy yard on the far side of the barn. When she was out of sight, she

turned so that the Mustang was again facing the road.

A few seconds later the other car raced past her position. It was going much faster than before. The driver was obviously panic-stricken because Nancy was no longer in sight.

Smiling in satisfaction, Nancy gunned her engine, swung onto the road, and zoomed off the way she had come. As she topped the rise, she glanced in her rearview mirror. The other car was about a hundred yards beyond the farm, doing a hasty three-point turn in the middle of the road.

All right, she thought. The chase is on!

Nancy quickly formulated her plan. A mile later she found the spot to execute it—another farm. The dirt yard surrounding the barn was even wetter than the one at the last farm. A tractor had gouged deep tracks in the mud, she could see. Thank goodness for the previous night's rain!

Quickly Nancy drove to the far side of the barnyard and turned right. Next, she pushed open her door and slumped down in her seat. From a distance, she hoped, it would look as if she had abandoned her car and run into the barn.

Twenty seconds later the engine of the other

car grew louder. As she had hoped, it immediately swung into the far side of the barnyard—the side that was the muddiest. With luck, the other car was now hubcap-deep in the mud. She heard its door close softly.

Nancy waited a few seconds longer, to give the driver time to get halfway to the barn. Then she sat up.

She wanted to check out the driver of the other car. One good look at his face was all she needed—

It wasn't a he. With a start, Nancy saw who it was.

Brenda!

The girl was trying to tiptoe gingerly through the mud. It wasn't going well. Her leather jacket, calf-length wool skirt, and expensive-looking boots just weren't right for the job. A grimace of disgust twisted her mouth as her right boot slid ankle-deep into the muck.

As she heard Nancy's door slam, she looked panicked and started back for her car. But her feet kept sinking.

Soon Brenda gave up. She stood still—and visibly sank deeper into the mud. "Nancy, you tricked me! I thought you were inside!" she yelled.

Nancy snapped open her door and climbed

out, trying hard not to smile. "Brenda, if you want leads for your stories, why not just phone?"

Brenda folded her arms. "Oh, sure, like you'd really help me!"

Nancy finally gave in to a grin. "Maybe I would, and maybe I wouldn't."

Brenda became indignant. "You can't stop me from reporting the news!"

Nancy shook her head. "I'm not 'news' and you know it. You're just hoping I'll do your thinking for you. Well, from now on you can do your own thinking, Brenda."

Brenda's jaw tightened. "I have. You're not the only girl in River Heights with a brain, you know. In fact, I even know who the insider at Hayward Security is."

Nancy was interested. Reaching inside her car, she switched off the ignition key. "Who is it?"

Brenda walked toward her, her boots making little sucking sounds in the mud. "I think it's Hayward's vice-president, Neil Masterson," she said. "If anyone can fiddle with the alarm systems, it's him. Plus he's got a motive," she hinted.

Now Nancy was *really* interested. "What motive?"

"His baby daughter."

Nancy recalled the photo on Neil's desk. What was the little girl's name? Tasha. She frowned. "What do you mean?"

Brenda finally drew near. "She has a congenital heart defect. She's had several operations. *Expensive* operations."

"So what? Neil's medical insurance pays for that," Nancy reasoned.

Brenda shook her head. "Only to a point. Most medical plans have a limit. I checked, and Neil has exceeded the Hayward plan's limit."

"Are you sure?" Nancy asked.

"Oh, yes. His little girl had three operations last year. We're talking about open-heart surgery, you understand. That adds up very fast. The total cost must have been hundreds of thousands of dollars."

There was no way that Neil Masterson could be making that kind of money. So how was he paying the hospital bills? Nancy would have to find out.

The corners of Brenda's mouth curled smugly. "So, what do you think? Is that excellent detective work, or what?"

Nancy shrugged. "Maybe, maybe not. Your father is a smart man. I know that, too."

Brenda recoiled as if stung. Bull's-eye, Nancy thought. It was her father who had found out about Masterson.

"Well, thanks for the tip," Nancy said, climbing back into her Mustang. "And good luck getting out of that mud."

"Aren't you going to help me?" Brenda wailed.

"You need a tractor. Or maybe a team of oxen," Nancy joked.

"Why, you—! Okay, I'll go find a farmer," Brenda said tightly. "But before you go, get this straight: I'm going to crack this case, Nancy Drew. And I don't need any help from you!"

As Nancy roared away, she shook her head in wonder. If Brenda truly wanted to catch the insider at Hayward Security, she wasn't going to do it by tailing a detective.

Nancy drove directly to Hayward's headquarters. Neil Masterson was in a good mood when she was shown into his office.

They talked amiably for a few minutes. Then, having broken the ice, Nancy leaned back in her chair.

"By the way, I saw on your job application that you were in the army."

"Six years," he said proudly.

"Did you have any demolitions training while you were enlisted?" Nancy asked.

"Some—why?" His tone grew cautious.

"Just wondering. Tell me, do you watch the eleven o'clock news on TV?" she went on conversationally.

"No, my wife and I usually go to bed around ten."

Nancy said, "So you were at home with your wife last night?"

"All night. Why are you asking?" Neil was definitely suspicious now.

"Just—"

"Wondering, yes, I know," he finished. "Nancy, you're checking on my whereabouts, aren't you? Does this mean you suspect that *I* might be involved in the robberies?"

"I have to cover all possibilities," Nancy said hastily.

"Where I spend my free time is my business! I don't owe an explanation to you or anyone else!" His face was red with anger. "Now, if you'll excuse me, I have to see some people." Rising, he walked quickly out of his office.

Nancy was stunned. Why was Neil acting so guilty? If anything, she was more suspicious of him now than before.

Later that afternoon Cindy Larson arrived at Nancy's house. She was carrying a file folder. Her face was flushed with excitement.

"Hi," Nancy said, pulling a second chair over to her desk. "We're going to write a profile of Stanley Loomis today," Nancy announced.

"Good. I've already begun his," Cindy said.

"You have?"

Cindy grinned. "He acted so suspicious on Saturday yelling at Tom over that loudspeaker and all, so today on the way over I stopped at the library and looked him up in *Who's Who in River Heights.* The Chamber of Commerce publishes it. Then I searched the indexes for the city newspapers and found some real old articles about him."

"Anything interesting?" Nancy asked.

"He used to be a burglar," Cindy announced.

"What!"

Cindy nodded. "That was a long time ago. He went to prison and reformed—or so he said. After his parole he went into the security business. He told his customers that he could protect them better than anyone else because he knew better than anyone else how to rob them!"

"Quite a sales pitch," Nancy said dryly. "Good work, Cindy."

Cindy beamed. "Anything else?"

"We need to write a profile on Tom's vice-president, Neil Masterson," Nancy said.

"You're kidding! He lives across the street from me." Cindy sat down. "Nancy, I can't believe he's a suspect. He's so nice! I've even baby-sat his daughter, Tasha."

"Even so, we're starting a profile," Nancy said grimly. "Hold on! You say he lives right across the street?"

"Uh-huh." Cindy looked troubled.

"Can you see his garage and driveway clearly from your room?" Nancy asked.

"Yes."

Nancy tapped her pencil on her desktop. "Fantastic. Cindy, how would you like to do some surveillance?"

"I—I guess so," Cindy answered uncertainly.

"Good. Watch his house tonight. If he leaves, jot down the time. Also write down the time when he returns. Don't try to follow him anywhere, though. Just watch."

"Will this prove him innocent?" Cindy asked hopefully.

"I'm pretty sure the thieves'll be working tonight. If Neil is one of them, he'll go out. If he doesn't—well, it may not prove that he's innocent, necessarily, but it will help."

"I'll do it, then," Cindy promised. "Boy, it sure is creepy to suspect one of my own neighbors! I feel like a traitor."

"When you're a detective," Nancy said, "you have to ignore your personal feelings and be objective about everyone."

When Nancy went downstairs for dinner that evening, her father was waiting for her. She had a pretty good idea of what he wanted to talk to her about.

"I guess you saw my car, huh?" she asked in a small voice.

Carson nodded gravely. "I did. Would you like to tell me what happened?"

She told him.

Carson wearily rubbed his eyes. He was still in his business suit and looked tired. "Nancy, it isn't worth the risk."

"Yes, it is. Dad, listen—" Nancy began.

Her father cut her off with an angry wave of his hand. "No, *you* listen. I won't let you risk your life. This time you're up against professionals, Nancy—ruthless, violent men!"

"Yes, but . . ." Nancy's voice trailed off. She knew he was right.

"Nancy—" Carson's voice softened. "It looks to me like you're trying to prove something with this case. What? Does it have something to do with your young assistant?"

"With Cindy? No. What makes you think that?" Nancy asked, genuinely puzzled.

"I thought that maybe you were trying not to let her down—to be professional yourself. A professional detective, that is."

"No, that's not it—not exactly," Nancy said. The truth was, she hadn't felt that there was anything special about this case—until now. But now that her father had pointed it out, she realized that there *was* something different. She sighed. "I guess it started when I spoke at the Career Fair on Saturday. Remember that?"

"Uh-huh."

Nancy went on. "Well, I hadn't realized it until now, but it got me wondering about my own career—you know, what I'm going to do with my life. I want to know what it would be like to be a real detective—a full-time, *career* detective."

"So you decided to try it out?" Carson guessed.

Nancy nodded. "Sort of. You see, on this case I've tried to be totally professional. I've tried to treat Tom like a client."

A smile grew on her father's face. "I understand. But, sweetheart, remember you've got plenty of time to choose your career. Years, in fact. You don't have to rush."

"No, I don't suppose I do." Nancy smiled, too. In a way, she felt a whole lot better thinking that. "But, Dad, now that I've started this case, I have to finish it. I'm not a quitter. You taught me that." But would he let her continue her investigation? She held her breath while he thought.

"Okay, finish the job," Carson said after a minute. "But promise me something—"

Nancy hugged him. "Anything!"

"From now on take Bess or George with you when you patrol the warehouse district," he requested.

"I promise," Nancy said.

That night Nancy positioned herself on a platform high up the side of a grain silo near the river. She was bundled in a thick wool sweater and her leather jacket.

George was with her. "Tell me again why we're up here?" her friend asked.

"Because it's a good surveillance point. And because this time I can stay still and let the robbers do the moving around," Nancy explained. She reached into her knapsack.

To help her she had borrowed a piece of equipment from Chief McGinnis. It was a Night Vision Device—an NVD, for short. It had a lens like the zoom lens on a camera, a slim rectangular body, and a binocularlike eyepiece. By adjusting the brightness control on its side, she could turn night into a high-contrast, green-colored day.

It was cold and windy on the platform, but the view was perfect. Peering through the NVD, she began to survey the rooftops below. Most robberies, she knew, involved a lookout. Where better to station one than on a roof?

For more than an hour she scanned the area, moving methodically up and down the grid of streets. She was already familiar with most of the buildings. From this angle, though, they looked vulnerable. Many had easy points of entry on their roofs.

Then Nancy caught a sudden movement. Swinging the NVD back, she searched a rooftop half a block away.

There!

She caught the movement again. By the

stairwell door. She focused. Nancy was looking at a hideous face. Its skin was rotted and blackened. Teeth and jawbone showed through a ragged hole in its cheek. Dried blood caked its empty eye sockets.

Then the face turned. Pupils shone from deep in the bloody sockets. It was staring right at her.

Chapter Nine

NANCY GASPED. Her heart began to pound. Then she forced herself to think rationally. Dead men did not move around. It was a rubber Halloween mask on a robber. And she was sure he couldn't see her in the dark.

"Nan, what's wrong?" George asked, but Nancy just waved her to silence.

Nancy continued to follow him as he looked over the edge of the roof. After scanning slowly right and left, he waved his arm. It was a signal—*all clear.*

The thieves were about to strike! Nancy

repacked her knapsack and tore down the ladder to the street, George close behind.

When they reached the street, Nancy tossed her keys to George. "Start the car and wait here. Keep the passenger door open. I may need to get in in a hurry."

"Where are you going?" George asked.

"Just to verify there's a robbery in progress. As soon as I'm sure, I'll be right back—then we'll drive to a phone."

It took only a minute to reach the corner of the building. She crouched low and risked a peek. No trucks, no robbers, no open loading bays. Everything was shut tight. What was going on? Nancy slid around the corner and started down the street, hugging the wall and darting between shadows.

Except for her, there was no movement at all on the block.

Suddenly forty yards ahead of her a door flew open. A figure darted out and ran down the street at top speed. Nancy could plainly see the rubber mask pulled over his head. It was him!

She took off. Her knapsack made running awkward, so she shucked it off and tossed it into a shadow. She would get it later. Right

now it was more important to follow the Dead Man.

The chase lasted for five blocks. It was the same guy she had chased two nights earlier, Nancy realized excitedly. She recognized the way he pumped his arms and lifted his knees. Track athletes ran that way. She saw that she was falling behind. Rats! She *couldn't* lose him—not now! She speeded up.

Then, halfway up the hill, Nancy saw a swirling red light bouncing off the buildings ahead. A police car was around the corner! The Dead Man saw it, too, and quickly darted down an alley. When Nancy reached it, she saw him sprinting up a fire escape to a roof above.

She decided not to follow. He was trapped, she knew. Catching him would only be a matter of surrounding the building and tightening the net. She ran to the corner to flag the approaching police car.

There were three of them speeding toward her. Nancy skidded halfway into the street and began to wave her arms. The first two whizzed by her at high speed. The third screeched to a stop. Chief McGinnis was in the passenger seat. He rolled down his window and shouted,

"Nancy, get in! There's a five-five-oh at Uptown Electronics."

"No! It's back at All-County, and one of the guys is on the roof of that building!" She pointed. "I chased him there!"

"What?"

Rapidly Nancy explained. The chief ordered his driver to dispatch four cars to trap the Dead Man. Satisfied, Nancy climbed in the backseat.

"But, Chief, I thought we were going to All-County Moving and Storage!" Nancy said as they pulled up in front of Uptown Electronics. "I saw the lookout signal an all-clear from that roof."

"I'm afraid you're mistaken, Nancy—see?" the chief said.

A pair of medics was wheeling out a stretcher. Strapped to it was a young man in a Hayward Security uniform.

"I don't understand," Nancy muttered. "This doesn't make sense, unless—"

"Unless what?" the chief asked.

"The lookout wasn't a lookout at all, but a decoy," she said dejectedly.

After Nancy returned with George, they quickly learned the facts. The gang had keyed off the alarm, grabbed the guard, knocked him

out, and made their getaway with fifty thousand dollars' worth of laptop computers. The police had been called by the guard after he came to.

The chief's men had not found the decoy. The man was obviously familiar with the area and had an escape route ready. Nancy felt terribly frustrated.

Nancy turned to Tom and the chief. "The laptop computers they took were worth a lot, but they could easily have taken more. They took only twenty-five boxes."

"It's almost as if they're robbing for the sport of it," George remarked.

The chief shrugged. "Usually profit is the motive behind a robbery."

Nancy excused herself to call Cindy Larson. It was late, but Cindy was still awake, watching out her bedroom window.

"Mr. Masterson came home at six o'clock and he's been inside ever since," Cindy reported with obvious relief.

"Okay, thanks. I'll see you tomorrow after school," Nancy said. "Oh, and Cindy—wear old clothes that you don't care about."

"Why?" Her assistant was curious.

"It's probably better if I don't tell you. See you then."

Nancy hung up and bit her lip thoughtfully. That Neil Masterson had an alibi didn't completely clear him, she knew. But it helped.

The following morning Nancy called Neil Masterson's office and found that Adam Reeves had not been on duty the night before.

Checking Stanley Loomis's whereabouts was even easier. The business section of *Today's Times* carried an article describing a speech he had given to the River Heights Retail Merchants Association the night before. In it he had stressed the need for reliable security. The alibi didn't clear him, but it did indicate he couldn't have taken part in the robbery.

Next she phoned Chief McGinnis to ask if there had been any sign of the stolen goods. The chief told her nothing had surfaced.

Nancy spent the rest of the morning focusing on the profiles of her three strongest suspects.

She went to check out Adam Reeves's apartment building. It was clean and well maintained. Not fancy, but nice. The refuse area behind the building was orderly. She had no trouble finding what she needed. After loading it in her trunk, she drove home.

She was studying Adam Reeves's credit report when Cindy arrived.

"So soon?" her assistant asked, pulling over her seat. "I thought it would take weeks for that to get here."

"I asked them to fax it to my father's office," Nancy told her.

"What does it tell us?" Cindy asked.

"Plenty. When you add up everything he's spending, it totals up to more than he's making."

"Where does he get the extra money?" Cindy wondered.

"Good question. This credit report lists only one employer, so it's a pretty good bet that he hasn't got a second job," Nancy said.

They went to the garage then, and Nancy backed out her car so they'd have plenty of room to work. After opening her trunk, she lifted out the plastic garbage bag she had taken from Adam's garbage can.

Cindy gulped. "Nancy, are we going to do what I think we're going to do?"

"Uh-huh," Nancy confirmed, spreading newspapers on the driveway. "That's why I asked you to wear old clothes."

They both donned gardening gloves, and Nancy slashed open the bag.

"Oh, gross!" Cindy said, her face twisted in disgust.

"Dig in." Nancy smiled. "We need to make a list of everything we find."

When it was done, the list was quite revealing. Adam dined on sirloin, and liked expensive cologne. The most interesting discovery, though, were several copies of a magazine for entrepreneurs.

"It could be that Adam is planning to open a business," Nancy surmised.

"How can he do that if he's spending more than he makes?" Cindy wondered.

"He may be expecting to get a big lump of money soon," Nancy explained. "Now, let's review. Both Neil Masterson and Stanley Loomis could have masterminded these robberies," she summarized. "They both have the expertise, and they both have motives. Stanley Loomis wants to hurt his competition—Neil Masterson has hospital bills to pay."

"But what about all the money Adam Reeves is spending?" Cindy asked.

"If you ask me, he is the strongest suspect," Nancy said. "He had more opportunities than the others to be involved."

"So where do we go from here?" Cindy asked.

"You go back to the telephone," Nancy said. "A line on those stolen goods would help a lot. I'm going to do something I should have done two days ago."

"What's that?"

"Tail Adam Reeves," Nancy declared.

Adam left work at five o'clock. From the warehouse he drove to his apartment building. Nancy followed at a discreet distance. Parking down the street from his building, she watched him go inside. Then she settled down to wait.

At ten minutes after six Adam returned to his car. He had changed from his uniform into a suit and topcoat. He looked sharp.

To Nancy's surprise, he then went to a house several streets from hers, where he picked up a date: an attractive blond girl.

They went to Chez Louis, an expensive waterside restaurant. Nancy went in and sat at the bar and sipped a soda—slowly. She secretly kept her eyes focused on Adam's table. The girl looked utterly bored.

At least, she did until Adam presented her with a long, flat box from a jewelry store. Her face lit up, and she opened it with a cry of delight that Nancy could hear all the way at the bar. Inside was a gold necklace.

Nancy had seen enough. This reinforced her conclusion that Adam was living beyond his means. In fact, she now had enough evidence to confront him. And once confronted with some hard facts, he might make a confession.

If he didn't, he would nevertheless feel the pressure, and crooks under pressure tended to make mistakes.

Nancy walked to the parking lot and unlocked the door of her car. As she was bending down to get in, she was suddenly jerked up and off her feet.

She was caught from behind in a choke hold!

Chapter Ten

NANCY COULDN'T BREATHE. She struggled, but it was pointless. The arm around her throat was like steel. She managed to squeeze out the words, *"Put . . . me . . . down!"*

"Not until you say why you're following me." The voice belonged to Adam Reeves.

"I can't—*aagh!*—breathe!"

Adam relaxed his grip. Nancy's toes met the ground, but he didn't let her go. She gulped in air. What should she say? If she blew it, Adam might kill her on the spot.

She decided to stick to the truth—part of it, anyway. "You worked at two of the warehouses that got robbed. Of course I'm following you —what did you expect?"

"Standard procedure, huh?" Adam mocked. He tightened his grip a notch. "You'll have to do better, Nancy."

"Okay." Nancy's windpipe hurt. She recited some facts. "You've got high balances on your credit cards. Your car payments are six hundred and forty-six dollars a month. You're planning to open a business, but you've got nothing in the bank. Get the idea?"

Adam suddenly released her, and Nancy slumped to the ground, gasping. But in a moment she was back on her feet and facing him with a cold stare.

"How do you know that stuff?" he demanded.

It was amazing how easily you could put someone off balance with a little research and intuition.

"Never mind how I know," she said, sounding more assertive than she felt. "You're in a lot of trouble, Adam."

"Baloney. That's not what *he* says."

"He?"

Adam caught himself. "Never mind who. Get to the point."

"The point is, my evidence shows that you're involved in something illegal. You'd better start cooperating."

Adam sneered. "You don't have anything solid on me."

Nancy was stuck. He was right. Surprising a confession out of him depended upon convincing him that she knew the whole story. But she didn't. Worried, she tried a new tack.

"Okay, Adam, I'll go easy. Just tell me where you did time." She mentally crossed her fingers.

Adam staggered back a step, as if struck. Nancy couldn't believe her luck. She had guessed right. A little more pressure and he might confess!

"You've done crimes before. And that choke hold—it's a mugger's move. Was that your game?"

"No! I—" Once more he stopped himself. He had amazing composure, Nancy realized in dismay. "You can't prove any of this."

Not yet, she couldn't. But she thought she knew how to. If only she could get his fingerprints.

Her eyes still locked on Adam's, Nancy reached behind her and began to open her car door.

Adam's hand shot out and shoved the door closed.

"Hey!" he growled. "I'm not done with you yet."

"Sorry," Nancy said sarcastically. "Look, since we aren't getting anywhere with this conversation, let's drop it."

For a moment Adam didn't move. Nancy was afraid he would grab her again, but he must have decided against it. Perhaps, she thought, he was remembering his date in the restaurant. What would she think if she was watching? With a hostile glare, he brushed past her and went back inside.

Nancy breathed a sigh of relief and got into her car. She wanted to get out of there—fast!

At home she immediately dusted the door of her car with a fine black powder.

"Nice fingerprints!" Chief McGinnis complimented her the next morning. "Almost a complete set, too. Where'd you get them?"

"From the door of my car," Nancy explained.

"Let's run 'em through the computer and see what turns up," the chief said.

Fifteen minutes later an officer came in with a manila folder. The chief opened it, scanned the contents, then handed it to Nancy.

"Well," she said when she had looked it over, "that explains where Adam disappeared to for six months. If you'll excuse me, Chief, I think I'll have a little talk with Tom Hayward about this."

"Prison?" Tom Hayward said, astonished. "A Hayward guard?"

"For grand larceny," Nancy affirmed. "Adam stole a car."

Tom shook his head. "But how can this be? We screen our employees thoroughly. We check for things like this. They take lie detector tests."

"An experienced liar can beat the detector," Nancy pointed out.

"But not that easily," Tom replied. "There's usually enough doubt about the results to disqualify the candidate."

"So how did Adam slip through?" Nancy wondered.

"That's what I'm going to find out," Tom

resolved. "It may take some doing, though. Adam was hired more than a year ago."

"Anything you find out will be a help," Nancy told him.

Tom tossed the fingerprint report onto the broad expanse of his glass-topped desk. His office was very large. Its corner windows overlooked green countryside and a man-made pond. In the pond a powerful waterjet shot an arc of water high into the air. Rainbow hues danced in the mist.

"I'll have to fire Adam, of course," Tom said.

"Wouldn't you rather leave him on duty so you can keep track of him?" Nancy suggested.

Tom brightened. "Good idea. We'll keep him off the streets."

"McGinnis will blanket the area with patrols tonight, right?" Tom inquired.

Nancy replied, "Yes, and I'll be watching our three main suspects."

"Three at once? How?" Tom wondered.

"Adam will be on duty at the CD warehouse," Nancy said. "My assistant has Neil Masterson's house under observation. That's two. As for Stanley Loomis, I'll follow him myself."

"I'm going with you," Tom announced.

Nancy was surprised. "You don't have to. I can cover him—with the help of some friends, of course."

"I believe you, but even so, I'm going. I'm tired of sitting around waiting for the next robbery to happen," Tom said with conviction. "I need to get involved."

"Fine with me," Nancy agreed. "It means I can give my friends Bess and George the night off. I'll pick you up here at sundown. Wear dark clothes in case we wind up on foot."

"No problem."

Just then the phone on Tom's desk trilled. He snatched up the handset. "Yes?" A pause. "Okay, put him on—"

The conversation lasted only a minute, but it was long enough to propel Tom out of his plush leather desk chair. He paced back and forth behind his desk, a worried look on his face. Concerned, Nancy watched as the phone cord stretched to its limit.

"Yeah . . . yeah . . . Can't you? No . . . okay . . . I see. Well, keep me informed."

Hanging up, he sank back into his chair with a weary sigh.

"Bad news?" Nancy asked.

"The worst," Tom said. "That was our banker in Chicago. The price of Hayward

Security stock has dropped another three and a half points. I have now lost three quarters of a million bucks. In one week."

"I'm sorry," Nancy said, stunned. "Let's hope we get some positive results tonight."

Nancy spent the rest of the day filling in the details on Adam Reeves. She read the court records of his trial, interviewed his neighbors, and phoned his ex-boss at the gas station. She found nothing unusual, though.

That evening she picked up Tom as arranged. Nancy got the feeling that he was itching for some action. He was tense and likely to be disappointed, she knew. For the most part surveillance was a passive activity.

Stanley Loomis worked late. At eight o'clock he drove to a steak house. At eight fifty-five he stopped at a video store and rented a movie. Then he drove home.

Nancy and Tom watched his house from her car for another hour or so. The lights were off except in the living room, where the bluish flicker of the TV could be seen through the window. At ten forty-five the lights went out. All was quiet.

"There's nothing happening here," Tom

said after a few more minutes. "Let's head down to the warehouse district."

"Fine by me," Nancy said. "We can check with the chief."

The warehouse district was quiet, too, according to the officers in a police car they stopped. Tom was impatient.

"They're around here somewhere. I can feel it!" he exclaimed, hitting Nancy's dashboard with his fist. "What do you say we check under the Interstate bridge?" Tom said.

"That's almost out of the district. There's nothing in that area except some scrap metal yards," Nancy countered.

"Exactly. See, I figure the gang hangs out somewhere near the warehouse district, not in it. They wait until they're sure the 'heat' has cooled, and then they move in."

"Sure," Nancy agreed, looking at Tom with increased respect. He was very sharp! "Why didn't I think of that? Let's go."

From a distance the bridge was a graceful, looping M outlined in lights. Up close it was a soaring steel dinosaur lumbering into the river on colossal concrete legs. Nancy coasted slowly through the wasteland that lay under the span. Wrecked cars and garbage were strewn about.

On the far side was a collection of auto salvagers, concrete mixing plants, and scrapyards. Twisted chain link fences wandered along the roadside.

"Looks deserted," Nancy remarked uneasily.

"Maybe, maybe not. Let's drive around," Tom suggested.

Yellow anticrime lights turned the area into something from a nightmare. Nancy turned left near a scrap metal yard.

"There! See him?" Tom exclaimed suddenly, pointing.

Nancy snapped her head around. Leaning against a chain link fence near the open gateway to the scrapyard was a figure in black. A rubber Wolfman mask was pulled over his head.

"Yes!" Nancy twisted the wheel and swung toward him. As her headlights swept over him, the Wolfman darted inside the yard. Strange, she thought. Hadn't he seen them approaching sooner?

"Let's go!" Tom said. "We can catch him!"

"Shouldn't we call—"

"There are two of us. We can corner him!" Tom had his door open already. As Nancy

braked to a halt, he leaped out and dashed into the yard in pursuit of the Wolfman.

Nancy grabbed her keys and followed. She was worried. Tom was taking a terrible risk.

On the other hand they now had one of the robbers cornered. The chain link fence was twelve feet high and topped with barbed wire. No way was the Wolfman going anywhere. This was their best break yet, she knew.

Inside, she looked around. There was no sign of either Tom or their prey. Which direction should she go?

"Nancy! Up on the scaffolding!" Tom called from somewhere nearby.

She turned toward the scrapyard's office building. It was an old wooden structure two stories high. Metal scaffolding enveloped it. Then she saw the Wolfman darting up a ladder.

"I see him!" she called.

Nancy raced to the ladder. Should she follow? She looked around. Still no sign of Tom. He was probably on the opposite side of the building, she realized, closing in on the Wolfman from the other direction.

She decided to risk it. This time she was not facing her adversary alone. Nimbly she sped

up the ladder. No Wolfman. She scrambled up another ladder and found herself on the roof. The stairwell enclosure in the middle of the roof provided the only cover. The Wolfman had to be hiding behind it!

Nancy's heart was pounding. Quietly she tiptoed to the edge of the roof and looked down. On the ground two stories below her was a collection of scrap metal. Razor-sharp edges glinted in the half light.

"Tom?" she called. Where was he?

Suddenly two hands smashed into her back. With a scream, she went hurtling off the platform toward the jagged metal below!

Chapter Eleven

As Nancy fell, a picture of her father flashed into her mind. He's going to be furious with me, she thought.

Then her fall was broken against a pair of strong arms, and she slid easily to the ground. It took her a moment to realize that she wasn't dead.

"I—I can't believe you were standing here!" she said to Tom. Another few inches and she would have been sliced to ribbons by the scrap metal.

He was amazingly calm. He said, "It's a lucky thing I was!"

"Thank you. I thought you were up on the scaffolding, too!"

She wanted to stay right there with his arms around her for a few minutes, but a troubling thought had struck her. "The guy in the wolf mask is still up on the roof."

"You're right," Tom agreed. "Look, we'd better call the police."

She raked back her hair with her fingers. "You don't want to trap him anymore?"

"Not after what just happened to you."

Before they were halfway to her Mustang, they heard an engine roar to life. A second later a low-slung car shot around the corner of the building.

"Look out!" Nancy yelled. Grabbing Tom, she pulled him out of the way. Together they tumbled to the ground.

The car shot past them and sped through the gate. Its lights were off, including the license plate bulb, so Nancy missed the number. She sprang to her feet, but by the time she had run into the street, the car was turning a distant corner. She saw its lights snap on as it did.

"Rats!"

Tom ran up next to her. "I didn't get the number, did you?"

"No!" she said in frustration. "I can't even say for sure what model it is."

"Maybe we can catch it?"

"Doubtful," Nancy predicted.

Tom shrugged. "At least we got close."

Nancy was suddenly angry. Stalking toward her car, she muttered, "Close isn't good enough, Tom. Not for me."

The first thing Nancy did upon arriving home half an hour later was to confirm the whereabouts of her suspects. She phoned Cindy.

"I hope I'm not calling too late," she said apologetically.

"No problem, but I don't have any news," Cindy reported. "Mr. Masterson has been home since a quarter past six."

Nancy thanked her and hung up. Next she dialed the nighttime number at Hayward Security headquarters. Guards were required to phone in every hour to confirm that they were on duty and awake. If they failed to report in, then headquarters dispatched a van to check on them.

The switchboard operator told Nancy that Adam Reeves had phoned in every hour.

"You spoke to him personally?" Nancy asked, to be certain.

"Sure. Well, sort of. The guards usually don't say much," the operator explained. "They give their ID number, say 'Reporting in,' and then hang up."

"Well, thanks a lot for your help."

Stanley Loomis was also a suspect, but she was positive that he had not been at the scene. He couldn't have left his house and driven to the area faster than she and Tom. Also, the Wolfman had been tall and agile. Loomis was short and fat. Still, that didn't put him completely in the clear. This gang had more than one member, and some of them might work for Loomis.

The next morning Nancy drove to Loomis's main office. Like Tom, Loomis had a fleet of vans, she saw. He had more than Tom did, in fact.

That meant he employed a lot of guards. Nancy needed to find out more about them. She went to one of the cafeterias in the warehouse district that was popular with workers.

It was nearly empty. The cashier was reading a paperback. Nancy asked for a pack of

gum. As she paid for it, she said, "Can I ask you a question or two?"

"What for?" the cashier asked warily, handing Nancy her change.

"My name's Nancy Drew," Nancy began.

The woman's face lit up. "Haven't I seen your name in the paper? Aren't you the girl detective they're always writing about?"

"That's right," Nancy confirmed. "And I'm trying to help a friend."

"What do you want to know?" the woman asked, smiling.

"Warehouse workers eat here a lot, right?" Nancy asked.

"They're our main customers," the cashier affirmed.

"Do the security guards ever come in, too?"

"Sometimes."

Nancy nodded encouragingly. "Do they ever talk about the companies they work for? Do they ever complain?"

The cashier laughed. "Nancy, every worker complains!"

"What about the security guards, though?" Nancy persisted.

"Why don't you ask that guy over there." The cashier pointed.

"Thanks," Nancy said.

The man was in his late forties and had a ruddy complexion. He was drinking coffee at a Formica-topped table by the window. Although he wasn't wearing a uniform, a Loomis & Petersen jacket was hanging over the back of his chair.

A newspaper was open in front of him. He was reading the want ads, Nancy saw. "Excuse me, may I ask you a few questions?"

"What for?" the man inquired without looking up.

Nancy ran through the same routine that she had with the cashier. Satisfied, the man offered her the seat across the table.

"Thanks," Nancy said, sitting. "You work for Stan Loomis?"

"Not anymore," the man said glumly. "Laid off a week ago."

Nancy lifted her eyebrows. "Why?"

"Things are tough everywhere, I guess," the man replied. "Company had to tighten its belt."

"Gee, I'm sorry. How long did you work for him?" Nancy asked sympathetically.

"Seventeen years! Still can't believe it," the man muttered.

Nancy leaned toward him. "You must be pretty angry."

"Well, I'd rather somebody else got laid off than me, I'll say that," the man grumbled.

Nancy zeroed in on her target. "Would you say Stan Loomis is honest?"

"Sure," the man said without hesitation. "Stan was on the wrong side of the law once. He told me all about it. But he reformed. He's as honest as my mother—and believe me, kid, that's honest!"

Nancy smiled. "I believe you. What about Hayward Security—think you might get a job working for them?"

"Wouldn't want it," the man said firmly.

"Why not?" Nancy was surprised.

"'Cause I've talked to their guards. The pay's lousy."

"Any other reasons?" Nancy asked.

The man stirred his coffee thoughtfully. "Not that I can put my finger on. The guys who work there are kind of—I don't know, unhappy. They don't have a lot of nice things to say about the company, you get my drift?"

"I think so. And thanks," Nancy said, rising. "You've been a big help."

* * *

When Cindy Larson arrived at Nancy's house that afternoon, she asked, "What can I do to help?"

Nancy slid the telephone toward her. "You can call more discount stores. I've listed numbers from the rest of the county. That will free me up to work on our profiles."

Cindy's face fell. "But I've called so many already! Isn't there something else I can do?"

"Getting bored?" Nancy asked with a smile.

"Well, a little," Cindy admitted sheepishly.

"Don't get discouraged. You never know when a clue will turn up."

"I suppose." Cindy reached for the phone.

Suddenly Nancy felt guilty. She placed her hand on Cindy's to stop her from dialing. "Actually, there *is* something else you could help me with—"

"Not more garbage, I hope?" Cindy groaned.

Nancy shook her head. "No. What time is the mail delivered in your neighborhood?"

Cindy looked at her watch. "Right about now."

"Does Neil Masterson's wife get it out of the mailbox?"

"No, Mr. Masterson does that when he gets

home from work. At least, that's what I saw him do the last couple of evenings."

"Good enough," Nancy said, rising from her chair. "Let's go."

They drove to Cindy's neighborhood. It was a new development—mostly ranch-style houses.

They cruised up and down the block several times, checking to see that no one was in Neil's yard. Then Nancy quickly pulled up to the curbside mailbox and took his mail.

"Nancy, isn't opening other people's mail illegal?" Cindy asked, aghast. She looked a bit pale, Nancy saw.

"We're not going to open it," Nancy said, driving away.

"Then why steal it?"

"We're not stealing it. We're borrowing it," she said.

"Now I'm *really* confused! Why borrow it if—"

"I'll show you why in a minute."

Back in her bedroom, Nancy opened her windows wide. Next, she sorted through Neil's mail. There was some junk mail and also what appeared to be a bill from River Heights Hospital.

In addition, there was an envelope from Loomis & Petersen. Interesting. Nancy put it and the hospital bill in the center of her desk. Then she went to her closet and took out a bottle of clear fluid. "This is highly flammable," she warned.

Using an eyedropper, Nancy dribbled some of the fluid on the envelope from River Heights Hospital. Instantly the wet part of the envelope became transparent.

As Nancy had suspected, it was a bill. The amount due was $5,425. A very hefty sum. Nancy blew on the wet spot. Within a minute the envelope was once again opaque.

"That's incredible," Cindy said, shaking her head.

Next Nancy dribbled fluid onto the envelope from Loomis & Petersen. Her eyes went wide. Inside was a check made out to Neil Masterson. The amount it paid him was exactly $5,425!

Chapter Twelve

THAT EXPLAINED how Neil was able to pay the bills for his daughter's operations. But what did Loomis get in exchange? Information about Hayward's alarm systems? Access codes?

Or was it more than that? And what about Adam Reeves? Where did he fit in? In an unguarded moment Adam had mentioned a "he." Who was that? Neil? Loomis?

Nancy needed definite answers. Time was running out. The price of Hayward Security

stock had dropped even farther that day. Tom and his shareholders were losing a fortune. She had to get to the bottom of things, and fast. It was time, Nancy decided, to call in her reserves.

Bess and George arrived at Nancy's right after dinner. Cindy stayed, too. The four parked themselves in Nancy's room.

"Starting tonight we have to keep a constant tail on Loomis, Masterson, and Reeves," she announced. "We want to know everything they do, everyone they meet."

"Okay!" Bess said. "Exactly what do we have to do?"

"Borrow your parents' cars, pick up your target, and stick with him. Keep a record of everything: locations, times—the works. George, you take Adam Reeves. But be careful. He can spot a tail."

"If he spots me, at least I'll have a shot at outrunning him," George joked.

Nancy warned, "Stay in your car. If he sees you, take off."

"Who do I get?" Bess asked.

"Neil Masterson," Nancy told her.

"Is he cute?"

The others howled in mock outrage and threw pillows at her.

"Hey! My hair!" Bess wailed. When the melee died down, she added, "I guess that leaves you with Loomis, Nancy."

"What about me?" Cindy asked.

"We need you to be our central contact. If there are any problems, we'll call in to you, and you can get word to one or both of the others."

"I just sit by the phone?" Cindy looked disappointed.

"You are our lifeline," Nancy told her seriously. "That's important."

That's dull, Cindy's expression said. But she only nodded.

"Okay, let's get going. We'll stick with our targets until they go home. Then we'll pick them up again in the morning," Nancy said.

That night was a washout. Adam worked at the CD warehouse, then drove straight home. Neil worked late, then went home, too, leaving Bess to spend the evening parked by Cindy's house while Cindy spent the evening by Nancy's phone.

Nancy herself traveled a bit more, but in the

end Stanley Loomis did nothing very unusual. His one unexpected stop was at a florist, where he walked out with a dozen pink tulips. He took them home. Nancy realized for the first time that he was probably married.

Saturday morning the team was at work early. Nancy was still sipping tea from her thermos when Loomis climbed into his car and drove to his office.

Nancy parked halfway down the block from his office—close enough to see him leave, far enough not to be noticed. Then she settled in for a long wait.

Tap, tap, tap.

The rapping on her window caught her completely off guard.

"Bess!" She rolled down her window. "What are you doing here?"

Bess grinned. "Same thing you are. I just parked a little farther way, that's all. When I saw your car I came over."

Nancy jerked herself upright. "But that must mean that Neil Masterson is—"

"You got it." Bess nodded. "He arrived at Loomis's office a few minutes ago. Do you think they're inside having some kind of pow-wow?"

"I'd lay odds on it," Nancy said. Reaching behind her, she got her knapsack. Inside the pack were her binoculars and a camera with a telephoto lens. "Let's go."

"Where?"

"Where we can see into Loomis's office. We should have a couple of rooftops to choose from."

"Rooftops?" Bess echoed nervously.

The building Nancy chose was diagonally across the street from Loomis & Petersen. In an alley next to it she leaped up and caught the lowest rung of the fire escape.

"But, Nancy—" Bess said in a worried voice.

"You can stay here if you like," Nancy pointed out.

Bess looked around the alley. "No, thanks. I'll go with you."

A minute later they were in position. A rooftop sign hid them. By peering with her binoculars through a gap in the sign, Nancy could see directly into Loomis's office without being detected. Neil Masterson was indeed meeting with Loomis.

"What are they doing?" Bess asked.

"Looking at some diagrams," Nancy re-

ported. "Neil is pointing things out with his pen. Loomis likes what he sees."

"What are they planning, I wonder?" Bess mused.

Nancy shook her head. "I don't know, but I'm pretty sure of one thing—Tom Hayward knows nothing about this."

That night Nancy switched places with George to tail Adam Reeves. Saturday night was a prime time for robbery since the warehouse district would be all but deserted. Since Adam was the suspect most likely to be part of an actual strike, she wanted to be the one covering him.

According to his work schedule, Adam was off. When he left his apartment, he was dressed all in black. Nancy's excitement grew as she followed him downtown because he doubled back a few times, obviously checking for a tail. Nancy countered his moves perfectly.

There was no moon that night. Nancy snapped off her headlights and used only the light from the streetlights. Adam finally parked in the warehouse district. Nancy did, too.

Finally, close to midnight, a van came up their street from the direction of the river. Adam started his car and followed it around

the corner. Her pulse quickening, Nancy got out and followed on foot.

Adam's destination was an audio components warehouse. She had passed it many times on her earlier patrols. As she watched from the shadows thirty yards away, Adam got out of his car—only now he wore the Wolfman mask. Nancy snapped a picture.

The van backed up to the loading bay. Another figure dressed in black got out of it—the Dead Man. Nancy recognized the grisly mask instantly. She took another shot.

The two men opened the back doors of the van and wheeled out handcarts. The Dead Man went to the alarm system keypad and pushed a sequence of keys. The red light that had been blinking on the panel went off. They rolled up the door.

As Nancy had expected, they worked mostly in the dark, using flashlights. They were fast, too. She saw them zoom between the warehouse and the van twice in less than a minute.

Nancy crept closer. She wanted to get as much on film as possible.

The Wolfman and the Dead Man disappeared inside the warehouse for more than a minute. Nancy crept closer. There was no sign of them.

She was now close enough to make out the lettering on the van. It said, "Hayward Security Systems." No wonder no one ever noticed them coming or going! They had the perfect camouflage: a vehicle that was totally familiar to people in the district. And to the police. And to her.

Was it a fake Hayward van or the real thing?

Nancy darted up to the loading bay. The thieves were now deep inside the warehouse.

She leaped up onto the loading platform because she needed a picture of the interior of the van, and that was the only way she could get it. She sighted through the viewfinder.

No good. She moved back, stepping carefully around a small aluminum ladder that someone had left set up inside the warehouse. She sighed again—still no good.

When she was twenty feet away she sighted again. Perfect. Then, through the viewfinder, she saw the aluminum ladder come into the picture. It was falling! It clattered onto the platform. Nancy froze.

She peered into the darkness and saw who had knocked the ladder over. *Cindy!*

"I'm sorry!" Cindy whispered.

"What are you doing here?" Nancy whispered back, furious.

"I—I wanted to get in on the excitement," Cindy replied, "so I followed you down here."

This was no time to lecture the girl, Nancy knew. "Let's get out of here before—"

It was too late. From inside the warehouse Nancy heard the sound of running feet. The Wolfman and the Dead Man were coming!

Chapter Thirteen

INSTEAD OF RUNNING down the street, Nancy grabbed Cindy and hauled her into the warehouse to fake out the robbers. Boxes of stereo parts were stacked on top of wooden pallets. The pallets were arranged in long parallel rows running from the front of the warehouse to the back.

Nancy yanked Cindy down the aisle that was closest to the right wall. The thieves weren't likely to come that way—she hoped.

When they reached the back wall, they found an aisle perpendicular to the others.

Nancy pulled Cindy behind the last pallet of components. Now they were no longer visible from the front of the warehouse.

Nancy heard the thieves run up to the loading bay door. A second later powerful flashlight beams shone down the aisles. Bright circles of light played against the wall to either side of them. The stack of boxes hid them, but Nancy knew that the thieves must suspect someone was there.

Nancy put her mouth to Cindy's ear and whispered, *"Don't move!"*

The warning was hardly necessary. Cindy was nearly frozen with terror.

Nancy looked around for a makeshift weapon. There was nothing within reach. Naturally, *this* warehouse would be spotless! The only thing available was her camera. Nancy was surprised, somehow, that she still had it in her hand. Too bad the flash attachment wasn't on. She might have been able to blind them temporarily.

Male voices conferred near the front. Then Nancy heard the van's rear doors slam. Hope seized her. Were they leaving?

Not right away, it turned out. The next sound she heard was that of a tool working on a pipe—a pipe wrench? What were they

doing? After a minute, a loud clanging began. They were hammering on a pipe. Why?

The loading bay door rolled down and was locked, leaving them in total darkness. There was the muffled sound of the van starting up, and then the engine fading in the distance. They were alone. Nancy whipped a penlight from her pocket, switched it on, and grabbed Cindy's hand.

"Let's get out of here!"

As they drew close to the front, Nancy stopped—and sniffed. There was an odor in the air.

"Gas! That's what they did! They ruptured a gas line!"

"W-we're going to d-die," Cindy whimpered.

"No, we're not, but we'd better get out of here soon," Nancy cautioned.

The loading bay door couldn't be opened. The control panel inside was identical to the one outside. The code had to be keyed in. A door in the office led out, too, but it was locked. Nancy searched the office for a key, but couldn't find one. She tried the phones. Dead.

"The wires outside were cut," she guessed.

Nancy found the light switches and flicked

them until the warehouse interior was completely lit. Then she raced to find the gas leak.

"Help me trace this line!" she ordered Cindy. "Maybe we can find a valve that will turn it off." But there wasn't one. If there was, it was on the outside.

The smell of gas was now heavy in the air. Nancy felt dizzy. How long would it take the warehouse to completely fill with gas? An hour? Fifteen minutes? She forced herself to think.

"An emergency exit! There has to be one!"

There was, set into the back wall. But it was chained shut.

"That's illegal!" Nancy fumed.

Nancy ran along the back wall, looking up. Yes! About ten feet up on the wall was a row of three lateral windows. They were too high up to reach with the aluminum ladder.

"We've got to build a pyramid out of boxes," she said urgently.

They began to move the stereo components, erecting a crude cardboard stairway. It was growing increasingly difficult to work, however. The smell of the gas was overpowering. Nancy felt like gagging. Cindy began to cough. They had to get out—soon!

At last they reached the windows, but the handles on them wouldn't budge. They were rusted in place. They would have to break the windows open, but with what?

"The ladder!" Nancy said.

The trip for the ladder was agonizing. The gas stung Nancy's throat and eyes. Returning to the rear wall, she gripped the ladder by two middle rungs, climbed up the cardboard stairway, and thrust the ladder against the window.

It bounced off. She tried again. This time, the window cracked.

"Hurry!" Cindy urged, her voice a series of choking coughs.

Two more thrusts and cool, fresh air was pouring in through a hole. A minute later the glass was completely out. Nancy cried in triumph, "We did it!"

She helped Cindy out first. Then she squirmed through the narrow space and dropped ten feet into the alley outside.

"N-Nancy, I'm so sorry! I almost got us killed," her assistant sobbed.

Nancy hugged her. "Cindy, it's okay. We got out. That's all that counts. Come on, let's call the police and the fire department."

* * *

As she slept that night, Nancy dreamed that she was choking. In the morning she barely touched her breakfast.

Later, in her bathroom, she developed the pictures she had taken the night before. She tried to think the case through, but no conclusions would come.

Her father was sitting across the room reading the Sunday paper. He asked conversationally, "How's the investigation going?"

Nancy said, "I don't know. It's frustrating—it doesn't add up. Means. Motive. Opportunity. I can't get a clear picture of who's planning it all."

Carson folded the front section of the paper. "At least the robberies aren't on page one anymore. Brenda wrote another article about them, but it's buried on page twelve."

Nancy smiled. "Sounds like she hasn't come up with any new angles." Knowing Brenda, Nancy decided, she must have been feeling very frustrated. The reporter loved to see her byline on page one.

"No, she hasn't." Her father opened the business section. "On the other hand, the

plunge in Hayward's stock price is top financial news."

Nancy went to see. Looking over his shoulder, she read that Hayward shares had now lost eighty percent of their value. Analysts were predicting that, barring a sudden change in fortune, the company would be bankrupt within a week.

"How awful," she groaned. "People are losing a ton of money just because of a couple of break-ins. And Tom's losing the most."

"Well, the ones who sell their shares are losing," Carson said.

Nancy suddenly stood upright. "Dad! What did you just say?"

"I said, the people who sell their shares at bargain prices are the losers. You see, a decline in a stock's price is really only a loss on paper. You have to sell to actually lose money."

"That's it!" Insight flooded Nancy's mind like a sudden burst of sunshine. She cried, "Dad, you just gave me the answer!"

"I did?"

Nancy threw her arms around his neck and kissed his cheek. "You said a drop in value is only a 'paper' loss, right?"

"Right."

"And isn't it also true that for every seller of stock there's a buyer?"

"True. A 'sale' is always an exchange between two parties," Carson agreed.

"Then that's it! Nancy exulted. "I've cracked the case!"

Chapter Fourteen

"There are just a few things I have to check," Nancy added. "Can you help me, Dad?"

"I'll try," Carson said. He was still in the dark, Nancy could see, but he trusted his daughter's abilities.

Nancy said, "I know the price of Hayward stock is down, but exactly how many people are selling their shares? A lot? A few? And how many people are doing the buying?"

"There's no way for us to know that for sure," her father explained. "But I can tell you

how many shares have been sold this past week."

Carson turned the pages in the business section. "Here we are. The number of shares traded this week was—wow, two million!"

"That's a lot?"

"Nancy, there are only six million shares in existence, and Tom owns slightly more than half of those."

"So about two-thirds of the other shareholders have sold out," she calculated. "I wish there was *some* way to know for sure who was doing the buying."

Carson studied her. "You know, I think I see what you're getting at. If you can supply enough evidence, then the Securities and Exchange Commission can subpoena brokerage house records and prove who did the buying."

"Really? That's great!" Nancy said happily. "Maybe you can help me with something else, too."

"Shoot."

"How much of Loomis & Petersen does Stanley Loomis own?"

"That's easy," her father said. "Forty-nine percent. Just under half. Roy Petersen controls the firm."

"Dad, how do you know that?"

Carson smiled. "I'm their lawyer."

That left only one point for Nancy to check. She walked to the phone. She hated to make this call, but it was essential.

"Hello, Brenda?" she said, once the connection was made. "It's Nancy Drew."

"Hello, Nancy," Brenda said frostily. "How's the case going?"

"Uh, okay. But I need to ask you a question."

"Oh? Why should I help you out if you won't help me?" Brenda asked.

Nancy took a deep breath. This was the part she had dreaded. "Because I've got the case nailed down. I just need to fill in a few of the details."

"What do I get in return?" Brenda asked bluntly.

"Some exclusive details," Nancy offered, "once the arrest is made."

There was a pause. "Okay, you're on."

"How did you first hear about the break-in at the CD Revolution warehouse?" Nancy asked.

"An anonymous caller phoned the city desk and asked specifically for me," Brenda said with a touch of pride.

Nancy's heart leaped. "And then you gave that caller your home number, in case he wanted to give you any more tips, right?"

"How did you know that?" Brenda asked, surprised.

"It doesn't matter. Is that how you found out about the Jumping Jeans warehouse break-in the next day?"

"Yes. Now, when are the police going to make the arrest?" Brenda demanded.

"Soon," Nancy said evasively. "Thanks, Brenda. Bye."

She hung up quickly and immediately dialed again.

Chief McGinnis was against her plan. It was much too dangerous, he maintained.

Patiently Nancy explained that while she now knew the identity of the gang's mastermind, her evidence against him wouldn't hold up in court. To be sure of convicting him they needed a confession. And their man would not confess to the police. He was far too cool for that.

Their only hope, she argued, was to surprise a confession out of him. That meant that he had to be confronted by someone he didn't fear—someone who would catch him off guard.

By the time she finished, the chief had no choice but to agree.

Even though it was Sunday, the front doors of the Hayward Security building whooshed open to admit her. Nancy wasn't surprised. She had known that they would be working.

There was no receptionist, so she walked straight back to Neil Masterson's office. Inside, the special ribbonless computer printer was busily clacking away. Tom Hayward was sliding a cardboard box under Neil's desk.

"One of the laptop computers?" Nancy asked.

Tom straightened. Without pausing, he said, "Yes, it's a laptop. A present. A bonus, you might say."

Smart. Very smart, she thought. "Too bad Neil won't get to keep it," she said. "The police will take it as evidence against you."

"Oh?" Tom arched an eyebrow quizzically. "Evidence of what?"

So it was going to be like that. Nancy steeled herself. She had known that she would have to do this the hard way.

"I first became suspicious of you that night in the scrap metal yard when you miraculously 'saved' my life," she began.

"Yes, that was a lucky coincidence," Tom agreed.

"I'm not a big believer in coincidence, though," Nancy went on. "You knew exactly where to stand."

"Nancy, you seem to be accusing me of something here." He raised his shoulders and turned up his palms.

"You're right. I should start from the beginning," she said, trying to hide her nervousness. "It's a simple story, but it took me a long time to piece it together."

The printer stopped clacking.

"It begins with something my father said. About stocks," Nancy explained. "He said that if the price goes down you only lose money if you sell. That got me thinking."

"About what?" Tom asked. He sat down in Neil's desk chair.

Nancy's voice grew stronger. "About buying. It hit me that although selling means losing money, *buying* could mean earning money—lots of it—*if* the stock price went back up again. In fact, you could double, triple, or even quadruple your money."

"Naturally," Tom said. "But what of it?"

She had him now, she could tell. He was

stringing her along to find out how much she knew. Her confidence surged.

"You've been trying to buy out your main competitor, Loomis & Petersen, in order to get what you want."

"Which is?"

Nancy looked straight into his eyes. "A monopoly. The security business all to yourself."

Tom's eyes narrowed.

"Now, Petersen was willing to sell out," Nancy went on. "He's old. Probably getting ready to retire. But Loomis wouldn't sell. I found that out one day when I visited their offices."

Tom didn't move, but his gaze was hostile now.

"You needed money to buy Petersen's controlling interest," Nancy continued, "and you knew you could get it by buying Hayward stock low and selling it high. The only problem was how to push the price of the stock up and down."

A muscle in Tom's jaw twitched.

"That's where the robberies came in," Nancy explained. "They were bad publicity. Investors lost confidence. They sold. You

bought, probably under another name. Once you had enough stock, your plan was to 'solve' the case, recover the stolen goods, and watch the stock price soar."

Finally Tom spoke. "You're saying *I* committed the robberies?"

"You and Adam Reeves," Nancy said. "At first I couldn't understand how a guy with a prison record could get hired at Hayward. Then I realized that you hired him yourself, before Neil Masterson started working here. He was willing to commit crimes for you when ordered," Nancy said. "You robbed your own customers with his help. But you didn't steal much. You didn't have to. Just enough to commit the crime."

Tom probed deeper. "And where are the goods now?"

"Probably stashed in another warehouse somewhere," Nancy guessed, "waiting to be 'discovered' by you at the right moment. That explains why none of us has been able to trace them."

Tom leaned back in his chair and pressed his fingertips together. "Okay, let's suppose your theory is correct. How did Adam and I arrange the break-ins? Adam only knew the code for the CD Revolution warehouse."

"Easy." Nancy glanced at the printer. "You just printed new envelopes and the computer assigned new codes. After the break-ins, you 'changed' the codes again for security reasons. No one knew they had been changed twice."

Tom nodded. "Clever. Seems you've figured out a flaw in the system."

"Stanley Loomis helped me with it," she admitted. "He told me that your system was as 'secure as a bureau drawer,' which anyone can open. I started from there."

"Go on."

Nancy took a deep breath. "There was only one more thing you needed—a fall guy. Someone to take the blame. You chose Neil. He has a motive. Plus he has the means. He could print new envelopes as easily as you. As for opportunity, he spends evenings with his family, but that's okay. The 'gang' took care of the robberies, Neil only cooperated with them. Which is enough to send him to prison, and which is why you are planting that laptop computer under his desk."

"Criminals," Tom said, "are so careless."

"Exactly. You even tried to point *me* at Neil, and for a while it worked. The evidence suggested he was guilty, but I couldn't square that

with what I knew of his character. He's an honest man with a good reputation."

"But what about Stanley Loomis?" Tom said. *"He* has a sordid past."

"He reformed long ago," Nancy said. "His only problem now is competition from you. He was working on it, too, planning new products and services."

Tom waved his hand as if to dismiss her entire story. "That's all very interesting, Nancy, but you are forgetting one thing: I have alibis for the break-ins. So does Adam, for that matter. One time I was even with you!"

Nancy smiled. "Oh, yes—Career Day. That's where you got really clever. On Career Day you and Adam robbed the warehouse early in the morning. Then you tied Adam to the chair, where he stayed all day. You, meanwhile, established your alibi by speaking at the Career Fair with me and Chief McGinnis. Late in the afternoon, Adam tripped the emergency exit alarm and told his hair-raising story."

"But Adam had to phone in to our headquarters every hour. How did he do that?" Tom asked. His voice was rising in pitch.

"He didn't. A recording did. It's easy to rig up. You use the same equipment that's used to make junk phone calls. Every hour it dials the

Hayward number, plays a brief recording, and hangs up. It was the same trick you used the other night to make it seem like Adam was working when he was actually waiting for us. The equipment is probably at your house, right?"

Tom's jaw tightened. He was starting to sweat, Nancy saw with satisfaction. "Okay, Nancy, I'll admit this all sounds plausible. But so what? Neil Masterson or Stanley Loomis could have masterminded the robberies, too. There's as much evidence against either of them as there is against me."

"Not true," Nancy said calmly.

"What do you mean, it's not true!" He was shouting now. "Look at their motives! Neil's debts! Loomis's hatred of me!"

"Those are facts," Nancy agreed, "but you see, I am positive you are guilty because I know something about Neil and Loomis that you don't know. Neil is moonlighting for Loomis on the weekends. He's helping Loomis plan his new systems and services. I took secret pictures of one of their meetings yesterday."

"No!"

"It's true. And Loomis sends Neil checks that are made to the exact amount of Neil's

hospital bills. I've seen them. All Neil and Loomis have to do to dismiss the case against them is tell the truth. By elimination, that will leave only one mastermind—you, Tom."

"No, no, *no!*" Tom pounded his fists on Neil's desktop. His face was red. "I knew I shouldn't have let you investigate."

He leaped up from his chair. Nancy was about to give a signal, when suddenly she was blinded by a bright light.

From the doorway an electronic flash bleached the scene white for a millisecond. Spots danced in front of Nancy's eyes.

"Nice going, Nancy," she heard Brenda say. "You got him cold. And I've got it all on tape! I was standing right outside. What a story this is going to make!"

"Yeah, some story," Tom said. As Nancy's vision cleared, she saw that he was holding a gun. "Too bad you won't ever get to write it, Brenda. Nancy, call off your backup!"

Chapter Fifteen

"HOW DO YOU KNOW I have a backup?" Nancy asked nervously. Having a gun pointed at her was not her favorite experience.

"Don't treat me like an idiot," Tom growled. "No way would you have pushed me so hard without a backup. Call 'em off!"

Nancy was wearing a blazer. Flipping up its lapel, she spoke into the tiny wireless microphone that was pinned there. "Chief, he's got a gun. We have to let him go."

"You mean, let *us* go," Tom clarified. Leap-

ing across the desk, he ran behind Brenda, threw his elbow around her neck, and pressed the barrel of the gun to her temple. "Lois Lane, here, is going with me."

Brenda gasped, her face white with fear.

"Wait! Take me instead," Nancy offered.

"Oh, no! You're too smart," Tom said. "Brenda here was dumb enough to let me use her to spread bad publicity about my company, but I think she's smart enough to help me get away without causing any trouble."

"Yes, that's why you were so willing to talk to her at the Jumping Jeans warehouse," Nancy said, stalling for time. "I thought that was foolish then, but—"

"I'm no fool and neither are you," Tom said. "Now, keep back!"

He wrestled Brenda out of the office with his arm still around her throat and the gun still pressed to her temple. Nancy followed at a distance as he took Brenda outside to his BMW. He forced her in through the driver's side. Then he climbed in and slammed the door.

"So long, Nancy!" he called. The BMW roared to life.

Nancy looked around desperately. Down the road in either direction—out of sight from

inside the Hayward building but visible now—were a dozen vans full of cops. They were useless now. Tom had a hostage.

He took off. Making a sudden decision, Nancy leaped into her Mustang and followed. She didn't know where he was going, but no way was she going to let him kidnap Brenda.

She caught up to him half a mile later. He was heading in the direction of the airport. In her rearview mirror Nancy saw the police vans pulling up behind her. Good. She needed backup for what she was about to do. They couldn't let him get on an airplane with Brenda!

Accelerating, she pulled up next to him and jerked her wheel sideways.

Wham! Her car smacked into his.

Wham! She hit him again, and this time kept swerving until he was forced first onto the shoulder and then off the road, where he skidded to a stop. Nancy stopped beside the car and leaped out, yelling at the top of her lungs. It was essential to distract Tom—to keep his mind off Brenda!

It worked. Brenda leaped out of the passenger side and began to run. Tom snapped open his door and climbed out. He looked first at Brenda, then at Nancy, unable to decide whom

to deal with first. It was enough time. The police vans roared up.

In an instant several police officers were out and crouching in firing position. Tom dropped his automatic and raised his hands.

Nancy gave a whoop of joy and ran after Brenda to make sure that she was all right.

Two days later Nancy sat in Chief McGinnis's office with her father, Brenda, Brenda's father, Bess, George, and Cindy Larson.

"Morning, everyone," the chief said, striding in. "I have some news. Tom Hayward will be arraigned before a grand jury later this very morning."

Everyone applauded.

Carson spoke up. "I have some news, too. After Tom's arraignment, Neil Masterson will become the acting head of Hayward Security. I'm assembling a pool of backers—Loomis & Petersen among them—who will pump fresh capital into the company to help it out of its tailspin."

"That's great," Nancy said. "It would be a shame if after all his trouble Neil had to lose his job, too."

Mr. Carlton spoke up again. "I've got some

connections at the hospital, and they tell me that Neil's little girl, Tasha, should be okay. Her last operation was a success, so she won't need any more."

Nancy's eyes moistened. That was the best news yet.

"There's one thing I still don't understand," George said after a moment. "Nancy, how were Tom and Adam able to know where you were every minute of your surveillance?"

"They didn't. Not every minute. But they planted a small transmitter on my car—the type that tells you if your target is getting closer or farther away—and that helped."

"What about when you were on foot?" George asked.

"They tailed me a few times," Nancy explained.

"Adam's testimony is going to be devastating to Tom's defense," Carson observed.

The chief agreed. "Thank goodness he agreed to cooperate with us. That and the recorded confession we got from Nancy's hidden microphone will make the DA's job a lot easier."

"Nancy," Cindy asked, "how did you know about the transmitter planted on your car?"

"Come outside and I'll show you."

The group went outdoors, where the temperature was surprisingly more like summer than autumn. Nancy's car was in the parking lot. The dents that she had put in it ramming Tom's car were gone. It also had a new coat of paint. Blue, as always.

"Wow, that was fast!" Bess remarked.

"You bet. From now on, this car is getting nothing but TLC," Nancy promised.

"Oh, right," George drawled. "You'd better sell it to someone else."

"Anyway, about the transmitter," Nancy said. "They found it while they were doing the bodywork yesterday."

A few minutes later the group broke up. Carson returned to his law office, Brenda and her father to their paper, and Bess and George took off for the tennis courts. Nancy was left alone with Cindy when Chief McGinnis went for coffee.

"Can I give you a lift?" Nancy offered. "Where are you going?"

"History class," Cindy said. "It's a school day. I have to go back."

"Too bad," Nancy said sympathetically.

"Oh, no. I'm looking forward to school. After this case, it seems like paradise. One

more time, Nancy, I'm sorry I put us in danger," she apologized. "And thanks."

"Forget it," Nancy said warmly. "Maybe you'll work with me again?"

"I don't know. I kind of doubt it," Cindy said, climbing into the Mustang's passenger seat. "It was interesting, but also—"

"Scary? Boring? Both?" Nancy climbed in and twisted the key.

"Both, and a lot more. What I mean, though, is that after this I think I'll just read about your cases in the paper, if that's okay. It was great to do it once, but I definitely think that detective work is for people who know what they're doing and love doing it!"

With a smile, Nancy released the brake and hit the gas. Her Mustang surged forward and blended into traffic.

She couldn't have agreed more.

Make No Mistake

Chapter One

"TALK ABOUT SLEAZY. Look at this headline," Bess Marvin said indignantly, sliding *Today's Times* across the kitchen table to Nancy Drew. "The poor guy's dead, and all anyone can talk about is his money."

Nancy pushed her reddish blond hair back from her face and looked up distractedly from the table, which was covered with the components of her car's tape deck. It kept eating her tapes, and she had taken it apart to see if she could fix it.

Picking up the newspaper, the slender eighteen-year-old glanced at the headline Bess had mentioned. It ran in big letters across the front page of the paper: "Glover's Millions Up for Grabs."

"It's pretty pathetic," she agreed after skimming the article. "That reporter was so busy writing about how big Mr. Glover's estate is that he hardly even mentioned his heart attack or any of the many donations Mr. Glover made to charities." She turned her attention back to the pile of components in front of her.

"I bet everyone in River Heights will be at his funeral tomorrow," said Bess, her blue eyes shining. "I mean, how often does a multimillionaire die without anyone to inherit his estate? His fortune's worth over ten million dollars!"

Nancy was fitting two tiny metal components together and pressing an even tinier metal spring between them. Without looking up, she said, "Oh, I'm sure there'll be somebody. A man with wings of hospitals named after him isn't going to forget to make a will. Now that I think of it, I remember my dad mentioned one."

Carson Drew, one of River Heights's most prominent lawyers, had been Clayton Glover's attorney. Nancy knew her father was involved with the settling of his estate, but she didn't know any of the details. "He'll probably leave most of his money to charity," she told Bess, "and a nice bit to Mrs. Adams."

"Oh, the housekeeper, that's right," said Bess. "Remember how great it was when we used to spend time out at Glover's Corners. You know, back when"—she paused uncertainly before finishing—"back when Matt was around."

Nancy and Bess had been in junior high when Matt Glover was reported missing in Colorado after an avalanche sent tons of snow tumbling into a mountain pass. He had been on a ski trip with four other boys in his freshman college class, Nancy remembered. Four bodies were discovered when the snows melted. Matt's was never found. It had made headlines in all the major newspapers in the area.

"I haven't thought about Matt much lately. I used to think about him all the time after he disappeared," Bess went on.

Something about the wistful note in Bess's voice made Nancy glance up to study her friend. There was a dreamy look in Bess's blue eyes, and she was twisting her long blond hair absently in her fingers. "Disappeared?" Nancy repeated. "You almost sound as if you think he could still be alive."

"I know there's no way he could be," Bess said slowly. "But for a while after he disappeared, I used to have this kind of fantasy—you know, where he would reappear, just like that, and we'd go back to skating and stuff out at the Corners. It was just wishful thinking, but I half convinced myself that he really *would* come back." She let out a little laugh. "I guess I have a pretty strong imagination."

Nancy smiled. "Well, it's understandable. Even though we were five or six years younger than Matt, he invited us all to skate and hang

out at Glover's Corners. He was almost a hero to us."

"Almost? He *was* a hero, at least to me. Too bad it was only in my mind that he survived that avalanche." Bess sighed, resting her chin on her hands. After a short silence, she said, "Speaking of heroes, how's Ned?"

A familiar warm glow spread through Nancy at the mention of her longtime boyfriend, Ned Nickerson. Ned attended Emerson College, which was several hours' drive from River Heights.

"He's fine," Nancy answered. "He might make it home for a visit next weekend. I hope he can. Since I'm not on a case, I'd be able to spend lots of time with him."

Nancy's talent as a detective was well known in River Heights. She wasn't a professional, but people often asked for her help in solving mysteries. Sometimes it seemed that her detective work took up all her time, though. She was always grateful for free time to be with Ned and her friends.

Her stomach growled, and Nancy realized she was hungry. Giving up on her tape deck, she swept the components into a plastic bag, then went over to the kitchen cabinets.

"Want some popcorn?"

"Don't tempt me," Bess said, eyeing the jar Nancy pulled from the cabinet. "I'm trying to lose a few pounds."

Nancy smiled. Bess was *always* trying to lose a few pounds, even though she was the only one who thought she needed to. Her curvy figure—now covered with hot pink leggings and an oversize pink- and white-striped sweater—was different from Nancy's slender, taller build, but it suited Bess perfectly.

Nancy held the popcorn out temptingly, and Bess frowned. "Pretty sneaky plan, Nan, trying to distract me from thinking about Matt with popcorn."

"Is it working?"

"Well . . ." The frown was slowly replaced by a big grin. "You bet! I'll get the popper," she offered, going over to the cupboard. "Anyway, I read somewhere that popcorn has hardly any calories as long as you don't add butter."

Soon they had a heaping bowl of fluffy, butterless popcorn on the table between them. Bess reached for a big handful, popping the kernels one at a time into her mouth.

"I know it's morbid," she said, "but I keep thinking about how great it was when Matt was around and we used to go out to Glover's Corners."

Nancy nodded. "It was fun." In the winter, she remembered, there'd been ice skating on the pond behind the house. In the summer the pond was fringed with low-hanging willow trees, and Mrs. Adams, the housekeeper, would bring them ice-cold lemonade after they'd swum.

"Poor Mrs. Adams," Nancy said. "Now that Mr. Glover is gone, I wonder what she'll do."

Rosemary Adams had been more than just a housekeeper to the Glovers. Since Matt's mother had died when he was only ten, she'd been like a mother to him. It was hard to imagine Glover's Corners without her.

The girls looked up from their popcorn as Carson Drew came into the kitchen. Putting down his briefcase, he greeted Nancy and Bess, and Nancy saw at once that he was preoccupied. His forehead was creased, and his eyes were red looking.

"Hi, Mr. Drew," said Bess. She peered at her watch, then hopped up and began putting on her red down coat. "I guess I'd better go. It's almost time for dinner."

"I might as well tell you both right now," Carson said, not listening to Bess. "It's going to be all over town soon enough."

Both girls looked at him expectantly.

"I had a call from Rosemary Adams at Glover's Corners," he said. "A young man came to the door this afternoon." Carson hesitated, almost as if he couldn't continue with what he had to say.

"What did he want?" Nancy prompted.

"He said he was Matthew Glover, and Rosemary nearly fainted from the shock."

Nancy's mouth fell open. She started to say something, but her words were drowned out by Bess's excited cry.

"You see," she shouted, her face flushed pink. "I was right all along. Matt's alive, and he's come home!"

Chapter Two

NANCY GLANCED from Bess's ecstatic face to Carson Drew's serious one. "Could it really *be* Matt?" she asked her father. "Is it possible?"

"Of course it's possible," Bess cut in impatiently.

"I haven't met him yet myself," Carson said, rubbing his eyes, "but Mrs. Adams swears that he looks and acts like Matt. But she's not sure he is Matt. Apparently, he says he had amnesia after his skiing accident. It wasn't until he saw Clayton Glover's picture in the paper that he remembered who he was." He shook his head and added, "As to whether or not he's telling the truth, I don't want to make any kind of judgment until I meet him."

"That's a good idea, Dad. And I think we

should do the same." Nancy stared meaningfully at Bess. "Right, Bess?"

"What? Oh—yeah, sure, Nan," Bess said, but the dreamy expression on her face told Nancy that her friend had already made up her mind.

"You were right, Bess," Nancy said in a low voice the following afternoon. "I think all of River Heights *is* here for Mr. Glover's funeral."

Nancy, Bess, and Bess's cousin George Fayne were entering the stone church where the service was to be held.

"It is really packed," George agreed. "I bet most of these people never even met Mr. Glover." Tall and slim, with short dark hair, George squeezed in next to Bess and Nancy in a pew toward the rear of the church.

Nancy peered toward the front of the church and found Rosemary Adams, dressed all in black. Nancy knew she must be in her sixties, but the silver-haired woman looked frailer than her years. Her face was dead white, and she was leaning heavily on Nancy's father's arm.

"Where is he?" Bess asked, craning her neck to scan the church.

Nancy didn't have to ask who "he" was. And from the amount of whispering Nancy heard, she guessed a lot of other people were wondering where Matt Glover was, too.

"Shh," said George. "The service is starting."

It wasn't until after the funeral that they got a

glimpse of Matt Glover. Many of the mourners lingered outside the church, and Nancy, George, and Bess paused, too.

Nancy was buttoning up her fleece-lined leather jacket when she heard Bess give a little shriek.

"There he is!" she exclaimed. "Wow, he's as great looking as ever!"

Nancy and George turned to follow Bess's gaze. Nancy spotted the tall, lanky guy at once. He was about twenty-three or -four, the age Matt would be, and he had the thick black hair and dark eyebrows Nancy remembered. He was approaching her father and Rosemary Adams, and Nancy saw his face light up with the wide grin that had been Matt's trademark.

"I'd die to have him look at me with that smile," Bess said with a sigh. "That's Matt, all right."

George rolled her eyes at her cousin. "That's your purely objective opinion, right?" she teased. Taking another look at the guy, she added, "I don't know. I don't remember Matt's shoulders being quite so broad."

"A man can change in five years," Bess said defensively. "He was our age when he died. When he disappeared, I mean," she corrected herself.

Privately, Nancy agreed with Bess. A lot of things about a person could change over time. Even so, this guy looked incredibly like the Matt

she remembered. If he was an impostor, he was a very good one.

"They're coming over," Bess said excitedly.

A moment later the three girls were saying hello to Carson Drew and Mrs. Adams. They tried not to stare too openly at the young man with Carson as he introduced him.

"I'd like you to meet my daughter, Nancy," Carson said. "Nancy, this is"—he hesitated before saying it—"Matthew Glover."

Nancy knew her father didn't necessarily believe the stranger's identity, but what else could he call him? Nancy realized that she, too, had already started to think of him as Matt, even though she wasn't convinced he was the *real* Matt.

Whoever he was, his smile was easy and unforced. Up close Nancy could see that he had Matt's deep blue eyes and dark lashes. Bess was right about one thing—he *was* great looking!

"Nancy Drew," he said. "I knew you'd grow up to be beautiful."

For a second she thought he was trying to flirt with her. But then he smiled in a friendly, direct way. When Carson introduced him to Bess and George, he was just as charming with them.

"It's great to see you again," Bess told Matt. Nancy could almost see stars in Bess's eyes. "I always kept up a tiny hope that you'd come back."

"Thanks, Bess. That means a lot to me," Matt told her as he flashed her one of his big smiles.

Nancy had the distinct feeling that someone was watching them. Glancing over Matt's shoulder, she met the intense gaze of a man who was staring at them from the steps of the church. He had short blond hair and was wearing a green parka with a hood. Nancy had the feeling that she'd seen him before.

Then she remembered—he was an environmental activist. Giralda, that was his name. Tony Giralda. She had seen his face on posters for a campaign to clean up River Heights's Muskoka River.

Matt's voice drew Nancy's attention back to the conversation around her. "I'd like you all to come back to Glover's Corners," he was saying. "Rosemary has prepared enough food to feed an army." He gazed at the housekeeper affectionately, but she didn't return the look. She continued staring straight ahead, slightly dazed.

"Poor Mrs. Adams," Nancy said a few minutes later as she, Bess, and George climbed into Nancy's blue Mustang.

"What do you mean?" Bess asked. "She must be having one of the happiest days of her life. She was like a mother to Matt."

George stared at her cousin. "I didn't exactly see her falling all over him," she said dryly.

"That's because she's too stunned," Bess retorted.

They swung out onto the main street and followed the stream of cars heading toward the outskirts of River Heights. Glover's Corners lay between two heavily wooded areas and was bordered by a low brick wall. The entrance drive curved into the property from a tall, wrought-iron gate. The gate stood open, but the house itself was well hidden behind some gently rolling hills.

"This is just as I remember it," George said as Nancy turned onto the twisting drive.

After rounding a few curves, they could see the house. Built of rose-colored brick, it was huge, with a main hall and two wings stretching out on either side of it. The wings curved slightly toward the front, circling a large garden. The pond was barely visible at the foot of a gentle slope behind the house. The old stables and the pond, Nancy remembered, were behind the house.

Nancy parked behind the other cars and climbed out to crunch over the gravel path toward the front door. Other people were also making their way toward the house, and Nancy noticed that one of them was Tony Giralda. He was getting out of a battered-looking van a few cars in front of Nancy's Mustang.

"Pretty impressive," George said, once they were inside. The entrance hall was huge. Directly in front of them was a stately mahogany staircase. There were two curved archways leading to the two wings of the house to the right and left of the hall.

"The guests are all going this way," Bess said, pointing to the left.

"That's right," said Nancy. "As I remember, the other way leads to the more private areas."

There were several open doors along the hallway, and the girls peeked into them as they passed. There was a paneled library, a living room, and a smaller sitting room, all elegantly furnished. Most of the guests had collected in the formal dining room, so the girls went in there.

"Mrs. Adams sure seems to be a lot happier now," George commented.

The housekeeper was rushing around, seeing that the big urns were full of coffee and tea, fussing over the plates of cold meats and bowls of salad. Nancy saw that the color had come back to her face, and there was even a smile on her lips now.

"I don't know about you guys, but I'm starving," Nancy said, eyeing the long table that stretched along one wall. It was piled high with food.

The girls got in line and took plates. Nancy was just spooning some pasta salad onto hers when a deep voice spoke up right behind her: "I can't tell you how it feels to be back."

She turned to see Matt standing there. "It must be kind of weird for you," Nancy said. "How *does* it feel?"

Matt gave a deep sigh. "Wonderful and strange

at the same time. In some ways I feel as if I've never been away."

"Oh, but you have," Nancy said. "Five years is a long time." It was almost creepy to be talking to him again. If he really was Matt, she reminded herself.

He ran a hand through his thick black hair. "I guess so. I just wish I could have figured out who I was before . . ." He broke off.

Nancy gave him a sympathetic look. "Your father was a wonderful person," she said sincerely. "We'll all miss him." After a pause she asked, "How did you find out who you were?"

"I saw the obituary in the Chicago *Clarion,*" Matt explained. "There was a photo of my father, and as soon as I saw it I had to sit down. I knew he meant something to me, something very important. I read the obituary three times, and each time things came back more clearly. I don't think you can imagine what it felt like, Nancy."

"Very few people could," she admitted. "But then, very few people have amnesia."

"That's what your father said. I was talking to him before you got here. He said he's never run across a case in all the years he's practiced law."

This might not be amnesia, either, Nancy thought, if he's not the real Matt Glover. Almost instantly she felt aggravated with herself for raising the doubt so automatically. Lighten up, Drew, she scolded herself.

"I'm starving," Matt said, breaking into her thoughts. He filled his plate, then started to make himself a thick roast beef sandwich. As she watched him, Nancy suddenly remembered something.

Everyone had always teased Matt about the huge mounds of mustard he added to just about everything. She paid close attention, holding her breath as he clamped the top piece of bread over the beef.

Matt didn't bite into it, though. Heading for the silver bowls filled with brown and yellow mustard, he opened his sandwich and plastered the beef with mustard the way the real Matt Glover would have.

Nancy shook herself for being so untrusting. So far there wasn't really any reason to doubt him. Matt was speaking with Bess now in a completely casual and natural manner.

Seeing her father across the room, Nancy crossed to him, but as they talked her eyes kept straying to Matt and Bess. Bess seemed to be doing most of the talking, and from the smiles on both their faces, they were enjoying each other's company quite a bit.

"Is something bothering you, Nancy?" her father asked. "I just asked you a question, and you didn't even hear me."

Nancy felt herself blush. "Sorry, Dad. I was just thinking, it's pretty amazing about Matt

coming back. Maybe it *is* him." She told him about the mustard.

Carson Drew followed her gaze. "A really clever impostor would know all about the person he's pretending to be," he replied, sounding thoughtful. "I honestly don't know what to think about him, Nancy. If you asked me whether that guy is Matt Glover or a con man, I couldn't give you an answer. Not yet."

Nancy took a bite of her pasta salad. "I guess the important thing is not to be biased either way."

"One thing's sure—he knows the house inside and out. When he first came here today, Rosemary said she asked him to get two trays for her from the second pantry. He got them in record time—not a false move."

Nancy thought of the huge kitchen with its many storage rooms and pantries in the back hall. It wouldn't be easy for a stranger to find the second pantry so quickly—unless he'd studied a blueprint of Glover's Corners.

"What's this about false moves?" George asked, coming up to Nancy and her father.

"We were just talking about Matt, and how he hasn't made any yet," Nancy told her.

"If he's an impostor, you mean," George added. "Well, so far he has two definite fans."

"You don't have to tell me who one of them

is," Nancy said with a laugh, nodding toward Bess. "Who's the other?"

"Mrs. Adams. I just heard her say something like, 'Maybe dreams *do* come true.' "

"She'd know better than anyone," Carson Drew commented. Putting his arm around Nancy's shoulders, he said, "I'm worn out. You girls won't mind if I leave early, will you?"

"Poor Dad," Nancy said. "Settling Mr. Glover's estate has been a lot of extra work for you, hasn't it? Here, I'll get your coat."

Out in the hall, Nancy paused to glance out the windows on either side of the front door. The day appeared to be colder and grayer than ever, and the cars lining the winding drive were covered with a frozen mist.

Shivering slightly, she went to the front hall closet and pulled her father's heavy overcoat from its hanger. She was just slinging it over one arm when a noise behind her made her pause.

Nancy swiveled around and saw someone emerge from the shadows near the front door. She recognized Tony Giralda's lean, wiry form as he strode toward her.

"So, you've been taken in by him, too," he said. Nancy saw that he had brown eyes, and there was a look of intense anger in them. In fact, it seemed to Nancy that his whole body was tense with a kind of nervous energy.

"What do you mean?" Nancy asked him.

"You're some kind of detective, right?" he

asked, but his angry voice made it sound like an accusation.

Nancy nodded.

Giralda's hands balled into fists at his sides. "I knew Matt Glover," he said, drawing the words out. "I knew him like my own brother. And that guy's not him."

Chapter Three

"How can you tell?" Nancy asked Tony. "What kind of proof do you—"

"I've got to go," he said suddenly. "If you want to talk, you can find me at my office. Giralda's Environmental Action."

"Tomorrow?" Nancy asked immediately. If Tony Giralda had any proof that the man inside wasn't Matt Glover, she wanted to know what it was as soon as possible.

He nodded. "Hours are noon until eight. I'll be there all afternoon."

When Nancy went back into the library with her father's coat, Carson Drew was nowhere in sight. George was just putting her empty plate with some others at one end of the long table.

"Did you see where my dad went?" Nancy asked, going over to her.

George pointed toward a doorway at the rear of the dining room, which Nancy knew led to the kitchen. "He went back there with Mrs. Adams."

The two girls found Nancy's father in the kitchen, holding Mrs. Adams awkwardly in his arms and patting her back. The housekeeper's eyes were red rimmed, and she had obviously been crying.

When Mrs. Adams saw Nancy, she said, "Oh, dear, please excuse me. I feel like smiling and crying at the same time."

"Rosemary is feeling a bit overwhelmed," Nancy's father said.

Straightening herself, Mrs. Adams stepped away from Carson Drew and wiped her eyes with one end of the kitchen towel she was holding. "At first I couldn't be sure that young man was really Matt, and yet I wanted him to be. I wanted it so much."

She sat down at the long oak table. "Mr. Glover was a very fine man," she went on after a long pause. "He took it so hard when Matt disappeared. My heart ached for him. He was a wonderful employer, but things were never the same here after Matt vanished. You remember, Nancy, dear, how happy the atmosphere at the Corners was. The picnics and barbecues, the skating . . ."

"Yes," Nancy said in a comforting voice. "My friends and I were talking about it earlier. Mr.

Glover continued to invite us out here, but it was never the same after Matt died."

"We have to stop saying that now, of course," Mrs. Adams said, smiling. "Matt didn't die, thank goodness, and now he's come home. It's just wonderful, isn't it? If only his father could have lived to see him again." She looked as if she might start crying again, but then she clapped one hand over her mouth and said, "Silly me, it was only because of Mr. G's death that Matt remembered who he was."

"Yes, he told me how the article in the *Clarion* sparked his memory," Nancy said. She paused, then asked, "Tell me, Mrs. Adams. When did you know he really was Matt?"

"I began to suspect it when we came back here after the funeral. He stepped into the hall and asked me where the old elephant's leg was." Mrs. Adams was beaming, unaware of the puzzled expressions on the others' faces.

"Elephant's leg?" Carson Drew inquired.

"Yes, the old umbrella stand. Mr. G's father brought it back from Africa years ago. It was a hollowed-out leg—a curio, really. Matt always loved it as a child. I had to tell him his father gave it away after he disappeared. Mr. Glover couldn't stand being reminded of Matt every time he saw the thing."

"I wonder why he didn't ask yesterday, when he first came to the door?" Nancy said.

Mrs. Adams appeared to be indignant. "You

don't think I let him into the hall yesterday?" she asked. "He didn't take one step inside, because I couldn't be sure who he really was."

"But now you're sure?"

The housekeeper nodded. "When we came back here today, he knew right where to find my trays, for one thing. And when he went up to see his old room, he came back amazed at how it hadn't changed. Only a boy who'd been raised here could know such things, don't you agree?"

Nancy smiled rather than answering.

"Still," Mrs. Adams continued, "there's always that little nagging doubt, isn't there? A fortune hunter could learn about the umbrella stand and about how Matt's father kept the room the way it had been. . . . "

"And where the trays were kept in the second pantry," Nancy added.

Rosemary Adams wiped at some imaginary dirt on the table with the kitchen towel. "But I really knew in my heart that he was Matt when he called me Addie."

"Addie?" Nancy asked.

"That was Matt's private nickname for me. He didn't use it when other people were around, but in private, he always called me Addie."

Mrs. Adams glanced at her watch, then got quickly to her feet. "My goodness, I've been neglecting my guests," she said.

"Don't try to do too much," Carson Drew advised her.

"Oh, but there'll be lots of work now that Matthew is back," she sang out in a happy voice.

"So you think he'll stay on here?" George asked. "This place is pretty big for one person."

"Two people, you mean," Mrs. Adams corrected. "Don't forget, Matthew will surely want to marry and raise a family, and I'd want to stay on and take care of them."

Nancy gazed after Mrs. Adams as she bustled back toward the dining room. The detective in her was beginning to be very intrigued by this situation. Whether or not the man she'd met that day really was Matt Glover, his appearance was definitely causing ripples.

"Did you ever hear Matt call Mrs. Adams 'Addie'?" George asked from the backseat of Nancy's car. She and Nancy and Bess were driving back toward town from Glover's Corners.

"I don't think so," Nancy said, "but Mrs. Adams said that he didn't use the name in front of other people."

"What's this Addie business?" Bess asked.

"Matt's private nickname for Mrs. Adams," George told her. She stretched her long legs out on the seat and leaned back. "It seemed funny to me, that's all."

"*I* think it sounds cute," Bess countered.

George rolled her eyes. "You think everything about Matt is cute."

"That's because it is," Bess replied. "Matt's a major heartthrob, you have to admit."

"He is handsome," Nancy agreed. She gave Bess a sideways glance. "But maybe you should hold off falling in love with the guy until everyone's sure he really is Matt."

"Who's not sure?" Bess asked. "Mrs. Adams is convinced. Who would know him better? And you saw how much mustard he put on his sandwich. How would he know how much Matt liked mustard unless he *is* Matt?"

"Well, Tony Giralda's not so sure." Nancy told Bess and George about the environmentalist's reservations.

Bess looked at her doubtfully. "Well, I don't remember anyone named Tony Giralda hanging around with Matt. How would he know?"

"Tony said he knew Matt like a brother," Nancy explained. "We were a lot younger than they were, don't forget. We don't know who Matt's friends were."

"Yeah," said George. "Just because we didn't know him doesn't mean Matt didn't."

Nancy steered the Mustang onto Bess's street and pulled up in front of her house. "Anyway, I'm going to talk to him tomorrow and find out what he has to say. It can't hurt."

"I don't see why you guys can't just admit that Matt's really back." Bess got out of the car, pausing with the door open while she looked back and forth from Nancy to George. "I would

think you'd at least believe Mrs. Adams if you don't believe me. Oh, well. See you." She closed the door and was gone.

Nancy dropped George off and was on the way home when a new thought struck her. It was something Mrs. Adams had said: "Don't forget, Matthew will surely want to marry and raise a family, and I'd want to stay on and take care of them."

Mrs. Adams had lived at Glover's Corners for over twenty years, and she loved the place. Where would she go if the estate was given to River Heights as a museum or a nursing home or if it was demolished to make room for development?

It was definitely in the housekeeper's best interests to have Matt show up. She knew Matt better than any other living person and could easily teach a stranger—a stranger who looked just like Matt—all the little things. Maybe she'd even made up that stuff about her nickname being Addie.

Nancy didn't want to believe it, but a part of her was whispering that the only one who knew enough about Matt and Glover's Corners to set up a giant fraud was Mrs. Adams.

Chapter Four

NANCY LET OUT a long breath. She could hardly believe that Mrs. Adams would deceive anyone, but she had to admit that it was possible.

A dog ran out into the road. Nancy swerved to avoid it, then forced herself to keep her mind focused on her driving for the rest of the way home.

She found a note from her father in the kitchen: "Went to bed early. See you in the A.M." Beneath it, he had scrawled, "Call Bess."

Picking up the kitchen extension, she dialed Bess's number, smiling to herself when her friend's bubbly voice came over the line.

"Nan! I have so much to tell you!"

Nancy leaned against the kitchen counter and cradled the receiver between her head and shoul-

der. "I just dropped you off ten minutes ago, Bess. How much could there be to say?"

"Matt called," Bess said, her voice shrill with excitement. "He told me how much it meant to him to have good friends like me after being away for five years. He mentioned you and George, too."

Nancy could practically see her friend's grin over the line. "I forgot to tell you guys on the ride home," Bess went on, "that he had told me his whole story—well, practically all."

"What did he tell you?"

Nancy listened to the story about the obituary to see if he'd told it any differently to Bess, but it was the same, almost word for word. "He doesn't remember the skiing accident in Colorado at all," Bess finished. "He didn't even know his own name until he read it in the paper. He had taken the name Gary Page. He was working as a journalist. Doesn't that sound familiar?"

"Yeah," Nancy agreed. "I remember that Matt was the editor of the high school paper. I think he even wrote a few articles for the *Morning Record.*"

"So that's more proof he's really Matt, right?"

"Maybe," Nancy said noncommittally. "Where'd he work? In Colorado?"

"He didn't say. He just said something made him want to keep moving east. He worked on a paper in Nebraska for two years, and then he

went to Iowa before going to work for the *Clarion* in Chicago."

They talked for a few more minutes, and then Nancy hung up. It seemed more and more as if Matt was who he said he was. It would be great if he were—especially for Bess—but Nancy knew she wouldn't be convinced until she had checked out a few things. Tony Giralda's doubts, for one.

Maybe she'd go to the Chicago *Clarion* office, too, to check on his background to see if Gary Page was the same guy as the Matt Glover she'd met that day.

Her father would be checking him out, too. Carson Drew was spending the whole next day with Matt. Apparently there were matters to be settled before Matt could be legally accepted as Clayton Glover's heir. If anyone could catch him in a lie, it was Carson Drew.

Nancy shook her head. She'd thought about Matt Glover enough for one day. She knew one way to get her mind off him. Grabbing the bag with her disassembled tape deck in it, Nancy sat down at the kitchen table, dumped the parts out, and concentrated on putting them back together.

When Nancy woke in the morning, light snowflakes were dancing outside her window. She had stayed up until after two A.M., working on her tape deck, and had slept much later than usual. It was ten by the time she had dressed in jeans and

a pale green cable-knit sweater and went downstairs.

Hannah Gruen, the Drews' housekeeper, was making chicken soup for lunch. Hannah had been living with the Drews since Nancy's mother died, when Nancy was just three, and she was more like a member of the family than a housekeeper.

"That smells delicious," Nancy said, sniffing appreciatively.

"Your father's at his office with that young man who says he's Clayton Glover's son," Hannah informed her. "I imagine they'll be there all day."

Pouring herself a glass of orange juice, Nancy popped two slices of bread into the toaster. "What do you think?" she asked.

"About what?"

"About the new Matt," Nancy said. "Do you think it's possible to have amnesia for five years and snap out of it when you see your father's obituary?"

Hannah considered Nancy's question. "It happens all the time on TV," she said, "which is enough for me to doubt it. On the other hand, *anything* is possible."

"I guess you're right—on both counts," Nancy said, laughing. When her toast popped up, she buttered it, then smothered it with strawberry jam.

"You're going to spoil your appetite for lunch," Hannah told her.

Nancy took a bite of toast. "Don't worry. I always have room for your soup."

At twelve Nancy proved it, eating a big bowl full of it. After mopping up the last of the soup with a thick slice of crusty bread, she checked her watch. It was early afternoon, and Tony Giralda would probably be in his office by now.

Pulling on her leather boots and heavy jacket, Nancy grabbed her tape deck from the small table in the front hall, where she'd left it the night before. Then she ran out to her car. A light snow was falling, but the flakes melted as soon as they hit the ground. Backing out of the driveway, Nancy put a tape in the deck and was pleased to hear that the sound was perfect and that the machine was no longer eating tapes.

Nancy drove toward the address she'd looked up for Giralda's Environmental Action office. Soon she pulled up in front of a building on the outskirts of River Heights's downtown area.

To call the Environmental Action building an office was stretching things a bit, Nancy thought as she studied the building through the window of her car. It was really just a long, low garage. Posters publicizing Tony's campaign to clean up the Muskoka River covered the area around the door.

Pulling the fleecy collar of her leather jacket

close around her ears, Nancy stepped out of the car, walked to the door, and knocked on it. A few seconds later Tony opened it.

"I was wondering if you'd show up," he said as she stepped inside.

It wasn't exactly an enthusiastic hello, Nancy thought, but at least his voice had lost some of the angry intensity of the day before.

"I said I would," she told him.

He took her jacket and hung it on a hook just inside the door next to his parka. Then Nancy followed him down a small hallway lined with closed doors. Nancy guessed they opened into closets—there really wasn't room for much more.

Tony led Nancy into an office. The room was crammed with posters and buttons. A table against the wall was piled high with letters and envelopes and so was the only desk in the room.

"This is pretty much a one-man operation," Tony explained. "I can't afford to hire anyone full time, so I have to depend on volunteers." He gestured around the empty office. "As you can see, they're not always dependable." Clearing off some posters that were on his desk chair, he offered Nancy the seat, while he leaned on the edge of the desk.

Nancy got right to the point. "You said you were convinced that the man at Glover's Corners isn't the real Matthew Glover."

"That's right—he's not," Tony replied.

"Do you have any evidence?"

Tony crossed his arms over his chest, and that dark, brooding look came back into his eyes. "Well, not hard evidence," he told her. "But I *know* that guy is a phony."

More opinion, Nancy thought. Opinion was a long way from being concrete proof. "Do you mean he doesn't look like Matt or sound like him?" she prodded.

"Oh, he looks like Matt would look now, if Matt were alive, and he sounds the way I remember Matt's voice. But he's not Matt."

"In other words, it's just a feeling you have?" Nancy said, trying to keep her disappointment out of her voice. This was turning out to be a total waste of time.

Tony nodded. "It's not just a feeling. It's a *gut* feeling, as strong as they come."

"Too bad they don't allow gut feelings to be admitted as evidence in court," she said. The words sounded more sarcastic than she had meant them to be, and Tony shot her an angry look.

"I'm sorry," Nancy said quickly, "but if you could just think of what it is that makes you so sure he's a fake, that would help. Was it the way he walked or some gesture he made? Matt was left-handed, according to my dad. I watched that guy yesterday, and he favored his left hand, too. But maybe there are some things like that that don't fit. Can you think of anything?"

Tony raked his fingers nervously through his short blond hair. "I can't think of anything specific, but I swear to you I'm right."

Great, Nancy thought. Getting up from the chair, she told him, "I don't see what you think I can do to help."

He pounded his hand on the desk so hard that Nancy jumped. "Can't you get to the truth about this guy?" he blurted out. Recovering himself, he went on more calmly. "I mean, you must have ways of working so that he wouldn't suspect you."

Nancy shook her head. "If he's an impostor, he'll suspect everyone. I'm sorry, but unless you can give me something more concrete to go on, there's nothing I can do." She stood up to leave.

Tony made a disgusted noise in his throat and turned away. Nancy walked out, casting a glance back over her shoulder. Tony's face was set in an angry grimace.

Nancy was surprised to find her father home when she returned from Tony Giralda's office. He was sitting at the kitchen table, eating a bowl of Hannah's soup. Nancy sat with him.

"I thought you were going to be tied up with Matt Glover all day," she said. "It's only one-thirty."

"I had to come back to pick up some papers," Carson said, tipping his bowl to scoop up the last of the soup. "You know, Matt is coming through

with flying colors so far," he told her. "He signed an affidavit, and the signature compares well with Matt's. There's a slight difference, but handwriting changes over time. Of course, I'll submit a sample of the writing to an expert, just to be sure."

"Did he sign with his left hand?" Nancy asked.

"Yes, and he did it completely naturally." Carson pushed the empty bowl away from him and then sighed. "Going over the writing samples could take a few days. It's a touchy situation, so we have to be very careful. Clayton's will is clear that his son is to inherit everything if he's ever found. That's usual in cases where a body hasn't been recovered. If Matt hadn't shown up, Glover's money was to be split up among several charities."

"He didn't leave any to Mrs. Adams?" Nancy asked.

"Oh, there's a nice bequest to Rosemary," he said. "But the rest, which amounts to several million dollars, was to go to charity."

"I suppose he left money to the hospital," Nancy guessed.

"Yes. There's also a large bequest to the hospital's day-care center and several bequests to smaller organizations and businesses."

A sudden idea occurred to Nancy. Leaning forward over the kitchen table, she asked, "I don't suppose Tony Giralda's Environmental Action group would be one of them?"

Carson was surprised. "Yes," he said. "As a matter of fact, it is. How did you know?"

Nancy told her father about her visit to the Environmental Action office. "From the look of the place, I can bet he has a hard time making ends meet. But he's incredibly devoted to his work. He seems practically fanatical about it."

"A hefty bequest from Mr. Glover could be the answer to his financial problems," Carson put in. "I see what you're getting at, Nancy."

Nancy's blue eyes were wide. "Maybe Tony Giralda is fierce enough about his work to want to cheat the real Matt out of his legitimate inheritance!"

Chapter Five

"It's a possibility, Nancy," Carson told her. "There's just one—"

Nancy didn't hear because she had already jumped up from the table and was heading for the front door. "I can hardly wait to tell Bess and George," she said excitedly as she grabbed her jacket from the closet. "See you later, Dad."

She drove over and picked up Bess, and then they went directly to George's.

"You mean Tony Giralda might be trying to frame Matt so he can get Mr. Glover's money?" Bess said after Nancy had told them about her encounter with Tony and the bequest to his organization. "That's disgusting!"

"Tony Giralda's not the only one who might be cheating to get a piece of the Glover fortune,

either," Nancy went on. She explained her idea about Mrs. Adams coaching someone to play the role of Matt.

George brushed a hand through her short, dark curls and seemed extremely dubious. "I don't know, Nan. She seemed harmless to me."

"Maybe," Nancy said. "The point is, whatever we're dealing with, there may be more people involved in it than just Matt. I'm going to keep an eye on Tony Giralda and Mrs. Adams—and I think I need to check out Matt, too."

"Where do we start?" George asked.

"Well, I'd like to check out Gary Page's credentials at the Chicago *Clarion,*" Nancy suggested.

George looked at her watch. "If we leave right now, we could be back by early evening."

"Well, *I* already believe Matt," Bess said. "But if it'll make you guys feel better, let's go."

Nancy frowned. "I wish we had a photo of him to take with us, to show the people at the paper."

"No problem," said Bess, blushing a little. "I just happen to have a very recent picture of him." She fumbled in her purse and drew out an instant photo of Matt.

"Where did you get that?" Nancy and George asked at the same time.

"I went over to the Corners this morning," Bess said, her whole face bright pink now. "When Matt called last night, he said I should feel free to stop by, so I did. Mrs. Adams was snapping pictures of Matt and gave me one."

"Pretty good detecting, Bess," Nancy joked. "It's just what we need. Let's go."

Bess grinned. "And I thought I was just flirting!"

The light snow had let up, so the three friends made good time. The *Clarion* offices were in the Loop, or downtown Chicago, and were in a building about five times as big as the one where the River Heights *Morning Record* was.

At the main receptionist's desk they were directed to the sixth floor, where another receptionist asked them what they wanted.

"We'd like to speak to someone about a reporter who worked here until a few days ago," Nancy said. "Gary Page."

The receptionist spoke into a phone, then told them, "Ms. McCoy will be with you in a moment."

They could hear heels tapping smartly down a hall, and then a tall woman with shoulder-length black hair came into the reception area. "I'm Sheila McCoy," she said. "I was Gary's editor—" She caught herself, then added, "I guess I should start calling him Matt Glover. I hope nothing's happened to him?"

Nancy introduced herself and assured Sheila McCoy that he was fine. "How long had he worked for you?" Nancy asked as the editor led her, Bess, and George back to her desk in the newsroom.

"About a year. He came with excellent references from a paper in Iowa City. He was a good reporter, and I'll miss him. They don't grow on trees, you know."

She opened a file and took out a cutting. "I don't think I've ever seen any reporter with a better memory for detail. Here, this is a copy of one of the first stories he did for the *Clarion.* It's about a local entrepreneur—kind of a rags-to-riches story."

Nancy glanced at the article with the Gary Page byline but didn't notice anything special about it. "What about his past?" she asked, looking up from the article. "Did Gary Page ever talk about his family or background?"

Sheila shook her head. "No," she said. "He was *very* private. To say that he kept to himself would be an understatement."

Pulling Bess's photo from her purse, Nancy asked Sheila if it was a good likeness of Gary Page. This time Sheila's eyes narrowed. "What's this all about, anyway?" she asked.

"We're, uh, working on an article for our local paper," Nancy lied. "Matt Glover's a real human-interest story back in River Heights—that's where we're from."

The smile returned to Sheila's face. "Well, good luck," she told them. "Great shot," she added after studying the picture. "Looks just like him."

"May I keep this?" Nancy asked, holding up the article.

"Sure." Sheila shook hands with them. "Say hello to Gary—I mean, Matt, for me."

"Now we have all the proof we need," Bess said, stirring her hot cocoa. After they'd left the *Clarion,* they had decided to stop at a diner for something to eat and drink before making the drive back to River Heights.

"Hold on," Nancy said. "We need to find out a lot more." She took a sip of her cocoa and stared out the window next to their booth. "All Sheila McCoy told us was that the man in the snapshot was the man she knew as Gary Page. That doesn't mean the guy is really Matt Glover."

"Well, at least he told the truth when he said he'd worked at the *Clarion,*" George said. She was flipping through the jukebox selections at their table.

Nancy pulled out the article the newspaper editor had given her and skimmed through it. It was dated a little over a year earlier and was about some man who had once been a gardener for a private estate. He had opened up a landscape gardening business in downtown Chicago and had become very successful.

"It's very well written," said Bess, reading over her shoulder.

There was a picture of the man, Jake Loomis,

but since it was a photocopy, the picture was a blur. Nothing about the article was helpful, and Nancy folded it and put it back in her jacket pocket.

"You know," George said, "that woman said something funny—about Gary Page being a loner."

Nancy nodded. "I was wondering about that, too. I mean, what kind of guy *never* mentions anything about his background during a whole year? Sheila McCoy saw him practically every day, but she says she knows nothing about him."

"Somebody might act like that if he planned to vanish," George proposed, downing the last of her cocoa. "A man who planned to impersonate someone who was dead wouldn't want people to know anything about him."

"Oh, come on, you guys," Bess cut in. "He had amnesia, remember. How could he tell anyone about his life? *He* didn't know anything about it."

Bess glanced out the diner window, and suddenly delighted surprise lit up her face. "Look!" she exclaimed. "There he is—in that phone booth!"

Following Bess's gaze, Nancy immediately saw Matt's unmistakable figure. He was speaking into a pay phone a few yards from the diner. There was a vintage sports roadster beside him, and Nancy recognized it as having belonged to Mr. Glover.

"What's he doing here?" George wanted to know.

"We'll know soon enough," Bess said, waving out the window until she got his attention. "He's coming over."

Matt was wearing a broad grin as he hung up the phone and headed for the diner. "Hi, you guys," he said cheerfully. He spoke to all of them, but Nancy noticed that he saved the fullest force of his deep blue eyes for Bess, and she was eating up the attention.

"What a treat," he told her. "I get to see you twice in one day." He leaned close to her and said jokingly, "We've got to stop meeting like this."

"Not if I can help it," Bess returned, laughing.

Nancy glanced across the table at George, who rolled her eyes as if to say, "She's really getting silly about this guy!"

Nancy knew just what George meant, but she wasn't sure what to do about it. "Um, I'll be right back, you guys. I'm just going to the ladies' room," she said.

She gave George a meaningful look as she got up and was glad when George said, "I'll come with you."

"Can you believe it?" George said, leaning against the sink when she and Nancy were alone in the ladies' room. "Bess adores that guy. She's only just met him again—I mean, if he really is Matt—and she practically worships him."

"I noticed Matt doesn't seem to mind a bit,"

Nancy added. "In fact, he seems to be egging her on. This could turn out to be a real disaster."

George nodded. "I know what you mean. What if he is a phony and just using Bess to gain credibility?" Her brown eyes were filled with concern. "I'd hate to see her get hurt."

Nancy nodded. "That's what I'm afraid of, too. For her sake, I hope Matt Glover really is who he says he is. Because if we prove that he's not, it will break Bess's heart."

Chapter Six

"WHAT DO YOU THINK we should do?" George asked.

"I think we'd better hurry up and find out the truth about Matt. Come on," Nancy said, reaching for the ladies' room door. "Let's get back to the table before Bess decides to elope with the guy!"

George laughed, but her expression became grim again when she and Nancy returned to their seats and saw the adoration written across Bess's face.

"Uh-oh," Nancy whispered. "We'd better break this up."

She cleared her throat loudly as she and George sat down again. Matt and Bess broke off their conversation to acknowledge them.

"I have to tell you," Nancy said to Matt, "that the reason we're in Chicago is because of you."

"Nancy!" Bess gasped, shocked. She looked nervously at Matt, obviously not wanting him to know they'd been snooping on him. Matt was staring in bewilderment at Nancy.

"It's important for us to be honest with you, Matt," Nancy explained. "We were checking up on you at the *Clarion.*"

"I told Nancy it wasn't necessary," Bess put in quickly.

Matt smiled at all of them. "Actually, I'm glad you checked up on me. I want you to trust me, and you're right, Nancy, we have to be honest with one another."

"Good," said Nancy. "I'm glad we understand each other."

"As a matter of fact, I asked your father if I could take a lie-detector test," Matt added to Nancy.

"Then everyone will have to believe you," said Bess.

He grinned at her again, then said, "Let's talk about something more pleasant."

"Like what?" Bess's eyes were shining.

"Like ice skating. The temperature out there must have dropped ten degrees since noon. The pond at home should be nicely frozen over tonight. What would you all say to a moonlight ice-skating party?"

"Just like the old days," Bess said.

"It's a great idea," Nancy said. The more they hung out with Matt, the more certain they could be that he was—or wasn't—Mr. Glover's son.

"Good." Matt got up to go. "I have to get back to the Corners and sweep the pond for tonight. The car holds only two, I'm afraid. Would you like to ride back to River Heights with me, Bess?"

Nancy held her breath, hoping that her friend would refuse.

"Sure," Bess replied breathlessly. "I'd love to."

"I'll pick you up in an hour, after I check in at home," Nancy told George as she dropped her off at her house.

After a quick hello to her father and Hannah, Nancy decided to go see Tony Giralda again. She had almost an hour before she had to pick up George and Bess, and she wanted to check out her theory that Tony might be trying to cheat Matt out of his inheritance.

Nancy changed her cable-knit sweater for a turtleneck and heavy ski sweater. She grabbed her skates and was almost out the door when the phone rang. She answered it in the kitchen.

"Ned!" she said, a smile lighting up her face when she heard her boyfriend's voice on the other end of the line. "Where are you?"

"Still at school. That's why I'm calling. I'm

afraid I won't be able to make it out to see you this weekend. I've got a killer test on Monday, and I've got to stay here and study. Sorry."

"That's okay," she said. "But I hope you know you'll have to make it up to me by being doubly sweet the next time you come, Nickerson."

It felt great to talk to him, and soon Nancy found herself telling Ned about Matt Glover.

"Yeah, I read about him showing up in the paper," Ned said when she was done. His voice was filled with concern as he added, "If he's an impostor, he's got a lot to lose if anyone exposes him. Be careful, Nan."

"You know me," she said in a teasing voice.

He sighed. "That's what has me worried."

Nancy said goodbye, then hung up and went out to her Mustang. It was already dark, but the porch light illuminated the outdoor thermometer, which read fifteen degrees. The pond would definitely be frozen.

Raising her eyes, she admired the pale three-quarter moon that was just rising. She thought of the old days Matt kept mentioning. If only she knew whether he remembered them himself, or whether he'd been coached to memorize the details of Matt Glover's boyhood by someone else. She remembered Sheila McCoy saying that Gary Page had the best memory for detail she'd ever known. Was it good enough to memorize all the details of someone else's life?

As Nancy pulled up in front of the Environ-

mental Action office, it was just before eight and she stopped thinking about Matt and started thinking about Tony. She frowned when she looked at the office. She didn't see any lights on. Maybe he'd left right on time that day.

Looking up and down the street, she saw that it was deserted and pitch-dark except for the weak glow of a street lamp a block away. Nancy reached into the glove compartment for her flashlight and flicked it on, before walking through the frigid night air to the office door.

She knocked and called Tony's name, but no one answered. Next, she tried the door. It opened. Great! She'd just take a quick look around for anything incriminating. Shining her flashlight so she could see where she was going, Nancy went down the short hallway, past the two closed doors, toward the garagelike office.

The door to Tony's office stood wide open, but the lights were off. In a soft voice, Nancy tentatively called his name again, just to make sure no one was there. Then she swung her beam around the room.

After flipping through the papers on his desk, she opened the top drawer. Nothing there but a candy bar and some old papers that had to do with a local law about industrial dumping into the river.

The other drawers were just as uninteresting, and they were dirty, too. Her nose began to feel itchy from all the dust she was creating.

Just then Nancy felt a prickly sensation at the back of her neck. It didn't make sense that Giralda had left the building unlocked, so he must be coming back soon. She knew she should leave, but she wanted to check out whatever was beyond the other doors leading off the hallway. Doing so was probably a waste of time, but she couldn't pass up the opportunity.

Quickly she went back to the hallway, swinging the beam of her flashlight back and forth. When she reached the first door, she tried the handle gingerly. The door pulled open with a creak, and Nancy peered into the dim interior. It was a closet, as she'd expected. It contained nothing but cleaning supplies and an ancient-looking mimeograph machine.

At the next door Nancy paused for a moment. Was that a noise she heard? She stood completely still, listening, but there was nothing.

I guess I just imagined it, she thought, shaking her head. *This place is starting to get me spooked.* Resolutely, she pulled open the door and stepped inside.

All of a sudden Nancy felt herself being roughly shoved forward. She fell to her knees. A second later she heard the door slam shut behind her and the lock turn. She was trapped!

Nancy swung the beam of her flashlight until she found the light switch, then turned it on. Keeping the lights off didn't matter anymore, since someone knew she was there.

She didn't have time to wonder who, though, because just then she heard a low growling behind her. Nancy whirled around.

Standing in the back left corner of the room were two very large dogs. They looked part German shepherd and part something else—something wild. Their teeth were bared, and their fierce eyes were trained on Nancy!

Chapter Seven

NANCY FROZE, trying to remember everything she knew about calming animals. "Good boys." She tried to keep her voice calm, but she could hear that it was higher pitched than normal. "What good boys, yes. There's nothing to be afraid of."

The dogs' teeth were no longer bared, she saw with relief, but they were still growling, so she kept talking. "I don't blame you for being angry at me. If someone burst into my house as I did into yours, I'd be furious. . . ." She trailed off, peering cautiously at the huge animals. Was it working?

She wasn't sure. "Good boys," she said again. The dogs seemed to be calming down, but Nancy

wasn't—especially when she heard a voice outside the door shout, "Who's there?"

It was Tony Giralda! There was no way she could hide from him now, so she called out, "It's me—Nancy Drew."

There was a pause, then the door was unlocked and opened. Tony was standing in the hall, a frown on his face. "What are you doing in there?" he asked. "What are you doing here at all?"

"Get me away from these dogs, first," Nancy said, stepping quickly around him and into the hall. "I didn't know you had attack dogs."

"Attack dogs?" Tony repeated, looking amused. "Fred and Max wouldn't hurt a flea. They're high-strung, but they're sweethearts." As if to prove it, Tony whistled softly, and the big dogs loped over to him, giving little yowls of happiness when Tony petted them. "Fred was probably terrified when you went in there. He's afraid of strangers."

"I didn't go in, I was pushed," Nancy told Tony. "Hard." She gazed intently at him.

Tony's mouth dropped open. "But nobody was even here. I was out getting dinner. When I came back and saw the door was open, at first I was afraid a burglar was in here. But I guess I just left it unlocked." He smiled sheepishly. "Sometimes I get so caught up in my work I forget to lock up."

He led her back to his office, switching lights on as he went and checking out the entire area.

"Whoever pushed you is gone now," he said as they sat down, Nancy at his desk chair and Tony in a gray metal folding chair. "Did you get a look at the person?"

"No. Anyone could have gotten in the front door."

"Mmmm." Tony frowned. "Well, nothing seems to be missing, so I guess if the person was a burglar, you scared him off. Hey, you still haven't answered my question," he said. "What were *you* doing here?"

Nancy watched him for a second before answering. She wasn't sure, but it didn't seem as if Tony had been the one to push her. He seemed genuinely surprised to see her. Besides, why would he push her into Fred and Max's room if he knew the big dogs wouldn't harm her?

On the other hand, if he knew Nancy didn't know the dogs were harmless, he could have locked her in the room just to scare her or to teach her a lesson.

Nancy frowned. The only thing the incident did was reinforce her feeling that she was right to be looking into the Matt Glover case. Someone didn't like her snooping around, and someone had tried to do something about it.

"I wanted to see you," she told Tony at last. It was true, even if she did get in a little snooping while she was at it. "I wanted to ask you some questions."

"Like what?"

She decided to confide in Tony—up to a point. "I went to the offices of the *Clarion* in Chicago this afternoon," she said. "I spoke to Matt Glover's editor. She identified a photograph of him and confirmed everything he'd said."

Nancy took out the article Sheila McCoy had given her and handed it to Tony. "Here's a sample of one of his earliest pieces for the *Clarion.* He was using the name Gary Page then."

Tony smoothed the crumpled photocopy and scanned it briefly. He was about to hand it back when something caught his eye. "Jake Loomis!" he exclaimed. "I always wondered what happened to him. He left town a few years ago."

Nancy felt a prickling sensation along the top of her scalp. "Jake Loomis used to live in River Heights?" she asked.

"Sure. He was the gardener out at Glover's Corners. He worked there for years. Wow, this brings it all back! Yeah, Loomis must have left when Matt was about fifteen or sixteen. He always had dreams about setting up his own business."

"He seems to have succeeded, judging by this article."

"Yeah." Tony leaned forward and said in an urgent voice, "Look, this is all beside the point.

What I want to know is, what are you doing about exposing this fake Matt Glover? I mean, surely you can see by now that I'm right about him."

No, Nancy couldn't. She didn't know whom to believe. She didn't really trust Tony *or* Matt. Tony wanted Matt to be a fake, so that Giralda's Environmental Action would get a piece of Mr. Glover's fortune. Since he hadn't mentioned the money he'd be receiving from the estate, maybe he wasn't playing straight with her.

She wanted to find out more about Tony's interest in the will, but she was afraid of pressing her luck. She'd already been accosted once, and she didn't want to risk it happening again in such a deserted place. She rose to go. "Thanks for the information. I'll be in touch."

Tony walked her out to her car. The moon had fully risen, and the gloomy street in front of the office was now bathed in silvery light. Suddenly Nancy had an inspiration. Why not ask Tony to Matt's skating party? Maybe she could learn something from how Tony and Matt behaved toward each other.

Tony reacted oddly to her suggestion. He seemed shy and unsure of himself. "I don't know," he said. "I haven't really been invited. I'm not sure I should come."

"I'm inviting you," Nancy said. "If you don't have skates, there are probably some there you

can borrow. Besides, I thought you said you knew Matt like a brother."

"The *real* Matt," Tony muttered. "Not this guy."

"That's the whole point. You'll be able to watch him on what's supposed to be his home turf. You can't afford to pass up a chance like this."

Tony rubbed his chin, considering. "Yeah, I guess you're right. Okay, I'll go," he said, but he didn't sound as though he really wanted to.

Nancy climbed into her car. "I have to pick up my friends first. Why don't you go ahead to the Corners and we'll meet you there."

Tony still seemed troubled, but he agreed.

Nancy couldn't help wondering why he was acting so strange. Why would he be reluctant to visit Matt—unless he had something to hide?

George was ready and waiting, dressed in red sweats and a heavy down vest. Her ice skates were slung over her shoulder, and she was eager to get on the ice. A natural athlete with terrific coordination, George was at her best when she was in action.

Five minutes later they were in front of Bess's house, and Bess, wearing a short pleated skirt, a pink turtleneck and tights, and a heavy sweater, was climbing into the backseat.

"Aren't you afraid you'll freeze in that?" George asked, gesturing at Bess's skirt.

"I have on three pairs of tights," Bess returned. She added in an anxious voice. "Do they make my legs look too fat?"

"Are you kidding? You look great!" Nancy said firmly. She was a little dismayed, though, because she knew exactly whom Bess wanted to look great *for.*

As they drove to Glover's Corners, Nancy told her friends about what had happened at Giralda's office. "Anyway, I invited him to come skating with us tonight," she said, finishing her story.

"What!" Bess and George exclaimed together.

"What did you do that for?" Bess went on.

"He has an interest in exposing Matt," Nancy said. "It may be greed on his part, or it may be something more honest. I have to find out."

"Oh, Nan," said Bess from the backseat. "Can't we forget about the case for tonight? I just want to have fun."

Nancy smiled at her in the rearview mirror. "Me, too. I'm just going to keep my eyes open, that's all." Turning into the driveway, she announced, "Here we are."

"Oh, it looks more gorgeous than usual," Bess said as they climbed out of the Mustang.

Nancy had to agree. Glover's Corners was blazing with light from every window. There

were white Christmas-tree lights strung in the bare limbs of the trees around the pond, and the moon had climbed high, shedding a warm glow on the skeletal maple trees and the carefully trimmed evergreen bushes by the house.

Suddenly Nancy blinked. "That's it," she said softly.

"What's it?" asked George.

Nancy quickly explained what Tony Giralda had told her about Jake Loomis's being the gardener at Glover's Corners. "You know, I thought there was something funny, and I just realized what it is."

Nancy took a deep breath, then went on. "All the article said was that Loomis had worked at a private estate. Mr. Glover's name was never even mentioned, even though, according to Tony, Jake Loomis worked there for many years. Don't you think that's weird?"

"Why?" Bess looked confused.

"Loomis is a pretty successful guy now," George said. "Maybe he didn't mention Glover's Corners because he wanted to play down the fact that he used to be a gardener for a rich guy. It might be embarrassing for him."

"Maybe," Nancy said slowly. "But what if Gary Page or Matt Glover—whoever he is—*purposely* didn't mention Glover's Corners in the article. What if he didn't want anything to connect Jake Loomis to the Glover family?"

"What are you getting at, Nan?" Bess was stamping her feet to keep warm.

Nancy took a deep breath. "It's quite possible that a fake Matt Glover and Jake Loomis are working *together* to steal Mr. Glover's fortune!"

Chapter Eight

INDIGNATION PLAYED OVER Bess's face.

"That's ridicu—" she started to say, but she broke off in midword, startled by a hissing noise from the darkness behind them.

"Pssst!"

Nancy, Bess, and George whirled around to see Tony Giralda step into the light of one of the lanterns lining the front drive. Nancy hadn't noticed his van when they drove up, but now she saw that it was parked under one of the huge, leafless maple trees.

"Why didn't you go in?" Nancy asked him.

"I don't know those people. I was waiting for you."

"But you must know Mrs. Adams—if you and Matt were such good friends," she said, studying

him curiously. "I thought you said you knew him like a brother."

The way that Tony scuffed his feet in the gravel told Nancy that he'd been lying. But why? "Well, forget it," she said after a minute. "Let's just go in. It's freezing out here."

Matt was waiting for them in the library. He looked amazingly handsome in dark pants and a royal blue ski sweater. The fire was roaring, and there was an enormous plate of sandwiches on the low table. The air smelled of cloves and cinnamon, and Nancy realized that Mrs. Adams must have revived one of her favorite recipes, mulled cider.

Matt gave them all a big hello. Then, turning to Tony, he said, "I'm glad you came, Tony. It's been a long time since we skated together."

Tony hesitated before he took Matt's hand, and when he shook it, it was with a strictly formal air. Then he went and sat stiffly in a leather chair.

Mrs. Adams came in a moment later, holding a freshly baked pie. "Hello, girls," she said. "This is a special night, with the house full of young people again."

She put the pie down on a silver stand and straightened. Her gaze landed on Tony, and she peered at him with a puzzled expression on her face.

"This is Tony Giralda, Addie," Matt said smoothly. "You must remember him."

"Yes," she said vaguely. "You were here after Mr. Glover's funeral, weren't you?"

Tony rose from his seat and nodded, an embarrassed flush in his cheeks.

So Tony *had* been lying, Nancy thought. Surely Mrs. Adams would have recognized him from the old days if he had known Matt as well as he'd said he had.

Matt broke the uneasy silence after Mrs. Adams left the room. "I thought we should get in some carbo-loading before we skate," he said, cutting into the pie and handing out plates to everyone.

"Definitely," Bess agreed. She took a big bite of her pie. Giggling, she added, "We wouldn't want to collapse from lack of energy."

As Nancy dug into her own slice, she couldn't help but admire Matt's friendly, easy way. He urged them to help themselves to sandwiches and went to the kitchen to bring back a tray with mugs for the mulled cider. It was easy to see why Bess was attracted to him.

"Don't get too comfortable," Matt warned them after a few minutes. He picked up a blue woolen hat and a pair of gloves and pulled them on. "We have some serious skating to do."

"All right!" said George, jumping to her feet. "Let's go!"

Nancy chuckled as Bess gazed longingly at the warm fire before saying, "I guess I'm as ready as

I'll ever be. I hope I don't turn into an icicle out there."

"You'll warm up in no time once you get moving," Matt assured her. The way he was looking at Bess, Nancy knew her friend would warm up in no time—from being with Matt, more than from skating.

They all grabbed their skates and made their way out the back door and down the long slope leading to the pond. Nancy was still lacing up her skates, sitting on one of the benches by the pond, when George slid onto the ice and began twirling in dizzying circles. Bess and Matt were the next ones on the ice, and they skated arm in arm. Tony, Nancy noticed, was less steady on his feet. He was wobbling a little as he made his way slowly around the pond.

"Hurry up, Nan, the ice is great!" George called.

"Ready!" She finished lacing up her skates and got up from the bench. Moving to the edge of the pond, she stepped out onto the ice. It was as smooth as glass. There were no twigs or dead leaves to mar it, and she remembered that Matt had gone home from the diner to sweep it especially for them.

She took a few tentative steps at first, then she was gliding in long, sure motions across the pond. Coming up next to Tony, she said, "Isn't this great?"

Tony gave her a weak smile. "I guess," he said.

He lurched forward unsteadily. "I was never very good at this."

"You must have had plenty of practice right here," Nancy said sweetly. "When you were a kid."

"Yeah, sure," he mumbled, but he wouldn't look at her.

Just then Matt and Bess whooshed up, laughing. "Come on, Tony," Matt said, "we'll tow you across the pond."

Tony started to protest, but Matt took one of his arms and Bess the other, and they skated off with Tony between them.

Nancy started doing easy jumps. She still wasn't sure what she thought about Matt or Tony, she realized as she curved around on the ice.

"Looking good, Nan," George said, breaking into Nancy's thoughts as she skated up. George's cheeks were red from the cold. She nodded her head toward Tony, who was still being held captive by Matt and Bess. "Maybe we should go rescue Tony. The poor guy."

Nancy laughed, but her voice was serious as she said, "I don't know if I feel so sorry for him. He's definitely hiding something."

"You mean about being such great friends with Matt?" George asked.

"Yeah. I mean, I was almost ready to think he wasn't the one who locked me in that room. He seemed really shocked. He acted completely nat-

ural at his office. I kind of liked him. But out here, around Matt, he's acting really strange."

George was skating in tiny circles in front of Nancy. "So maybe he *is* trying to steal Matt's money," she said. Digging the tip of one blade into the ice, she stopped to study Nancy with concerned eyes. "I'm not sure what to believe. But someone's afraid of you, Nan. You'd better be careful or you might really get hurt."

Suddenly Matt was in front of Nancy, making a dramatic, sweeping bow. "May I have your arm?" he asked, doffing his blue cap to her.

Had he overheard? Nancy had no way of knowing. Giving Matt her sweetest smile, she dropped him a curtsy and took his arm. Then they were off, gliding across the pond. They skated well together, and Nancy decided to take Bess's advice and just enjoy herself—for the moment.

As if reading her mind, Matt asked, "Having fun?" He grinned down at her and gave her arm a friendly squeeze.

"You bet," she said. And it was true. They didn't say anything for a few minutes, and Nancy let herself enjoy the crisp cold air and the smooth motions of the skating. Inevitably, the case crept back into her thoughts, though.

That article, for one thing. It was quite a coincidence that the person Matt interviewed turned out to be his father's ex-gardener. Nancy

was about to ask him about it when someone yelled behind them.

Tony had fallen on the ice and was having a hard time getting back on his feet. Matt sped over and helped him to one of the benches to catch his breath. A moment later George had skated over to Nancy again.

"Do you think Matt heard what we were talking about?" she asked in a low voice.

Nancy shrugged. "I don't think so, but I'm not positive. I thought of something else, too, about that article. But I didn't have time to ask him about it." She looked over to where Matt, Bess, and Tony were sitting, then went on. "Why would the picture of Matt's father jog his memory about the past, when seeing Loomis in the flesh didn't? And why didn't Loomis recognize him?"

George shrugged. "I don't know—maybe Matt never really saw the gardener. They wouldn't necessarily have run into each other."

"I guess you're right," Nancy said, letting out a sigh. "I'm going to sit down for a minute. I need to clear my head."

Bess and Matt were just stepping back onto the ice as Nancy got off and sat down next to Tony on the bench.

"I should be going, Nancy," he said, bending over to unlace his skates. "Give my thanks to Mrs. Adams."

"Sure. Did you notice anything special about Matt?"

He glanced up and shook his head. "It's amazing," he began. "If I didn't know better—" He broke off his sentence, and suddenly he became extremely animated.

"There *is* something special, but I didn't think of it until now," he said. "Once when I was here, Matt had an accident."

"A serious one?"

"Not really." Tony pursed his mouth as he tried to remember. "Someone tripped him when he was skating, and he cut his wrist on a piece of sharp ice. It bled pretty badly. We were only about ten at the time."

Nancy looked at him, confused. "I'm not sure I see what the point is."

Tony's excitement continued. "The cut left a scar, that's the point. Right here." He pointed at his left wrist. "A half-moon shape. Check it out—see if it's there. I'll bet you it's not. And if it isn't, we have proof that this guy's a fake!"

"Hot chocolate," said George, grinning.

Bess chimed in, "And marshmallows, too! This is perfect, Mrs. Adams."

"If anything can un-numb my fingers, this is it," Nancy said, taking a mug from the beaming housekeeper.

The girls and Matt had left their skates and boots in the kitchen and were back in the library. Matt was reviving the embers of the fire, and they

were all leaning on oversize pillows on the hearth rug.

"If you'd stayed out any longer, you'd have frozen to death," Mrs. Adams said, taking in their bright red cheeks. "Well, I'm off to bed." Matt kissed her cheek, and she blushed with pleasure.

Nancy had made a point of sitting next to Matt. She wanted to get a good look at his wrist. If Matt didn't have a scar—and if Tony was telling the truth—then Matt was a phony.

"I think my watch is fast," she said, shaking her wrist. "It says eleven forty-five, but it can't be that late."

Without hesitation, Matt hiked up the sleeve of his sweater and consulted the old-fashioned gold watch on his left wrist.

Nancy leaned over his shoulder. There was the scar, all right, exactly where Tony had told her it should be.

Before she could take a closer look, Matt shrugged the sleeve of his sweater back down and said, "What do you know. It really is a quarter to twelve." He shot one of his big grins across the room at Bess. "I was having so much fun with you guys that I lost track of the time."

Nancy rubbed her chin. Chalk up another piece of evidence in Matt's favor, she thought. Still, she wished she'd gotten a closer look. There was something . . .

"That's a neat watch you have, Matt," she said suddenly. "Do you mind if I take another look at it?"

"Sure." He pulled the sweater sleeve back up and said something about how the watch had belonged to his grandfather and Mrs. Adams had told him to wear it.

Nancy barely listened to his words, however. All of her attention was focused on the puckered skin that formed a half-moon on his wrist. She wasn't an expert on scars, but she was pretty sure that they faded to normal skin tone or paler with time.

But Matt's scar still was pinkish red—as if it was only a few months old—not ten or fifteen years!

Chapter Nine

"HEY, NAN, I could really get used to this, couldn't you?"

Bess's cheerful voice brought Nancy's attention back to the conversation in the library. Focusing on Bess and George, she saw that they had their stockinged feet stretched toward the glowing fire. Bess was munching on one of the sandwiches that had been left over from before they went skating.

Beside Nancy, Matt laughed and said to Bess, "You're welcome as often as you like." His blue eyes shone as he added, "And I hope it will be *very* often."

"It's really wonderful here," Nancy agreed, sipping her hot chocolate and checking out the glistening oak bookshelves and antique furni-

ture. Inheriting Glover's Corners would definitely be worth an impostor having plastic surgery to give him a scar like the one the real Matt had had, Nancy added silently. She wished she knew for certain how old his scar was.

Nancy's brain was so full of *possible* scams. Maybe Matt was an impostor with a phony scar. Or maybe Tony was trying to cheat Matt out of his inheritance. Or maybe Mrs. Adams, or the ex-gardener Jake Loomis, was working with Matt. Her brain felt like a computer on overload —nothing would compute.

Boy, will I be relieved when tonight's over and I'm back home in bed, she thought. A good night's sleep is the only hope for me!

Over breakfast the next morning, Nancy told her father about the skating party and Matt's scar.

When she was done, Carson rubbed his chin thoughtfully. "The young man is taking a lie detector test down at city hall this morning," he said. "The test isn't always a hundred-percent reliable, but his willingness to take it is in his favor."

Nancy nodded. After her father had left to meet Matt, she poured herself a second glass of juice and sat back down at the kitchen table. Even after a good night's sleep, she wasn't sure where to start. She pulled out the article about

Loomis and began to reread it. Maybe there was something she had overlooked.

It wasn't until she was reading it for the fourth time that Nancy suddenly paused and drummed her fingers on the kitchen table. According to the article, Loomis Landscaping had its office in downtown Chicago. *Hmmm.* Matt might not have recognized Loomis during their interview a year ago, but had Loomis recognized *Matt?* It was a long shot, but she had to ask.

On an impulse, Nancy picked up the phone extension in the kitchen and called George. "Are you up for another trip to Chicago this morning?"

"Not another visit to the *Clarion?*" George's voice sounded skeptical.

"Nope. I want to talk to Jake Loomis this time."

"Good idea," George said. "Ready when you are, which, knowing you, is probably about ten minutes ago!"

Next, Nancy called Bess, but there wasn't any answer, so she headed out to her Mustang. It was as cold as ever outside, and the sky had a heavy, gray look to it.

"I hope it doesn't snow today," George said as she climbed into the car ten minutes later. "It looks as though the sky's going to open up and dump a huge pile of it on us."

Nancy shrugged. "That's fine with me—as

long as it holds off until we get back from Chicago."

"What's our story going to be?" George wanted to know as Nancy turned the Mustang toward the highway. "Are we still reporters?"

"I guess so. We'll say we're doing research for a *Who's Who in Chicago Business.*"

"Get him off his guard by buttering him up and making him feel important, eh?" George grinned. "Sounds good to me."

The traffic was heavy, but by midmorning they were in Chicago, and Nancy was winding her way through the crowded city streets to St. Paul Street, where the Loomis Landscaping office was. Luckily, she was able to park right outside.

"This is pretty familiar," Nancy said, getting her bearings before she and George went into the building. "If I'm not mistaken, the *Clarion* building is only a block east of here."

"Whatever you say." George grabbed her arm and pulled her toward the entrance. "It's a little cold for a geography lesson, Nan. Let's get inside."

In the marble-floored lobby, George let out an impressed whistle. "Not too shabby," she said in a low voice.

Nancy nodded her agreement. "It looks as if Jake Loomis has done pretty well for himself."

The office of Loomis Landscaping was a huge space that looked as if it had been converted from a warehouse. It was partitioned with low

walls and tastefully decorated with plants and framed photos of colorful gardens. A blond woman sitting behind a wide reception desk asked the girls if she could help them.

"We'd like to see Mr. Loomis," Nancy said.

"Do you have an appointment?"

"No," said Nancy, "but we won't take much of his time." She gave her *Who's Who* spiel.

When she was done, the receptionist gave them a wide smile and said, "I'm sure Mr. Loomis won't mind giving you a few minutes." She picked up her phone and spoke into it briefly.

A moment later a man dressed in an expensive-looking suit emerged from a room at the far end of the office and headed toward them. He had salt-and-pepper hair with a beard to match and a burly, muscular build.

Jake Loomis received them with a big smile. Nancy and George followed him back to his office, which was large and furnished with a mahogany desk and leather-upholstered chairs.

"You girls look pretty young to be doing such important work," he said, gesturing for them to sit down in the leather chairs.

"We're older than we look," Nancy assured him, smiling. "Younger reporters do all the footwork, and the older ones get all the credit."

"Well, you can't have everything right away," he said. "Look at me. I didn't start to be successful until I was twice your age—at least." He spoke with a self-satisfied air, and Nancy sus-

pected that he had probably made the same comment many times before.

George leaned forward and said, "We wanted to check up on something in the article about you in the *Clarion*—the one that came out about a year ago."

"Good article," Loomis said.

Ignoring his smug tone, Nancy went on. "It said that you had been a gardener for a private estate before you came to Chicago. Could you tell us whose estate it was?"

The smile left Loomis's craggy face, and he grunted. "What possible difference could it make?" he asked.

"It's important to know some background of the men and women we select for *Who's Who,*" Nancy said, pressing him.

Jake Loomis rested his chin on his thick knuckles. "Oh, well," he said at last. "It can't matter now. The man is dead, quite recently, as a matter of fact. He won't know."

Nancy arched an eyebrow. "I'm sorry, I don't understand," she said.

"Let's just say we weren't exactly friends when I left. I quit after an argument with him. Glover was stubborn as a mule. That was his name, Clayton Glover. He was a hot-shot millionaire in River Heights." Loomis glowered at Nancy as he remembered. "The old man never would admit he was wrong. But I didn't want to make his life worse by mentioning him in that article."

Nancy pretended to take notes. She didn't understand why Loomis couldn't just mention Mr. Glover's name without bringing up whatever their fight had been about, but she didn't want to put him on the defensive.

"What do you mean, 'make his life worse'?" she asked.

Loomis shook his head. "You see, Glover was absolutely shattered after his only son died in an accident," he explained. "Matt was a great kid. I taught him everything he knew when he was small. I was more like a father to him than his own dad, if you know what I mean. The kid was only twelve or so when I left. I really missed him. Too bad his father and I couldn't see eye to eye."

Nancy nodded politely. She was curious as to what the argument had been about, but there was another important question she needed answered first. If Loomis had known Matt so well . . .

"You must have been happy to hear that Matt's alive," George said to Jake Loomis. "It's amazing, isn't it?"

Way to go, George! Nancy thought. *You were reading my mind!* She quickly added, "Yes, and it must have been a double surprise to you that Gary Page, the reporter who interviewed you, was really the long-lost Matt Glover." She watched Jake Loomis extra closely as she asked, "Did you recognize him at all when he interviewed you for the article?"

For a fraction of a second, Loomis just stared at Nancy and George. But then his heavyset face took on its smug expression again. "Yeah, well, I did notice the resemblance, but I didn't make much of it since I thought Matt was dead." Loomis let out a soft chuckle. "It sure was a surprise to see his picture in the paper, though."

"Oh, a lot of people were surprised, Mr. Loomis," George put in.

Loomis sat back in his chair and laughed out loud. "I'll bet. I understand a bunch of businesses have been waiting like vultures to get their hands on Glover's money. With Matt back, the hospital and the environmental people and the rest of them are all out of luck."

Nancy was about to ask Loomis if he'd tried to contact Matt at all since his return. She didn't have time to ask him any more questions, however, because just then the receptionist buzzed to announce another visitor.

"I'm sorry, girls, but I'm afraid I'll have to end our interview now," Loomis told them, getting up from his desk and showing Nancy and George to the office door. "When is this *Who's Who* coming out?" he asked.

"We'll let you know," George said hastily as they scooted out.

When they got outside, they saw that it had begun to snow. Nancy turned on the windshield wipers as they drove back to River Heights.

"What do you think?" George asked, popping

a tape in Nancy's newly repaired tape deck. "Was he telling us the truth?"

"I'm not sure, George. It certainly *could* be the truth," Nancy replied. "He didn't lie about who he'd worked for. But when he talked about Matt, I couldn't decide if he was telling the truth or not. I couldn't read him."

"Well, I didn't like him. He's too full of himself." George was tapping her foot to the beat of the music, but there was a frown on her face.

"Yeah," Nancy agreed. "And there's something else, too. He seemed to know an awful lot about the will, for someone who hasn't seen Matt or Mr. Glover in over ten years." She sighed. "But all that is supposing that Matt Glover is a phony. And if we're trying to find the most likely person to be an accomplice in a scam, I'd say Mrs. Adams wins. She'd know Matt better than anyone else."

George shook her head. "Oh, Nan, she's such a nice woman. I'd hate to think she's guilty of anything."

"So would I, but we can't rule out the possibility. I want to talk to her again.

"In fact, let's make a quick stop for some soup, then head over to Glover's Corners," Nancy suggested as she pulled up in front of her house.

The snow was falling very heavily and starting to accumulate by the time they set off for Glover's Corners. Switching on the weather report, the girls heard that more snow was expected.

Nancy drove very slowly and carefully. The snow was now almost a blanket of white against the front windshield, and she almost missed the gate to the Corners.

"I'm going to try to get a look at Mrs. Adams's room," Nancy said, creeping up the long, winding drive at a snail's pace.

"Where do I come in?" asked George.

"I need you to distract Mrs. Adams so I can search. If we're lucky, Matt's still with my father, taking that lie detector test."

"And how do I distract her?" George was staring at the ledges of snow being pushed off by the windshield wipers.

Nancy shrugged. "We'll just have to play it by ear, I guess."

Pulling to a stop in front of the house, she and George trudged through the snow to the front door. Nancy rang the bell and then heard it echoing somewhere deep in the old house.

"Listen," said George.

Nancy cocked her head to the side. She could hear Matt's voice, and it seemed to be coming from somewhere quite close. His tone sounded angry, although she couldn't distinguish his words.

Putting a finger to her lips, Nancy gestured to George to follow her. The snow cushioned the sound of their boots as they backed away from the door and moved toward the left wing of the house, where Matt's voice was coming from.

Walking almost to the screened-in porch at the end of the wing, Nancy could make out Matt standing on the porch. Despite the cold, he was wearing only a button-down shirt and jeans, and he was talking on a cordless phone.

"Nancy! George! What are you doing here?"

The two girls jumped in surprise and saw Bess leaning out a living room window.

Nancy gasped, knowing that Matt must have heard, too.

When she looked back to the porch, she saw that Matt had stopped talking into the cordless phone—and was now staring at her with cold, unwelcoming eyes.

Chapter Ten

NANCY GAVE MATT a tentative smile and waved at him. Instantly an answering smile spread across his face, making her wonder if she'd just been imagining his angry scowl.

"It's freezing out there," Bess called to Nancy and George as they made their way back to the front door. "Hurry up and come in!"

As the girls brushed the snow off themselves and stepped inside, Bess asked again, "What are you guys doing here?"

"I guess we could ask you the same question," said George.

Bess spoke in an excited rush as she explained. "I ran into Matt downtown at the bakery. He was buying a cake for Mrs. Adams. It's some kind of

tradition they have or something. Anyway, he suggested I come back and share it. I thought it would be rude to say no."

"So you were just being polite, eh?" said George, rolling her eyes. "I don't suppose that the opportunity to spend time with the super-gorgeous Matt Glover had anything to do with your decision?"

"Absolutely not," said Bess indignantly. Then she blushed. "Well, maybe a little. I mean, I know he's not going to fall in love with me or anything, but I just think he's so *romantic!*

"Now it looks like we're getting snowed in," Bess went on. From the flushed look on her face, Nancy could tell that being snowed in with Matt Glover would be Bess's idea of paradise.

Nancy couldn't help smiling at Bess. It was great that she was so happy. Nancy just hoped she wouldn't be disappointed.

"I hope we're not ruining your romantic afternoon," Nancy said apologetically. "We really came to see Mrs. Adams."

"I'm glad you're here." Bess looked around. "Matt must still be on the phone. I guess we can just go to the kitchen."

As they walked down the hall, Bess turned to George and Nancy and said, "Oh, by the way, it so happens that Matt passed the lie-detector test with flying colors. I think you owe him an apology, both of you."

Nancy was surprised. "Did Matt tell you himself that he passed?" she asked. If so, there was a chance he was lying.

"Nope. Your father did. I saw him just as he was leaving his office, before I ran into Matt."

"Lie-detector tests aren't infallible," Nancy said, "but passing is definitely a good sign for Matt." If Matt was an impostor, she would have expected the lie-detector results to be inconclusive at best.

Bess frowned. "'A good sign'? That's all? You're such a skeptic, Nan. When are you going to admit that Matt Glover really is back?"

"When all the evidence is in," Nancy said, pushing through the door to the kitchen.

Mrs. Adams was sitting at the long oak table. Nancy was surprised to see that her eyes were red, as if she had been crying. She was staring out the kitchen window and didn't even seem to notice that the three girls had come in.

"Anything wrong, Mrs. Adams?" George asked gently.

The housekeeper jumped half out of her seat, then relaxed when she saw Nancy, George, and Bess. "Oh, I am jumpy lately, aren't I?" she said, smiling wanly. "I—I suppose it's all this excitement, what with Matt coming home so suddenly."

Nancy wondered if Mrs. Adams had heard that Matt had passed the lie-detector test. If so, she didn't seem very happy about it. In fact, she

seemed more depressed than Nancy had seen her since Mr. Glover's funeral.

"Isn't it great news about the lie-detector test?" Nancy said, taking a seat beside the housekeeper at the table. Bess and George sat down opposite.

"Yes, yes," Mrs. Adams said halfheartedly. "Wonderful news." She heaved a deep sigh, then rose with effort and went to cut slices from a chocolate cake that sat on the silver server where the pie had been the night before.

"Would you girls like a slice of this lovely cake?" she asked. Her voice sounded even more distraught to Nancy, and there were tears in her eyes now. "Matt was good enough to bring it home from the bakery."

"No, thanks," Nancy said. "Maybe later."

"Speak for yourself, Nan," George put in. "I'd love a piece."

"Me, too," Bess chimed in. In response to her cousin's questioning look, she said, "The first piece I had wasn't very big."

Nancy and George chuckled, but Nancy noticed that Mrs. Adams didn't even crack a smile as she expertly cut slices for George and Bess, slid them onto two plates, and passed them over. The housekeeper's hands were trembling.

Nancy was about to ask Mrs. Adams what was wrong but stopped herself when she heard Matt's voice, just outside the kitchen.

"Hey, everyone," he was calling. "The radio says this is a blizzard!"

Matt entered the kitchen like a comet and turned a big smile on Nancy and George. "I'm so glad you're both here," he said, his voice bubbling with enthusiasm. "I was thinking we could go for a sleigh ride."

"But there aren't horses at Glover's Corners anymore," George pointed out between bites of chocolate cake. The estate stables had once held two or three horses, but after Matt's disappearance Mr. Glover had sold them off, Nancy remembered.

"There's a stable a short walk from here, though," Matt said. "Thurston's. They rent sleighs along with the horses. I just called to check it out. Come on, now. You have to come—it's all set up."

"In a blizzard?" Bess inquired nervously.

"It's supposed to let up before long," answered Matt. "And we have plenty of spare scarves and gloves and stuff to bundle up with."

Bess still looked dubious, but she said, "Well, okay."

"Let's do it!" said George.

"It'll be fun," Nancy agreed. She was glad for a chance to see more of Matt. When they came back, maybe she'd be able to check out Mrs. Adams's room and find out if what was bothering her had anything to do with Matt.

"Great. I better get to the stable before we're

completely snowed in." Before he left the kitchen, Matt looked over at Mrs. Adams. "Have a piece of cake, Addie," he said warmly. "I got it especially for you."

Mrs. Adams began to cry as soon as Matt left the room. Nancy put one arm around her shoulders. "What is it, Mrs. Adams?" she asked.

The housekeeper reached for a paper napkin and rubbed at her eyes. "It's really nothing, dear, nothing for you to worry about. I have the most terrible headache—it just won't go away."

"Can I get you some aspirin?" George offered.

Mrs. Adams shook her head. "No, thank you, dear. I think I'll just lie down for a while."

"I'll help you to your room," Nancy said.

"I don't know what's the matter with me," Mrs. Adams said as Nancy led her up the stairs. "I should be so happy, under the circumstances. . . ." Her voice trailed off.

Nancy wanted to find out what was upsetting Mrs. Adams, but she was afraid any questions would only upset her more. Nancy kept her arm firmly around the older woman's shoulders until they reached her third-floor room.

It was large and comfortable—everything was neat as a pin. The windows had a gorgeous view of the back garden and the pond, even though it was distorted by the thick sheets of heavily falling snow.

Mrs. Adams sat on the edge of her bed and let her head fall into her hands. Moving over to her,

Nancy noticed that there were three photographs on the bedside table. One was of Matt as a little boy, sitting on a pony. Another was of Clayton Glover, and the third was of Mrs. Adams and Matt sitting side by side on one of the benches that circled the pond.

She knew she shouldn't let her emotions get in the way of the case, but she just couldn't imagine that Mrs. Adams would do anything to deceive the Glover family, even after Mr. Glover's death. Obviously, they had been the most important people in her life.

Gently, Nancy helped Mrs. Adams to lie back on the bed, then went back downstairs. She paused at the landing to phone home to let her father and Hannah know that they were all waiting out the storm at Glover's Corners.

Nancy found Bess and George in the library. George was feeding pine cones to the fire, while Bess was lazily flipping through the pages of a magazine. Nancy picked up a magazine to look at, too.

"How's Mrs. Adams?" Bess asked at last, putting her magazine down.

Nancy plopped down on the sofa beside her. "Resting. I'm sure she'll feel better in a while."

"She's had a lot to deal with, what with Matt coming back and all," Bess said sympathetically.

"If it really is Matt," George added quietly. "I'm sorry, Bess," she said in response to the

dark look her cousin shot her, "but you've got to be prepared for that possibility."

"I just know it's Matt," Bess insisted. "I would be able to tell if it weren't." She was about to say something else, but paused before going on excitedly, "Listen—the sleighs!"

They all rushed to a window. The storm had begun to let up, and Nancy could see that fresh snow lay deep and thick around Glover's Corners and in the woods beyond. The sun was low on the horizon, and the sleighs and snow all had a pinkish glow to them.

"There's Matt!" Bess exclaimed, pointing to a figure in an Eskimo-style parka driving the first sleigh.

"That must be someone from Thurston's stables in the other sleigh," said George.

Bringing up the rear was a four-wheel-drive Land Rover—the only kind of vehicle that could make it through the snow before the plows came.

"I wonder why he rented two of them?" Nancy asked. "One is big enough for the four of us."

George was already heading for the front closet, where their jackets and boots were. "Who cares why? It'll be so much fun. Let's go!"

They struggled into the warmest clothes they could find in the cloakroom. Bess wound a long, fluffy, red muffler around her neck and picked up a pair of matching mittens. "Hey, Nan," she said, pointing to a bright blue woolen hat hang-

ing from a peg, "you should wear that. It'll look fantastic with your hair."

Nancy's hat was still wet so she pulled on the cap, then the girls went outside. As they tromped through the snow to the sleighs, the man who had driven the second sleigh was climbing into the Land Rover. "We'll be back in an hour," Nancy heard him tell Matt. "Enjoy your ride."

Matt's face was glowing from the cold. "Hey, my hat looks good on you," he complimented Nancy.

For a second Bess looked the tiniest bit jealous of the compliment, but at Matt's next words her face lit up. "I thought Bess and I would take one sleigh and you two the other," he said to Nancy and George. "You do know how to drive?" he asked Nancy. She nodded.

"We'll follow the old trails through the woods and meet back here in an hour if we split up."

"Terrific!" said Bess, hopping up next to Matt in the first sleigh.

As Nancy and George climbed into the second sleigh, George commented in an undertone, "Bess's nervousness sure disappeared in a hurry."

"I'll say," Nancy agreed, pulling the heavy lap robe over their knees. "Her crush on Matt is getting even bigger. I just wish she'd back off a little until we're sure about him."

Nancy watched as Matt and Bess led the way,

starting out for the woods. Taking the reins, she urged their horse to follow.

There seemed to be no sounds in the world but the jangling sleigh bells, the creak of leather, and the snorts of the horses as they went forward in the snow.

"This is great." George sighed. "I'd forgotten how wonderful a sleigh ride can be."

"It *is* beautiful," Nancy agreed.

Soon they were deep in the woods, with its mixture of tall pines and sturdy oaks. The sun was very low now, and deep shadows had settled around the tree trunks, but the snow still shone with a beautiful, pearly glow. Nancy felt herself relaxing as she followed Matt and Bess's sleigh, which was about twenty yards ahead of them.

Seeing Matt's sleigh veer off onto a narrower path to the left, Nancy said, "I guess we should follow." She began to maneuver their horse to turn left. "I don't want to get lost out here."

The path was just wide enough for the sleigh, and lined by trees on both sides. Their horse was moving at a good trot now, and the tree branches seemed to whiz by them. Nancy had to concentrate to see clearly through the thick shadows.

Suddenly she started. At first she just saw a blur, then she realized it was someone in a red hunting jacket stepping out from beneath the pines, right into the path of her sleigh!

Instinctively, she gripped the reins hard and

pulled back, but she could see the sleigh was moving too fast to stop in time. "Hey! Get out of the way!" she yelled, but the figure in red hurtled onto the path directly in front of them and streaked by under the horse's startled nose.

"Watch out!" George shouted.

The horse reared in panic, and Nancy gripped the reins harder. Then she felt them snap in two in her hands. She watched in horror as the leather strips slid from her grasp and dropped behind the wild horse, leaving her with two useless ends. A second later the horse bolted and took off into the woods.

The horse was still attached to the sleigh by the traces, but there was no way to control the animal. The sleigh teetered and then went careening after the horse, into the woods and down a slope. Tree branches whipped at Nancy's face, and the forest went by in a blinding blur.

"We're going to go over!" she heard George yell beside her.

The last thing Nancy saw was a huge oak rushing toward her. Then everything went black.

Chapter Eleven

WHEN NANCY OPENED her eyes again, the first thing she saw was Mrs. Adams's worried face floating above her.

Nancy's head was pounding, but when she gingerly moved her legs, then her arms, she found that they worked. Turning her head, she looked around, squinting, and saw she was lying under a goose-down quilt in a bedroom at Glover's Corners.

"What?" she began, but Mrs. Adams put a finger to her lips and said a doctor was on the way.

Nancy looked over Mrs. Adams's shoulder at the snow-covered tree branches outside the bedroom window. She blinked, dimly remembering

the runaway sleigh, the startled horse, and the oak tree. There was something else, too, but her mind felt so foggy she couldn't concentrate on it.

Letting out a sigh, she shut her eyes again. That was when it came to her—the figure in red hurtling across the path in front of them. Someone had deliberately frightened the horse. But who?

Nancy felt a cool, soothing cloth being placed on her forehead. Opening her eyes again, she asked Mrs. Adams, "Is George all right?"

"George landed in a snowbank. She's fine."

Nancy tried to tell the housekeeper that someone had startled her horse on purpose, but Mrs. Adams told her not to talk until the doctor had examined her. Nancy stared at the ceiling, trying to get her thoughts together. Her head felt woozy. She could hear the muted voices of George, Bess, and Matt from somewhere beyond the bedroom door. The sound was lulling and comforting.

She must have drifted off, because when she opened her eyes again a kind-looking man was sitting by her bed. Mrs. Adams introduced him as Dr. Biddle. This time Nancy felt wide-awake and clearheaded. She greeted the doctor with: "I'm really fine—you shouldn't have bothered to come out on my account."

"Now, hush, young lady," the doctor told her with a smile. He examined her eyes with a little penlight and asked her if she was feeling dizzy.

Nancy shook her head. "I just have a king-size headache."

"It's no wonder," Dr. Biddle told her. "You must have the hardest head in River Heights, to have gotten the better of that tree you ran into. If you had a concussion it was a very minor one. I don't think X rays will be needed."

After the doctor left, Nancy took some aspirin. When the pounding in her head had lessened a little, she went downstairs to the library. Matt was standing on the hearth by the fire, and Bess and George were sitting on the couch. They all looked worried. Matt rushed over to Nancy when she stepped into the room.

"Nancy, are you all right?" he asked. "You really gave us a scare back there." He led her over to a chair beside Bess and George and poured her a steaming cup of tea from a china tea service on the table in front of the couch.

"Someone gave my *horse* a scare," Nancy replied evenly. She took a sip of the tea. "Mmmm, this tastes good. I'm starting to feel better."

Bess looked up, her blue eyes filled with concern. "That's awful. You guys could have gotten killed, and Matt and I didn't even know anything was wrong until George screamed for us."

"You wouldn't have seen anything, unless you were looking back," Nancy said. "A person dressed in a red jacket ran out from the trees right in front of us."

Matt nodded. "That's what George said. Did you see who it was?"

"No, and I don't even know if it was a man or a woman. It all happened so fast."

"I do remember one thing," George said, leaning back against the plush pillows of the couch. "Whoever it was had a ski cap pulled low so it was impossible to see the face clearly."

"I don't suppose it could have been an accident?" Bess asked.

"Oh, come off it, Bess," George told her cousin. "People don't wait around in the woods in a snowstorm and charge out in front of a horse by accident. Whoever did it meant for Nancy or me to get badly hurt, maybe even killed. And somehow I don't think whoever it was was after me."

Matt looked troubled. "If someone is trying to hurt Nancy, it must be because of me—because of the investigation she's been doing to see if I'm who I say I am." He held up a hand as Nancy started to speak. "Yes, I know you haven't been sure about me. I heard Bess telling you about the lie-detector results earlier. I do understand your suspicion, believe me. I know it's a strange story to swallow, but I hope soon you'll believe I'm telling the truth about who I am."

Watching Matt as he paced back and forth in front of the fire, his blue eyes earnest and troubled, Nancy was almost positive he was telling the truth.

"What we have to think about is who could

have done such a thing," Matt went on. He paused to look at Nancy. "Do you have any suspicions?"

Nancy shook her head, waiting for him to speak. He stopped his pacing as if he had an idea.

"I hate to say it," Matt said at last, "but it must be one of the people who would have inherited my father's fortune if I hadn't reappeared. Like maybe Tony Giralda."

So Matt had thought of that possibility, too, Nancy thought with a touch of admiration.

"You could be right," she told him. "There's something else we should consider, too. I don't think the attacker was necessarily after me. It's just as likely that the person was trying to get *you* out of the way, Matt, so that your father's money would be distributed to the causes named in the will."

Bess gasped. "Oh, no!" she wailed.

"That makes sense," said George. "Whoever it was could have mistaken our sled for Matt's. It was pretty shadowy out there, so it would have been hard to tell who was in which sled."

"I'll bet it *was* Tony Giralda," Bess said emphatically. "He's so intense!"

"His work is his whole life," Matt pointed out. "If he loses it, he loses everything. He's barely surviving as it is. He needs that money."

Matt came over and knelt in front of Nancy's chair. He put a hand on her shoulder and stared into her eyes. "I'm sorry that I've caused you so

much trouble. If anything happened to you because of me I'd—I don't know what I'd do."

Nancy studied Matt's blue eyes carefully, but there was nothing in them but sincere concern. "Thank you, Matt," she said.

As Matt went over to put another log on the fire, Mrs. Adams came in with fresh tea. She smiled at them, but Nancy saw that the housekeeper still had a pained look on her face, and her step had lost its usual energetic bounce.

As she bent to place the fresh teapot on the table, she leaned close to Nancy and whispered very softly, "I have something to tell you."

Nancy blinked, surprised. Obviously Mrs. Adams wanted to talk with her in private. Getting to her feet, Nancy picked up the tray with the cold teapot on it and said, "Here, Mrs. Adams, I'll help you clear this."

In the kitchen Mrs. Adams didn't waste any time telling Nancy what was bothering her.

"There's something I want you to know," the woman began. She leaned over the counter and began chopping carrots and tossing them in a big stewing pot. "Ordinarily I'd wait until you were feeling better, but this can't wait."

"I'm fine, don't worry about me," Nancy reassured her. There were some stalks of celery on the counter, too, and Nancy went to work on them, chopping and tossing them into the pot.

"When you came into the kitchen earlier to-

day, I suppose you could see I'd been crying." Mrs. Adams sniffled, and Nancy waited quietly until she continued.

"I was so happy when Matt came home. It seemed like a dream come true. But now—now I don't know what to believe, Nancy." She lowered her voice to a whisper. "I don't trust him anymore."

Nancy looked curiously at Mrs. Adams. "I'm sorry, but I'm not sure I understand," she said. "Why don't you trust him?"

Mrs. Adams took a deep breath. "You know how it is when you want to believe something so badly, you overlook all sorts of things in order to convince yourself?"

"Sure," said Nancy.

"Well, it wasn't like that at all with me," Mrs. Adams said defiantly. "I didn't have to overlook signs that Matt wasn't my Matt, because there simply weren't any. Everything he did, everything he said, was exactly what I expected of the Matt I remember. He even remembered to bring me a cake today, when he had so much on his mind."

She pressed her hands to her mouth to stop the trembling of her lips. "You see, it was a custom in this house, way back when Matt was little. I would bake a pie, or a cake, and when it was finished, Mr. Glover would bring us a new one from the bakery."

"What a nice way to show his appreciation of you," Nancy said, reaching for another celery stalk.

Mrs. Adams wiped away a tear with her finger. "That's what Mr. Glover said, that I deserved to be spoiled, the way I looked after them. Made me feel like one of the family. I told him I loved baking, but he insisted. He was such a considerate man. And now that he's gone, Matt is continuing the tradition."

"I'm sorry, Mrs. Adams, but I don't quite see what you're leading up to," Nancy said, a puzzled frown on her face.

The housekeeper looked at Nancy with anguished eyes. "The cake," she said. "It was—"

"Nan, your father's on the phone." Bess had come into the kitchen. "Need any help, Mrs. Adams?" She crossed the room and took the knife Nancy had put down on the counter. "I'll give you a hand while Nancy talks to him."

Nancy assured her father that she was all right and said she'd be home as soon as the snowplows cleared the road. When she returned to the kitchen, however, she saw that George and Matt had joined Bess and Mrs. Adams there, and they seemed prepared to stay for a while.

So much for learning Mrs. Adams's secret about Matt, Nancy thought, frustrated. She didn't have a chance to get Mrs. Adams alone again until after they'd eaten a dinner of beef

stew and salad, and finished up the chocolate cake.

"That was delicious," Bess said, pushing her empty plate away from her. "I couldn't eat another bite."

George shot her cousin a teasing look and said, "That's good, because I doubt there's another bite left after those two servings of everything you ate."

"How about watching a tape on the VCR," Matt suggested, getting up from the table. "My dad had a pretty good selection of old movies. They're in the den."

As the others followed him toward the den, Nancy stayed behind to help Mrs. Adams clear the table.

"What were you saying before about the chocolate cake?" she asked the housekeeper, picking up the conversation they'd started earlier.

"It was chocolate," Mrs. Adams said.

Nancy stared at her. "Is there something strange about that?"

Fresh tears sprang to Mrs. Adams's eyes as she explained in a quiet voice, "It's anything chocolate. I'm terribly allergic to it. The one kind of cake Matt Glover would never bring me is the one he brought today."

Nancy thought for a moment. "Is it possible that he's forgotten?" she suggested. "After all these years, maybe—"

"He'd remember this," Mrs. Adams interrupted. "It's a very severe allergy. When he was a little boy, I ate something with chocolate in it by mistake. My throat swelled up, and I could hardly breathe. Mr. Glover had to send for the doctor. It scared Matt half to death, I remember."

Nancy nodded. "You're right, he wouldn't be likely to forget anything as dramatic as that."

"That's why I don't think that boy is Matt Glover. It breaks my heart to say so, but he's not Matt."

Mrs. Adams's words were still ringing in Nancy's ears when she joined the others in the den. She could hardly concentrate on the movie —some spy thriller about a Russian double agent. She kept stealing glances at Matt, who was sitting next to Bess on the couch and acting as charming and natural as ever.

When the movie was over, Nancy glanced out the den window and was relieved to see that a plow had come to clear the driveway. That must mean the roads had been plowed, too. Her head had started to pound again, and all she could think about was going home and getting into bed. While Bess and Matt rewound the video, Nancy and George went out to the front closet.

"I'm exhausted," said Nancy, opening the closet door. She pulled her jacket off its hanger and pushed aside some other coats to get to

George's. That was when she saw it—a flash of red peeking out from beneath some raincoats.

Her heart pounded in her chest as she pulled the raincoats aside. An old red hunting jacket hung on a peg near the back of the closet. Reaching out, she fingered the sleeve. It was slightly damp.

"George!" she gasped. "It's the red hunting jacket! The one the person wore to spook our horse!"

"You're right!" George exclaimed, peering into the closet over Nancy's shoulder. "But what's it doing here?"

"Whoever scared our horse put it here."

George frowned. "But we're the only ones around here, and none of us was wearing it, because we were all *in* the sleighs."

Nancy's voice dropped to a whisper as she said, "Not *all* of us. There was one other person around—someone who wasn't in the sleighs, someone who knew that we were." She paused. "Rosemary Adams."

Chapter Twelve

GEORGE STARED AGAIN at the red hunting jacket. "Nan, do you really think a sixty-year-old woman would go tromping out in knee-deep snow to try to kill someone?" she asked doubtfully.

"It does seem pretty unlikely," Nancy replied, smiling at the ridiculous picture George's words painted in her mind. But her face swiftly grew grim again as another point occurred to her.

"George, this case just gets more complicated the more I get into it," she complained. She told her friend what Mrs. Adams had said about Matt bringing home the chocolate cake.

"So Mrs. Adams doesn't think that guy is really Matt Glover," George summarized when Nancy was done.

"Right, and there's something else. Remember I was wearing Matt's blue wool hat on the ride?"

"Yeah. So?" George prompted.

"So I looked like Matt," Nancy said excitedly. "Don't you see? That makes it even more likely that whoever spooked our horse expected to get Matt's sleigh. Especially if that person was someone who would recognize that cap as Matt's. Someone like Mrs. Adams."

"You're saying that Mrs. Adams spooked our horse in an effort to kill Matt? Why? Because she was angry at him for being a phony?" George's brown eyes were skeptical. "Sorry, Nancy. I don't buy that."

"I know it sounds far out, but it is possible," Nancy said. She snapped her fingers as she remembered something else. "Or if you don't like that, try this one on for size. Matt was wearing that blue cap the night we went skating —and Tony Giralda was there."

"Hey, I like that better," George said. "He does have a big reason for wanting Matt out of the way. But if it was Tony, how'd he get hold of this jacket?"

Nancy pulled out George's coat and handed it to her. "Well, when we left the house for the sleigh ride, Mrs. Adams was resting in her room. He could have come in while she was upstairs, taken one of the old jackets, and replaced it after causing our accident." Then her face fell. "Actu-

ally," she said, crestfallen, "just about anyone could have done that."

"Not quite anyone," George put in. "Even if Matt is a phony, the way Mrs. Adams says, he couldn't have done it."

"No, he's in the clear since he was in the other sleigh with Bess," Nancy agreed. "Anyway, I'm not sure the chocolate cake business is enough to prove that this Matt is an impostor. Sure, it would be frightening for a child to see someone having a violent allergic reaction, but Matt wouldn't necessarily remember that it was caused by chocolate. After all, Mrs. Adams still made hot chocolate for Matt and the other kids, didn't she? It wasn't as if the whole household was deprived of chocolate just because their housekeeper was allergic to it."

"Now, *that* would be something you'd remember," George put in, grinning. "Amnesia or not."

Nancy laughed, but her voice was serious when she said, "On the other hand, Matt's new-looking scar *is* kind of suspicious, and—" She snapped her fingers.

"What is it, Drew?" George said. "I know that look, and it usually means you're about to get us into some crazy situation."

"Not this time," Nancy said, laughing. "But it just occurred to me: What if Matt hired two sleighs because he *knew* something was going to happen—because he planned it! It's possible."

"In that case, it would have to have been Matt's accomplice." George sighed. "Who do we think that is?" she asked plaintively. "I'm so confused!"

"The most likely person to be Matt's accomplice is Jake Loomis," Nancy reminded George. "I think we can rule out Mrs. Adams on that score, since she's now claiming that Matt isn't really Matt—if you know what I mean."

George groaned. "I guess so." She peered down the hallway. "I keep expecting Bess and Matt to come out of the den. They're really taking a long time to rewind that video, don't you think?"

At that moment Bess and Matt appeared. Bess's face was suffused with happiness. After they had said goodbye and the girls had climbed into the car, she said in a dreamy voice, "You guys, Matt asked me to go to the movies this weekend. I'm beginning to think I really might have a chance with him."

"Bess, he's much older than you," George objected. "Get real!"

Nancy didn't say anything, but she made a silent vow: one way or another, she was going to have this case solved by the weekend. She couldn't sit by not knowing the truth—not when her friend's happiness might be at stake.

Half an hour later Nancy pulled up in front of Tony Giralda's Environmental Action office. Her

mind was racing after finding the red jacket, and she felt too agitated to just go home.

During the drive she had made a mental list of the three suspects for the accident with the sleigh. The first, Mrs. Adams, might have done it hoping to scare or hurt Matt, whom she believed to be a phony. Nancy knew that possibility was slim, so she set it aside. She'd check out the others first.

She had to consider both Giralda and Jake Loomis as likely suspects; Tony because he wanted to get Matt out of the way, Loomis because—if Matt was a phony, and he was Matt's accomplice—he wanted to get Nancy off the case. Anyway, the sooner Nancy checked these two out, the better.

Good, he was working late. The lights were still on, Nancy thought as she parked in front of Tony's office. The fresh snow was up to the tops of her boots as she made her way to the front door. Finding it unlocked, she let herself in quietly. She was about to call out when she heard Tony's voice. It sounded as if he was on the telephone.

"I'm sorry, ma'am," he was saying. "I know I'm a little late with the rent, but if you can just wait a few more days I'll—Yes, I know, but—"

Nancy listened attentively. It was obvious that Tony was having money troubles.

Silence. Then, "Please believe me. I'm expecting some donations this week. It's not a case of being desperate, it's—" His voice took on an

angry tone. "Look, this is a small operation. I'm practically waging a one-man war against pollution in our river—"

The person on the other end of the line kept cutting Tony off, so Nancy didn't hear much more of his side of the conversation. At last he put down the phone.

Nancy called out to let Tony know she was there.

He was frowning as he came through the doorway to the hall, but when he saw Nancy, his expression lightened. "What a nice surprise," he told her. "I was expecting a lady with an eviction notice, and I get Nancy Drew instead. What brings you here tonight?"

Tony beckoned Nancy into his office. Nancy hesitated when she saw Fred lying next to the desk chair, but the big dog's tail began to wag when he saw her so she sat down tentatively.

"I couldn't help but overhear," she began.

Tony shook his head and told her, "Some people don't understand that it's a struggle to make ends meet around here. They act as if my Environmental Action was funded by the Rockefeller Foundation or something." He sighed. "I mean, I work day and night. People like my landlady don't realize how tough it is."

But it would be a lot easier if Matt Glover turns out to be an impostor and you get some of Mr. Glover's money, Nancy thought. Clearing her throat, she said, "Do you mind if I ask where

you were this afternoon between, say, five and six o'clock?"

"Right here, where I always am," Tony replied. "What's this about?" he asked irritably.

The look on his face darkened as Nancy explained, and finally he blurted out, "Look, if anything's happened, it was caused by that jerk who's calling himself Matt Glover. Didn't you check out his scar?"

Nancy nodded. "He has a scar, but it looks kind of fresh—maybe too new to have been gotten when he was a kid. I couldn't tell, though."

She took a deep breath. "I'd like to trust you, Tony, but you're not being totally open with me. There's something you've never mentioned."

Tony glowered at her as he raked a hand through his blond hair. "Yeah? What's that?"

"Clayton Glover's money," Nancy said.

He put up his hands in a gesture of helplessness. "I won't deny that I'll miss the money. Mr. Glover used to make a donation to me every year, but what can I do? He can't give from beyond the grave, can he?"

"I didn't mean his donations, Tony. I meant big money, enough to let you run this place in style."

"Where's that supposed to come from?" he asked, giving her a skeptical look.

Leaning forward, she told him, "Giralda's

Environmental Action is in Mr. Glover's will. It was one of the charities he provided for. Because of Matt's reappearance, you stand to lose a lot, Tony. Obviously your interest in proving him to be an impostor goes beyond just a 'gut feeling.' "

Tony's jaw hung open in disbelief. "And you thought I *knew* that?" he asked. "I had no idea!"

His reaction was so shocked that Nancy had a hard time thinking he could be lying. But she was puzzled. "If that's true, then why is it so important to you to expose Matt? I mean, could you really have known him well enough to be so convinced he's a phony?" She shot him a sarcastic look and added, "I think we can drop the idea that you knew him like a brother."

Tony flushed. "Okay, maybe I stretched the truth a little when I said that Matt and I were really tight, but only because I thought you wouldn't take me seriously otherwise."

He took a deep breath before continuing. "I wasn't part of his circle of close friends or anything. They were pretty elite, and I didn't feel comfortable around them. But Matt was a regular guy. He was always really nice to me—not stuck up at all. We used to talk a lot at school, and he did invite me out to the Corners a few times." He smiled sheepishly. "Not as much as I made it sound, though."

"But you still think you knew him well enough to know that this Matt is a fake?" Nancy asked.

"It's just a feeling I have. Maybe it's because I'm a guy and I'm not distracted by his good looks."

Nancy ignored his annoying comment. "Look, Tony," she told him, "I promise you I'll expose Matt if he isn't who he claims to be."

Nancy got up to leave, and Tony walked her to her car. "So Mr. Glover really left me something in his will, huh?" He looked both proud and surprised. "That was pretty decent of him."

After saying good night, Nancy drove back toward her house. Could she scratch Tony off her list of suspects? He claimed he hadn't even known he had anything to gain from Mr. Glover's will. But he could have found out—the provisions of the will seemed to be common knowledge to other people.

Nancy rubbed her temples. Her head was still aching, and she was ready to get some sleep.

"Talk about long days," she said to her father as she entered the house. "Today was a killer."

Carson Drew was sitting in the living room, reading. He looked up at her with concern. "You almost *did* get killed," he reminded her. "Promise me you'll be careful, Nancy."

"Dad, you know I always am." She sat down on the sofa next to him. "Bess told me Matt passed the lie-detector test."

Her father held out the sheets of paper he'd been reading. "Yes," he said. "In fact I was just

looking it over more closely. I want to make sure of the results before we wrap this up."

"And?" Nancy looked at him expectantly.

"Matt did extremely well. The important things checked out in his favor. The test shows he's telling the truth when he says that he is Matthew Glover, that he was born in River Heights, that he is the son of Clayton Glover—essential things like that."

"Was there anything that *didn't* check out?"

"Only one thing. We asked him the same question several times, and he always answered yes. But the machine went haywire, indicating that he might not have been telling the truth."

Nancy looked at her father. "What was the question?"

"It was," said Carson Drew, " 'Have you ever been in Colorado?' "

"You're kidding!" Nancy exclaimed. "But the real Matt would have to have known he'd been in Colorado. That's where he was lost in the avalanche!"

Chapter Thirteen

NANCY STARED at her father. "If Matt was lying about being in Colorado," she said slowly, thinking out loud, "he must have been lying about all the other stuff, too." She paused, frowning. "But the test showed that he was telling the truth. Why?"

Carson held up his hands. "These tests aren't always reliable," he said. "There can be all sorts of inconsistencies."

Nancy yawned, then rubbed her head, which was still throbbing. "Well, I won't be able to think straight until I get a good night's sleep." She said good night, then went up to her room, dropping off almost as soon as her head hit the pillow.

The following morning she woke up with only a ghost of her headache. Her first thought as she sat up in bed was about the way the reins had felt as they snapped apart in her hands right before the accident.

She blinked as the thought struck her—reins didn't simply rip in two. A stable that rented horses and sleighs couldn't afford to let their leather get so dried out that their clients were in danger.

"Somebody tampered with them," she said aloud. Jumping out of bed, she dressed quickly in jeans, a white turtleneck, and a blue sweater. After eating a bowl of cereal and gulping down some juice, Nancy grabbed a jacket and went out to her car. "First stop, Thurston's livery stables," she said.

The sun reflected off the fields of dazzling snow in a blinding glare, and Nancy had to squint to see as she drove to the stables, a few miles outside of River Heights. She turned into the entrance, marked by a sign in the shape of a huge horse's head. It read: "Thurston's Livery—Horses for Hire, Sleigh Rides in Season."

Nancy parked in a lot in front of a big red barn that had that same horse's head and motto painted on it. A wooden shack jutted out from the barn on one side of the entrance, and Nancy went over to it.

She knocked on the door, and a young man

with ruddy cheeks opened it and gestured for her to enter. He introduced himself as Charlie Murphy.

"What can I do for you?" he asked, all smiles.

Inside, the pungent odor of horses and hay struck Nancy immediately. A rear door in the shack opened into the barn, and Nancy caught a glimpse of stalls against one wall.

"I just wanted to check on something," Nancy said, returning Charlie's smile. "When things like reins get old, and the leather becomes thin, is there a way to mend them?"

"Mend them?" Charlie's smile faded. He pulled out a chair for her and perched on the edge of his makeshift desk. "We wouldn't let our reins be used if they were old and thin. When they start to wear out, we replace them. Why do you want to know?"

He seemed to be a little alarmed, and Nancy guessed he thought she might be an investigator, checking to see if Thurston's was renting unsafe equipment.

"I'm not here to accuse Thurston's of anything," she reassured him. "The fact is, there was an accident yesterday involving one of your sleighs."

"What kind of accident?"

Instead of answering, Nancy said, "Let's say some equipment of yours was damaged, entirely through the negligence of the renters. What

would happen? Would they have to pay for what they'd damaged?"

"Sure." Charlie continued to look at her suspiciously. "I'm not sure what you're getting at, but I don't think I should say anything more until Mr. Thurston gets back." His jaw was set in a straight and stubborn line.

I'm not getting anywhere! Nancy thought, frustration building inside her. "Look," she blurted out. "I was in that accident yesterday. As you can see, I'm still in one piece. I don't plan to sue Thurston's, but I do want to know who sawed into a set of your reins yesterday and nearly got me killed!"

Shock played over Charlie's face. "That's terrible!" he said sincerely. "I'm sorry. I guess I'm a little protective of the stables." He paused for a moment. "What was it that you said about the reins?"

"I think someone sabotaged them, but I need to be sure."

Charlie rubbed his jaw and let out a low whistle. "Sabotage— So that's what Mr. Thurston was yelling about yesterday."

"What do you mean?" Nancy asked.

"Well, when Mr. Thurston gets mad, I try to keep out of his way, so I didn't exactly hear everything. But he was going on about some jerk who'd ruined a brand-new set of reins. Mr. Thurston was really burned up about it. The guy didn't get his deposit back."

Nancy leaned forward excitedly. "Do you know who it was?"

Charlie picked up a ledger from the desk and flipped through it until he found the right page, then ran his finger down a column of names. "Here it is. Glover. Matthew Glover."

Nancy drove back toward River Heights, still reeling from what she'd learned. Matt Glover had to have sabotaged her sleigh. Someone had ruined a brand-new set of reins. How many brand-new sets could have been ruined in a day? It had to have been her set, and it *had* to have been Matt. He was the one who had gotten the sleighs from the stable. No one else had gone near them until she, Bess, and George joined him for their ride. He had deliberately tried to hurt her, and that could mean only one thing: Matt was afraid she was going to expose him as a phony. He *was* an impostor, and he had to be working with someone—the person in the red jacket who had spooked her horse.

Nancy braked for a red light. Well, Matt was about to find out she didn't scare so easily! she fumed. The problem was, she still needed concrete proof. She knew the broken reins weren't enough evidence to convince a court that he was an impostor.

When the light turned green, Nancy turned in the direction of the River Heights library. All copies of the local papers for the last ten years were on microfilm there. She intended to check

every shred of information about Matt's disappearance five years earlier. Something would come to her. It had to.

Forty-five minutes later Nancy still hadn't found anything that would break the phony Matt's story. Letting out a frustrated sigh, she closed her eyes and massaged them with her fingers. The microfilm was making her headache come back.

Suddenly she felt a strong hand grip her shoulder. Her eyes popped open and she looked up—straight into the blue eyes of Matt Glover.

"Still at it, I see," Matt said. He was using his old teasing voice, but Nancy could hear the undercurrent of steely anger. Or was she just imagining it?

Was it just a coincidence that he was there? Or had he followed her? Suddenly Nancy was glad she was in a public building and not some isolated place. "Still at it," she admitted, trying to act casual.

"Well, you'd better work fast," he said. "By noon tomorrow I'll be granted my rightful place as Clayton Glover's son. The lawyers are drawing up the papers now."

Rightful place! What a bunch of baloney!

Matt gave her his trademark grin, then with a casual wave he sauntered off. Now that Nancy knew for sure he wasn't the real Matt, he seemed smug and arrogant, not charming. He was right

about one thing, though. She had to work quickly if she was going to prove he was an impostor before noon the next day!

Nancy returned the microfilm, stepped out into the cold winter air, and briskly walked the short distance to her father's law firm.

"This is a surprise," Carson Drew said, smiling as she came into his office. "Uh-oh. From the dark look on your face, you're not here to tell me I'm the number-one father of the year."

Nancy laughed and gave him a quick hug before taking a seat. "Well, you are, Dad, but I came about something else." She told him what she had figured out about Matt. "He has to be working with someone else, and I have an idea who, but I don't have a shred of proof." She explained about Jake Loomis.

"Well, maybe we can dig something up just by talking. Why don't you talk through what you know about the case and see if we can figure anything out," her father suggested.

"It's worth a try," Nancy agreed. Leaning back in her chair, she began reconstructing her investigation for Carson Drew.

When she got to the part about Tony Giralda, a concerned look came into her father's face. "Nancy, that was privileged information you gave to Tony. Nobody is supposed to know the terms of the will but the lawyers and Matt."

"What?" Nancy leaned forward, beginning to feel excited. "You're sure no one but you and

some other lawyers and Matt knew the terms of the will?"

"Positive. Well, there was one other person who knew." He pointed a finger at her, an amused smile on his lips.

Nancy quickly told her father about her visit to Jake Loomis. "The point is," she finished in an excited rush, "when we talked to Loomis, he said he hadn't seen Matt since he was interviewed by him. But he knew all about which businesses would inherit Mr. Glover's money. He *must* have found out from Matt. There's no other way, is there? So they've definitely been in touch."

She remembered seeing Matt on the telephone by the diner that day in Chicago. He might have been speaking to Loomis.

Carson Drew frowned. "This is very serious, Nancy. If Matt told Loomis about the will, that must mean—"

"That we can *prove* he and Matt are partners in a giant scam to steal Mr. Glover's fortune!"

Chapter Fourteen

NANCY JUMPED UP. "I've got my proof. Loomis and Matt—I mean Gary Page—set up the whole scheme." She gave her father a big hug. "Thanks, Dad. You just helped me clear everything up."

She was already halfway to the door when Carson asked her, "Where are you going?"

"To catch some criminals!" she called over her shoulder.

Her mind was racing as she got back into her Mustang, the pieces of her plan falling together. She had to set a trap to bring Loomis and Matt together, where she could confront them and get hard evidence—evidence to stand up in court. She knew just how to do it, too.

Bess was the answer. There was no way Matt

would let his guard down with Nancy, but he would have no reason to suspect Bess. She had believed in him from the start. As far as Matt was concerned, she was his loyal dupe. Of course, Nancy would first have to convince Bess that Matt was an impostor—something she wasn't looking forward to at all.

First Nancy drove to Tony Giralda's office. After parking in front of his building, she pulled a small notebook and a pen from her purse and carefully composed a short script.

> This is Mr. Loomis's client in River Heights. I'm having trouble with my garden, and I need to see Mr. Loomis at seven this evening—in person.

When she was done, she reread it, satisfied. If she could get Tony to call Jake Loomis's office and say exactly that, she was sure it would be enough to set Loomis up.

"You want me to do *what?*" Tony boomed when Nancy proposed her plan to him. He stared at the words.

"You won't be talking to Loomis," she explained. "You'll be speaking to a receptionist. Just give her the message and hang up. There'll be no way he'll ever connect you to the call."

"I don't know. . . ." Tony said.

"Come on, Tony. Where's your sense of justice?"

"Why can't *you* make the call?" he argued.

"It has to be a man's voice, or Loomis will know it wasn't really Matt who called," she told him.

Tony shook his head. "I don't know. I'm not very good at this kind of thing."

"Please, Tony, just practice it a few times. Think of it as a rehearsal for your part in bringing justice to River Heights."

Reluctantly, Tony took the paper and read woodenly. His face was flushed bright red, and he stumbled on every other word.

"Lighten up," Nancy said with a smile. "Try it again."

His second attempt was even worse. Nancy had to struggle to keep from laughing. "You sound like a taped announcement," she said.

"Did I ever say I was an actor?" he retorted irritably.

Nancy read the message out loud, showing him where to pause so that he would sound natural. He got better with each try, and at last Nancy punched out Loomis's number on Tony's phone and handed him the receiver.

Tony clutched it tightly, perspiration beading his forehead and color rising in his cheeks. "I feel like a dope," he said, but then the line was picked up in Chicago. He straightened up and said his piece, then hung up.

"She started to ask questions, so I figured I'd better get off." He let out a huge breath of relief

and told her, "I'm shaking all over. Is that what stage fright is like?"

"Not bad, Tony, not bad at all," she said. "You might be headed for a new career."

"Cut it out," he said, but now the pink in his face came from pleasure.

After thanking Tony, Nancy left his office. She braced herself as she drove over to Bess's house. This part of her plan she was dreading.

"Nancy Drew, you're trying to ruin everything!" Bess wailed. "Why can't you just accept that Matt Glover really has come back? Give the guy a break, would you?"

Bess was wearing pink sweats, sitting on the exercise bike in her room.

Nancy sighed and plopped down on Bess's bed. "Come on, Bess. You can't ignore the evidence—"

"That's what you keep telling me," Bess retorted, pedaling furiously, "but I don't see what's so conclusive about it. There's no proof that Matt cut those reins, and you said yourself you weren't sure about his scar. If you want me to go along with some stupid plan to trap him, you can just forget it." She crossed her arms over her chest and said defiantly, "In fact, I think as his *friend* —which you obviously aren't—I should warn him."

"You can't!" Nancy sat up straight on Bess's bed. She *had* to make her understand—and fast.

In an urgent voice Nancy explained again about how Matt must have been the one to tell Loomis which charities were to receive money. "Don't you see? Loomis lied to us when he said he hadn't seen Matt since the interview. That means Loomis and Matt *have* to be working together. It's the only answer.

"And it's not just a matter of the charities who'll be cheated," Nancy continued. "What about Matt, the real Matt? What about his father? It would be an insult to their memories. I'm trying to protect them, too."

Bess still didn't look convinced, but Nancy saw her expression soften a little. "I don't like it," she said dubiously. "What if you're wrong? I'd never be able to forgive myself for being so sneaky. Why do I have to be involved at all?"

"If I could do it, I would, but I can't. Matt doesn't trust me. He wouldn't give me the time of day. He might let down his guard with you, though. Look at it this way, Bess. If he really is Matt Glover, isn't it worth it to prove it beyond any doubt? That way we could all be happy for him."

Bess sighed. "When you put it like that," she said slowly, "it sort of makes sense." She smiled shakily. "What is it I'm supposed to do?"

"I want you to catch him out in a lie, except it won't be a lie he tells. It'll have to be something he says he remembers. Something that never really happened. A lie in reverse."

"What if he says he doesn't remember it?"

"Then I guess we'll know he's the real Matt Glover," Nancy replied. "I'll apologize to you for all my doubts, and everyone will live happily ever after."

Bess grinned. "That's the version I like," she said, "and I'll bet you that's what happens." Her expression grew serious, and Nancy was afraid she might change her mind.

"What's the matter?" Nancy asked.

Bess climbed down from the exercise bike and went over to her closet. "Well, I was just wondering. . . ." She threw open her closet door and started rummaging through her clothes. "What should I wear?"

Nancy grinned. "At least you haven't lost sight of the really important things in life—like the perfect outfit!" She got up from Bess's bed and helped go through her closet. "Whatever you wear should have deep pockets," she said. "I want you to have my tape recorder going, so we'll have proof."

Bess's eyes widened. "That's the kind of thing *you* do," she said.

Nancy pulled out an oversize red sweater with two big patch pockets. "This will be perfect, and you'll look great!"

"Okay." Bess sat down on the edge of her bed and asked, "So what kind of lie do you want me to catch him in?"

"It has to be something from a big event in his

life," Nancy said. "Something he'd remember because of when it happened. *Nobody* could have filled him in on every little detail, it just isn't possible. You know, like his eighteenth birthday, when he got that great sports car— Hey, Loomis had left by then! Hold on, I think I've got it."

She told Bess her plan and then called Mrs. Adams at Glover's Corners. "Are you alone?" she asked. The housekeeper told her that Matt had gone downtown.

Nancy quickly told Mrs. Adams what she had figured out and what she planned to do about it. "Leave the side door open," Nancy instructed after sketching out her scheme. "And when Bess and Matt are safely in the library, come and tell me."

"This isn't going to be dangerous for Bess, is it?" Mrs. Adams sounded concerned.

"No," said Nancy. "Matt won't even know he's been trapped, but we'll have it on tape. By the time I confront Loomis and Matt this evening, Bess will be long gone, and I'll have the police with me. Once they hear the tape, I'm sure the authorities will be eager to take Matt into custody."

The housekeeper promised to let them know the moment Matt returned to the house. When Nancy returned to Bess's room, Bess was wearing the red sweater over a black knit skirt, red stockings, and black boots.

"You look great!" Nancy told her. Seeing

Bess's sad expression, she added softly, "I wouldn't even ask if I didn't think it was very important. I hope I'm wrong, Bess, really I do. But you've got to be prepared for the worst."

Bess nodded shakily.

Nancy had just showed Bess how to use the minirecorder when Mrs. Adams called back and told them that Matt had returned to Glover's Corners.

"This is it," she told Bess, feeling a rush of energy flow through her. "We're on!"

It was late in the afternoon when Nancy eased her Mustang through the gates of the Glover estate. The sun was setting, and the house and grounds were shrouded in dark gray shadows. Nancy was happy for the cover of darkness; Matt would be less likely to see her.

"We'd better park here so he doesn't see my car," she told Bess, stopping just inside the gates. "You can tell him you got dropped off. I'll wait till you're inside, then circle around by the trees to the side door."

Nancy watched as Bess trudged up to the house. As soon as she was inside, Nancy made her way to the side door and flattened herself against the wall so no one could spot her from inside. She checked her watch. Five o'clock.

Twenty minutes later, Mrs. Adams appeared at the side door, opening it soundlessly. "They're in the library now," she whispered. "I'll be in the kitchen."

Nancy slipped inside and tiptoed up the two steps from the side door. Now she was in a hall, with the dining room to her left and the library to the right. The library door wasn't closed, but Nancy was sure she couldn't be seen from this angle.

Once more she flattened herself against the wall just a few feet from the door. If Matt came out for any reason, he would probably use the door that led to the back hall and the kitchen. And if he headed for the door where she was eavesdropping—well, Nancy had to hope that Bess would find some way to warn her so she could duck back to the outside door in time to avoid being seen.

Bess's voice floated out from the library and Nancy heard her leading the conversation to the topic of parties. She said something about having to buy a present for her cousin Louise's birthday party. Nancy grinned—she didn't think Bess even had a cousin named Louise.

"I never seem to be able to choose just the right present," Bess was saying. "When I was a kid I bought some aquarium gravel—you know, the kind that comes in rainbow colors—for a boy who had tropical fish. He started crying when he opened it, and when I asked him what was wrong, he told me all his fish had died the week before."

Matt roared with laughter. "Poor Bess," he said.

Nancy had to suppress her own laughter as she listened to the wild stories Bess was inventing about terrible gifts she had given. She sounded completely natural, and Matt was laughing and egging her on.

"Still," Bess said, her voice dreamy now, "the best party ever was your eighteenth, Matt. It wasn't just that gorgeous car your father gave you, it was—everything!"

"It was a spectacular party," he agreed.

"I was only in junior high back then," Bess went on, "and I remember my friends and I were completely amazed that you invited us. It was the high point of our entire year! I don't think I've ever seen a cake as big as the one you had, not even at weddings."

Nancy caught her breath. This was it.

There had been two cakes, one in the shape of the number one and the other, number eight. Both had been iced in mocha fudge, Matt's favorite at the time.

"Was it your father who thought of having a cake the shape of a giant football, or was it you?" Bess was asking.

"It was me," Matt said, without missing a beat. "I guess I wanted everyone to remember my shining career on the varsity team. Not very modest of me, was it?"

Nancy's breath caught in her throat. He'd fallen for it! Now Bess would know for sure that the guy in there with her *wasn't* Matt Glover.

Nancy knew she had to be devastated by the realization. Now Nancy listened even more attentively, hoping Bess wouldn't give herself away.

"And iced in purple and white," Bess said. Her voice was trembling now, but Matt didn't seem to notice.

"The colors of River Heights High," he said, chuckling.

Nancy silently urged Bess to make some kind of excuse and get out of there. She was sure Bess wouldn't be able to keep up her facade much longer.

Suddenly a loud *crack* rang out from the library. Every muscle in Nancy's body tensed. What was going on? Was Bess in trouble? She heard Matt give a grunt of surprise, then Bess said, "Who's that?" Nancy heard panic in her friend's voice.

A split second later, Bess let out a cry of alarm. Nancy gasped as she heard the sound of something metal clattering onto stone. The flagstone hearth?

The tape recorder! Matt must have found it—and that meant Bess was in danger!

Chapter Fifteen

NANCY SPRANG for the doorway, her heart pounding. But just inside the room, she stopped short as her gaze fell on a second man. Jake Loomis!

Nancy realized with dismay that her plan had gotten totally fouled up. Loomis wasn't supposed to arrive for about another hour. But there he was, holding both of Bess's arms behind her in one of his huge hands. In his other hand he held the minirecorder. His face was twisted with fury, and just the sight of it made Nancy shiver.

He glanced at her, his eyes narrowing with recognition. "You!" he spat out. Turning to Matt, he muttered, "She's the one who came snooping around my office. There was another girl with her

but not this one." He indicated Bess with his head.

Matt whirled around to face Nancy. "What are you doing here?" he asked.

Ignoring Matt, Nancy said to Jake Loomis, "Let Bess go."

Bess's eyes were wide with fear, and she was trembling. Her arm was twisted painfully behind her, but Loomis didn't release his grip.

"Let her go," Nancy said again, using as firm a voice as she could muster. "What are you afraid of? Do you really have to use all your strength to terrorize someone who's one-third your size?"

Loomis dropped Bess's arms and took a threatening step toward Nancy. "You're a troublemaker," he said. "I should have known—all that nonsense about *Who's Who.*"

"What are you doing here?" Matt directed his curt question to Loomis, biting off each word.

Loomis glared at him. "You should know, you sent me a message to come."

Matt looked surprised. "A message? I didn't send any—" He broke off, staring at Nancy. "She tricked you, Jake."

"Look who's talking about being tricked," Loomis said. "You've let these kids make a fool of you."

"It wasn't easy," Nancy cut in. "He was very good, Mr. Loomis. Almost too good. You have great skills as a coach."

"I don't know what you're talking about,"

Matt said. "Nothing's changed. Bess and I were just talking about parties—nothing heavy—and all of a sudden Jake comes in like a lunatic."

"Come off it," Nancy told him. "You don't think we'll still fall for your charade, do you?"

Unperturbed, Matt turned toward Bess and gave her one of his dazzling smiles. "You believe me, don't you, Bess?"

Nancy watched Bess turn brick red with anger and humiliation. "No, I don't! It so happens, Matt Glover, or whoever you *really* are," Bess fumed, "that your birthday cake was nothing like the one I invented. A cake shaped like a football! A purple and white cake, for the high-school colors? I don't think so."

She gave a scornful laugh, but it turned into a cry of pain as Loomis grabbed her arm and twisted it behind her back again.

"Okay, girls," he said in a cold voice. "I didn't want anything to happen to anyone, but you've brought it on yourselves. You"—he gestured to Nancy—"get over here with your friend. I think we're going for a drive."

Nancy stayed where she was, playing for time. "If Bess and I disappear, don't you think it will make it harder for Matt to claim his legacy? After all, my father *is* the lawyer in question."

"I don't care if your father is the president," Loomis snarled. "Get over here, you little—" He checked himself. "It must have been fun for you to come to my Chicago office and pass yourself

off as a researcher for *Who's Who in Business.* You really thought you were putting one over on me."

"Not at all," said Nancy. "I knew right away that you were a smart criminal, even if you are slimy. I'll bet you've always been looking for the chance to pull off this kind of scam."

Loomis smiled. "And my chance came, didn't it? It came in the form of a reporter named Gary Page." He turned toward Matt and said, "The second I saw you, you reminded me so much of Matt Glover I knew my time had come."

"I'm warning you, Jake," Matt barked. "Shut up."

"You're warning *me?"* Loomis laughed. "Who do you think you are? Without me, you'd be nothing, a two-bit hack, a nobody!" He gave Matt a smug look. "I created you, and you're throwing it all away over these—" He threw a look of loathing at Nancy and Bess.

"Stop running your mouth, Jake," Matt said harshly.

As the two men argued, Nancy frantically looked around for a way to escape. There was no way she and Bess were a match for the two men, physically. If they ran, Matt and Loomis were sure to overpower them. She could only hope that Mrs. Adams had heard and called the police —if Loomis hadn't already gotten to her. Nancy shuddered at the thought. For the moment, Nan-

cy decided, all she could do was keep distracting them.

"How did you give yourself that scar on your wrist?" she asked Matt.

Matt glared at her but said nothing.

"Give the girl some credit," Loomis said. "She's on to you."

"And I'm on to *you,* too," she said, turning to Jake Loomis. "It wasn't enough for you to succeed in the landscape gardening business, was it?" she asked Loomis. "When the *Clarion* sent Gary Page to interview you, it seemed like a perfect chance. He looks like Matt would have looked—he's athletic and charming like Matt, and he's even left-handed!"

Loomis shrugged. "Page was a natural. Had a memory like an elephant, too. I knew he could pull off acting like Matt."

Nancy turned to Matt. "Tell me something," she said. "What made you decide to go along with it? Did it take lots of persuasion, or did you agree immediately?"

He glared at her for a moment, before grumbling, "Oh, who cares if we tell you. Where you're going, it won't make any difference." The grin on his face was smug. "It was the money, of course. I'd have been a fool to turn down a chance like this."

"It must have been easy meeting every day," Nancy said. "The *Clarion* is so close to Loomis

Landscaping. You must have been awfully busy, Gary. Working full time as a reporter and then taking lessons from Loomis in your spare time. He must have drawn you a map of Glover's Corners. But you had to memorize all sorts of other details, too. You had to remember to call Mrs. Adams 'Addie,' and to plaster mustard on your sandwiches. You had to learn all the little customs of life at Glover's Corners, like bringing pies and cakes to Mrs. Adams so she wouldn't spend her whole life baking."

Nancy took a deep breath, then pressed on. "You made a terrible mistake with that chocolate cake. You didn't know Mrs. Adams has a violent allergy to chocolate. The real Matt saw her nearly die from eating some by mistake. It's not something he would have forgotten."

Matt grimaced. "I think I can still finesse that one," he said to Loomis.

"It was a class act, Gary," Nancy said, "but you were bound to mess it up. Nobody could have learned all the little details that make up a person's life."

"Like two cakes in the shape of the number 18," Bess piped up.

"I don't see why you're making such a big deal of this." It was Gary Page speaking. "Who would have been hurt? I make a wonderful Matt."

"Oh, brother, I've had enough of this," said Loomis. "Get over here!" he shouted at Nancy.

For emphasis, he twisted Bess's arm viciously, making her shriek again.

Nancy had no choice but to do as he ordered. Her heart was beating hard as she went to stand next to Bess, but she was determined not to show either of the men that she was afraid.

"This is what we're going to do. We're going to drive out into the countryside. It's a deep freeze out there."

Bess started to cry, and Nancy saw that her whole body shook. Ignoring her, Loomis went on in an eerily calm voice. "I'm going to let you out of the car in a field somewhere, twenty miles from any town."

Bess moaned and bit her lip.

"Mother Nature will do the rest," Loomis said. "I won't have to lay a hand on either of you."

"No one will believe we died by accident," Nancy said. "They'll connect it to Gary, and he won't go down without taking you. You played your game, and you lost. Why not just admit it?"

"I'm not a loser, kid." Loomis sneered.

"Wait a minute," Gary cut in. "Maybe we can talk this over. If you girls could keep a secret, we still have a way out of this. There might even be some money in it for you. I'd be willing to share—there's more than enough to go around."

He looked beseechingly at Bess and shot her that same flirtatious look, but she just glared at him.

"Shut up," Loomis said harshly. "If you think these girls could keep a secret, you're crazier than I thought." He shoved Nancy. "Let's get going," he said, "and don't bother to scream. Nobody will hear you. I've already tied up your gray-haired friend in the kitchen. She'll have to go with you girls, of course.

"Now move it!"

Before she could do anything, Nancy heard a crashing noise come from the hallway.

"What the—?" Loomis turned toward the doorway as the crashing noises came closer. Suddenly his face went slack with shock.

Following his gaze, Nancy saw two enormous dogs come hurtling into the room, growling and baring their huge teeth. Grabbing Bess's arm, Nancy tore her friend away from Loomis just as the dogs made a flying leap toward them.

Chapter Sixteen

NANCY AND BESS BARELY managed to jump out of the dogs' way. Loomis, too, leapt back, but the enormous dogs kept after him, cornering him on the couch.

Nancy had recognized Tony Giralda's dogs, Fred and Max, at once. Her experience with the dogs had shown her that they weren't fierce, but Loomis didn't know that. He had scrambled over the sofa and was cowering against the wall in panic.

That took care of one criminal, she thought, but there was still one more.

Nancy spun around and looked for Gary, who was edging away from the group. Seeing her, he took off at a run toward the rear door, the one Loomis must have used to get in unseen by

Nancy. Nancy sprinted after him, catching up to him just before he reached the doorway and immobilizing him with a quick judo kick to his side. Gary let out a groan as he fell and lay curled up on the floor, clutching his ribs.

"Way to go, Nancy!" a deep voice called out behind her.

Turning, she saw that Tony Giralda had come into the library. Mrs. Adams was there, too, and she and Bess were standing close together on the opposite side of the room from Fred, Max, and Loomis. They seemed to be as frightened as Loomis was of the big dogs, who were now standing with their paws up on the sofa and growling deep in their throats.

"Hello there, Mr. Loomis, glad you could be here," Tony said, going over to the sofa.

"Someone should call the police," Nancy said.

"Over my dead body," Loomis said, but his voice was shaky.

"That can be arranged," Tony told him. "Fang and Claw here are trained attack dogs. I have only to say the word and they'll tear you to shreds." Nancy had to suppress a laugh at the aliases Tony had given Fred and Max. "I called the police as soon as I found Mrs. Adams tied up in the kitchen."

Nancy saw that Gary was getting to his feet, still clutching his side, and she gestured for him to walk over and stand by the couch, where Fred and Max could keep an eye on him, too.

Fred was still making that deep, menacing sound in his throat, and Nancy hoped he wouldn't stop—at least until the police showed up.

Holding out her hand, Nancy spoke to Loomis in a firm voice. "I'd like my tape recorder back, please. Hand it over to me very carefully. We don't want to alarm Fang."

Loomis held the minirecorder out and tossed it on the couch. "It won't do you much good," he scoffed. "It hit those flagstones pretty hard before. The thing's probably broken."

"I wouldn't be so sure," Nancy said, picking it up. She rewound the tape a little and then hit the Play button. Bess's voice came into the room, loud and clear. "Was it your father who thought of having a cake the shape of a giant football, or was it you?"

Behind Nancy, Bess giggled nervously at the sound of her own voice.

"That doesn't prove anything," Gary said. "Who remembers a cake from years ago? You'd be laughed out of court with that evidence."

"Maybe you've forgotten all the things you just confessed when you thought it didn't matter, since you planned on leaving us to die in the snow," Nancy pointed out.

"*I* haven't forgotten," Bess called from behind Nancy.

"We'll both testify to everything in court," Nancy said. "You two are going to jail for a long time."

Loomis's face had turned a deep purple color. With a cry of rage, he lunged at Nancy, hands raised, but she ducked aside easily. Loomis crouched, ready to spring at her, but he hesitated as the high-pitched whine of a siren filtered into the room.

A moment later two squad cars with flashing red lights raced up the drive and screeched to a halt in front of the house.

"The police!" Mrs. Adams exclaimed. "And not a moment too soon."

"Well, it's been quite an evening!" Mrs. Adams said. She, Nancy, Bess, and Tony sat around the kitchen table. None of them had wanted to remain in the library after the police took Gary Page and Jake Loomis away.

"We're lucky it ended the way it did," Nancy said, taking a sip of her cider. Mrs. Adams had made a big pot of it, and now the scent of cloves and cinnamon filled the air.

"It wasn't all luck, dear," Mrs. Adams reminded her. "The police were delighted that you had that tape.

"I'm just glad it's over. I thought I would drop dead of fear when I saw those beasts," the housekeeper added, chuckling. "I thought they were the most fearsome-looking attack dogs I'd ever seen."

"That makes two of us," Bess said. "Who would have known they were such sweethearts?"

Nancy glanced affectionately at the big dogs, who were lying contentedly at Tony's feet, chomping on pieces of beef bone that Mrs. Adams had put in soup bowls for them.

"They deserve that reward for coming to the rescue," she said. "Which reminds me, how did you know to come here, Tony?"

"I started thinking of that phone call you had me make," he began, reaching down to pet Max. "The more I thought about it, the more dangerous I thought the situation was. I went to your house to warn you, but your housekeeper said you weren't home. That's when I got a pretty good idea of where you were, and I drove out here. I saw your car parked down at the end of the drive, and I had a feeling—"

"A gut feeling?" Nancy asked, grinning.

"Right, a feeling you were in danger. I parked down by your car, then came up to the house by foot. I saw through the window what was going on. Luckily the side door was open. Anyway, when I got inside, I found Mrs. Adams tied up in the kitchen." He held up his hands and smiled. "The rest is history."

"But how did you get Fred and Max to act so threatening?" Bess asked, a puzzled look on her face.

Tony reached down again to pat the big dogs, who had finished chewing on their bones and were sleeping with their muzzles resting on their huge front paws. "There's one thing that drives

Fred and Max crazy. They can't stand getting a bath, and always put up a big fight."

"So you dumped some water on them, and presto—enter Fred and Max, barking ferociously," Nancy guessed. "I was wondering why the fur around their heads was wet."

"I didn't like doing it," said Tony, "but I figured it would be the best way to stall until the police showed up. By the way, who locked you in my office with Fred and Max the night we went skating?"

"It had to be Gary, since Jake wasn't around then. He must have followed me to see what I was up to," Nancy replied.

"I want to thank you for everything, Tony," Bess said. "If it weren't for you, Nancy and I might have ended up as icicles a hundred miles from anywhere."

"My mistake was in thinking that Loomis wouldn't get here until later," Nancy said. "Tony told him seven o'clock in our phone call, but he obviously decided not to wait until then. In fact, I think he was already here. I bet he never left the area after causing our sleigh accident yesterday."

Bess's blue eyes went wide. "You mean he's been here all along?" she asked.

"Not here at Glover's Corners, but close by. There are lots of motels around."

"He must have called his office for his messages," said Tony, "and the receptionist said that

stuff about his client in River Heights having trouble with his garden."

"And now his car's out in *our* garden," Mrs. Adams said. "I do hope the police will take it away."

Bess looked at the housekeeper and asked, "Where will you go, Mrs. Adams? When all this is over, I mean."

"I imagine I'll go to Florida," Mrs. Adams told her. "I have a sister there, you know. Besides, the winters here are beginning to get to me. Old bones don't like the cold as much as young ones do.

"Still," Mrs. Adams went on, on a dreamier note, "it was lovely, having you all here again. I suppose I was fooling myself to think we could bring the old days back."

"But it *was* like the old days," Bess insisted.

"No, dear," corrected Mrs. Adams, "it only seemed like them. In the old days that handsome young man who skated with you had a good heart. Matt was a wonderful person, just like his father. The man out on the pond this time was wicked, through and through."

She turned shining eyes on Nancy, Bess, and Tony. "But thanks to you, he'll get what he deserves."

"You bet," said Bess, grinning. "He might have been hoping for ten to twenty million, but now he'll get ten to twenty years!"

Chapter Seventeen

"WELL," SAID TONY, scraping his chair back, "I have to get back to my office."

"We should go, too," Nancy said to Bess. "I'd like to go to my house and tell my dad the case is over. We could stop by to pick up George on the way."

Nancy, Bess, and Tony hugged Mrs. Adams, then trudged down the long drive to their cars.

"Nancy?" Bess asked after Tony had driven off. Nancy saw that there was a wistful look in her friend's eyes. "Weren't you ever taken in by Matt—I mean, Gary Page? Not even for the tiniest minute?"

"Sure," Nancy answered. "Especially when we were out on the pond, in the moonlight, and we

were having so much fun. I was just as fooled as anyone."

Bess sighed.

"Don't feel bad, Bess. You really wanted it to be true that Matt was alive. And Gary Page put on a really convincing act. He was charming, handsome, generous—he said and did everything exactly right. No one could ever blame you for believing in him."

Bess smiled sadly. "When he fell for that lie about the cake, *I* was the one who felt like a fool at first. I mean, I actually thought I could fall in love with that guy! But then I just got madder and madder at him for being so deceitful." She shook her head. "What a jerk."

Nancy gave Bess a warm smile. She knew Bess must feel sad that Matt had turned out to be a fake, but at least she was mad at him, too.

Nancy and Bess climbed into the Mustang and went to pick up George. As the three girls then drove toward the Drews', Nancy and Bess told George what had happened out at Glover's Corners.

"You're kidding!" George exclaimed. "I can't believe I missed the wrap-up of the whole case!"

"I wouldn't have minded missing it a bit," said Bess. "It was pretty scary."

"It was even scarier if you knew Fred and Max's true nature," Nancy added with a laugh. "I was afraid they'd start wagging their tails and making friends with those goons."

The lights were on at the Drews' house, and Carson Drew greeted the girls with a big smile as they came in the front door.

"The police chief just called and told me what happened," he said. "He said to tell you that Jake Loomis and Gary Page both gave signed confessions." Carson smiled proudly at his daughter. "The police have an open-and-shut case. Page and Loomis will be going to jail, I can promise you that."

"Great!" Nancy said. She and Bess sat on the den sofa, while George settled herself in an easy chair.

"By the way," Carson went on, "that was clever of you to have Tony Giralda's guard dogs to protect you. Otherwise you would have been in great danger."

The three girls looked at one another, then dissolved in laughter, leaving Carson to stare at them and shake his head.

"There's one thing I don't understand," Bess said, still giggling a little. "How could Gary Page have aced that lie-detector test?"

"I don't understand it either," Nancy put in. "I know they're not completely reliable, but how could he have done so well? And what made him so eager to take it, when he knew he was lying?"

"I have a theory about it," Mr. Drew said. "The conspiracy to commit fraud between Gary Page and Jake Loomis was no small thing. It was

planned on a grand scale. If it succeeded, they would split a huge fortune.

"They were smart enough to know they couldn't carry it off without a lot of preparation. In a sense, Gary went into training as an athlete would."

"He went into training to *become* Matt," Nancy said, nodding. "That makes sense."

"Yes," her father continued. "To become Matt. Not to imitate him perfectly, but to *be* Matthew Glover for the rest of his life. He submerged himself in so much detail, he worked so hard at being Matt, I think in the end he might really have believed he *was* Matt."

"Then why did the test indicate he was lying about having been in Colorado?" Nancy asked.

"It turns out he never had been in Colorado. He's from Nebraska. He did work on a paper in Iowa City, but he's never been west of Omaha."

"Why should that make any difference?" George wanted to know. "He lied about everything else easily enough. Why couldn't he lie about being in Colorado?"

"I think I know," Nancy said. "Colorado, the accident itself, wasn't a part of his training with Loomis. Why should it have been? He'd had amnesia, and even if he snapped out of it when he saw his father's obituary, he might not remember the actual accident, anyway."

"Yes, I think you're right, Nancy," Carson Drew said.

"In other words," said George, "he couldn't believe in anything Loomis hadn't prepared him for."

"Well put, George," said Nancy's father. "Think of Loomis as the trainer and Gary Page as a racehorse."

"A racehorse that finally tripped on a hurdle," said Nancy.

There was a giggle from Bess before she put in, "A hurdle shaped like a football and iced in white and purple."

At that moment the phone rang. Nancy went to answer it.

"Hi, Nan," came Ned's voice. "Sorry to call so late, but no one was at your place all day except Hannah."

Nancy felt a familiar warm tingle at the sound of his voice. "It was one of those days," she told him.

"One of what days? What happened?" he asked. "You sound a little tired."

There was so much to explain. "It's a long story," she said into the phone. "And I've got company. I'll call you back and tell you everything as soon as Bess and George leave, okay?"

She talked with him a few more minutes, then said goodbye and hung up. When she returned to the living room, Bess and George were eating chocolate-chip cookies from a plate on the low table in front of the sofa.

"Solving cases with Nancy always makes me so hungry," Bess said, biting into one of the chewy cookies.

Nancy was reaching for a cookie herself when her father commented, "I'm sure there'll be some interesting reading in the papers tomorrow."

Bess sat up on the sofa. "About how we caught the criminals?"

"No," Carson replied. "About Mr. Glover's will. Now that nobody's contesting it, the information can be published."

"Since the ban of secrecy has been lifted," Nancy said to her father, "can you tell us who's going to get all that money?"

Carson Drew pulled a sheet of paper from his jacket pocket and unfolded it. "As a matter of fact, I have a copy of the press release that's going to the media." He began to read aloud.

" 'The will of Clayton Glover leaves his magnificent residence, Glover's Corners, to the town of River Heights. It is to be used as a historical museum and gathering place for citizens of the community. In an unusual move, Glover's will dictates that the grounds of his estate be turned into a park and that the pond be used for ice skating in season.' "

"Way to go, Mr. Glover," George said, clapping her hands.

Carson glanced at the girls and smiled. " 'The entire complex will be called the Matthew Glover

Park,'" he went on, "'in memory of Mr. Glover's son, who was killed five years ago on a skiing holiday in Colorado.'"

Carson then skimmed over the names of the local charities who would receive money. As Nancy had known, Giralda's Environmental Action was on the list.

"Great," said Nancy when her father told them the annual sum Tony would receive. "Now he'll be able to expand and get the help he deserves."

"Let's hear it for Fred and Max!" George shouted.

"What about Mrs. Adams?" Bess asked.

"A trust fund is to be set up for her," Carson assured the girls. "Mr. Glover mentioned special thanks to her for her faithful service. The press release also mentions Matt." He read again from the paper. "'None of these bequests would have been possible if Mr. Glover's son, who would be twenty-three, had lived. We can only speculate as to how Matthew Glover would have used the vast wealth his father would have left to him.'"

Carson refolded the paper and looked up. "That's it."

A deep silence followed. Nancy looked at Bess, who wore a thoughtful expression. Nancy hoped hearing about Matt hadn't upset her too much.

"Well," Bess said at last, "something good came out of all this."

"Definitely," George agreed. "Mr. Glover

made it possible for the good old days to go on forever."

Bess shook her head. "That's not what I meant, although it's certainly a good thing."

"What *did* you mean, Bess?" Nancy asked.

"The real Matt Glover might still be wandering around with amnesia," Bess said. Grinning, she reached for another chocolate-chip cookie. "He could still come home."

George rolled her eyes in disbelief, but Nancy reached out and hugged Bess. "You know what?" she said. "You're probably right."

Poison Pen

Chapter One

"Mmm, this is the life," Nancy Drew said with a contented sigh. She draped her fluffy rainbow-striped towel at the foot of the lounge chair and sank down into the soft cushions. Her reddish blond hair spread out around her head like a halo, glowing in the bright sunlight. "Nothing beats a long, lazy day at the River Heights Country Club pool."

"Don't I know it," agreed her friend Bess Marvin. Bess was stretched out on the lounge chair next to Nancy's, her eyes closed and her fair skin glistening with sunscreen. "Don't you wish summer would last forever?"

"Not me," piped up Bess's cousin George Fayne from the other side of Nancy. "I'd hate to give up skiing." Leaning on one elbow, she ran her fingers through her short, dark curls,

which were still wet from swimming. "But don't worry, Bess. It's only June. We've still got the whole summer in front of us!"

"With heat like this, it's hard to believe the summer is just beginning," Nancy commented. "I heard the temperature was supposed to hit ninety today." She plucked at the fabric of her neon green two-piece bathing suit. "I think it's about there now, and I think I'm almost ready to jump in the pool."

Bess opened her eyes and stared gravely at first Nancy and then George. "Tornado weather," she said with a shudder. Her gaze drifted lazily in front of Nancy, but then her blue eyes suddenly flew open wide. "Hey, Nancy," she said in an urgent whisper. "Who is that *gorgeous* guy?"

"Gorgeous guy?" George repeated, sitting up straight. "Where?"

"Over there," Bess said, gesturing.

Shading her eyes with her hand, Nancy gazed over at the other side of the pool, where a young man of about nineteen or twenty had just settled into the lifeguard's chair. He had shining black hair and classic chiseled features. His skin was tanned to a deep, glowing brown, which emphasized his slim yet muscular build. He was talking with a tall, lanky blond guy who stood by the chair.

"You mean the guy in the chair or the guy next to it?" George asked. "They're both

pretty awesome looking, if you ask me. Hey—doesn't the tall one look familiar?"

"I can't believe you don't recognize David Park and Jonathan Evans," Nancy said, shaking her head. "They were only a year ahead of us in high school."

"That's David Park?" Bess whispered. "That dark-haired hunk is the skinny, quiet guy who used to work in the library?"

"The one and only," Nancy replied, laughing.

"Jonathan Evans!" George seemed flabbergasted. "Boy, has he changed."

"Yeah, they both blossomed late," Nancy agreed. "I guess I shouldn't be teasing you about not recognizing them. I might not have known them myself, except that they go to Emerson College now. They're friends of Ned's."

Bess's eyebrows shot up. "Well, why didn't you say so? You can reintroduce us."

"Good idea, Bess," George put in, her brown eyes still focused on the two guys.

"Fine by me. They're really nice." Nancy swung her long legs over the edge of her lounge chair and stood up. "Let's go!"

The girls made a striking trio as they walked around the pool to the lifeguard's station. Nancy was slender and lithe, with shoulder-length reddish blond hair and sparkling deep blue eyes. George was a bit taller than Nancy,

with dark eyes and curls and the streamlined build of a natural athlete. Petite, curvy Bess had long blond hair, blue eyes, and a flirtatious smile.

"George, does my hair look ratty?" Nancy heard Bess whisper next to her.

"How could it? All you've done since we got here is brush it," George replied.

"That's not true!" Bess began indignantly.

Nancy chuckled as she listened to them argue. Bess and George were almost complete opposites, despite being cousins. One loved sports, the other hated exercise. One was quiet and a little on the shy side, the other bubbly and outgoing. And yet they were practically inseparable. They bickered some, but Nancy knew that under it all they were the best of friends.

"Hi, David. Hi, Jonathan," Nancy called as she approached the lifeguard's station.

The guys glanced over, and David broke into a wide grin of recognition. "Hey!" he greeted her. "How've you been, Nancy? Where's Ned? I haven't seen him since the end of spring semester."

Nancy shrugged. "I wish I saw more of him, too," she admitted. "But Ned's been really busy with his summer job at the insurance company."

"We know what that's like," Jonathan chimed in. He adopted an exaggerated,

martyrlike expression and said, "We lifeguards have it pretty tough, sitting out here day after day in the hot sun."

"My heart bleeds for you," Nancy said dryly. Then she gestured toward Bess and George. "You remember Bess Marvin and George Fayne, don't you?"

David's dark eyes sparkled with interest as he took in the cousins, but Nancy noticed that his gaze lingered longer on Bess. "Well, if I didn't, I sure won't forget them now," David declared. "You three look great!"

"George Fayne?" Jonathan gazed at George, and Nancy saw a glint of recognition and then admiration in his eyes. "You were on the school tennis team, right?"

George nodded, her eyes bright. "That's right. And you were the track team's star sprinter."

Nice work, Drew, Nancy congratulated herself. "Hey," she said suddenly as an idea struck her, "are you guys going to the concert at the lake tomorrow night?"

"You bet," Jonathan replied. "Ice Planet's the greatest."

"Well, I'm having a barbecue at my house—just Ned, Bess, George, and me. Why don't you guys come? We can all go to the concert together afterward," Nancy suggested, glancing at Bess and George with a hint of a smile.

"I'll be there," Jonathan said immediately.

"Count me in," David said at the same time.

"Great!" Nancy said. "Come over around six. See you then."

As the girls walked back to their lounges, George whispered to Nancy, "You never said anything to us about a barbecue at your house tomorrow night."

Nancy's blue eyes gleamed mischievously as she explained, "That's because I didn't think of it until just now!"

"That's what I call good thinking." Bess nodded her approval.

Nancy was just lying back on her lounge when Bess demanded in a horrified tone, "Hey, what do you think you're doing?"

"Well, last time I checked, it wasn't a federal crime to lie in the sun," Nancy said, gazing quizzically at Bess. "But I have a feeling that's not what you have in mind."

"You've got that right," Bess retorted. "Come on, you two, get out of those chairs and stop being lazy. We have work to do!" She grabbed Nancy's hand and pulled her to her feet. "The concert's tomorrow night, we're going with three gorgeous guys, and I for one have nothing to wear. We've got to shop!"

"Okay, we're getting there. All I need is a pair of pants to go with the top I just bought," Bess announced. "And maybe—"

"Here we go," George muttered. "And may-

be some new shoes, and some new makeup, and a dress in case the top and pants don't look good—"

Nancy laughed. "You should talk," she said, pointing at the bulging shopping bag in George's hand. "You did pretty well yourself."

It was afternoon and the girls had just left Vanities, a trendy boutique at the River Heights mall. Suddenly a familiar, gloating voice rang out from behind them: "Well, if it isn't Nancy Drew."

Even before she looked, Nancy knew who the speaker was: Brenda Carlton, girl reporter and major nuisance. Brenda's father owned *Today's Times,* one of River Heights's daily newspapers. He occasionally let Brenda write articles for the paper, and this had given her the idea that she was an ace crime reporter.

That in itself wasn't so bad. The real problem was that Brenda constantly tried to show Nancy up by meddling in her investigations—often landing herself and Nancy in hot water.

Just recently Nancy had been working to clear Ned of a murder charge, and Brenda's constant interference had almost landed Ned behind bars for life! And to top it off the reporter had had nerve enough to write an article for the paper in which she'd taken credit for solving the case! Needless to say, Brenda wasn't exactly on Nancy's list of her favorite people.

Nancy sighed and turned around with a smile in place. The reporter was wearing a beige silk blouse, tailored slacks, and pumps, and her dark hair was twisted into a French braid. Nancy had to admit she looked very pretty.

"Don't tell me you girls were actually shopping at Vanities," Brenda said with disdain.

"Hi, Brenda," Nancy said in a neutral voice.

George leaned close to Nancy and said in a low voice, "She's probably just jealous. Her dad must have taken away her credit cards this week."

Nancy saw a flash of annoyance in Brenda's dark eyes. "I heard that," Brenda said. "For your information, my cash flow is fine. In fact, I was hoping you three would let me treat you to a late lunch at the Eatery—if you haven't eaten already."

Nancy, Bess, and George exchanged startled glances. Brenda wasn't exactly known for her generosity—especially toward them. Nancy couldn't help wondering if she was up to something.

There was only one way to find out. "Uh, sure. We haven't eaten yet. That'd be nice," Nancy answered.

The four girls took the escalator up to the Eatery, a cafeteria-style restaurant on the mezzanine level. After going through the line, they carried their trays over to an empty table and sat down.

Nancy swallowed a bite of her chicken salad sandwich. "So, Brenda, what's up?" she asked.

Brenda's face radiated an innocence Nancy knew not to trust. "Up? Nothing's up. I was just wondering what kind of plans you have for the summer."

"Oh, I don't know," Nancy said guardedly. "I'm between cases at the moment. I don't really have any special plans."

Bess laughed. "My plan is to have as much fun as possible," she said.

"Mm-hm. Well, I don't think *I'll* have too much time for fun and relaxation," Brenda said, shooting Nancy a significant look.

Here it comes, Nancy thought. "Uh—why not, Brenda?" she asked, taking the bait.

Brenda leaned forward. "I've been given a very important assignment at the paper," she said in a confidential tone.

"Oh!" Bess exclaimed. "You mean your new column. I saw it the other day."

"What column?" Nancy asked, surprised.

"If you ever read a paper, you'd know," Brenda snapped. Then, with a smile at Bess, she added, "At least *you* seem to be concerned about current affairs. So how do you like the column?"

"Well, I've—uh—only seen it once or twice," she answered, sounding a bit embarrassed. She turned to Nancy and George. "Brenda's writing an advice-to-the-lovelorn

column," Bess explained. "So far I've seen only one column, though, and it seemed as if there weren't many people who needed advice."

Brenda's cheeks flamed with color. "Yes, there are!" she cried. "The letters have been pouring in. I just—I just haven't had a chance to answer them yet. I've been busy with other important assignments."

Nancy stifled a laugh. The last story of Brenda's she'd seen was on the theft of twelve dollars from the Elks' Lodge petty cash box. Now, that was hot news! Aloud she merely said, "I'm sure more letters will come in, Brenda. People are always getting their hearts broken, falling in love."

"Well, Nancy Drew," Brenda snapped, "it may surprise you to know there are secrets in River Heights that even *you* haven't heard of."

There she goes again, trying to show me up, Nancy thought with a sigh. "I'm sure there are," Nancy returned. "People are bound to have concerns that no one else knows about—or *should* know about. Some matters are just private."

Brenda glared at her. "But there are some things that shouldn't be kept secret, don't you agree?" she retorted.

"Like what?" Nancy asked, picking up her sandwich to take a bite.

"Like murder."

"What? What do you mean?" Nancy demanded, her eyes open wide.

Brenda folded her arms and leaned back in her chair, a satisfied smile on her lips. "I mean—when was the last time *you* got a letter from someone who's afraid they're going to be murdered?"

Chapter Two

MURDERED?" Nancy repeated, feeling dazed. She put her sandwich down on her plate. "What are you talking about? Who's going to be murdered? Brenda, this could be serious."

"It's nothing for you to worry about," Brenda replied secretively.

"Brenda, are you saying that you got a letter from someone who fears for his or her life? Who is it?" Nancy pressed, leaning forward on her arms.

"None of your business," Brenda retorted. "A reporter never reveals her sources. Anyway, I don't have time to discuss this right now—I have places to go and people to see." She slid her chair back and stood up.

"Wait!" Nancy cried, but Brenda just smiled down at her and grabbed her purse.

"I'm sure I'll see you around town," she said, and flounced away.

The three girls stared after her. Then Bess turned to George and Nancy and asked, "You don't think she's serious, do you?"

"It *would* be just like her to make up something like that," George said, forking a tomato from her chef's salad. "Brenda will do anything for attention."

"That's true," Nancy said slowly. "I'm not sure what to think. Let's go over to the newsstand and check out this column of hers."

Bess and George agreed. After finishing their lunches, the three girls wandered down to a newsstand on the main level. Nancy bought a copy of *Today's Times,* and the girls sat down on a polished wooden bench to read it.

"'Tornadoes Ravage Chicago Suburb,'" George read aloud, peering over Nancy's shoulder at the headline on the front page. "That's awful."

"Yeah. Some friends of my parents live in that town," Bess commented. "They lost their garage."

"They're lucky it was only the garage," Nancy said soberly. "I mean, that's bad, but just think how much worse it could have been. Look at this photo." She pointed at a grainy black-and-white shot of the ruins of a house. One wall was oddly intact, but the rest had totally collapsed.

"Twenty-seven families have been left

homeless," George murmured, still reading the article. "Those poor people!"

"It's this weather," Nancy murmured. "All this awful, heavy heat. Tornadoes breed in it."

Bess blew out her breath in a long sigh. "Please, you guys, let's change the subject," she begged. "All this stuff about tornadoes scares me."

"At least there's no tornado watch set for River Heights yet," Nancy said.

"Well, actually, there was one of those minitornadoes—what do you call them, microbursts—here last weekend," George said. She pointed at some scaffolding set up near one end of the mall's main concourse. "Right over there. It barely touched down. Luckily for the mall, the only damage was to a skylight—oh, and the roof was ripped up a little bit."

Bess looked as if she'd rather be anyplace but where she was right then. "I wish you hadn't told me that, George," she said nervously. Then she gasped. "Oh, no! I just thought of something *really* awful! What if there's a tornado watch tomorrow night? They might call off the concert!"

"Well, there's nothing we can do about it," Nancy pointed out. "Come on, let's read Brenda's column." She flipped through the paper until she came to the Lifestyles section. "Here it is—'Just Ask Brenda.'"

Bess leaned in to get a better look. "Hey, that's a great picture of her."

Nancy peered at the photo. Brenda had a sweet, helpful smile on her face. "I've never seen her look like that in real life," she commented, laughing.

"Read us the first letter, Nan," George suggested. "Let's see what terrible problems Brenda is tackling today."

"Okay, here goes." Nancy went on to read a long, whiny complaint about a neighbor's overgrown, unkempt lawn. " 'I have asked her repeatedly to do something about her unsightly property, but she ignores me. What can I do?' " Glancing at Bess and George, Nancy told them, "The letter's signed, 'Fed Up.' "

"Whew!" George exclaimed. "What a boring letter! Are there any others?"

Nancy scanned the column. "Just one. It's from a girl who wants to break up with her boyfriend because the only place he ever takes her is the video arcade."

"What's Brenda's advice?" Bess asked.

"Brenda says it's probably because the girl isn't very interesting," Nancy replied.

George let out a low whistle. "Talk about unsympathetic!"

"Yeah," Bess added. "I think this column would be the last place anyone would turn to if they *really* needed help."

George nodded her agreement. "She was

probably making up what she said just now about someone being afraid."

"If anything exciting ever does appear in this column," said Nancy, tapping the folded-up paper in her lap, "I bet it will be right out of the overactive imagination of Brenda Carlton."

Nancy got up from the bench and dropped the newspaper into a nearby garbage can. "Come on, guys, let's get out of here. I want to get home and see if I can talk Hannah into making something wonderful for dessert for tomorrow night."

"But I never bought a pair of pants," Bess objected.

"Oh, come on," George scolded. "You already have at least ten pairs of pants at home that would look perfect with your new top."

Bess considered for a moment. "Yeah, I guess I do," she agreed. "Okay."

The three girls picked up their shopping bags and headed out to the parking lot to Nancy's blue Mustang. Nancy was the first one through the doors that led from the mall out to the asphalt lot. Heat struck her in a searing wave, and she could feel perspiration bead on her brow.

Suddenly, from somewhere to her right, a sharp screech of rubber tore through the summer air, followed by the loud crashing of metal on metal.

"What was that?" George cried.

Nancy was already running toward the noise. She didn't even turn around as she yelled back, "It sounded like an accident. Come on! Someone might need our help!"

Chapter Three

As Nancy sprinted toward the sound, she could see a crowd gathering around two cars in the parking lot. One of the cars, a silver sedan, had apparently struck the other, a red sports car, on the left front fender.

As Nancy ran up, the driver of the sedan was just climbing out of her car. The woman was about forty, with short ash blond hair, and was wearing an expensive-looking linen suit. Nancy was relieved to see that the woman didn't appear to be injured, although she seemed to be shaken.

Nancy's eyes widened when she saw who the driver of the other car was. Brenda Carlton—and she looked furious.

"Look what you did to my car!" Brenda raged, pointing at her dented front fender. "Don't think you won't pay for the damage!"

"I'm so sorry!" the woman exclaimed. Her voice shook, and there were tears in her eyes.

The poor woman sounded as if she was about to break down. Stepping forward, Nancy asked, "Can I help? Is everyone all right?"

"Just barely, no thanks to her," Brenda said, jerking a thumb at the blond-haired woman. "She steered right into me!"

"I tried to stop, really I did," the other woman said shakily. "I kept pumping the brakes, but the car wouldn't—" She broke off with a sob.

"That's crazy!" Brenda declared. "You just weren't paying attention. Someone call the police!"

"I think someone already went to do that," George put in.

"P-police?" The woman's voice quavered. "Oh, dear!"

"Don't worry," Nancy told her, putting an arm around her shoulders and steering her away from Brenda. "It's just routine. The police have to be informed so that they can make a report to your insurance companies. You look pretty shaken up," she went on. "Why don't you sit in your car until the police get here? Here, let me help you."

"Thank you so much," the woman said gratefully. "I'm Mrs. Keating—Maggie Keating. I just don't know what happened," she went on as Nancy led her to the sedan. "I couldn't stop. It was so frightening!"

"I'm sure it was," Nancy said, trying to soothe her. "You should probably have your brakes checked."

"Yes, I'll do that," Mrs. Keating agreed.

Nancy settled Mrs. Keating in the driver's seat, then straightened up to find herself gazing into an extraordinary pair of eyes. One was a deep, vivid blue; the other was golden brown.

The effect was so startling Nancy nearly jumped. The eyes belonged to a muscular, handsome man of medium height, who was standing only a few feet away. He had curly, light brown hair and a square jaw. His face was creased by a slight grin as he stared, first at Nancy, then at Mrs. Keating. Then, turning, the man stepped back into the crowd and was gone.

"Nan, what's wrong?" came Bess's voice.

Blinking, Nancy turned back to her two friends. "Nothing, really," she told them. "It's just that there was an unusual-looking guy here. He had one blue eye and one brown eye. . . ." She let her voice trail off. "I don't know why he seemed so odd, though," she said at last.

"One blue eye and one brown eye? Sounds very unusual to me," George commented. "Like a villain from a romance novel."

"Or a hero," Bess put in. "Was he cute?"

Nancy laughed. "He was pretty good-looking but definitely older. Close to thirty, I'd say."

"Nancy! I hope Ned doesn't hear about this," George said in a mock disapproving voice. "I can't believe you're talking with strange older men in parking lots."

"Here comes a patrol car," Bess cut in, pointing toward the entrance to the mall parking lot. "Do you think they'll need us as witnesses or anything?"

"We should probably stick around, just in case," Nancy said. She threw a quick glance at Brenda, who was now regaling the crowd with a dramatic, blow-by-blow account of the crash. "If the police don't get any story besides Brenda's, poor Mrs. Keating might end up in prison for life!"

"I don't believe this," Nancy muttered to herself the following morning. She had gone out after breakfast to pick up a copy of *Today's Times*. Now, as she scanned the opening sentences of "Just Ask Brenda," her eyes widened in amazement. The column had certainly taken a turn for the dramatic since the day before.

Nancy's father Carson Drew had already left for his law office, but Hannah Gruen, the Drews' housekeeper, looked up from the plant she was repotting by the kitchen sink. A pleasant-faced middle-aged woman with graying brown hair and warm eyes, she had lived with the Drews since shortly after the death of Nancy's mother, when Nancy was

three. "What don't you believe?" Hannah asked.

Nancy was about to read to her from Brenda's column when the doorbell rang. "I'll get it," she offered. Still holding her copy of *Today's Times,* Nancy went to the foyer.

"Hi, beautiful," a warm male voice greeted her after she threw open the front door.

"Ned!" Nancy's heart leapt with pleasure as she took in her boyfriend's tall, broad-shouldered frame and handsome face. "What are you doing here? Aren't you supposed to be working?"

"I am working," Ned replied, stepping inside. "I had to come into River Heights to pick up some papers, but they won't be ready for another half hour. So I thought I'd come visit my favorite detective. Hey, don't I get a kiss?"

In answer Nancy put the paper down on the hall table and threw her arms around Ned's neck. "You asked for it," she warned, then gave him a warm, lingering kiss.

"Mmm. How about seconds?" he murmured when their lips finally parted.

Nancy ruffled his brown hair and chided, "Don't be greedy!" Then she picked up the newspaper and led the way into the living room.

"What's going on? You don't usually read that rag, do you?" Ned asked, catching sight of the *Today's Times* logo.

"Not usually," Nancy agreed. "But Brenda Carlton has a new column, and I wanted to check it out. Here, take a look." She handed Ned the paper, still opened to Brenda's column, and pulled him down beside her on the couch.

He glanced at it briefly. "What is this, some kind of advice column?"

"Uh-huh," Nancy told him, nodding. "The previous column I read was pretty silly stuff, but this one seems to be spiced up with some 'creative' writing."

Nancy told him about running into Brenda and how Bess had teased her about the column being a little dull. "She got mad and hinted that things were going to get more exciting soon. Lo and behold, the first letter in her column today is from a girl who thinks her mother is going insane. And listen to the second one!"

She took the paper back from Ned and read, "'Dear Brenda, I turn to you in fear and desperation. Please help me. I think my husband is trying to kill me!'"

"What?" Ned exclaimed, alarm in his brown eyes.

Nancy read on.

"It started several weeks ago, when I opened a kitchen cabinet and a heavy silver platter fell from the top shelf and just missed

my head. I don't usually keep the silver in that cabinet! What if he put it there hoping it would fall and kill me?

"A week later I was climbing a ladder to prune our apple tree, and my foot slipped on one of the metal rungs. I nearly fell. When I checked the rung, I found it was covered with grease!

"Two days ago I went out to the garage and found my husband under my car with a pair of pliers in his hand. He says he was adjusting the steering, but I'm not sure I believe him. I haven't driven my car since, and I know he wonders why.

"Brenda, I don't know why he's doing this, but I'm sure my suspicions of him are right. I have no one else to turn to. Tell me what to do!

"Desperate."

"I see what you mean," Ned said slowly. "She definitely could have made up something like this. So what's her advice?"

"It's not very good, in my opinion. She tells Desperate to sit tight and do nothing." Nancy pursed her lips. "My advice in this situation would be to tell the woman to go to the police."

Ned gave her a probing look. "But I thought you said you didn't think this letter was real?"

Nancy pressed her lips together. "It would be pretty sleazy—even for Brenda—to lie

about something as serious as murder," she said after a moment. "But I guess I wouldn't put it past her. In fact, I think I know where Brenda got the idea for the last part of the letter—the bit about the car, I mean." Nancy told him about the accident in the mall parking lot.

"Brenda was in a fender bender, huh?" Ned remarked.

Nancy nodded. "And Mrs. Keating—the woman in the other car—claimed her brakes weren't working properly," she explained. "I'll bet you anything that's what gave Brenda the idea about the husband sabotaging the car."

"I don't want to bet," Ned said, grinning at her. "I'm sure you're right. Now, stop thinking like a detective for a second and tell me about tonight."

"Okay." Nancy told Ned about the barbecue she'd planned for before the concert.

"So you and I are playing matchmaker, eh?" Ned said. "Sounds like fun!" Glancing at his watch, he added, "Hey, I've got to go. My half hour is almost up." He got to his feet. "Listen, I'll see you tonight."

"I'll be counting the hours, dahling," Nancy said, waggling her eyebrows at him. Then she jumped up and planted a quick kiss on his lips.

"You're a lunatic," Ned said affectionately.

After he left, Nancy spent a couple of hours making potato salad and marinating chicken for the barbecue. Then, at noon, she headed

over to the mall to meet George and Bess for some last-minute accessory shopping before the concert.

"What are you going to wear tonight, Nan?" George asked as they walked down the mall concourse.

"I think my aqua dress—you know, the one with the palm trees and flamingoes on it," Nancy replied. "I'd like to find some really fun earrings to go with it, too."

"Let's go to Zigzag," Bess suggested. "They have the best jewelry."

As they approached the little store, Nancy was surprised to see a familiar dark-haired figure moving toward them. "Brenda Carlton—two days in a row," she murmured. "Just our luck."

"Hello, you three," Brenda called. She stepped around the scaffolding in the middle of the concourse and gave it a disapproving glare. "Seen the newspapers this morning?" she chirped.

"If you mean, did we read your column, I did," Nancy replied.

"So did I," Bess spoke up. A troubled expression crossed her face. "Are you sure you gave that woman the right advice, Brenda? I mean, if her husband really is trying to kill her, wouldn't it be wiser for her to go to the police?"

Brenda couldn't keep the satisfied smile off her face. "That shows what you know," she

said smugly. "Going to the police wouldn't help anything. I'm handling it."

"Oh," Bess said in an uncertain voice.

"Bess is right," Nancy declared. "If someone came to me with a problem like that, I'd definitely tell her to go to the police." She studied Brenda silently. "On the other hand, *I* don't have a newspaper column to spice up."

Brenda's nostrils flared with anger. "Just what are you trying to say?"

"You tell me," Nancy said evenly.

Suddenly Brenda tossed her head. "You're just jealous because my client didn't come to you, Nancy." She drew herself up haughtily. "If you must know, in tomorrow's column I'm going to tell this woman to get in touch with me. *I'll* get to the bottom of this case. After all, it's the least I can do—the woman asked for my help."

Then Brenda whirled around and marched away.

Staring after her, Nancy said, "I shouldn't have baited her. Now she's going to use her column to prove how great she is at solving a problem, which she probably made up in the first place. This whole dumb thing could go on forever."

"Nancy," Bess began, obviously troubled. "What if Brenda didn't make up that letter? It sounded real to me, and—well, she could really do something to make things worse for that woman."

"That's a pretty scary thought," Nancy agreed. "But think about it. It just seems like too much of a coincidence that you were teasing Brenda about how dull her column was only yesterday, and today—"

She never got to finish her sentence because at that moment, she heard a man cry, "Look out!"

Nancy spun, instantly alert. About fifty yards away Brenda was standing by the metal scaffolding in the middle of the main concourse. She was staring up, her face pale as death. She seemed to be frozen with fear.

A massive wooden beam had apparently slid off the workmen's platform, four stories above —and was hurtling straight at Brenda!

Chapter Four

BRENDA!" NANCY SHOUTED. She sprinted forward, but as she moved, she knew she didn't have a chance of getting to Brenda before the beam struck.

Nancy's voice must have awakened Brenda from her trance, though. Suddenly the young reporter gave a shrill scream and threw herself backward. A split second later the beam crashed down with a deafening clatter and bounced on the marble floor—right where she had been standing.

Nancy raced to Brenda's side. "Are you all right?" she asked breathlessly.

Brenda was unable to speak. She only nodded, her teeth chattering and her dark eyes round as two buttons. Nancy followed Brenda's horrified gaze to the beam, and her

breath caught in her throat. The four-inch-thick plank was cracked along its entire length from the fall. There was no way Brenda would have survived being struck by it!

"I saw it," Nancy heard someone say. She raised her eyes to see a woman in a baker's cap and apron. "I was standing right over there behind the counter, and I saw the whole thing." The woman shook a finger at Brenda. "You're lucky to be alive!"

Bess and George had rushed over right behind Nancy, and a few other people were coming over to see what was wrong. Bess put an arm around Brenda, who looked as if she might faint.

"Whew," George said softly to Nancy, glancing at the fallen beam. "If that thing had hit Brenda . . ."

Nancy nodded gravely. "It was close," she said. Her gaze traveled up the sides of the scaffold to the platform at the top. It appeared to be deserted. Nancy checked her watch. One o'clock—the workers were probably at lunch.

"If there's no one up there, how did the beam fall?" she wondered aloud.

Nancy heard Brenda draw in her breath sharply. Looking over, she saw two spots of color flaming in Brenda's pale cheeks.

"You don't look well," George told her.

"Maybe I should call an ambulance," the woman from the bakery offered.

"An ambulance?" Brenda's voice was shaky,

but she managed a scornful laugh. "I think you'd better call the police."

Bess frowned. "Police?" she said. "Surely for an accident like this—"

"Accident!" Brenda shrieked, twisting away from Bess. "You *would* think it was an accident. Well, it wasn't, let me tell you. Someone just tried to kill me!"

"What?" Nancy's jaw dropped. "Brenda, what are you saying?"

The reporter's dark eyes glittered. "Isn't it obvious?" she retorted. "I'm talking about my column. Someone clearly doesn't want me to be in touch with that woman. The person must know I'm about to uncover the truth!"

"How do you figure that? Did you see someone up there?" Nancy asked dubiously.

"No," Brenda said with an impatient flick of her fingers. "I was just minding my own business and—wham!"

"How could anyone have dropped that beam on you?" Nancy asked. "There was no one up there to drop it."

"Exactly," said Brenda triumphantly. "The perfect alibi—or so the murderer thinks." She pointed dramatically at the platform. "That board should be dusted for fingerprints. I want to talk to the mall manager, and then I want to talk to the police. This was a deliberate attempt on my life, and I want them to do something about it."

Nancy suppressed a groan. Leaning close to

Bess and George, she whispered, "I think what we're seeing here is an attempt to get some free publicity for Brenda's column."

"You mean she's making up all that stuff about someone wanting to kill her?" Bess demanded, sounding outraged.

Nodding, Nancy said, "I think so. I'm going to ask around, but I doubt anyone saw anything—there probably wasn't anything suspicious to see."

Sure enough, none of the people the girls questioned had noticed anything unusual. Nancy even tracked down some of the construction workers and talked to the manager. By the time the police arrived and Brenda began her story again, Nancy was completely fed up.

"Come on, let's get out of here," she said to Bess and George.

The three girls were turning to leave when Nancy's eye was caught by an amazingly good-looking young man in the crowd around Brenda. The guy was well over six feet tall, with a mane of unruly blond hair and piercing green eyes. He was staring at Brenda as if he were seeing a ghost.

Nancy stopped short. What's the matter with that guy? she wondered with a prickle of unease.

Almost as if he sensed her gaze, the guy turned and stared directly at Nancy. A deep

flush spread over his tanned face. He quickly averted his eyes and hurried away, pushing through the crowd.

"Boy, this is my week for spotting faces in the crowd," Nancy mumbled. She gestured with her head at the young man, who was just turning for a last look at Brenda. "Now, *he* looks like a guy with a guilty conscience."

"He just looks gorgeous to me," Bess said appreciatively. "If you want to follow him, Nan, I'm game."

Nancy and George broke into a laugh. "Thanks. I'm sure you're offering only out of the goodness of your heart," Nancy teased.

"What about David Park?" George asked. "Yesterday he was your idea of a total dream."

Bess's blue eyes sparkled with mischief as she retorted, "So I have a lot of dreams. Come on, let's go home and get ready for tonight."

"Wow, you look fantastic!" Ned exclaimed when he arrived at the Drews' that evening. His brown eyes held a warm glow of admiration.

Nancy pirouetted in front of him. The silky skirt of her dress flared out around her slender legs in a riot of bright, tropical colors. "Like it?"

"I love it," Ned said, pulling her into his arms for a kiss. "I just hope Dave and Jonathan aren't as dazzled as I am. After all, they're

supposed to be with Bess and George. So how was your day?"

"Very weird." Nancy told him about the incident with Brenda at the mall. "So now she's going around saying someone is trying to kill her," she concluded. "Can you believe it?"

Ned shrugged. "Maybe someone *is* trying to kill her."

"I don't think so," she said. "I mean, I actually asked around, just in case, but no one saw anything."

"Are you sure?" Ned asked, his eyes gleaming mischievously. "Someone might want revenge for the advice Brenda gave in her column."

"Hey, I never thought of that," Nancy said, giggling. "You could be right."

The front bell rang, and Nancy opened the door to let Bess and George in. Bess looked terrific in her new, thigh-length dusky pink blouse with a pair of white leggings underneath. George wore a black sleeveless blouse and a black miniskirt with chunky gold earrings.

"Wow! You guys are really dressed to kill," Ned said when he saw them. "Those guys don't stand a chance!"

Jonathan and David arrived soon after. Nancy had already started the coals, and before long the six were sitting on the back porch, their plates piled high with food.

"Well, the tornadoes seem to have held off,"

David commented as he took a second drumstick from the platter on the table.

"Keep your fingers crossed," Bess said. She spooned more potato salad onto David's plate and flashed him a dazzling smile.

Nancy peeked discreetly at George and Jonathan, who were sitting a little apart. George leaned forward, her dark eyes sparkling as she nodded agreement to something Jonathan was saying.

"Pretty good matchmaking, Drew," Ned whispered in her ear.

"I am the best. Aren't I?" Nancy whispered back.

The sun was just setting when they headed over to the lake. Nancy and Ned drove in his green Chevy, while the others went in David's car.

"We've still got about forty-five minutes before Ice Planet starts playing," Jonathan said after they met up in the parking lot. "Just enough time to get a soda and find a spot to sit."

They had almost reached the refreshment stand when Nancy felt a tug on her arm. "Hey, there's Brenda," Bess said. "She doesn't seem to be with anyone—do you think she came alone?"

Nancy followed Bess's gaze over to where Brenda was standing by herself. She looked very pretty in a white jumpsuit, but she seemed to be very uncomfortable.

"Seems that way. She looks lonely," Nancy said. Sighing, she added, "I'll probably regret this, but I'm going to ask her to join us."

Threading her way through the crowd of fans, Nancy tapped Brenda on the shoulder. "Hi," she said. "Have you recovered from this afternoon?"

"Oh—hi." Brenda seemed taken aback. "Yes, I'm fine."

"Did the police find any prints on that beam or on the scaffolding?" Nancy asked politely.

Brenda flushed. "No," she admitted.

Nancy just nodded. Brenda already looked embarrassed about the fuss she had made at the mall. It would be mean to rub her nose in it, though, so all Nancy said was, "I'm here with a bunch of people. Do you want to join us?"

Brenda was obviously torn between suspicion and eagerness. "Well, maybe for a little while," she said at last, making it sound as if she were doing Nancy a big favor.

The reporter followed Nancy back to Ned and the others, but it seemed to Nancy that she was distracted. Brenda hardly joined in the conversation, and she kept peering around at the crowd. Finally she murmured an excuse and wandered away, heading closer to the open-air stage.

"Was it my perfume?" George joked, nodding her head after Brenda.

"Oh, well, we tried," Nancy said, shrugging.

Just then she stiffened. "Look!" she cried, gripping George's arm. "It's the guy I saw at the mall this afternoon."

"The one Bess thought was cute?" George asked.

Nancy nodded distractedly, her eyes still on the tall stranger. He seemed to be strolling aimlessly—but Nancy noticed that his circular path was taking him closer and closer to Brenda Carlton.

Now, why is he following Brenda? Nancy asked herself. She didn't like what she was thinking, but she couldn't avoid the thought. Brenda had already had one narrow escape that day—and the tall stranger had been there when it happened.

It seemed farfetched, but what if this guy was responsible? Was it possible that he was planning to cause *another* "accident"?

Chapter Five

IN A FLASH Nancy made up her mind. It would be better to make a fool of herself and be wrong than to let something terrible happen to Brenda.

"I'll be right back," she said over her shoulder to the others. Then, without waiting for an answer, she strode purposefully after the tall blond guy.

Within seconds she was in the thick of the crowd that was drifting toward the stage. The sun had set, and with only the last vestiges of daylight to help her, Nancy was having a hard time keeping sight of her quarry. Then, to make things worse, a big, beefy guy in a tank top stepped in front of her, blocking her view completely.

"Excuse me, please," she said, but he didn't seem to hear her. "Uh—excuse me," she

said again, in a louder voice. "Could I get by?"

"Huh?" The guy turned and broke into a wide smile as he saw Nancy. "Hey, what's your hurry, Red? You here alone?" he asked.

Nancy frowned and tried to get around him, but he moved to block her way. "My name's Al," he said. "You're cute."

Nancy could hardly contain her impatience. "My name is Nancy," she told him. "I'm in a real hurry. And I'm here with my boyfriend. His name is Ned, but most people just call him Mad Dog."

Al's mouth fell open as he stepped aside.

Nancy hurried on, but to her dismay she'd lost sight of the tall, blond guy. "Oh, no!" she muttered. He probably wasn't up to anything, she reminded herself. But what if she was wrong?

Maybe I should look for Brenda instead, Nancy reasoned. In that white jumpsuit she shouldn't be hard to spot.

Nancy pushed her way closer to the stage, her eyes darting over the growing crowd. The platform had been set up at one end of a grassy lawn enclosed by a split-rail fence and rimmed by a line of towering oak trees. The whole thing was about a hundred yards from the lakeshore. Nancy was almost to the fence when she spotted Brenda, standing alone by the gate. The reporter looked at her wristwatch once, then once again.

At almost the same instant Nancy's eye caught a flash of movement in the trees. A quick glance was enough to give her a good idea of who was lurking among the old oaks. She circled around to the side, her heart pounding.

She wasn't mistaken. The tall, blond stranger stood in the shadow of a massive tree, his hair a bright golden patch in the deepening evening gloom. The guy was definitely studying Brenda. If his intentions were good, why would he be hiding behind a tree?

I guess I might as well be direct, Nancy thought. Stepping quietly up behind the guy, she cleared her throat, causing the stranger to whirl around. He gaped at Nancy, his green eyes wide with alarm.

At his first move Nancy had tensed, ready to defend herself if necessary. Now she relaxed, but only slightly. He doesn't *look* dangerous, she thought. But she knew that didn't mean much—she had met plenty of criminals who had looked as harmless as this guy.

"Excuse me, but I saw you over here in the trees, and I thought you might be lost or something," she said. "Can I help you?"

"Oh, uh, thanks, th-that's very nice of you," the guy stammered. "The fact is, I'm new in town. Well, sort of new—that is, I'm not here permanently. I'm a college student. I'm just here for the summer, staying with my aunt and

uncle." He stopped talking abruptly, gave a nervous laugh, and held out his hand. "My name's Rick Waterston."

He's babbling, Nancy thought. What's he so nervous about? She decided to come right out and ask him what he was up to.

"I'm Nancy Drew," she said in a firm, matter-of-fact voice. "I saw you at the mall this afternoon, and you seemed very interested in my friend over there—" She gestured toward Brenda, who was still by the fence gate. "Or at least in the near-accident she had just had. And tonight I saw you following her. I'd like to know why."

Rick's eyes sharpened with interest. "You know her?" he asked quickly. "That's Brenda Carlton, isn't it?"

Folding her arms across her chest, Nancy stared at Rick and asked, "Why do you want to know?"

Rick hesitated for a moment and stared at the ground. "This is going to sound really weird," he began.

"Try me," Nancy offered.

"I need to talk to Brenda," Rick said. "When I saw her this afternoon at the mall, I thought I recognized her. I tried to talk to her there, only then that beam nearly fell on her, and with all the excitement I didn't have a chance. So I left a message at the newspaper she writes a column for and asked her to meet me."

"What do you want to talk to her about?" Nancy pressed.

Rick hesitated again, raking a hand through his thick blond hair. "It's her column," he said at last. "See, there was this letter in it this morning, and my aunt and uncle—well, they haven't been getting along very well lately, and in the last couple of weeks I've noticed some weird things. . . ." Rick trailed off.

Nancy couldn't believe what she was hearing. "Wait a minute. Are you saying your aunt—" she began, but she was interrupted by a shout.

"Nan! There you are. I've been looking everywhere for you."

It was Ned. "Oh, hi," she greeted him distractedly, then introduced him to Rick.

"Nice to meet you," Ned said. He turned back to Nancy. "What's with the disappearing act? The concert's about to start."

Nancy glanced quickly at Rick. "I, uh—I needed to talk to Rick," she said. "He was just telling me something very interesting about his aunt and uncle." Speaking directly to Rick, she added, "I'd like to hear the rest of your story."

But Ned's presence seemed to have put a damper on Rick's willingness to talk. "Oh, it's nothing—it's dumb," he mumbled. "Look, I've got to be going. It was nice meeting both of you."

"Wait," Nancy said. But Rick was already

gone, hurrying along with the crowd that was settling in on the lawn in front of the stage.

Ned looked at her questioningly. "What was that all about?"

"I'm not sure," Nancy said thoughtfully. She told Ned about seeing Rick at the mall, spotting him following Brenda, and then his story about Brenda's column. "But the guy just clammed up the minute you came along," she finished. "I wonder if he was really trying to tell me he thinks his aunt wrote that letter to Brenda?"

Ned turned as the sound of clapping and whistling broke out. "Well, let's not talk about it now. Ice Planet must be getting ready to come onstage. Come on." He grabbed Nancy's hand and pulled her toward the stage. "The others went ahead to scout out a good spot for us, but if we don't get a move on, we'll never find them."

"Okay, okay," Nancy said, hurrying to keep up with him. As they entered the grassy enclosure and picked their way through the crowd, she craned her neck trying to spot Rick or Brenda, but neither was in sight.

The band launched into its first number, just as Ned and Nancy found the blanket their friends had spread out on the grass. Bess scooted over to make room on the blanket for Nancy and Ned.

Ice Planet was one of Nancy's favorite groups, and she began bobbing her head in

time to the music. Even so, her thoughts kept returning to what Rick had started to tell her.

Was there really a woman in River Heights who was afraid her husband was trying to kill her? Did that person really try to kill Brenda? Unless Rick had made up what he'd told Nancy—and she didn't know why he would—it was beginning to look as if maybe Brenda *hadn't* made up that letter in her column.

I've got to find out the truth, Nancy thought, because if this woman does exist, then she needs help. And Brenda is putting both herself and the woman in even more danger by publishing those letters and telling the letter writer not to do anything.

"Hey, Nancy, wake up," George scolded. "The concert's over."

"Huh?" Nancy said, blinking. "That was kind of short, wasn't it?"

"They played for over an hour," George informed her, giving her a quizzical look. "They even did that great long version of 'Frozen Out.' Weren't you listening?"

"I guess I was a little bit out of it," Nancy admitted sheepishly.

"Uh-oh," said Bess, leaning around David's shoulder. "I smell a mystery."

Nancy wasn't sure there *was* a mystery, but she wanted to find out if there was before anyone got hurt.

As they were walking back toward the parking lot, Nancy kept an eye out for Rick. They

were almost back to Ned's car when she finally spotted him. He was standing a few yards away, by a parked van—and he was talking to Brenda.

Nancy paused to take in the scene. Rick was leaning forward, an intent expression on his face as he spoke. Brenda, her back against the van, was gazing up into his eyes with an intimate smile. As Nancy watched, Brenda placed her hand on Rick's arm.

That's funny, Nancy thought, her eyes narrowing. Rick had led her to think he'd never met Brenda—but that hardly looked like a conversation between two people who didn't know each other.

Nancy knew Brenda well enough to suspect the reporter would stretch the truth if it suited her. She didn't know anything at all about Rick, but she was beginning to get the feeling he hadn't been totally honest with her, either. In any case, Nancy was increasingly sure of one thing—both Rick and Brenda had something to hide.

Chapter Six

NANCY FROWNED at the couple. She had to find out once and for all if there really was a murder plot in the planning stage, or if Brenda and Rick were somehow in cahoots and making the whole thing up. She didn't know why Rick would get involved, but there was only one way to find out.

Twining her arm around Ned's waist, Nancy nodded in Rick and Brenda's direction and asked, "Why don't we walk over this way, Ned? I want to check something out."

Ned gave her a puzzled glance but agreed.

After saying good night to the others, Nancy and Ned strolled over to where Rick and Brenda were. Nancy leaned her head on Ned's shoulder, her eyes half-closed, a dreamy smile on her face. But her ears were wide open,

straining to catch Brenda and Rick's low-pitched conversation.

"I wish I could, but I can't give you a ride," Brenda was saying. "Daddy is sending his driver to pick me up, and the guy is under orders to take me straight home. Daddy's worried about me, after what happened at the mall today."

Rick's reply was too quiet for Nancy to hear, but apparently it pleased Brenda. She giggled. "That's so sweet of you," she cooed.

"Uh-oh," Ned whispered. "Rick really seems to be fooled by Brenda's sweet act."

"Shh!" Nancy whispered back, stifling a laugh. "You're ruining my concentration."

Just then a long, sleek silver car pulled up beside Brenda.

"Here's my ride," Brenda said to Rick. Her voice sounded genuinely regretful, Nancy thought. "I guess I'd better say good night."

"Okay." Rick sounded hesitant. "Would you have lunch with me tomorrow?" he asked at last. "That is, if you're up to it."

Nancy sneaked a look at Brenda from under her lashes. Brenda's dark eyes were shining. "I'd love to," she said. "Call me at the paper in the morning. *Ciao!*"

With that she climbed into the back seat of the silver car. Before Brenda closed the car door, she caught Nancy's eye, and Nancy saw triumph in the look. Then the door closed, and the big sedan surged away.

Ned looked at Nancy. *"Ciao?"* he echoed in a dubious tone.

"Leave it to Brenda," Nancy said with a sigh of disappointment. She hadn't learned anything at all yet, though the look Brenda had given her made Nancy think *something* was up.

"Hey, look who's coming toward us," she murmured a moment later.

It was Rick. He approached them with a smile. "Hi," he said. "I'm glad to see a couple of familiar faces."

Nancy raised her eyebrows. It was a bit of a stretch to call her and Ned familiar.

"I was wondering," Rick went on smoothly. "I took a cab here tonight, and Brenda tells me it's hard to get a cab to come out here this late. Would it be too much trouble to give me a lift back to town?"

Nancy was puzzled. Why was he being so friendly now, when before he'd practically run away from them? She couldn't help wondering if this was part of some plan he and Brenda had hatched. What was his game?

Nancy was glad when Ned said, "Sure, no problem." He gestured down the row of cars to their right. "My Chevy's parked right over there."

Now, at least, she'd have a chance to dig deeper into Rick's story about his aunt being in danger. "So, Rick, you were telling me about your aunt and uncle before," Nancy said

casually as the three of them walked to Ned's car.

"Oh, right," Rick said. "Listen, forget about it. I shouldn't have been going on about their problems—it's really none of my business."

"You know, Nancy is a detective," Ned put in. They reached his car, and he unlocked it. "If you're really worried, talk to her. She can get to the bottom of anything."

"A detective? No kidding!" Rick exclaimed. From the too-bright tone of his voice, Nancy was almost positive Ned's comment wasn't news to him.

"Maybe you *can* help me," Rick said. He gave her a disarming grin. "Do you really want to hear my story?"

Nancy climbed into the passenger's seat. "Definitely," she said. He sounded as if he had rehearsed every word. This ought to be good! Nancy told herself.

Rick climbed into the back seat, and Ned slid in behind the wheel. A moment later he was pulling into the stream of traffic leaving the concert.

"I've always been close to my aunt," Rick began, leaning forward and resting his arms on the back of Nancy's bucket seat. "She's my godmother, too, and—well, several months ago she invited me to spend the summer with her and her new husband. But when I got here, he seemed very put out about my being here."

"You said he's your aunt's new husband?" Ned asked, glancing at Rick in the rearview mirror. "If they're newlyweds, maybe he just wants time to be alone with his bride."

Rick shook his head. "They're not newlyweds. I meant to say he's her *second* husband. They've been married over a year. No, he just doesn't want me around. I even heard them arguing about it one morning, when they thought I was still in bed. At one point Bi—my uncle said, 'Why did Rick have to come *now?*' "

Nancy was sure Rick had been about to say his uncle's name before he stopped himself. Why wouldn't he want her to know who his uncle was? Aloud, she asked, "What did your aunt say?"

"She didn't say anything," Rick answered. "She just burst into tears. She's been doing that a lot lately. And that's not like my aunt. She's usually a really fun-loving type."

"Mmm. Go on," Nancy prompted.

"Well, this morning we were having breakfast. My uncle had already left for work. My aunt was reading *Today's Times,* and suddenly she let out a funny little noise. She had turned totally white and appeared to be really shaken up." Rick blew out his breath. "I asked her what was wrong, but she wouldn't give me a straight answer. She gave me some line about how she'd been reading about tornadoes and how much they scared her. But I knew she was

lying, because *I* had the news section. She was reading Lifestyles."

"So later you checked out the Lifestyles section, and you saw the letter in Brenda's advice column from the woman who thinks her husband is trying to kill her," Nancy guessed.

Inwardly, she was thinking, Oh, you're good, Brenda. You actually convinced this guy to back up your claim about someone being in trouble. She still couldn't think of why Rick would go along with the story, though. Maybe he just had a crush on Brenda.

"Right," Rick was saying. "And I made a connection—" He broke off abruptly. "Wait, let me backtrack." His voice grew sober. "See, I wouldn't have thought anything about that letter, except that just yesterday my aunt was in a car accident. And the letter had something in it about the husband sabotaging the wife's car."

"But didn't the woman who wrote the letter say that she hasn't driven her car since she saw her husband tampering with it?" Ned pointed out, wheeling his Chevy into a right turn.

Rick shrugged and sat back. "Sure, but so what? That letter was probably written a few days ago. The accident was yesterday. Maybe something made her change her mind about driving.

"I wanted to see the letter Brenda got," Rick continued. "I called the newspaper office this

morning, and the receptionist told me Brenda had just left for the mall, so I went there to find her," Rick said. His voice grew sheepish. "The hardest part was getting up the nerve to approach her. A girl as gorgeous as Brenda—well, I was afraid she wouldn't even give me the time of day."

In the driver's seat Ned turned and raised his eyebrows at Nancy. Rick sure was laying it on thick. Brenda must have loved coaching him on this part of their story!

Rick leaned forward again. "I recognized Brenda from her picture in the paper. I was sort of following her when she stopped to talk to you, Nancy. Then the next thing I knew, she was practically killed by that beam, and Brenda was saying someone did it on purpose because of her column." He gave a little laugh. "Let me tell you, that really shook me up."

Turning in the front seat to look at Rick Nancy commented, "Well, you and Brenda seemed to hit it off tonight. Did she show you the letter?"

"Not yet," Rick admitted. "She has good reasons not to—she said it would be a violation of the writer's privacy, and it would compromise freedom of the press. But I'm still trying."

Nancy had to admit that Rick and Brenda had thought of all the angles. But it was suspicious that he hadn't actually mentioned names. "Rick, if you don't mind my asking,"

Nancy said, "don't you think you should go to the police with this information? What's your aunt's name, anyway?"

"Oh, you wouldn't know her," he said in a rush. Rick seemed immensely relieved when Ned broke into the conversation.

"Excuse me, Rick," said Ned. "Where should I drop you off?"

"The corner of Grange and Spruce," Rick said.

"It's no problem for us to take you right to your aunt's house," Ned protested.

Rick seemed a bit flustered. "No—no, really, it's not necessary. Grange and Spruce is just fine. Really."

"Okay," Ned agreed, shrugging. "Whatever."

A moment later, following Rick's directions, Ned pulled over at the intersection of Grange and Spruce, and Rick climbed out of the back seat. After thanking Nancy and Ned, he walked off into the darkness.

"Hmm," Nancy mumbled as she gazed around. "Recognize this neighborhood, Ned?"

He peered through the windshield to where the headlights illuminated a big stone house. "Looks pretty ritzy."

"It is," Nancy informed him. "And it just so happens Brenda Carlton's house is only about a block away."

Ned whistled. "Hey. Are you saying Rick is on his way to see Brenda right now?"

"I wouldn't be surprised," Nancy said. She crossed her arms and frowned out into the night. "You know what? I think Brenda is using this guy Rick as part of some kind of campaign to convince the world—or me, at least—that the letter in this morning's column was serious."

"You mean he's lying about his aunt?"

"I think so," Nancy said uncertainly. Shrugging, she added, "Rick seems to have a crush on Brenda. She could be using that to get him to feed us this whole story. It's—"

Nancy was interrupted by a shout, followed by the echoing sound of rapid footsteps on pavement. Peering out her window, she saw a muscular man of medium height dash through the beams of the headlights. Close on his heels was a taller figure.

"It's Rick!" Nancy exclaimed, recognizing the second figure.

The shorter man was faster than Rick. He raced forward and snapped his head back briefly to check out his pursuer.

Nancy gasped when she saw his face. It was the man she'd seen the day of the car accident—the guy with the mismatched eyes!

Chapter Seven

In a moment he was gone, swallowed up in the darkness of the tree-lined street. Rick continued to tear after him.

"Ned, I've seen that guy before!" Nancy cried, jumping out of the car. "He was in the mall parking lot the day Brenda had her accident."

Ned climbed out of the car, too, and came around to stand by Nancy. "So what does that mean?" he asked, looking baffled.

Just then Rick reappeared and crossed the street toward Ned's car. He was frowning, and his face was shiny with sweat. "I lost him," he panted. Bracing his hands against the hood of the car, he bent over, inhaling deeply.

"Rick, what happened?" Nancy asked urgently.

"I saw that guy prowling around my aunt and uncle's house," Rick replied. He straightened up indignantly. "I'd better go call the cops."

Nancy laid a hand on Rick's arm as he was turning to go. "Did you get a good look at him?" she asked. "The police will need a description."

"I only saw him from the back," Rick said, shaking his head.

"Well, I saw him," Nancy told him. "He shouldn't be too hard to spot—he's unusual looking. He has one blue eye and one brown eye."

At her last words Rick blinked, and a wary expression spread over his face. Nancy had the distinct impression that her description rang a bell with Rick. "Do you know anyone like that?" she asked him.

"Uh—no," Rick said quickly.

Why was he lying? "Maybe I should be there when you talk to the police," Nancy pressed. "I seem to be the only witness who actually saw the man's face."

"I don't want to put you out. In fact, maybe I shouldn't go to the police. The guy is probably long gone by now, and it would only scare my aunt if she knew he'd been around." Rick had suddenly become nervous and in a hurry to leave. "Well, good night and thanks again."

Back in the car Ned turned to Nancy. "What do you think made him change his mind about

going to the police?" he asked. "That was weird."

"I thought so, too," Nancy agreed. "He seemed to recognize the man's description, but he sure wasn't about to tell us who it was."

Whatever Ned was about to say was interrupted by a tremendous yawn. "I'm beat. I'd better get you home," he said. "Why is it that so many of my dates with you turn into major adventures?"

"I just like to keep you on your toes, Nickerson," Nancy retorted playfully.

As they drove the short distance to the Drews' house, questions whirled dizzily in Nancy's mind. Who was the man with the different-colored eyes? Did Rick really have an aunt? And if so, who was she? Was her husband trying to kill her? Had she really written a letter to Brenda's column? Or were Rick and Brenda trying to pull a hoax?

Suddenly Nancy found herself yawning, too. I'll get a good night's rest, she thought to herself, and tomorrow I'll start digging out the real story behind the letter in Brenda's column!

Nancy glanced out the window of her second-floor bedroom, toweling her hair dry after her morning shower. Heat was already rising in shimmering waves from the shingles of the porch roof. It was going to be another scorcher.

After putting on a pair of shorts and a maroon T-shirt, she went out to her Mustang and drove to pick up a copy of *Today's Times.* When she returned, her father was seated in the dining room, eating a breakfast of French toast, juice, and coffee. He greeted Nancy with a smile that crinkled the corners of his dark eyes.

In contrast to Nancy's reddish hair, Carson Drew's was dark brown, though it was now flecked with silver at his temples. His face was square, while Nancy's was a delicate oval. But both father and daughter had the same straight nose—and the same gleam of intelligence and determination in their eyes.

"Morning, Dad," Nancy said cheerfully, setting the paper on the table as she sat down. "I hope you saved me some breakfast."

"There's a stack of French toast in the warming dish," Carson answered, pointing to a covered dish on the table. "And there's bacon and melon slices. Hannah's out doing errands, but she made sure we wouldn't starve."

Nancy helped herself. "You must be busy—you've been at the office late a lot this week."

"I've been swamped." Looking over his coffee cup at her, Carson said, "As a matter of fact, I have to ask a favor. I need a cashier's check from my bank, but I can't get there today—I've got meetings until six o'clock tonight. Would you mind going for me?"

Nancy shook her head. "No problem."

"Thanks." Carson pushed his chair back and stood up. "I've got to get going. I'll call you from the office and let you know the exact sum."

Nancy blew him a kiss. Then she opened her copy of *Today's Times* and turned to Brenda's column.

"Wow," she muttered. Brenda hadn't printed any letters that day. Instead, the entire column was a dramatic plea to the woman who was afraid her husband was trying to murder her.

"Please contact me!" the column trumpeted in big letters. "You can't survive this terrible crisis alone. You need the help of a sensitive, intelligent, resourceful person. I am that person, but you have to come to me."

"Oh, brother," Nancy muttered out loud. Brenda was really coming on strong.

Setting the paper back down on the table, Nancy thought through her plans for that day. After she went to the bank, she'd go to the paper to see if she could get her hands on the letter that woman had supposedly written. It was definitely time to get to the bottom of this.

"You'll have to get an approval from the bank manager, miss." The teller raised her eyebrows apologetically at Nancy. "I'm not authorized to dispense that kind of cash."

Letting out a sigh, Nancy thanked the teller

and headed for the manager's office. The office door was open, and Nancy could see a stocky man with gray hair cut short in military style behind the desk.

It was just her luck that he was busy with another customer. She'd already waited in line for twenty minutes, but she had no choice but to take a seat and wait some more.

After a few minutes she began to get impatient. The bank manager didn't seem to be in any great hurry. In fact, he and his customer seemed to be swapping war stories!

"And frankly, Bill, I was *scared,*" the customer was saying. "But I crawled on my belly until I reached the arsenal, and then I pulled out my last grenade and chucked it in. And then I ran. Brother, those were some fireworks!"

The bank manager chuckled. "I'll bet. Say, did I ever tell you about the time I blew up a convoy of enemy supply trucks in a tunnel?"

Ugh, what a gruesome conversation! Nancy shifted uncomfortably on the hard plastic seat outside the office.

"It was so simple, it was beautiful," the manager declared. "The tunnel had been sealed at one end by a rock slide. It was a protected location, in the heart of a mountain —impossible to bomb, and so deep in enemy territory they never thought they'd have to worry about security."

Nancy was trying not to get annoyed. She'd

heard of good customer relations, but this was carrying it a bit far.

"I parachuted in at night," the manager was saying, "and slipped into the tunnel before the convoy arrived. I planted a bottle of ether at the sealed end. Then I went to the open end, lit a candle, and left. A few hours later the ether fumes reached the candle flame, and—boom!"

Nancy began tapping her foot against the carpeted floor, letting her gaze roam around the manager's office. Suddenly she sat up straighter in her chair as she read the name-plate on his desk. William A. Keating.

Wait a second— Could he be related to Maggie Keating, the woman who'd crashed into Brenda at the mall? It wasn't a very common name; it made sense that they could be related.

Then another idea hit Nancy. The previous night Rick had cut himself off in the middle of saying his uncle's name. He'd said "Bi—" and then changed it to "my uncle." What if he had been about to say "Bill"? As in Bill *Keating?*

Nancy's eyes widened. If Mr. Keating was Rick's uncle, and Mrs. Keating was Rick's aunt, and she had had a car accident . . .

Could it be that Rick's story was true and the letter was genuine? Could Maggie Keating have written it? Could the bank manager be a killer?

"Can I help you?"

Nancy came out of her thoughts with a start to see Mr. Keating in the doorway, beckoning to her. His other customer had gone.

Nancy managed a smile. "Sure." She handed him her withdrawal slip and asked him to approve it.

Just then the speaker phone on Keating's desk buzzed.

"Excuse me." Leaning over the intercom speaker, he said, "Yes?"

"Mr. Keating, the auditors want to move the inspection up to next Monday. Will that be all right with you?" inquired a tinny voice.

"Monday? What was wrong with Wednesday?" Keating asked sharply.

"I don't know, sir," the voice replied.

Keating frowned. "All right, fine. Make it Monday." The intercom clicked off.

Keating looked up at Nancy. "Excuse the interruption," he said, smiling. He scrawled his initials on the slip and handed it to her. "There you are, young lady. Have a nice afternoon."

"Thanks," Nancy told him. "You, too."

Nancy could barely bring herself to wait for the teller to make out the cashier's check. When she finally got it, she drove it over to her father's law firm. He was between meetings, so she took it into his office herself.

"Thanks," her father said when she handed him the draft. "Did you have any trouble?"

"Not really, but I had to get an approval from Mr. Keating, the bank manager." Nancy sank into a red leather chair by her father's desk. "Dad, what do you know about him?"

"Who? Keating?" Carson asked, sounding surprised. "Not much. Why?"

Nancy briefly told him all that had been happening the past few days, and about the possible connection she'd just made between the Keatings and the letters in Brenda's column.

"I'd hate to think Maggie could be in any trouble," Carson said when Nancy had finished, a frown creasing his forehead. "She's a fine person, used to be married to a lawyer I knew, Wilford Trout. He passed away about five years ago, and last year Maggie married Keating."

Leveling a serious look at his daughter, Carson went on. "I have to admit I don't know much about Bill. He hasn't been in town long—the bank brought him in from Chicago several years ago.

"I hear he's a bit of a high roller, though. Some of the bank's directors feel his investment policies are risky." He shrugged. "That's all I know."

"All?" Nancy cried. "Dad, you're amazing!" Thinking out loud, she added, "I doubt Mr. Keating would want to kill his wife just to get back at her for not being wealthy. So what's his

motive?" She drummed her fingers on the chair arm, deep in thought, then snapped up straight and said, "Unless he's going to *get* money by murdering her—insurance money, for instance."

Carson leaned forward. "Nancy, this could be serious. Don't you think it's a matter for the police?"

"So far I'm just guessing, Dad. I'm not even sure Mrs. Keating really is Rick's aunt or that she's the woman who wrote the letter to Brenda." Nancy jumped to her feet. "But I'm definitely going to find out."

Nancy swung her Mustang right onto the street where the Keatings lived and started scanning the numbers for 357, the address she'd found in the phone book. She located it just down the street from the corner where she and Ned had dropped Rick off after the concert the night before.

Well, at least Rick wasn't lying about where his aunt lives—if Mrs. Keating really is his aunt, Nancy reminded herself.

At first Nancy saw only the long, sloping lawn edged with tall, leafy trees. It wasn't until after she turned into the driveway that the house came into view. Set back from the street, it was large and ornately Victorian, with round turrets, lots of gingerbread woodwork, and a sloping roof over the porch.

Nancy didn't see any cars in the driveway, but then Mrs. Keating's sedan was probably in the shop after her accident with Brenda. After braking her own car to a stop, Nancy got out, went to the front door, and rang the bell.

When the door opened, Nancy saw that Mrs. Keating still appeared to be distraught and that there were dark circles under her eyes.

"Mrs. Keating," Nancy began, "you may not remember me, but I was at the mall when you had your accident the day before yesterday. I'm Nancy Drew."

"Yes, of course," Mrs. Keating said, without smiling. She reached up with one hand and nervously patted her ash blond hair. "Is there some problem?"

Nancy wanted to clear one thing up right away. "I'm a friend of your nephew's—"

Mrs. Keating's expression brightened slightly as she said, "Rick? Well, I'm afraid he's not here at the moment. Now, if you'll excuse me—"

She began to close the door, but Nancy stuck out her hand to hold it open. "Mrs. Keating, please. I'd like to talk to you about the accident. Rick seemed very worried, and I—"

"Please! There's nothing to say." Mrs. Keating was visibly shaken by Nancy's insistence, but then slowly she got her feelings under control. "I'm sorry," she went on in a calmer voice, "but I'm late for an appointment. Now,

goodbye." With that she closed the door in Nancy's face.

Shaking her head, Nancy walked back to her car. Whatever Mrs. Keating was nervous about, she wasn't about to fill Nancy in on it. So now what?

After driving home, Nancy phoned Ned at work.

"Hi, it's me," she said into the receiver when he answered. "Will you do me a big favor?"

"If I can," Ned answered. "What's up?"

"I need information on someone who may be a client of Mutual Life," Nancy told him.

"I can't give you information about policy-holders," Ned protested. "It's confidential. I could get fired for doing that."

"I know, and I hate to ask," Nancy replied. "But this is important." Quickly she explained her idea about Mrs. Keating being the letter writer. "I need to find out what kind of life insurance Mrs. Keating has. If it's enough to kill for . . ."

"Then she's in trouble," Ned finished. "Okay. I'll see what I can find out."

Five minutes later he called her back. "She is one of our clients, all right. I had to go into the mainframe computer files to check out her coverage," he reported. "That's where the big-ticket policies are maintained."

"Big-ticket?" Nancy repeated. "What's that?"

"Any coverage over two hundred thousand

dollars," Ned said. "Mrs. Keating's policy has only been in the big-ticket file for six months."

Nancy felt a rush of anticipation. "What does that mean?" she asked excitedly.

"It means that six months ago, Mrs. Keating's life insurance coverage jumped—to a cool million dollars!"

Chapter Eight

NANCY TIGHTENED HER GRIP on the receiver. "Ned, are you serious?" she gasped.

"You bet. Mrs. Keating has had a policy with us for almost ten years," he explained in a grim voice. "Her coverage was a hundred thousand dollars—until January. That was when Mr. Keating arranged for them both to receive much more substantial policies."

"Wow," Nancy murmured. She picked up the phone, carried it over to the sofa, and sat down. "I can't believe this. Maybe Brenda has stumbled onto a real case."

"And she's totally botching it up," Ned added. "We've got to do something, Nan."

Nancy thought for a second. "How about this?" she suggested, glancing at her watch. "It's four now. Can you leave work a little early?"

"I guess so," Ned replied after a moment.

"Great. Meet me here at my house. You and I are going to pay a little visit to Brenda." Nancy's brows drew together in a determined frown. "It's time we got a straight story from her."

"On my way, chief," Ned said, then hung up.

Nancy raised her eyes as Hannah bustled into the room. "I thought I heard you in here," the housekeeper said. "I just came in from the garden. My, but it's hot today! Come on into the kitchen and I'll fix us both some iced tea."

"Mmm, sounds good," said Nancy, following Hannah into the kitchen. Still deep in thought, she reached distractedly for two glasses and filled them with ice.

"By the way, Bess called while you were out," Hannah said, pouring tea into the glasses. "She wants you to call her back late tonight. She sounded very excited—said something about a date with someone named David."

"Hmm? Oh, that's nice," Nancy said vaguely.

"Let me guess—you've got a new mystery."

With a start Nancy realized that the housekeeper was peering at her closely. "You're right, Hannah. I guess you know me pretty well."

"I should say so!" Hannah replied firmly.

They sat down at the kitchen table, and Nancy told Hannah about the Keating case. As she was finishing, Ned arrived, flushed and scowling.

"The air conditioning in my old clunker is out," he said. "I'm just about roasted. Let's take your car, Nan."

"Sure," Nancy agreed, grinning as Ned downed in one giant gulp the glass of iced tea she had poured for him. She put both their glasses in the sink, then headed for the front door, calling over her shoulder, "I'll be home for dinner, Hannah."

They drove to the *Today's Times* offices, in downtown River Heights, only to be told by the receptionist that Brenda had left. Ten minutes later Nancy guided her blue Mustang up the Carltons' steep driveway.

"Here we are," Nancy announced. "Finally."

As the house came into view, Ned exclaimed, "Wow! I'd forgotten what a castle this place is."

The Carltons' enormous white house was perched on a knoll overlooking several acres of grounds. Manicured green lawns swept down to a high, well-trimmed hedge. Beyond the hedge a thick belt of trees all but hid the neighboring house, a huge brick mansion.

"It's pretty impressive," Nancy agreed. She steered her car into a gravel turnaround and parked. Then she and Ned got out, went up to

the pillared porch, and rang the doorbell. A uniformed maid answered.

"Hi," Nancy said. "We're friends of Brenda's. Is she home?"

"Miss Carlton is out by the pool," the maid replied. "May I tell her who's calling?"

"Oh, don't bother to announce us," Nancy said quickly. "We'd like to surprise her." She didn't want to give Brenda the chance to avoid them.

The maid hesitated briefly but then led them through the house and out a set of glass doors that opened onto a flagstone patio. "Right down those steps," she directed.

Brenda, clad in a white two-piece bathing suit decorated with long fringe, lay on a chaise longue by the kidney-shaped swimming pool. When she saw Nancy and Ned, her expression was anything but welcoming. "What do you want?" she demanded.

"Some answers," Nancy shot back.

"Hey!" a new voice broke in. Nancy turned and was surprised to see Rick Waterston emerging from the bathhouse, wearing a pair of swim trunks. "Hi!" he called, waving. "I didn't know you two were coming over. Did you bring your suits?" he asked.

Although she hadn't expected to see Rick, Nancy was glad for the chance to question them both. "We're just here for a moment," she told him. "May I ask you something?"

"Shoot," Rick replied, grinning easily.

"Why didn't you tell us Maggie Keating is your aunt?"

Rick's smile faded, and he sputtered, "How'd you know—hey! Has something happened to her?"

"Not that I know of," Nancy told him. After a short pause she added, "Not yet, anyway."

"What are you trying to say?" Rick asked.

Taking a deep breath, Nancy explained, "I'm saying that I believe your aunt is in serious danger from her husband. I'm sorry I doubted your story last night." She glanced at Brenda, who wore a look of blank surprise on her face. "But if we work together now, it may not be too late to save your aunt."

"Tell me what to do," Rick said instantly.

"Rick!" Brenda protested, jumping up from her lounge and going over to him. "Didn't I tell you I could handle it?"

"Yeah, but if Aunt Maggie really is in trouble, I'll take all the help I can get." Rick's voice was apologetic but firm.

Brenda opened her mouth to say something, but Rick put his hand gently over it. "Please."

To Nancy's amazement, Brenda subsided.

"Incredible!" Ned murmured. Brenda shot him a dirty look but remained quiet.

Nancy and Ned pulled up deck chairs and sat.

"Rick, why was it such a big deal for you to keep your aunt's identity a secret?" Nancy asked.

With an apologetic glance at Brenda, Rick said, "It was Brenda's idea. I just—"

"You don't have to go sticking your nose in every single case that comes along, Nancy," Brenda said hotly. "We were doing just fine on our own!"

Ignoring Brenda's outburst, Nancy asked Rick, "Can you add anything more to what you told us last night?"

Rick began pacing up and down by the edge of the pool. "Not a lot," he admitted, frowning. "All I have is a bunch of vague suspicions."

Nancy glanced at Brenda, half expecting her to interrupt again, but the reporter just stared sulkily. Turning back to Rick, Nancy urged, "Tell us about your uncle. What's he like?"

"Well," Rick said, pausing to look at her, "to be honest, no one in my family is too crazy about Uncle Bill. He's one of those gung-ho types. He used to be in the army, and he never stops talking about the service and all the incredible missions he was on. I think he probably exaggerates."

Nancy smiled slightly, thinking of the story she'd overheard in the bank earlier that day.

"Is he nice to your aunt?" Ned asked.

"I guess so," Rick replied, shrugging. "My mom thinks he married Aunt Maggie for her money, but I don't know about that. She isn't rich. Her first husband had some family money to start out with, I think, but by the time he

died, there wasn't much left. Uncle Wilford spent most of it on racehorses. The Trouts—that's Uncle Wilford's family—are famous for their expensive hobbies, and Aunt Maggie's a pretty big spender herself."

Rick gave a short laugh. "If Uncle Bill did marry her for her money, he must have been pretty disappointed."

I'll bet, Nancy thought.

"That's the thing I don't get," Rick went on. "Why would Uncle Bill want to kill her? If he's after a wife with money, why doesn't he just divorce Aunt Maggie?"

Nancy and Ned exchanged a knowing glance. Clearing his throat, Ned explained about Mr. Keating's increasing the insurance policy on Rick's aunt to a million dollars.

Rick drew in his breath in a shocked gasp. "Oh, no," he murmured, his face a ghostly white.

"We think he's after that million dollars," Nancy added. "But we need some hard evidence. Unless we can prove our suspicions to the authorities, we can't help your aunt." She leaned forward to take in Brenda.

"What are you staring at *me* for?" Brenda demanded hotly.

"You're the one who holds the key to this case," Nancy said. "The letter from Mrs. Keating. You have to show it to us."

Brenda glared. "No way! I can't reveal my

source," she protested. "It would ruin my reputation as a reporter."

"We already guessed who wrote the letter," Ned said angrily. "Besides, a woman's life is more important than your reputation as a reporter, Brenda. That letter is the only solid piece of evidence in this whole case. Without it the police won't even listen to us."

"But the letter was confidential," Brenda objected stubbornly.

"Please," Rick begged. He took Brenda's hands in his and stared into her eyes. "My aunt's life is at stake. I need your help."

Brenda looked torn but remained silent. Gazing at her, Nancy was struck with a sudden thought—one she didn't like at all.

"Brenda, when did you get the letter?" she asked.

Brenda flushed. "Tuesday," she said. "The day I had the accident at the mall."

"Morning or afternoon?" Nancy demanded quickly.

"Morning, I think," Brenda mumbled, looking flustered.

"What did it look like?"

"Wh-what do you mean?" Brenda stammered.

"What did it look like?" Nancy repeated. "Was it handwritten?"

"Yes—I mean no. It was typed."

Aha! That was Brenda's first slip. "How long

was it?" Nancy asked, continuing to grill the reporter.

"I don't remember." Brenda's voice was becoming shrill. "What does it matter? I don't like the third degree, Nancy!"

"You don't?" Nancy asked sharply. "Then show us the letter, Brenda."

"I can't show it to you," Brenda insisted. "I can't. Now, stop bugging me!"

Nancy folded her arms and gave Brenda a piercing look. "I think I know why you can't show it to us," she said.

Brenda glared at her but said nothing.

"You can't show it to us because there *is* no letter," Nancy accused, unable to keep the anger from her voice.

"What—?" Rick said, an expression of shock coming over his face.

Brenda took one look at him and buried her face in her hands. "You're right," she confessed in a muffled voice. "I made the whole thing up!"

Chapter Nine

FOR A MOMENT Nancy just stared at Brenda. She was furious with the reporter, but what made it even worse was that she herself had ended up buying Brenda's dumb stunt.

"Wait a minute," Rick said, his green eyes bewildered. "You mean you made the letter up? This woman whose husband wants to kill her—she doesn't exist?"

Brenda fiddled nervously with the white fringe on her bathing suit. Without looking up, she nodded.

"And the accident in the mall, with the beam. You said someone was trying to kill you," Rick said. "Were you just making that up, too?"

Brenda nodded again, shamefaced.

"Why?" Rick asked. "What was the point?"

When Brenda didn't answer, Nancy spoke

up. "It was for publicity. Brenda wanted to make a splash with her new column, so she invented an exciting, dramatic scenario. Right, Brenda?"

Brenda lifted her head and tossed back her dark hair. "Well, it *could* have happened," she said indignantly. "People need to know that things like that can happen. In a way, you could say I was just being a responsible journalist."

"Come off it, Brenda," Rick said angrily. He moved to the edge of the pool and sat down with his back to Brenda, his feet dangling in the water.

Brenda seemed to have lost some of her spirit as she turned to Rick. "I had to do it," she said, pleading to his back. "My father threatened to cancel my column because I wasn't getting any interesting mail. I figured if I got just one exciting letter, others would follow. So I decided to write one myself. I'm sorry," she added weakly. "I never meant for it to get out of hand like this."

That reminded Nancy of something she had wondered about. "Brenda, how did you come up with that particular letter?"

"I got the idea after the crash in the parking lot. Mrs. Keating kept talking about how her brakes weren't working, and I thought, suppose they were deliberately sabotaged?" She shrugged and seemed to be faintly pleased

with herself. "The idea just took off from there."

"I thought that might be it," Nancy murmured, shaking her head. "I should've listened to my instincts."

"I couldn't believe it when Rick told me about his aunt, and I realized I had made up a story that was actually happening!" Brenda went on. Nancy noticed that she made it sound as if she'd done something really great.

A moment later, however, Brenda's expression deflated as she glanced at Rick, who had been sitting silently by the edge of the pool. Beams of late-afternoon sunlight shimmered on the surface of the water and outlined his slumped figure with a golden glow.

Nancy saw Brenda bite her lip uncertainly. Then the reporter rose from the chaise longue and went to sit beside Rick. She made little swirls in the water with her feet and stared down at them, as if unable to face Rick directly.

"Rick, I really am sorry," she said softly.

Nancy and Ned looked at each other in surprise. Brenda actually sounded humbled!

"I know I shouldn't have left you in the dark the way I did. I should have told you from the beginning that the letter was a fake." Brenda laid her hand on Rick's arm.

"The thing was," she went on, "when I first met you, I didn't want to tell you the truth

because I was worried you'd tell people and then my column would be ruined. Then, when you told me about your aunt, I thought I really could help." Her eyes flashed defiantly as she snapped her head back at Nancy. "I *still* think I can help—if you want me to, that is." Brenda's voice faltered as she added, "I guess the real reason I didn't tell you is because I knew you'd be upset. I was afraid you'd think I was a terrible person."

"What does it matter to you what I think?" Rick asked her.

Brenda was obviously on the verge of tears. "It matters. I—I really think you're terrific, Rick. I know you probably don't feel the same about me after what I did, but I wanted to tell you that anyway."

Nancy never thought she'd see Brenda acting in a sincere and sensitive manner. She must be in love!

Rick turned to Brenda with a shy smile. "Hey, it's okay. I wish you'd told me sooner, but I guess there's no harm done."

From his deck chair Ned put in, "The question is, where do we go from here?"

Nancy leaned forward and propped her elbows on her knees, her attention once more on the case. She quickly told the others about her visit to Mrs. Keating. "She seemed pretty scared, but what I don't get is, if she's afraid her husband's going to kill her, why doesn't she go to the police?" Turning to Rick, she

asked, "What do *you* think? You see them every day. How do they act toward each other? What's the atmosphere in the house?"

"Tense," Rick replied without hesitating. "Aunt Maggie's been on edge in general. But I don't know if it's because she thinks Uncle Bill is trying to kill her or if something totally different is bothering her. Uncle Bill seems pretty jumpy, too. I asked Aunt Maggie about it, but she just said he was under a lot of pressure at work."

"That doesn't mean much," Ned commented. He cleared his throat. "Phew! I'm thirsty. Sitting out here in the sun has dried me out."

"I have an idea," Brenda said, shaking the water from her feet and standing up. "Let's go get a soda and finish this discussion in a nice, air-conditioned restaurant. I want to take my car for a spin, anyway. It's just back from the shop, and I want to make sure it's running okay."

"Let's take my car," Nancy said to Ned as Rick and Brenda went into the bathhouse to change. "I should probably go straight home from the restaurant if I want to be on time for dinner." Flashing Ned a wide smile, she asked, "Want to come over? Hannah's making homemade strawberry ice cream for dessert."

"I'll be there," Ned said enthusiastically.

A few moments later Rick and Brenda reappeared, Brenda in a yellow minidress that

showed off her tan, and Rick in shorts and a T-shirt.

"I have to get my car out of the garage," Brenda announced. Slipping her arm through Rick's, she suggested, "How about riding with me, Rick?"

"Those two are getting pretty cozy, aren't they?" Nancy remarked in a low voice as she and Ned followed Brenda and Rick around to the three-car garage at the top of the driveway.

"Mmm." Ned chuckled. "I hope he knows what he's getting into."

"Actually, I'm sort of glad for Brenda," Nancy said. "She really seems to like Rick. And he's a nice guy. It could be good for her to be around someone like him. She might learn something. You know, Brenda isn't dumb, even if she acts it most of the time. And she's very pretty—"

"She sure is," Ned put in.

"Ned!" Nancy exclaimed, but then she saw the teasing twinkle in his brown eyes. "You'd better watch out, Nickerson," she said, giving him a playful jab in the arm. "I almost took you seriously. Then you would have been in trouble!"

Just then Brenda's red sports car rolled out of the garage. "Nancy, follow me," Brenda called through the open window.

Nancy and Ned got in her Mustang, and Nancy pulled in behind Brenda.

"This driveway would be great for sledding

in the winter," Ned remarked as they drove down the hill. "It's steep, and it barely has any curves."

"How can you even think about winter when it's this hot out?" Nancy said, shaking her head in amazement. When he didn't answer, she glanced sideways and saw that Ned was peering through the windshield at Brenda's car, a slight frown creasing his brow.

"She's going too fast to make the turn at the bottom," he mumbled.

"Brenda drives the way she talks," Nancy replied. "Fast and—"

Nancy's voice broke off as Brenda's brake lights suddenly flashed on. With a screech of tires her red car fishtailed wildly across the driveway.

"Something's wrong!" Nancy cried, braking. "Brenda's car is out of control!"

Nancy watched helplessly as the red sports car barreled out of the drive and straight across the street. Then, with a terrible crunch, it slammed headlong into a huge tree!

Chapter Ten

"Oh, no!" Nancy cried. She jammed on the Mustang's emergency brake, threw off her seat belt, and jumped out of the car. Ned's footsteps echoed right behind her on the pavement as she raced toward Brenda's car.

The red sports car had thrown up a huge cloud of dust when it plowed into the dry earth around the tree. At first it was hard to see through the dense cloud.

"Brenda! Rick!" Nancy yelled, coughing from all the dust as she and Ned reached the car.

Ned yanked open the driver's side door and pulled at Brenda's safety belt. A moment later she fell out into his arms. "I couldn't turn the wheel!" Brenda cried. "I lost control!"

"Rick?" Nancy called, alarmed. She bent down and peered into the interior.

Rick was in the passenger seat, still wearing his seat belt. He stared at Nancy with a dazed expression. "I'm okay," he said. Then he managed a shaky grin. "It's a good thing I remembered to buckle up."

"Boy, am I glad you did," Nancy said fervently. She hurried around to his side and helped him out of the car. "Are you hurt at all?"

"I don't think so." Rick rubbed his neck gingerly. "My head snapped back when we hit the tree, but it doesn't feel too bad."

Rick's knees were wobbly, so Nancy supported him with an arm around his waist. They went around to the driver's side, where Brenda stood shivering, her arms crossed tightly across her chest and her dark eyes brimming with tears. "Three times in three days," she said.

It took Nancy a moment to make sense of what the reporter was saying. But then she realized it was true—the crash in the parking lot, the beam falling inside the mall, and now this. Could they *all* be accidents?

"What happened?" Nancy asked gently.

"I don't know," Brenda answered, turning to face Nancy. "I just couldn't move the steering wheel. It felt as if there were a heavy weight on it." The tears spilled over and ran down her cheeks. "And—and I was going too fast to stop—" She broke into a sob, and Rick put an arm around her shoulders.

"The whole thing happened like that," he said, snapping his fingers. "We didn't even have time to react."

Brenda dried her eyes on the back of her hand, then looked at Ned and Nancy. "I thought the wheel felt stiff when I took the car out of the garage," she explained. "I didn't pay any attention to it, though. Then all of a sudden we were flying down the hill, and I couldn't turn." Her lip quivered again. "I hit the brakes, but we still crashed."

Nancy didn't like the sound of that, but she kept quiet. No use scaring Brenda for no reason. "If you hadn't slammed on the brakes," she said reassuringly, "the accident would have been a lot more serious. Come on, let's get over to my car. You two need to sit and calm down."

Once Brenda and Rick were seated in Nancy's car, Nancy, keeping her voice light and casual, said, "Ned and I'll be right back. I just want to take a look under your hood, Brenda."

"Okay." Brenda was holding Rick's hand tightly. She still looked frightened, but Nancy thought she seemed to be recovering from her scare—and that she was definitely enjoying Rick's attention.

As they crossed the street again, Ned asked Nancy in a low voice, "What's going on? Do you think there's something wrong with Brenda's car?"

Nancy simply shrugged. She'd had a sudden, frightening idea, but it was such a long shot she didn't want to tell Ned about it until she checked it out.

The red car had hit the tree hard, but fortunately Brenda hadn't been going fast enough to do much damage. Ned managed to raise the hood without too much trouble, and they peered inside at the tangle of bolts, fans, and hoses.

"Uh-oh," Nancy said after a moment, frowning. Reaching down, she tapped on a white plastic container that was bolted to the car's chassis. "Look at that, Ned."

"Wow!" he exclaimed, grimacing. The container looked as if someone had attacked it with a buzz saw. The plastic was ripped to shreds. Thick yellowish fluid oozed sluggishly down the sides. "That's the steering fluid reserve," he said.

"You mean it used to be," Nancy amended. "No wonder Brenda couldn't turn the wheel," she said grimly. "The hydraulic system that controls her power steering is completely wrecked.

"Ned, is there any way this damage could have happened when Brenda hit the tree?" Nancy asked.

"No way," he told her. Ned gave a tight smile. "I'd say we're definitely looking at a case of sabotage."

Nancy took a deep breath. "That's what I

was afraid of. Listen, I don't want to say anything to Brenda until I know for sure," she added, biting her lip. "She's already practically hysterical about what just happened. First I want to check out the lock on her garage door and see if it's been tampered with. If not, I suppose there's still a chance that this happened by accident at the garage."

"If any garage is hiring mechanics who can shred a steering fluid unit that way by accident," Ned retorted as they walked back to the Mustang, "then I hope I never take my car there for repairs."

"What were you two doing over there?" Brenda asked as soon as Nancy and Ned walked up. "Why were you looking at my engine?"

"We just wanted to check something out," Nancy replied evasively. "Come on, let's go back up to your house."

"What were you checking out?" Brenda persisted as they all trudged back up the long hill. Her voice had regained its sharp edge. "You'd better tell me. It's my car, after all."

Rick took Brenda's hand. "I'm sure she'd let you know if there was anything to worry about."

Nancy was amazed by the way Brenda seemed to respond to Rick. A big smile spread across Brenda's face, and for the rest of the way up to the Carlton house, she was silent.

"Now what are you doing?" Brenda called

when Nancy and Ned headed for the garage. She hurried after them. "You guys are being awfully mysterious."

Nancy was already bending down to examine the lock on the garage door. It was just as she had guessed. The edges of the metal lock plate had several shiny new scratches. Someone had taken the plate off and picked the lock.

Nancy's mouth was set in a grim line as she turned to Brenda and Rick. "Okay. It's time I told you the whole story," she said.

"Whole story?" Rick repeated, faintly alarmed.

Nancy nodded, then made direct eye contact with Brenda. "That 'accident' you had just now was no accident," she said quietly.

"Your steering fluid container was slashed," Ned explained.

Brenda's mouth fell open.

"Is this a joke?" Rick asked incredulously, turning from Nancy to Ned.

"Sorry, but it's not," Nancy answered. She gestured at the lock on the garage door. "Someone picked this lock. I think we're looking at a case of sabotage."

"Oh, no. No way," Brenda burst out suddenly. "You're not going to pin this one on me!"

Nancy stared at her, mystified. "What are you—" she began.

But Brenda wasn't about to be interrupted. "I don't believe you!" she cried, angrily plant-

ing her hands on her hips. "You can't seriously think I'd stage something like this, just for the publicity. Wreck my own car? Put my life—and Rick's—in danger? I don't think so. Face it, Nancy. This accident was just as real as the one with the beam—" She broke off suddenly, the color draining from her face as the meaning of her own words sank in.

"Exactly," Nancy said. "I'm not trying to say you had anything to do with staging either accident, Brenda. But *someone* did."

"Oh," Brenda said in a tiny voice.

Rick gasped. "Are you saying someone really is trying to kill Brenda?" he demanded, horrified. "But why? What for?"

Raking a hand through her hair, Nancy explained, "The accident with the beam happened the day Brenda ran that phony letter in her column. I think seeing that letter upset someone."

She took a deep breath before saying, "It's only a guess, but if you ask me, all these accidents are further proof that there really *is* a murder scheme. Whoever's behind it thinks Brenda knows about it, so now he or she's trying to kill her, too!"

Chapter Eleven

"OH, NO!" Brenda wailed, burying her face in her hands. "I've got a murderer after me!"

Rick put his arms around Brenda and stroked her hair, but his attention was still focused on Nancy. "You're serious, aren't you?"

Nancy nodded.

"You think it's my uncle." It was a statement, not a question. "He really *is* trying to kill my aunt. And now he thinks Brenda knows, so he's trying to kill her, too." Rick's brilliant green eyes were troubled.

"There's no proof that it's your uncle," Nancy said cautiously. "At this point, for all we know it could be someone we've never even heard of. But from what you've told me about your aunt and uncle, and from what Ned and I found out about their insurance policies, it

seems reasonable to start our investigation with them."

Brenda raised her head and glanced nervously over her shoulder. "I feel very exposed out here," she complained. "The murderer could be lurking right now, waiting for another chance to get me!"

Nancy grimaced at Brenda's overly dramatic flair, but she had to admit the reporter had a point.

"Why don't we go inside," Nancy suggested. "We can discuss what to do next over some cold drinks."

The four trooped inside the big white house, and Brenda directed the maid to bring a tray of sodas to the den.

Unlike the rest of the house, the den had a warm, lived-in feeling. The furniture was mismatched but cozy looking, and the big desk was cluttered with papers and books. A few framed college degrees and journalism awards hung on the walls, and Nancy guessed this was where Brenda's father, Frazier Carlton, worked.

Ned collapsed gratefully into a deep, well-worn armchair. "Whew, the air conditioning feels fantastic," he said, wiping his brow. Then, looking at Nancy, he asked, "So what's the plan?"

"We need evidence to prove our theory," Nancy began. She sat in another chair while

Brenda and Rick plopped down on a leather couch. "There are several things we should be doing. I think—if it's okay with everyone—that we should divide up the tasks and work in teams."

"Rick and I will work together," Brenda said immediately.

"Brenda, I'm sorry," said Nancy. "But you can't be on any of the teams."

"What?" Brenda cried. "Are you still trying to get back at me for that phony letter, Nancy?"

"No," Nancy said, trying not to lose her patience. "Someone has already arranged at least one, maybe two deadly 'accidents' for you, Brenda. We have to assume the person is going to try again. Your best protection is to stay put and not get yourself into even more danger."

"Nancy's right," Rick said to Brenda. "You are in danger. We can't risk losing you."

Brenda's eyes had been flashing angrily while Nancy spoke, but at Rick's words she calmed down, obviously touched by his concern.

The maid came in with their refreshments just then. After she left, Nancy went on. "Rick, you're our inside man at the Keatings' house," she said. "You have two jobs. One is to keep an eye on your aunt and make sure nothing happens to her. The other is to find out what

you can about your uncle. Does he have a study?"

Rick nodded. "He does a lot of work at home."

"Check it out," Nancy told him. "There may be a paper trail—you know, records or documents that prove he's got serious money problems."

"Got it," Rick said eagerly.

Nancy leaned back in the chair and stretched her long legs out in front of her. "I think I'll call Bess and George in on this, too," she said. "They can go around to Mrs. Keating's hairdresser and places like that and scout out some gossip on her." She held up a hand to silence Rick, who was looking indignant. "You'd be surprised at how much people know about other people's private concerns," she said. "We may learn something useful."

Ned swallowed some soda and set his glass down. "What about you and me, Nan?" he asked.

"Don't worry," Nancy told him, smiling. "I have it all figured out." She turned to Rick. "Do you know where your aunt's car was towed after the accident with Brenda?"

He thought for a moment. "A place called Westlake Auto, I'm pretty sure."

"Is it still there?" Nancy asked.

Rick nodded. "It should be. They aren't scheduled to start work on it until tomorrow. Why?"

"Because that's where Brenda's car is going for repairs," Nancy told him.

"I don't use Westlake," Brenda protested.

"For now, you do," Nancy told her, grinning. "Have the car brought in under my name. That'll give Ned and me a chance to get in and look at Mrs. Keating's brakes."

"I don't see why *I* couldn't do that," Brenda muttered sulkily. "It wouldn't be dangerous."

"Too risky," Nancy said firmly. Turning to Ned, she said, "We'd better go. There's nothing more we can do tonight, and anyway, we're late for dinner."

As they were leaving, Nancy looked back at Brenda. The pretty brunette was standing on the porch with Rick, watching them go. Nancy didn't miss the determined, rebellious expression on Brenda's face.

Uh-oh. She's going to make trouble before this case is over, Nancy thought. I just know it.

Nancy cradled the receiver of her phone between her chin and shoulder and dialed George's number. Then she sat back on her bed, counting the rings until her friend answered.

"Hi," she said when George picked up after the third one.

"Hey, Nan. Great timing. Bess is over, and she's dying to talk to you!"

"What for?" Nancy asked.

"Uh, I think she wants to tell you herself,"

George warned, laughing. Then her voice became fainter as she said, "Okay, okay, I'm giving you the phone! Stop grabbing."

"What's going on?" Nancy asked.

"I'll tell you what's going on," came Bess's voice over the line. "I had a date with David Park last night! Did you get my message?"

"Oh!" Suddenly Nancy remembered Hannah's giving her the message from Bess the day before. She'd been so preoccupied with the case that she had totally forgotten to return Bess's call the night before. "Oh, Bess, I'm sorry," she said sincerely. "I got it. I just had a lot on my mind."

"Mmmm. I'm not surprised," Bess replied. "I could see it coming the other night at the concert. You have a new case, don't you?"

"Guilty," Nancy admitted with a laugh.

"So—what is this case?" Bess asked.

Nancy could hear George's voice faintly in the background. "A new case? Tell her to come over and fill us in, pronto. She's not about to do anything without our help!"

A warm feeling spread through Nancy. She could always count on Bess and George. They were the greatest!

"I'll tell you about it in a second," she said to Bess. "But first, I want to hear all the details of your date!"

"So what do we do, Nan?" Ned whispered.

"I'm not sure," Nancy admitted. She

stepped around a heap of oily engine parts, carefully holding the hem of her white dress away from them. "I guess we'll have to improvise."

It was ten-thirty in the morning, and Nancy and Ned were standing by Brenda's car, amid a hum of activity, at Westlake Auto. Ned had taken the morning off so that he could go with Nancy to check out the brakes on Mrs. Keating's car.

Nancy frowned, considering. "We can't just tell the mechanic we suspect the brakes were sabotaged," she said quietly. "He'll think we're crazy!"

She straightened away from Ned as a harassed-looking man in stained white coveralls walked toward them, wiping his hands on a rag. The name Ernie was embroidered on a patch on his chest.

"Can I help you folks?" the man asked.

"Yes. Uh, I'm Nancy Drew," she began hesitantly. "I—"

The mechanic interrupted her, scowling. "Oh, you're the one who owns this car. Look, I didn't appreciate your attitude on the phone yesterday."

What was he talking about? Nancy wondered. Then she realized Brenda must have said something rude to the guy. "But I—" she began again.

Ernie cut her off. "I'm sorry, but there's no way I'll be able to get to your car before tomorrow." He waved a hand at the crowded

shop. "You can see how backed up we are. We're so busy I can't even keep track of what my men are doing."

The place did seem a little frantic. Men in white Westlake Auto coveralls hurried back and forth among dozens of cars in the huge space. As she looked around, Nancy had an idea.

She was wearing white, too. If Ned could keep Ernie occupied, she could find Mrs. Keating's car and look at the brakes. In the bustle the odds were that no one would notice her.

"Oh, but you *have* to fix the car today," she whined. "We need it." She grasped Ned's arm possessively. "Today is our one-year anniversary, and this is the car that we rode in on our very first date. We have such a big day planned, and if I don't get to ride in this car *today,* I'll just have a *fit!*" She squeezed Ned's arm. "Honey, can't you talk to him?"

Ned glanced down at her in surprise, and Nancy gave him a discreet kick on the ankle.

"Er—that's right," Ned said quickly. He leaned toward Ernie, lowering his voice. "Let me tell you, you don't want to be around this girl when she's having a fit. It's not a pretty sight." Looking back at Nancy, he shot her a quick wink.

Oooh! I'll get him for that later, she thought.

Ernie's expression was doubtful. "All the same," he said, "I can't get to it right away."

"Oh, *please!*" Nancy made her lower lip tremble. "If our plans are ruined I'll—I'll cry."

Ned put an arm around Ernie's shoulder. "Can we talk about this for a minute, man to man?" Still talking, he led Ernie toward the office.

Nancy watched them go, stifling a laugh. Not bad! Now I'd better get to it before they come back.

It took only a few seconds for her to recognize Mrs. Keating's silver sedan. It was parked near the back of the garage. As she wandered over, Nancy saw a pair of legs in white coveralls poking out from under the car's body. Someone was apparently working on it already.

That's probably good, Nancy realized. If she played this right, she could even get an expert's opinion on Mrs. Keating's brake trouble.

Bending down, Nancy said, "Excuse me."

There was a clattering sound as the mechanic slid out from under the car on a small, wheeled board. He stood up, dusting off his hands. Then he raised his eyes straight at Nancy. Her heart leapt into her throat.

"You!" she cried.

She was facing the man with the mismatched eyes!

Chapter Twelve

THE MAN gave Nancy a quizzical smile and asked, "Have we met?" But she was sure she saw a glint of recognition in his eyes.

Her thoughts were in a whirl, and her gaze kept flicking back and forth between the man's blue and brown eyes. In all the excitement of Brenda's accident, she'd completely forgotten him. Yet he'd been at the mall the day of Brenda's first car accident and near the Keatings' house the night of the concert. What was he doing working on Mrs. Keating's car now?

"No, you don't know me," Nancy responded after a moment. "But I've seen you before." She decided not to mention anything about seeing Rick chase him the night of the Ice Planet concert.

"You seemed very interested in an accident involving this car," she went on carefully.

"Ah, of course. You were the good Samaritan," the man said easily. "How could I forget a face as pretty as yours?" He unzipped his coveralls and stepped out of them. Underneath, Nancy noted, he had on an expensive-looking suit.

"Oh, I don't actually work here," he explained when he saw her look of surprise. "I just slipped in and—er—borrowed this extra coverall when the office was empty."

Nancy folded her arms, unsure of what to make of the guy. He was smooth—almost too smooth—and she didn't really trust him. "Why?" she asked bluntly.

The man shrugged. "It was more convenient than trying to explain to the mechanics that I wanted to examine one of their cars to see if its brakes had been doctored."

"*What?*" Nancy couldn't contain her surprise.

"Well, surely you suspect the same thing," the man said in a reasonable voice. "After all, you were the one who told Maggie to get her brakes checked in the first place."

From the familiar way he used Mrs. Keating's name, Nancy guessed he knew her. "Just who are you?" she demanded. "And what are you up to?"

"Oh, excuse my rudeness," the man said

with a charming laugh. He held out his hand. "I'm Maggie Keating's brother-in-law. Name's Chris Trout."

Brother-in-law? Suddenly Nancy recalled her father telling her that Mrs. Keating was the widow of a lawyer named Wilford Trout. This guy must be Wilford's younger brother. But what was he doing in the garage?

Reaching out, she took Trout's hand and shook it. "I'm Nancy Drew," she told him.

"Delighted," Trout said in that same supersmooth tone. Reaching into the pocket of the coveralls, he drew out a flat, oddly shaped piece of silvery metal. "Well, Nancy, you can be my witness. This is the proof that Maggie's brakes were sabotaged. I just found it."

Nancy's mind was racing. What was Trout up to? Could he somehow be involved in the plot to kill Mrs. Keating? He had been at the mall when she ran into Brenda. Could that be a coincidence? Nancy had to find out more!

"I didn't see you find that thing," she pointed out, hoping to goad more information from him. "Anyway, I don't even know what it is. You say it's proof of sabotage, but how do I know you're telling the truth?"

"Very good!" Trout said approvingly. He held the piece of metal up so Nancy could examine it. "This is a brake shoe. Notice the wear here and here." He pointed to two uneven spots on the surface of the metal piece

and went on to explain, "Now, wear is usual in everyday driving but not quite like this. If you look closely, you can see file marks."

Nancy caught her breath. He was right!

"It's very subtle, though." Raising his eyebrows, Trout added, "I doubt a regular auto mechanic would even catch it. It's just that I have some expertise on the subject of brakes."

"How so?" Nancy asked cautiously.

"I drive Formula One race cars," Trout told her. He made a sigh that seemed a little exaggerated. "Unfortunately, racing is a very expensive hobby, what with the cost of the cars themselves, maintenance, entry fees, and so forth. I've been forced into temporary retirement, due to lack of funds."

His mismatched eyes held a strange gleam as he added, "But my luck may be changing. I think you can look for me on the racetrack again in the near future."

More questions whirled in Nancy's head. Was he making some weird reference to the plan to kill Mrs. Keating? But then, why would he tell her about the sabotaged brakes if he was in on the plot? Unless he just wanted her to *think* he was trying to protect Mrs. Keating to throw Nancy off the track—

Nancy shook herself. It was all guesswork until she came up with proof. Clearing her throat, she said, "About the brake shoe—"

"Oh, yes. The brake shoe." Trout looked

down at the object in his hand, then gave Nancy a sudden, wolfish grin. "Don't worry. I'll make sure the proper people see it."

Before Nancy could even open her mouth to ask what he meant, Trout strode jauntily away.

"Nancy, I think we're going to have to give up for today," Ned's voice came from behind her.

Startled, Nancy turned around. Ned stood there with the mechanic.

"What?" Nancy asked, her mind still on the strange conversation with Trout.

"I said, I think we're going to have to give up on getting the car fixed today," Ned replied.

"Well, we'll live," Nancy said distractedly.

"Gee, you're sure you're not too disappointed?" Ned asked, frowning at her.

Suddenly Nancy remembered they were supposed to be putting on an act for Ernie. "Oh, of course I am," she said, pouting. "I'm *very* disappointed. Ned, let's go. I think I'm going to cry."

Doing her best to look upset, Nancy led the way out of the garage. As soon as they were around the corner and out of sight, though, she grabbed Ned's hand. "Listen to this!" Quickly she filled him in on her encounter with Chris Trout.

Ned whistled when she was done. "This Trout guy sounds like bad news," he commented.

"I agree," Nancy said. "He acted like he

wanted to help, but—I don't know, I got the feeling he was hiding something. If he really wanted to help Mrs. Keating, why would he run off like that with the brake shoe? Maybe he's actually in on some plan with Mr. Keating." Her blue eyes had a determined gleam in them as she added, "One thing's for sure."

"What's that?" Ned inquired.

"I've got some homework to do on both Bill Keating and Chris Trout."

"Wow, Nancy," Bess said wistfully. "This guy Chris Trout sounds kind of romantic."

"I don't know," said George. She poured herself a refill of soda and went back to her seat at the Drews' kitchen table. "Sometimes the most charming guys are the ones who make the most trouble."

Nancy nodded her agreement. "The question is, what kind of trouble?"

The girls had just eaten dinner, and now they were comparing notes on what they had learned that day.

"He's definitely a slippery kind of guy," Nancy went on. "The only solid information he gave me was that he drives Formula Ones—you know, race cars. So I called some racing people, and they actually thought I was trying to track Trout down for money. The guy said something like, 'Look, lady, you'll have to wait in line behind me and half of Chicago.'"

"Maybe he's not so romantic after all," Bess commented, taking a sip of soda.

"But it sounds like he's definitely broke," said George.

"Right," Nancy said with a nod. "I called my dad about it, and he told me both Wilford and Chris Trout inherited a lot of money from their parents. But both of them let it slip away within just a few years. Wilford still made good money as a lawyer, though, and my dad says Wilford was always giving money to Chris. I wonder if Chris hoped Wilford's widow would continue with the handouts," she added, thinking out loud.

"Maybe he's trying to kill Mrs. Keating and get it blamed on Mr. Keating so that he can inherit whatever she has," Bess suggested. "Ugh," she added, shuddering.

"That doesn't make sense unless Mrs. Keating put a special provision for Chris in her will," Nancy pointed out. "He's not Mrs. Keating's next of kin. He's not even really related to her."

"Besides," said George, "from what I heard today, I don't think Mrs. Keating has much money to leave to anyone."

Nancy nodded. "That's what Rick said, too. What exactly did you find out?"

"Well, I talked to Mrs. Keating's hairdresser, Maurice," began George, reaching for the last of Hannah's chocolate chip cookies. "He has this chic salon, but he was pretty chatty. I

went in to talk to him about a new look." She grinned and patted her dark curls.

"You didn't!" Bess cried admiringly. "Oh, this sounds fun. I wish I'd rescheduled my dentist's appointment so I could have gone with you."

George crunched into the cookie, then went on with her story. "After a while I got the conversation around to Mrs. Keating," she said. "Maurice is upset with her because she bounced three checks in a row. He says that right before Mrs. Keating married Mr. Keating, she was talking a lot about how much money she was going to have after the wedding. Maurice thinks *she* married him for *his* money."

"Now, that's interesting," Nancy said. "It's beginning to look as if both Mr. and Mrs. Keating went into their marriage thinking the other one would make them wealthy again."

"And they were both disappointed," Bess added excitedly. "Hey, maybe they're trying to kill each other!"

Nancy smiled at Bess. "Maybe," she allowed. "But so far we have no evidence that anyone is trying to kill *Mr.* Keating."

The three girls turned as Ned appeared in the kitchen doorway. "Hannah let me in," he explained. "What's up?"

Nancy was about to start filling him in when the telephone rang. She reached for the kitchen extension. "Hello?"

It was Brenda. She was beside herself with excitement. "Guess what?" she cried. "I just got an anonymous phone tip!"

"What?" Nancy asked. "Calm down, Brenda. What are you talking about?"

"It happened just five minutes ago," Brenda said. "The phone rang, and when I picked it up, this muffled voice told me I could get information that would help the woman who wrote the letter in my column. All I have to do is show up at Bluff Bridge at nine o'clock tonight."

"Brenda," Nancy said sternly, feeling a prickle of unease, "the letter was a fake, remember? This could be a trap."

"I know that!" Brenda said scornfully. "I'm not an idiot, Nancy. I'm just calling to tell you I'm going to set a trap for *him.*"

"You can't go!" Nancy yelled into the receiver. Was Brenda actually dumb enough to try to outsmart a potential murderer? Then Nancy remembered something. "Your car's still in the shop," she pointed out, heaving a sigh of relief. "You don't have any way to get there."

There was a sulky silence. "Well, how are we going to catch this guy?" Brenda asked at last.

Nancy glanced at her watch. It was already eight thirty-five! "I'll go in your place," she said, thinking fast. "I'll take Ned. And can you call Rick? Tell him to be on the far side of the bridge at ten of nine—and to watch for anyone approaching from that side."

After slamming down the phone, Nancy grabbed Ned and herded him toward the door. "I'll explain later, you guys," she called back to Bess and George.

In the car she told Ned about her conversation with Brenda. "We're going to set a trap for the 'trapper,'" she finished.

"Let's just try to stay alive until we get there," Ned said, sounding worried. "You're going awfully fast, Nancy."

"We have to beat him there," Nancy insisted, maintaining her speed.

At eight fifty-two Nancy parked in the shadow of some trees by the bridge. The steel arc soared high over the Muskoka River, with tall cliffs on either side. A few yellow street lamps gave it little light.

"You stay out of sight and guard this end of the bridge," she told Ned. "Rick should be on the other side. I'll go meet our mystery man."

"Nan, be careful," Ned said. He kissed her.

"I will," she promised.

Taking a deep breath, she walked toward the bridge. It appeared to be deserted, but there were plenty of dark, shadowy areas at both ends. Gnarled old trees hung out over the bridge, curtaining it off in a way that Nancy found sinister. She didn't like to think it, but a dangerous man could be hiding within just a few feet of her.

Her senses extra-alert, Nancy walked under the curtain of trees and stepped onto the

bridge. She paused to look around, struck by the odd feeling that someone was watching her. It's just Ned and Rick, she told herself sternly.

Nancy had taken a few more steps out onto the bridge when suddenly something thudded down behind her. Nancy jumped to one side—but not fast enough.

Hands slammed into her back and shoved her violently. Before she could do more than scream, Nancy found herself lurching forward, then falling—right over the guardrail of the bridge!

Chapter Thirteen

NANCY FELT the blood rush to her head as she slid headfirst over the side of the bridge, her legs scraping against the sharp edge of the rail.

"Help!"

She twisted her body in midair, and her hands shot out to make one desperate grab at a steel post. In a flash the metal was slipping through her palms, and Nancy clenched her teeth in despair.

Then, her scrabbling fingers locked around an edge of the post, and with a wrenching jerk her body stopped its fall. Pain shot through her arms, and she saw white stars behind her closed eyelids. But she wasn't falling any longer!

Panting, Nancy hung onto the post. After a

moment she worked up the courage to open her eyes. She was dangling below the level of the roadbed, amid a crisscrossing mesh of support beams and girders. Wind moaned through the steel web and whipped her hair into her eyes.

She risked a cautious peep downward—and immediately wished she hadn't. A hundred feet below, the Muskoka sent back a faint reflection of the bridge's lights. One small slip, and she'd be history!

The wind gusted, pulling at Nancy's entire body. Her heart jumped as she felt her fingers slip a fraction of an inch. She wouldn't be able to hang on much longer. Think clearly, Drew, she ordered herself.

Above her there was a confused babble of voices. Nancy tried to cry for help, but all that came out was a faint croak. Swallowing to moisten her dry throat, she tried again. "Help me!"

"Nancy?" Rick Waterston's blond head poked out over the rail. "Oh, no!" he cried as he spotted her. In an instant he had swung his long legs over the rail and was climbing down the girders. "Hang on! I'm coming!" he shouted.

Nancy's hand slipped again, until she now clung by just the tips of her fingers. "Hurry!" she called back frantically. "I'm about to fall!"

The wind gusted again, and Nancy's heart lurched as the metal bar slipped away from her

fingers. Just in time Rick's strong hand closed around her left wrist.

"I'm going to pull you up," Rick told her. "Trust me—I've done a lot of climbing."

Nancy's breath came in heaving gulps. Talk about close calls! But she still wasn't out of trouble. Looking up she could see the strain in Rick's face as he hauled her up. At last she was high enough that her feet found a ledge to support her weight. Slowly, with Rick guiding her every inch of the way, she climbed up the web of metal and over the lip of the bridge. Finally she lay collapsed on the road, gasping.

"Thanks," she said to Rick when she could speak again. "You saved my life."

"Don't thank me. I blew it," he said gruffly. "And our man clobbered Ned and got away before I could grab him."

"Is Ned hurt?" Nancy asked anxiously.

"I don't know. Brenda's checking," Rick said.

"Brenda?" Nancy repeated, suddenly wary. "What's she doing here?"

At that moment Brenda herself appeared from the shadows, supporting a limping, scowling Ned.

Jumping to her feet, Nancy ran to him and threw her arms around him. "Ned, are you okay?"

"I'm all right." Ned held her close. He spoke lightly, but Nancy heard a tremor in his voice. "I thought you were a goner, though, Nan."

"I'm fine," she assured him. "Now, tell me what happened."

Ned's face immediately darkened again. "Ask Brenda. She's the only one who saw anything, after that stupid camera flash of hers blinded me."

"Brenda!" Nancy exclaimed.

Beside Ned, Brenda flipped her dark hair back defiantly. "I was only trying to help," she muttered. "I thought it might be a good idea to come and get a picture, in case you guys let the crook get away."

"He wouldn't have gotten away if I had been able to see him!" Ned retorted furiously. "But I couldn't see a thing. The guy swung out of the trees and attacked you," he told Nancy. "I was running for him when Brenda popped up behind him and clicked her camera. The flash went off in my eyes, and the guy bolted. On the way he took time to flatten me." Ned rubbed his jaw and winced.

"Brenda, how did you get here?" Nancy asked, facing her.

Brenda's eyes flicked toward Rick, who stepped up beside Nancy.

"I brought her," Rick confessed in response to Nancy's questioning glance. "She really wanted to come, and I didn't think it would do any harm as long as she stayed in the car." He gave Brenda an angry look. "You promised you would," he reminded her.

Brenda hung her head and said nothing.

"Well," Nancy said with a sigh, "it's done. At least none of us got seriously hurt." Turning to Brenda, she added, "Get your film developed right away," she said. "Maybe there'll be a clear shot of our mystery man."

"Why do you keep calling him the mystery man?" Rick wanted to know. "There's no question that it's Uncle Bill, is there?"

"Yes, there is," Nancy told him. "First, we still have no hard evidence that this case involves the Keatings at all. Second," she went on, thinking out loud as she spoke, "even if it does involve them, there's still a lot of unexplained stuff going on. I'm pretty sure Chris Trout fits into this, but I'm not sure how."

She turned to Rick, remembering something else. "You knew it was him outside your aunt's house the other night," she said. "Why didn't you want to admit it?"

Rick's face took on an apologetic expression. "I didn't even know Uncle Wilford's brother was around until you described him. I couldn't figure out what he was doing there, but the whole thing really got me scared. Aunt Maggie's been so afraid to talk about what's going on that I guess I just clammed up, too. I was afraid something terrible might happen if I said anything—I'm not sure why."

He shook his head slowly, as if confused by his own actions. "And then I was so freaked

out by Brenda's accident and what you told me about my aunt's insurance, I forgot all about Uncle Chris."

"Well, there's a chance he could have set up this meeting," Nancy said, trying to piece things together in her mind. She thought of the brake shoe and Trout's words about getting it to "the right people." Could he have meant Brenda? But why would he want to give it to her?

"Speaking of hard evidence," Rick said, breaking into Nancy's train of thought, "all I found when I searched Uncle Bill's study today is evidence that he's weird."

"What do you mean?" Ned asked him.

Rick shrugged. "He has this folder full of clippings. Mostly it was stuff about the military, but there were lots of articles about tornadoes."

"Tornadoes?" Nancy was puzzled.

"Well, not tornadoes, exactly," Rick corrected himself. "Actually, they were all about microbursts. You know, those minitornadoes that all the meteorologists are warning about these days. The ones that appear out of nowhere, zap your house, and disappear before you even see what hit you." He grinned sourly. "Maybe Uncle Bill is trying to come up with some way to develop them into the army's newest secret weapon."

"Maybe." Nancy let out a heavy sigh. Her

head was beginning to pound, and she couldn't think straight anymore. "Let's all go home," she told the others. "We can start again tomorrow, after we've seen Brenda's photographs."

The sound of the telephone awakened Nancy from a deep sleep the following morning. Through bleary eyes, she checked the clock on her bedside table. Ten o'clock. Then she reached for the phone and mumbled, "'Lo?"

It was Rick. "I'm at *Today's Times* with Brenda," he said. "We just developed the film from last night."

Nancy sat up in bed, shaking herself awake. "Anything?" she asked.

"Nope. It's useless," came Rick's unhappy voice. "She got one shot. It shows a blur which we think is the attacker's shoulder—but it could be something else. And there's a great shot of Ned looking surprised."

It wasn't exactly good news, but Rick sounded so down Nancy decided to try to cheer him up. "Look, why don't you two take a break. I'll figure out our next move."

After she hung up, Nancy got up and showered. She was a bit stiff from her adventure the night before, and the air seemed thick and close, even in the air-conditioned house. Glancing out the window, Nancy wasn't surprised to see that the sky had a yellowish cast to it.

Tornado watch today, I'll bet. Still wearing her towel, she went over to the clock-radio by her bed and switched it on.

"The watch is in effect for the Chicago area," the newscaster was saying. "And for you folks in the River Heights area, look out. Twisters have been sighted heading your way, and we have reports of at least two microbursts touching down. Fortunately, no casualties have been reported. For live coverage, we go now to . . ."

As she listened to the tornado warning, several things suddenly clicked into place. The tornadoes—the folder full of clippings about microbursts—

Nancy reached down and snapped off the radio, cutting off the newscaster's voice. Her mind was racing. She could hardly believe what she was thinking—it was too farfetched.

"Oh, no!" she groaned out loud. "Could he really do it?" She didn't know how, but she suspected Mr. Keating was somehow going to use the tornado warnings to fake some kind of fatal "accident" for his wife.

After throwing on a pair of jeans and a polo shirt, she raced downstairs and headed for the door.

"Nancy?" Hannah Gruen's voice came from the kitchen. "Don't you want any breakfast?"

"No time!" Nancy called over her shoulder. "I've got to stop a murder from happening!"

In her car Nancy floored the gas pedal. She smiled grimly. If Ned griped about my driving last night, it's good he's not with me now!

Five minutes later she pulled up the driveway to the Keatings' big Victorian house. There was only one car in the garage, a white station wagon. Seeing it made Nancy pause. Suddenly she realized she had no idea what she was going to do next.

Improvise, she told herself fiercely. A woman's life is at stake!

Nancy hurried up and rang the bell, and a moment later Mrs. Keating opened the door. She looked even more shaken up than when Nancy had spoken with her last, but at least she was alive!

"Hi," Nancy said, vastly relieved. "May I come in?" Without waiting for a reply, she bustled inside, herding Mrs. Keating in front of her.

"You may not remember me," she went on, speaking softly and quickly. "I'm Nancy Drew. I was there when you had the accident at the mall."

"Yes, of course," Mrs. Keating said. She was wringing her hands, and her large brown eyes had a look of tense bewilderment in them.

"We don't have much time," Nancy hurried on. "I know this will sound strange, but I think you'll have some idea of what I'm talking about."

"I'm afraid I don't have any idea yet."

"Look, I'm a detective. I know about your husband trying to kill you," Nancy said bluntly.

Mrs. Keating's brown eyes looked as if they might pop out of her head. "You—you know?" she whispered in a shaky voice.

"Yes. And I'm sorry to have to say this, but I think he's about to try again. You should leave the house right away. You're in danger here."

Mrs. Keating was still staring, not moving. Suddenly Nancy realized that the woman wasn't looking *at* her, but rather *behind* her. A sixth sense shouted at Nancy to turn around.

It was too late. As she started to turn, a thick cloth pad was clapped over her mouth and nose. She gasped as a bitter, acrid stench assaulted her nostrils.

Then, abruptly, there was blackness.

Chapter Fourteen

NANCY SWAM SLOWLY UP through a sea of dark mist. "Oooh," she groaned as her eyes fluttered open. The inside of her head felt as if someone were pounding at it with a sledgehammer.

"What . . . ?" Gradually the objects around her came into focus, and Nancy realized she was in a leather recliner in a darkened room.

Where am I? she wondered, frowning.

Heavy velvet curtains shrouded the room's two big windows. To Nancy's left was a massive maple rolltop desk stacked with color-coded folders. Bookshelves flanked one wall, with a lumpy-looking velvet sofa in a shadowed recess between them. The adjoining wall was covered with framed photographs.

Feeling too weak to get out of the chair, Nancy squinted to bring the photos into focus.

Most of them were black-and-white group shots of men in uniform.

Soldiers . . . Bill Keating. Suddenly what just happened came flooding back.

She had come to warn Mrs. Keating. In her mind Nancy pictured the look of panic on Mrs. Keating's face—just before those hands came from behind and held the drug-soaked cloth over Nancy's mouth and nose to knock her out. She shuddered at the memory.

"I must be in the Keatings' house," she said aloud. In fact, she guessed she was in Mr. Keating's study. Keating must have come in and caught her, she realized. But what had become of Mrs. Keating?

A slight movement from the lumpy sofa made Nancy's eyes snap over to it. She hadn't noticed before because the couch was set back in the shadows, but now she made out a human form lying there!

Forcing herself up and out of the recliner, Nancy made her way painfully across to the sofa. "Mrs. Keating?"

Nancy's eyes widened as she saw not Mrs. Keating, but Chris Trout lying on the sofa. His eyes were closed, and even in the dim light she could see that he was deathly pale. A bruised swelling marked his forehead just above the left eye.

He's out cold, Nancy realized. But why? What's he doing here?

Suddenly a wave of dizziness hit her. She

had to grab on to the bookshelf to keep herself from falling over. Clenching her teeth, she held on and waited for the spell of nausea to pass.

This is bad, Drew. If you don't pull yourself together, you'll never get out of here!

As she gazed around the room, the dim sound of a car engine starting floated in through the window. Nancy went over as fast as her wobbly legs would carry her. Pulling aside the heavy red curtain, she gazed out, shielding her eyes from the abrupt rush of sunlight.

She saw that she was in a room on the second floor that looked out over the porch roof. The white station wagon that she had seen in the garage when she arrived was now in the driveway. As she watched, the driver's side door opened, and Bill Keating got out.

"Come on," he called, beckoning to someone who was apparently standing on the porch below Nancy. "We don't have time to argue about it now! Just get rid of the car. We can't leave any evidence that the girl was here. Then get out of sight!"

His words barely registered. Nancy tried to cut through the pounding fog in her head and think clearly. Whom was he talking to? She didn't have to wait long to find out. A second later someone hurried down the porch steps and ran to Nancy's car.

Mrs. Keating!

Nancy's stomach did a flip-flop. "Uh-oh,"

she muttered. "I think I've been missing one big piece of the puzzle."

She put a hand to her aching head. "Think, Drew!" she told herself, scowling fiercely. It wasn't easy. Whatever Keating had used to knock her out must have been pretty strong. But even in her weakened state, some very disturbing ideas were beginning to surface.

I came here thinking that Bill Keating was trying to kill Maggie Keating to collect her insurance money, she thought. And I got that idea from reading the letter in Brenda's column. But I know that Brenda made that letter up—it wasn't real. She didn't know anything about Mr. and Mrs. Keating when she wrote it.

So isn't it reasonable to assume that the letter wasn't right? Isn't it possible that Brenda got part of the plan right—but was wrong about other parts?

What if Mrs. Keating isn't Mr. Keating's victim after all? Nancy reasoned. What if she's his accomplice?

"Of course. Why not?" Nancy murmured. It made sense, in a sick way. Both Mr. and Mrs. Keating had married thinking that the other partner was rich, and Nancy's investigation had shown that both were disappointed. But instead of trying to kill each other, they had teamed up to remedy the situation!

It all clicked. "That's why Mrs. Keating didn't want the police to come when she had

the accident with Brenda," Nancy said aloud. "That's why she wouldn't confide in Rick after she saw Brenda's letter in the paper. She wasn't afraid her husband was trying to kill her—she was afraid Brenda had found out about the plot to *fake* her death and collect that million dollars in insurance! She was afraid of being caught!"

That also explained the way Mrs. Keating had been staring behind Nancy just before Mr. Keating knocked her out. Nancy shook her head in amazement. She sure had misread the situation. Now that Nancy thought about it, she realized that the odd look on Mrs. Keating's face hadn't been panic—it had been expectation.

She was just waiting for her husband to sneak up on me, Nancy thought angrily. And I thought she was in trouble!

The roar of the Mustang's engine made Nancy look down at the driveway again. Mrs. Keating had started the car. As Nancy watched, she drove away.

Hey, that's my car! Nancy wanted to shout. But she didn't think it would do much good. Besides, she had more immediate problems. Obviously, the Keatings planned on getting rid of her. She had to get both herself and the unconscious Chris Trout out of there before Mr. Keating came back to finish them off!

Still feeling unsteady, Nancy went over to

the study door and tugged on the knob. It didn't turn. The door was locked, of course. She'd expected as much.

She bent down and examined the latch. Not pickable. She couldn't see the locking mechanism, but from the look of it it was the sort where a section of the doorknob turned, too. A one-way lock. Strange—usually those were set up so that a person could lock and unlock the door from *inside* the room.

I'll bet Mr. Keating just took this one off the door and switched it around, Nancy guessed. It wouldn't be hard, and it would keep us in here very efficiently.

Going over to one of the windows, she struggled to raise the sash, but it didn't budge. Then she noticed that two stout nails had been driven into the wooden sill from the outside. They were holding the window shut.

She gazed out through the glass. If she broke the window, maybe she could shout loud enough to get someone's attention. . . .

That hope faded as she remembered the thick belt of trees that surrounded the Keatings' property. The place was isolated. From where Nancy stood, she couldn't even see any other houses. No one would hear her cries.

Just then another wave of sick dizziness swept over Nancy. She gripped the doorknob, but the whirling feeling grew stronger. Gasping, she slid down the wall to the thickly

carpeted floor and put her head between her knees.

She shook her head, trying to clear it, but if anything, she felt worse than she had five minutes earlier.

Suddenly she caught a whiff of that same bitter scent that she had smelled right before she lost consciousness. It was strangely familiar, but she couldn't place it. Nancy racked her fogged brain. *I know that smell, but from where?*

Just then a scene flashed into her head of her high-school chemistry lab. The teacher was holding up a beaker of some liquid and lecturing about it. "Quite dangerous . . . highly explosive . . ." And that same acrid taint hung faintly in the air. . . .

"Ether!" Nancy cried, snapping her fingers.

So that was what Keating had used to knock her out. He must have left some of it in the house, and the fumes were seeping into the air as it evaporated.

Nancy stood up and sniffed. The smell was strongest around the door and near the ceiling, so the ether was probably in the attic.

That was bad, she realized with a sinking heart. Besides the fact that the fumes were making her progressively weaker, if there were any sparks or open flames going anywhere in the house they might set off an explosion. . . .

Suddenly the war story she had heard Keating tell the other day in the bank rang in her

ears with a dreadful significance. He had built ether bombs during the war. All it took was a bottle of ether and a lit candle. She could hear his voice, saying, "A few hours later the ether fumes reached the candle flame, and—boom!"

Nancy had a sudden, sinking feeling in the pit of her stomach. "So that's how he's going to do it," she whispered.

The entire attic is a bomb, and when it goes up, Trout and I go with it! The authorities will find a demolished house—and two very demolished bodies.

It was a horribly clever plan. Not only were the Keatings getting rid of Nancy, but they were also providing themselves with a stand-in for Mrs. Keating's body. Because all that would be left of Nancy were some unidentifiable remains!

Chapter Fifteen

THAT'S WHY Mr. Keating had all those clippings about microbursts," Nancy said, thinking out loud.

She knew she was talking to herself. Over on the sofa Chris Trout still hadn't stirred. Somehow, though, hearing her own voice made her feel a little less alone.

"It was research," she said. "He's going to pretend that a minitornado touched down and demolished the house. It's perfect. No one can predict those things, and they touch down so fast that it's easy to miss them. Besides, there are no neighbors close enough to be witnesses.

"And that's why the ether bomb is up in the attic," she continued. "The house has to be wrecked from the top down, so that the microburst story will be convincing." She glanced over at Chris Trout. "And poor Mrs.

Keating and her brother-in-law just happened to be in the study upstairs when it happened," she added grimly.

It was a horrible thought. Nancy shuddered. "What am I going to do?" she asked.

She did have one thing going for her, she realized. She was sure Keating hadn't expected her to regain consciousness before the blast came. That was why he hadn't tied her up. He'd secured the doors and windows to minimize the risk, but he couldn't chance tying Nancy's arms and legs. If rope fragments were found in the wreckage, that might raise awkward questions.

She glanced over at Trout again. Still out. She couldn't count on his help—he might not wake up as long as they remained inside. The ether fumes were keeping him under.

How much time do I have? Nancy wondered desperately. She thought about Keating's story again. He'd said the ether bomb took a few hours to detonate. But the tunnel Keating had blown up must have been huge, big enough to hold an entire convoy of trucks. The Keatings' house was much smaller. Even if the candle flame was downstairs on the first floor, the ether fumes would reach it much more quickly.

Nancy felt a bone-chilling shiver. Groaning, she sat down on the leather recliner and dropped her head in her hands.

But then anger swept over her. "Get up,

Drew!" she told herself. She'd been in tight spots before. And she'd always found a way out. Nancy shook her head to clear it of useless doubts. She had no choice. She *had* to get them both out.

She stood up, ignoring the spots that were beginning to dance in front of her eyes. Grabbing Bill Keating's maple desk chair, she dragged it over to the nearer of the two windows.

All she had to do was pick it up and swing it through the glass. Come on, you can do it! she told herself.

But it looked so impossibly heavy, another part of her moaned.

"Do it!" she said out loud in a harsh voice.

With a tremendous effort Nancy picked up the wooden chair and heaved it forward, smashing it into the glass pane. Sparkling shards flew outward, showering onto the sloping porch roof.

Nancy stuck her head out the window and greedily gulped air into her lungs. It was warm and tangy, but at least it didn't have ether in it!

After wrapping her hand in the velvet curtain, she knocked the remaining splinters of glass out of the window frame. Then she crossed the room and stood over Chris Trout, who still hadn't budged. This part was going to be really hard.

"Okay, Mr. Trout, are you ready?" she asked him. He didn't answer.

"Shall I take that as a yes?" Nancy giggled, suddenly light-headed. "Well, ready or not, here I come—and here you go."

She stooped, grabbed Trout's limp arms, and hauled him up to a sitting position. His head lolled to one side. "Boy, you're a heavy sleeper," she chided him.

Twisting around so that her back was to him, she draped his arms over her shoulders and clasped her hands around his wrists. Then, slowly and laboriously, she began dragging him toward the open window. It was incredibly hard. Trout's muscular frame was heavier than it looked, and Nancy was already quite weak.

Suddenly she felt resistance. Looking down, she saw that one of Trout's dragging feet had gotten stuck between two pieces of furniture. Not now, Drew. You don't have the time or strength!

Nancy had to put him down to free him. She had such difficulty lifting him again that for a few dreadful moments she thought she might not be able to do it.

"Come on, Mr. Trout," she pleaded, gasping for breath. "Can't you help?" But he didn't stir.

Finally she got him onto her back again. Perspiring from the exertion, she lugged him the last few feet and draped his limp form over the windowsill. Then she reached for his feet

and unceremoniously shoved him forward. He slid through the window and landed in a heap on the porch roof.

"Okay, me next," Nancy panted. She climbed through the window and out onto the roof. "Phase one complete," she murmured.

Next Nancy grabbed Trout by the feet and slid him down the gently sloping roof. It was easier than dragging him across the carpet, but Nancy was already thinking ahead to what had to come next. She wasn't certain she could handle it. Somehow she had to get him off the roof without breaking his neck—or her own—in the process.

Leaning over the edge of the roof, she peered down. Good. The drop didn't look to be more than eight or nine feet. Directly below her was the front lawn, and the grass looked soft and springy. That's the first thing that's gone right today, she thought with a wry smile.

She sat back and took a deep breath. Then she turned Trout over so that he was lying on his stomach with his feet pointing toward the edge of the roof.

Inch by inch she lowered him over the edge of the roof. At last, when his legs and lower torso were dangling, Nancy could no longer hold him. She let go, and he slid the rest of the way off the roof, landing in the grass with a thud.

Without pausing, Nancy sat on the edge of

the roof and then pushed off with her hands. She dropped heavily to the ground beside Trout.

Her muscles were aching, but she couldn't rest yet. She knew they were still too close to the house. If the attic was to go up now, they could still be seriously injured. Gritting her teeth, Nancy grasped Trout's hands and began to drag him away from the house, toward the thicket of trees and bushes that surrounded it.

They had crossed the driveway and were nearly at the trees when the explosion hit. A muffled thud came through the air from the attic. It sounded strangely soft, and at first Nancy didn't know what it was. Then the shock from the blast knocked her right off her feet, sending her sprawling in the grass. She threw her arms over her head to protect herself.

Peeking up, Nancy watched as the top of the Keatings' house erupted. It was as if the attic were a huge balloon that had been filled too full and had burst. Chunks of roof flew straight up into the air, and bits of wall blew out in every direction. Brick, mortar, and wood hailed down onto the lawn.

When the dust settled, Nancy saw that the entire upper half of the house was gone. Here and there orange flames shot up out of the ruins. She gulped. If we'd still been in there, she thought. If we hadn't gotten out . . .

Nancy started at the sound of a car door

slamming behind her. Had someone come to rescue them? Maybe Ned—

As she got to her feet and turned around, the welcoming words died on her lips.

Mr. Keating had come back! He stopped on the driveway, giving her a cold smile. "Miss Drew, isn't it?" When she nodded, he shook his head, and said, "It's a good thing I came back to check the damage. You keep popping up when I don't expect you," he said. "It was you on the bridge last night, wasn't it?"

Again Nancy nodded. She knew he planned to kill her. Her eyes darted around her, but she couldn't think of any way to escape. After what she'd been through, she knew she was far too weak to struggle against him.

Come on, Drew! her thoughts clamored. You just got yourself out of one of the worst messes you've ever been in. Surely you can come up with some way to outwit this goon. At least you can stall him until Trout comes around!

"Who'd have guessed, when you came to me for approval of that withdrawal the other day, that you'd be causing me so much trouble in such a short time?" Keating said, sighing.

Nancy raised her head and forced herself to smile. "I can be quite a troublemaker," she said, hoping she sounded more confident than she felt. "And I think you've already found out that I'm very hard to get rid of."

"Mmm, yes." Keating looked thoughtful. "I

don't know how you managed to get this far, but I do congratulate you. You're a resourceful girl."

Nancy didn't like his smug tone. He knew he had the upper hand, but she wasn't about to just buckle under. "Well, Mr. Keating," she said firmly, "it looks as if your plan has failed."

"Oh, I doubt that," Keating said coolly. He glanced up at the house. "No, I think the situation can still be repaired."

"How?" Nancy asked. She didn't really want to know, but she needed to keep distracting him.

"I saw enough in the war to know that the body of someone who's been in a fire is very difficult to identify. And there does seem to be a flame or two up there." Keating pointed up at the second story of the house. "I think I'll just put you back there and let nature take its course. It will be easy to claim your body as my wife's."

He turned toward her. Horrified, Nancy tried to back away, but the combination of fear and exhaustion had made her muscles utterly useless.

He was coming at her, and she couldn't move!

Chapter Sixteen

NANCY STARED HELPLESSLY as Mr. Keating began to cross the driveway toward her.

The sound of a car engine made her turn, and Nancy saw her blue Mustang roar up the drive, heading straight for Mr. Keating.

He leapt backward with a shout. "What the—?"

The Mustang's door flew open, and Mrs. Keating stepped out. Her gaze lit on Nancy, and Nancy thought she saw relief in the woman's eyes. Then Mrs. Keating turned to her husband and said in a shaking voice, "We can't do this, Bill."

"Listen to your wife, Mr. Keating," Nancy called to him. "She's trying to save you from a life behind bars."

Keating ignored her. "Maggie, what kind of

nonsense is this?" he demanded of his wife. "You know we can't stop now. We're in way too deep."

"No, Bill," Mrs. Keating pleaded. "You're wrong! If I let you kill these people, *then* it'll be too late. Cheating the insurance company was one thing, but I can't go along with murder!"

"You already have," Keating snapped. He gestured toward Nancy. "If this girl hadn't managed to get out before the house went up, you'd be an accessory after the fact right now. So don't get self-righteous with me."

Stepping around the car, he continued toward Nancy. She tensed, but she knew she couldn't hold him off for long—she was still too weak. "It's up to you, Mrs. Keating," she called. "You're the only one who can stop him from making the biggest mistake of his life."

"She won't stop me," Keating scoffed. "My wife is in this up to her neck."

Just then tires squealed on the Keatings' winding driveway, causing Mr. Keating to glance over his shoulder. A second later a green Chevy sedan came into sight. Ned!

As the car screeched to a halt, Nancy felt a rush of relief so intense that she thought her knees would buckle. As Ned leapt out of the car, Brenda's red sports car pulled up with Bess, George, Rick, and Brenda all crammed inside. All five of them raced over to Nancy.

"Am I glad to see you guys!" Nancy cried. But then, looking over Ned's shoulder, she saw

the desperate look on Mr. Keating's face. In a flash he turned and started across the lawn at a run.

"Don't let him get away!" she cried, pointing.

Ned and Rick caught up to him in a flash and wrestled him to the ground. Keating's face twisted with fury. "You punks!" he growled, still struggling. Then Ned stunned him with a well-placed blow to the jaw.

As Keating went limp, Ned rubbed his fist and looked satisfied. "That was for last night," he said. Leaving Rick to handle his uncle, Ned rose to his feet and rushed back to Nancy, putting his arms around her. "Are you okay?" he asked tenderly.

Nancy hugged him as hard as she could. "How in the world did you know I'd be here?" she asked.

"I called your house, and Hannah told me you'd gone tearing out ten minutes earlier shouting something about stopping a murder," Ned told her. "Well, I know my Nancy," he went on, grinning affectionately. "I figured you had either gone here or to Brenda's. I called Brenda, and you weren't there, so that left here. So I told Brenda to call Bess and George for backup, and then I drove over. I want you to know I broke the speed limit all the way."

"I'm glad you did," Nancy said, giggling. She felt giddy now that she was out of danger, but she knew it wasn't over quite yet. Turning

to Bess and George, she said, "Guys, there's some rope in the trunk of my car. Maybe we should tie Mr. Keating up, just in case he wakes up and wants to go somewhere."

"Okay, boss." George made a salute and headed for Nancy's Mustang. "I'll run to a neighbor's and call the fire department, too."

"Nan, you're kind of pale," Bess said anxiously. "Are you really all right?"

With a grateful smile Nancy assured her, "Now that you guys are here, I am." She looked over at Mrs. Keating, who was standing by herself next to Nancy's car.

"Mrs. Keating, I guess I owe you some thanks, too," Nancy said, going over to her. "If you hadn't had second thoughts, I probably wouldn't be standing here right now."

"Aunt Maggie!" Rick exclaimed, rushing to his aunt's side. "Hey, are you okay? He didn't hurt you, did he?"

Mrs. Keating glanced from her nephew to Nancy with a pale, blank expression. She looked as if she'd been carved from a block of ice.

"Aunt Maggie?" Rick repeated when she didn't answer. "Hey, what's the matter?"

Nancy cleared her throat. Suddenly she felt sad—sad for Rick, who was about to learn the awful truth about his favorite aunt, and even a little sad for Mrs. Keating herself.

"Rick," Nancy said softly. "I think your aunt has something to tell you."

"What do you mean?" Rick looked puzzled.

Instead of answering, Nancy looked expectantly at Mrs. Keating.

"All right!" Mrs. Keating burst out suddenly. "I'll tell him." She turned to Rick, her eyes filling with tears. "Your uncle wasn't trying to kill me, Rick," she explained in a shaky voice. "The whole thing was a scam, from beginning to end. Bill and I planned to fake my death in an accident, so that we could collect the insurance money and start fresh somewhere else."

A shocked silence fell over the group. Rick's jaw dropped, and he stared at his aunt.

Poor guy, Nancy thought with a pang. She was pleased when Brenda moved forward and took his hand without a word. Rick hardly seemed to notice. He just continued gazing at his aunt, a look of horror on his face.

"Don't stare at me like that," Mrs. Keating cried. She turned her back, and Nancy saw her shoulders heave with her sobbing.

After a moment she went on. "It was Bill's idea, but I didn't have to be talked into it," she said. "We both like spending money so much, there just never seemed to be enough of it—"

"Enough for what?" Rick asked in a low, bitter voice. "Uncle Bill has a good job! Why don't you just admit you were greedy?"

Mrs. Keating sighed. "All right, it's true. We *were* greedy. But we also had some problems. Bill had been trying to pad out his salary with some risky gambles on the stock market. A

couple of those went sour, and we lost a lot. So he took a—a loan from his bank."

A loan? Nancy remembered how upset Keating had gotten when his secretary told him the bank's auditors were coming. "Mrs. Keating, do you mean your husband embezzled money from the bank?"

"Maggie, don't tell them anything!" came Mr. Keating's furious voice.

Turning, Nancy saw that he had come to, and was struggling against the ropes that bound his wrists and ankles. Ignoring him, Nancy repeated her question to Mrs. Keating.

The older woman glanced hesitantly at her husband. "Well, I—oh, what's the use! Yes, that's what I mean. He embezzled."

"I see," Nancy said with a nod. "Go on."

"At first we were going to stage a phony car accident. We were going to drive my car over the cliff and into the river. Then I'd disappear, and Bill would convince the authorities that I'd been in the car when it went over." Mrs. Keating shrugged. "The current was strong there. No one would question the fact that there was no body in the car."

"Ugh," Bess said softly. "That's creepy!"

Mrs. Keating looked at Brenda. "The day that I ran into you in the mall parking lot, I was trying to establish that my car had bad brakes," she explained. "I never thought you'd make such a fuss and draw so much attention

to me, and I certainly never dreamed you'd put me in your column the next day."

"I'm a journalist," Brenda boasted. "It's my job to make things public."

"But Brenda made up that letter," Rick said to his aunt. "She didn't know anything."

Mrs. Keating nodded. "I know that now, but at the time all we could think of was that somehow she'd found out about our plan. Bill was furious. I was just scared—I wanted to call the whole thing off then and there, but he refused. He told me not to worry about it, that he'd make sure Brenda didn't talk." Her brown eyes were filled with shame as she added, "When Rick told me about Brenda's nearly being hit by the beam at the mall, I wondered if Bill had had anything to do with it, but I was afraid to ask."

"Did you, Mr. Keating?" Nancy called to him.

"What do you think?" Keating suddenly flared. "Of course! It was a piece of cake. My bank was one of the principal backers of the mall when it was built. I have the blueprints in my office—I know every inch of that place. I followed the girl there, and then I sneaked up to the roof by way of one of the catwalks and waited for her to walk under the broken sky-light." His chest swelled with pride. "It was a calculated risk—but I've never been afraid of risks. I'm a winner."

"Most gamblers say the same thing," Nancy pointed out. "But they all lose sooner or later."

Keating just glared at her. After a moment Nancy turned back to Mrs. Keating. "Please go on with your story."

Mrs. Keating brushed back her ash blond hair and swallowed hard. "Well, after Brenda's column came out, things started happening fast," she said. "Bill told me that the bank auditors were coming in to do an investigation. We thought they might discover the missing money, and we couldn't let that happen. So we had to speed up our timetable. If I 'died' over the weekend, then Bill would have a plausible reason to be out of work next week. Without him the audit couldn't be held, and the auditors would have to reschedule, probably to sometime in the fall—that's the way these people work. And by that time we'd be long gone with the insurance money."

"Devious," Ned said, shaking his head.

"Yes, but the problem was that on Friday afternoon the mechanic from the garage where we'd had the car towed called to say that they'd discovered one of the brake shoes was missing."

"Ah!" Nancy said softly. "Enter Chris Trout." She was pretty sure she knew what was coming next.

Mrs. Keating nodded. "Right. Shortly after that, my brother-in-law showed up at our

door," she said. "He had the missing brake shoe, and he knew it had been filed down. He'd pretty much figured out what we were trying to do. He said he wouldn't tell anyone about it—as long as we gave him half the insurance money, once we got it.

"Our plans were falling apart," Mrs. Keating went on. Nancy had the impression that it was actually a relief to her to confess everything. "It was too risky to try the phony car accident—the mechanic knew my car had been tampered with. But we had to try something. Chris was pressuring us for money. We didn't know what to do—until this morning, when we heard there was a tornado watch."

"I heard that report, too," Nancy told her.

"Bill had been keeping a file of clippings on microbursts—he's very interested in natural phenomena," Mrs. Keating said. "I think he'd been turning over the possibility of staging a phony microburst for some time. At any rate, he knew how to do it. It seemed our problems were solved."

"Until I turned up," Nancy guessed.

"Not exactly. Chris came about ten minutes before you, to push us about the money," Mrs. Keating corrected Nancy, nodding toward Trout's still-unconscious form. "Bill knocked him out and took him up to the study. *Then* you came along."

"And you knocked me out, too, figuring that

when the blast was over, the authorities would find our remains, and everyone would think that I was you," Nancy concluded.

Mrs. Keating nodded. "But I couldn't go along with that," she whispered. "I couldn't."

"Maybe that will help you in court, Aunt Maggie," Rick said.

There was an uneasy silence. Finally, after a long moment, Nancy spoke up. "Well, I suppose one of us should go call the police. With Mrs. Keating's confession, and all these witnesses, I don't think we'll have much trouble proving this case."

"Just think," Brenda gloated. "If it hadn't been for me, we never would have stumbled on this case in the first place!"

Nancy rolled her eyes. Rick's whole family was falling apart, and Brenda could think only about herself!

But Brenda seemed to have realized her own mistake. She was actually looking remorseful. "I'm sorry," she said softly to Rick. "I didn't mean it to sound that way. I wasn't thinking."

Rick's face softened, and he smiled down at her. "I know you didn't mean it," he said. With a deep sigh he added, "I'm just glad to finally know the truth. And at least Aunt Maggie's still alive."

"I guess that's what really counts," Brenda told him, giving Rick a sympathetic smile.

Nancy grinned. Maybe Brenda *would* learn!

* * *

"Well, Brenda," Nancy said after the police had taken all their statements and carted the Keatings and Chris Trout away, "I think we can drop the contest about whose summer is more exciting. We're even now, at two attacks apiece—and I, for one, would rather not compete anymore!"

"Hear, hear!" George cried.

"Yeah, I hate competition," Bess put in.

Ned laughed. "I have an idea. I say we all just concentrate on having as much fun as possible this summer."

"That's the best idea you've had in a long time," Nancy declared. Then she kissed him.

Books in The Nancy Drew Files™ Series

For orders other than by individual consumers, Pocket Books grants a discount on the purchase of **10 or more** copies of single titles for special markets or premium use. For further details, please write to the Vice-President of Special Markets, Pocket Books, 1633 Broadway, New York, NY 10019-6785, 8th Floor.

For information on how individual consumers can place orders, please write to Mail Order Department, Simon & Schuster Inc., 200 Old Tappan Road, Old Tappan, NJ 07675.

MORE MYSTERY.
MORE FUN.
MORE OF YOUR FAVORITE TEENAGE DETECTIVE!

With three thrill-packed mysteries, **THE NANCY DREW FILES™ COLLECTOR'S EDITION** gives you the chance to read, share, and enjoy the best Nancy Drew stories ever—again and again and again!

Savvy and resourceful, Nancy matches wits with some of the most clever and sinister criminals ever to hit River Heights. But much more than that, she also makes new friends and dates new guys—and some of them can be dangerous, too!

Don't miss this special volume. It's a book you'll treasure forever.